The Texas Frontier

1866

They were dozing in the sunshine when they lost sight of the other riders over the horizon. Two boys in the new spring grass with the drool of their nap slung across their cheeks, bellies full from a lunch of jerked meat and cornbread. The gnarled oaks on the prairie leaned softly with the breeze and the rolling grass-covered hills swayed hypnotically in the glorious springtime sun.

The boy named Ewell came out of a half dream and rose up from his slumber with his eyes dumb and fuzzy. Out on the meadow a deep rumble thundered and the songbirds chirping playfully became silent and wary.

He rubbed his eyes and peered out. Hey Billy, look yonder. Is that them? He nudged the other boy. Billy sat up mumbling and looked about squinting into the sun.

Huh?

They jumped up and set off at a trot for a ridge that would offer a clear view of two men running their horses all out back toward them. They were leaned low in the saddle and shouting and kicking their horses and flailing at them madly with heavy strips of braided rawhide.

By the time the gear was gathered and they had mounted up with their horses kicked up and running they could hear the highpitched yip cries of the warparty piercing the air. They were fanned out charging from the hills, eighteen, twenty of them, and they vanished into a draw and then reappeared again on the horizon whooping all the louder, gaining ground on the fleeing riders who were turning back and firing their pistols aimlessly.

They could see the heavier white man on the dun horse had an arrow buried in his left arm. His partner had been shot in the leg and blood was flowing and flying with each gallop. Each of their horses had taken arrows and they were losing ground, slogging along and loping and foaming at the mouth.

Get to the creek! Billy's dad yelled out, and as he spoke the boys veered to their right but there wasnt enough time. When the men arrived they dismounted and gathered their saddle holsters with their guns and ammunition and scurried down with the boys for the cover of the creek bed but before they could get settled the raiders began to surround the small depression. Arrows whistled by, thumping the dirt, clattering off the rocks.

A group of riders poured over the ridge and another handful on foot scurried around on each side of the scraggly draw and all around them the Texans could hear the click and clink of rocks and the rustling of brush. Pistolfire rang out.

Ewell was drawing his gun and as he looked up for his mark an arrow flew through the soft flesh of his left cheek clear out the other side. He bowled over jabbering and kicking in a spasm. His father scrambled over to see about him when a warrior came flying from the ledge swinging his warclub and crushing the man's skull into a heap of mush. The man crumpled up, jerking and twitching. Billy's dad was reloading his pistol and shouting orders to his son when he was swarmed from behind and bludgeoned with a battleaxe.

Billy scrambled for a clearing on the far side of the wash and as he came running out a painted horseman appeared from the ledge to ride him down. He stumbled and fell, was clambering madly in the rocks on his hands and knees and by instinct rolled up in a ball when the right front hoof of the warhorse came pounding down into his kidney. He was in shock by the time they hauled him up on the horse to carry him away. He could hear them talking, a strange staccato mumble.

The indians pilfered the bodies and readied to ride out. Billy was barely conscious and before he passed out he looked back to see the leader hovering over his dead father. He kicked the man over face down and sliced a half-circle about his skull and placed a foot upon his upper back. He mumbled something to himself as he sucked in a big breath. Then he took hold of the man's hair with both hands and ripped away the scalp.

The San Saba River springs to life in the western fringes of the Texas Hill Country. It emerges from crystal clear springs that gurgle and gush from the Edwards Plateau and it slides and swirls one hundred miles east-northeast along the edge of the plains until it falls at last into the Colorado River.

In the late afternoon of a sun-dazzled day the Terry brothers were wandering carelessly through the muddy, rock-strewn fields along this river. They were sunburned and worn out from tending cows all day and ready to head home but they were looking for the last calf like they'd been told.

Charlie picked up a small rock and chucked it at a sparrow perched upon a limb. He looked at his big brother. Sam, was that a tornado last night?

Sam had his head down observing a grasshopper and he did not look at his brother. No, it was just a big storm.

What do you think a tornado would sound like?

How would I know? I guess lots of wind howling. Things flying around. Rocks and stuff smashing against things. Boards cracking.

But Sam, if you've never been in a tornado how would you know what it sounds like?

Sam sighed and shook his head in irritation.

Charlie looked up at him, innocently, for an answer. Mother says it would sound like a train.

Charlie.

What?

If you knew that why did you ask?

He didnt respond. They kept walking. He was kicking rocks as he shuffled along.

Sam, when's Father going to be back?

I dont know.

Tonight?

I dont think so. Prolly a few more days.

Do you miss him?

A little, I guess.

I do.

I know.

Sam paced out ahead and was quiet as he looked across the roiling muddy water of the river up to the bluffs of the valley. He knew to keep an eye on the hills. There were a few vultures cruising slowly against the blue and just below the rim he saw a herd of deer camouflaged by the brush. This was a fertile valley thick with grass and wildflowers, the oaks newly molted and full of green, and beyond them, an untamed country controlled by wild bands of Kiowa and Comanche indians.

Sam, what does a train sound like?

Charlie, how would I know!

I dont know.

There's no trains out here.

Oh.

The brothers followed the creek up and away from the river to a narrow gametrail lined by agaritas and persimmons. The trunks of the live oaks stained dark from the overnight storm, leaves perking vibrantly in the cool, crisp air. The wind barely whispered. They were walking through a field where water had pooled up in the granite escarpments and as the sun began its descent over the western hills the little pools glistened like random mirrors that had dropped and broken all about the countryside.

How long would it take us to walk to Mexico, Sam?

Sam clenched his fist and flung it down in anger. I have no idea! he said. A year probably. Charlie… I mean, why do you ask so many questions?

Would it take a year?

I dont know. Maybe longer.

Charlie was rubbing his eyes and dragging his feet through the rocks and the wet grass. His shirt was half untucked and his right pant leg was bunched into his boot. He was slouching and huffing and cold.

When are we going home?

Soon, but I dont want Father to be mad at us. We need to keep looking.

But that thing is not over here.

Dont be such a baby.

I'm not.

Look, it's getting dark. Let's just try a little bit longer.

I just want to go home. I'm hungry.

I promise we'll head home soon, okay?

Okay.

On a rise overlooking the river they came upon the crumbled ruins of an old presidio where pricklypear grew from jumbled clumps of stone. A rat snake slithered away for cover and a lizard scurried about the rocks. Deer grazing cautiously in the fields, turkeys flying to roost in the pecans along the river. A gust of wind picked up and then died. The boys passed through the remains of the dilapidated entrance gate and Sam stopped to look at the symbols engraved in the stone. Charlie, come look at this, he said. He reached up and touched the cold rock and he slowly whispered the letters under his breath as he traced the carving with his fingers. B O U I E. He stepped back and looked at the letters and wondered what they meant.

Charlie looked out over the hills and his mind wandered. Sam, are you scared of indians?

Sam said nothing. He was deep in thought.

Sam! I asked you, are you scared of indians?

Charlie, stop it! There's no indians out here. He took a long sweep of the surrounding country with his eyes. The light dying, sky fading to orange. The animals of the night now appearing in the dusk, silent and wary and watching.

But it does feel sorta creepy out here, he said. Like something is watching us.

Like what?

I dont know. Maybe ghosts.

Sam looked at his little brother. It was fun to put a scare into him. They stood there looking about uneasily, barely a breeze, hearing the wilderness listen. Charlie was watching Sam.

Well, I guess it is pretty late, said Sam. Let's see if it's over here and then we'll head home.

He walked along a trail and Charlie followed. Nearby hunkered down inside a clump of brush the warparty watched them, silently observing the boys and awaiting a signal from their leader.

An enormous warrior dressed in a buckskin vest raised his hand to restrain his men. He wore red paint over his face and his thickly muscled torso and he had dark black eyes framed by a round face. He was a nudge over six feet in height and he held a war shield adorned with red and yellow cloth and an image of a sun circled by two rings and he was petting the shriveled head of a sandhill crane that hung from this holy armament.

The brothers had split up along divergent trails. There were no sounds about the country but the fading quibble of their young voices. The savages watched them. Their chief was rubbing his face in thought and he plucked a chin whisker and turned to survey his men where they awaited his command and then he turned back and watched the two boys as they became more distant in the dying light. His face was serene and contemplative like a priest. The muscles around his left eye jerked in spasm. He felt a clicking in that ear. He began to lightly flick the soft brown hair of the white woman's scalp that dangled from his shield and as he watched the boys his thoughts took him further down the river where they would find a homestead full of women and children and a stable full of horses.

By now Charlie had wandered off alone. He kicked rocks and carelessly made his way, thinking nothing of the lost calf. He was humming a tune and his mind drifted to the evening at home. Daddy was away but it would be good to eat supper with Mommy and play games, tell stories, sing songs before bed.

Sam had taken a different path through a grove of pecans. Crisp evening chill at dusk. Sliver of a moon. He thought about the stories he'd been told about the indians.

He made his way into a clearing in the last of the light. A cold wind. Dark under the trees. He walked along with his head down quietly listening to the throated, guttural call of a crow in the distant dusk and he sensed something out of the corner of his eye and he stopped. Twenty yards to his left almost hidden in the grass was a red-tailed hawk. He held his breath. The hawk had been hammering at the skull of a crippled jackrabbit and it stopped and looked up at him and let out a rasping scream as it flapped away to a nearby perch.

The hare lay there semi-alert, almost normal except for the hole in the back of its head. Poor little guy, said Sam. Mr Hawk got you, didnt he? The rabbit looked up and he could see its heart pounding furiously. He approached it, cheeks red and nose running, thumbing an old greenriver knife his father had given him. He crept toward it very slowly. Sorry friend, he said aloud. When he got near enough to grab it he took a firm hold of it by its ears and when it began kicking he held it tight and swiped a sharp slash across its neck. Then he turned it upside down to let it bleed out and headed on home with a special surprise for the family supper.

The father is Robert Lee Terry. He is lean and wiry in his frayed wool pants and linsey-woolsey shirt. He ranges the open country herding the tallgrass prairies overrun with unbranded longhorn cattle, exploring the uncharted plains beyond controlled by the last wild indians. He has a pregnant wife back home and two young boys who suffer from the conditions he has placed them in. He lives each day singularly, like all men his destinies are perhaps predetermined. He lives by his own unique faith but succumbs to the mysteries of fate.

Dear Heavenly Father. Thank you for this meal. For all the blessings you impart. I trust you to take care of me, moment by moment, day by day. In Jesus' name. Amen.

He's been dragged along by the footsteps of his Scotch-Irish forbearers in a continual migration west. As a child he was hauled from Tennessee to Texas in a wagon and then orphaned by the age of five. The father never returns from the Mier expedition, the mother dies of cholera while he is away. He rides on, tired and burned. He is driven by a ruthless work ethic and yet deep inside him lies the demon of gamble and drink. He is born of frontier stock, destined to become an authentic outrider of the Texas plains.

As a young man he finds wages in the Northern Cross Timbers region. He rarely stays in one location for more than a few days at a time. Horseback all day, boils flaring his backside. He rides as far north as the town of Paris, loyal to the newborn barons of frontier cattle ranching.

Massive herds, open ranges near running water, controlling pastures by right of occupancy. Hands coated in axle grease. Silhouetted against the sun slouched in the saddle slumbering in and out of his dreams. The lone brave horseman who can be relied upon in a stampede to stop the cattle and put them into a mill.

During the war he is based out of Fort Belknap, on the edge of the indian frontier of the American West. He joins Company B of the Texas Rangers to scout the western country for indians. Twenty-seven days on horseback. At night the gypsum water rips through his bowels, tossing in a semi-conscious slumber to the cries of the lobo wolf echoing across the plains. They hunt turkey and deer, buffalo and black bear. They watch herds of pronghorn in the thousands, bison in the hundreds of thousands, and he follows the trail of the Comanche and Kiowa raiders and sees country that has never been looked upon by white eyes. He is born for the saddle. He is slender but has broad shoulders, ingrained durability. He is naturally bowlegged. His face is lean and sun-gnarled, ruggedly handsome with eyes in a perpetual squint. He rides among men of all races, all breeds, men of every character. Horse thieves, heroes, greenhorns, cardsharps. Men running from trouble into this lawless land, men searching for opportunities in the uncertain times of Reconstruction. He rides sunup to sundown and sleeps under the stars, obsessed with his work for he knows it is in his blood but he dreams for more.

He takes an interest in a trading post on Mukewater Creek serving men like himself who ride the trails to the northern markets. He cow-punches for Oliver Loving, chases rustlers for John Chisum. He takes his pay from these ranchers in cattle and holds herds in McCullough and Menard Counties and it is here on this range in the spring of eighteen and sixty-six where he finalizes his plans and gathers up his herds to join the first cattle drives west into the unknown desert for the crossing of the Pecos and the northern markets of New Mexico Territory.

Now in his thirty-first year, he sets out alone on the wagon road south from Chisum's Home Creek Ranch headquarters, a man full of hope, a man in search of his destiny. A two-day hard ride back home to the family that has almost forgotten him. They are just barely existing in their leaking, dirt-floored cabin, a mother and her boys, eating cornbread and beans seven days a week.

He prods his horse from the confluence of the Concho and Colorado running gently through the hills and he follows the polestar across the Fort Mason road. He shucks pecan shells with his teeth and sucks in great breaths of the fresh Texas air, thinking to himself how good he feels, wondering why he does not feel that way more often. Then he stops himself. Be careful, he thinks, as he has become wary of those times in his past when fate turned and the good feelings vanished and he was left to face the ever-present darkness that lingers, the inevitable evils that lie in wait, restlessly, at every turn.

It took him most of the morning to ride within range of the San Saba valley. He had made his way up a rocky plateau and stepped his horse through a granite outcropping to a window in the packsaddle with twenty-mile views to the south. He scanned the country slowly. A peregrine turned down off of a ridge, soaring in the cool air rising from the valley. He admired it. It had a broad wingspan and it screamed in annoyance and flapped twice and floated to the west. It turned in the sun, calling a wild, piercing *kee-eeeee-arr*, echoing. Then it flew on. RL watched it and took a deep breath and exhaled slowly.

He dismounted and led the horse along a ridge in search of the trail down, hat in hand, right arm held out for balance. The bright sun warmed his face. He cussed the route he'd chosen. Great lumps of rocks and thick brush and cactus. The horse was breathing hard.

He inched his way into a clearing, enormous boulders framing the trail down. Blackjack oaks and yuccas and junipers. He put his hat back on and mounted the horse and raised his eyes from the trail out onto his new perspective of the valley. That was when he first saw the spires of smoke, the vultures swirling.

He sat up tall and looked out over the country again. The pecan grove blocked most of his view of the valley floor but there looked to be fire smoldering through the trees. He let the reins drop and pushed his hat back on his head. He sighed deeply. Damn, he said. The Herd place. He just sat there thinking. He watched the vultures riding the currents.

When he rode into the wasted homestead he swung the rifle from a leather sling on the saddlehorn and butted the gun against his thigh. He reined the horse. It was jerking its head and he checked it harder as he scanned the yard, looking for someone, any sign of life. Tevis! he called out. Feathers and smoke swirled and floated in a light breeze and he could hear the low roar of the flames, the crackle of burning wood. Buckets and broken tools and shredded personal items were strewn about. He dismounted and approached the house, listening. He could feel the heat of the fire.

He shook his head and began to walk slowly through the scattered remains. He was thinking that he should have headed home a few days earlier and then he pushed the thought away. He saw drag marks in the dirt streaked in muddied blood. The gates to the pens were wide open and sheep were slain and the horses and cattle gone. He cleared his throat and spat and squatted. He tried to convince himself the indians would miss his place.

He stood up and went for the horse, out away from the home over to the crumbled rock fence at the edge of the property. There were buzzards pecking at the stinking and swollen family dog, struggling to get at the flesh for all of the arrows. A sheet had wrapped onto a tree limb and it was flapping rhythmically in the breeze. It was the only noise out there and it just kept popping. He stood there thinking. His heart was racing. He broke into a cold sweat. Then he pictured the raiding party riding all over the country, heading toward his home. Well, he said. One night. You just had to stay that one extra night, didnt you? And for what? You better get home. Now.

He turned and broke into a jog for his horse and then he ran and by the time he'd jammed the rifle in the scabbard and mounted up riding west he had a feeling that his life was about to change beyond anything that he could ever even pretend to comprehend.

The old man had been thinking about their family bible study as he watched his grandsons play in the field on that late Sunday afternoon and he was thankful that the sun had been shining brightly all day long. Sam Terry bear-hugged his little brother and hurled him to the ground. When Charlie got up in a screaming rage and charged at his brother all the women near the cabin stopped their chores and looked about the commotion.

The old man hollered back. Pay em no mind now Sally, he said. They're just bein boys.

The boys ran on. A big sheepdog named Gus rumbled along jumping playfully behind them. The women had been preparing an early supper over an open fire just off the front porch and they went back to work. Sally Terry leaned forward, all concerned, and kept her eyes on her boys.

Sam Haden! Charlie Warren! Come on in now it's about time to eat.

I'll round em up here in just a minute, Sally.

Thank you Daddy.

She walked inside the crude log home. She was smiling at her sister Sarah and there were other women milling around and more children playing about the two-room dogtrot cabin.

Now Wilma I'm just gonna tell it like it is, she said to her niece. I dont mind the menfolk being gone at all.

You can say that again!

It's just so much more relaxing.

Aint it the truth.

Not just for us, but those kids too.

Oh, they sure love getting to play together, dont they?

I know it, just look at them.

Sally, how's that baby feeling in your belly?

Oh, this baby is doin just fine. I tell you what. Fine and dandy.

Outside Charlie was chasing his brother and they ran into a thicket of oaks away from their grandpa. He smiled, gentle old man, and looked over the landscape and caught his breath. The sun was beginning to drop below the distant clouds and it was bright and it warmed him. A gust of wind swayed the surrounding oaks. In the distance the women and children were laughing. He could hear the congestion welling up from deep inside his lungs and he could feel the rhythmic thumping of his ever-weakening heart. High above some geese flew in a majestic V formation. They were honking and they flapped out into the sun and dropped and veered and passed overhead, gliding slowly out there in the pristine blue. He sauntered along. He was a joyful old man, surrounded by his family, and he reflected on the day at hand, fine days like this from the long ago. In the pasture that fronted the home was a small round stone that caught his eye as something that was perhaps used to grind seeds or grain in a mealing stone. He tripped and stumbled. He righted himself, wobbling, and reached down to grab the stone and as he studied its texture a four-foot mulberry shaft with a flint arrow drove through his wrinkled neck without slowing down and flew on whistling through the air before settling unseen in a thick tuft of bunchgrass.

He stood paralyzed, the pain rushing to his brain. He reached for his throat and he turned around, stumbling, looking about wildly in a crazed wonder as a second arrow hissed by and then a third thumped into his back. From his neck the blood shot out in rhythmic spurts as his old heart pumped away and when he cried out his voice faded weakly into a gurgled muffle. Then he began to hear a sound like a fountain of water being released under high pressure and then a final arrow lodged into the back of his thigh and he dropped to his knees and slumped forward with his face in the rocky soil and he burbled blood and dirt in those last breaths, the arrow shafts poking innocently into the air like ceremonial grave markers. The old man raised his head. His eyes rolled back into the depths of his skull and he may have had one good look at the horde of horse barbarians who rode howling from the trees and commenced circling the field. The women and children were watching with mouths agape from the cabin porch.

As they came pounding down into the pale rocky pasture Charlie came running out of the woods with his head down, arms and legs pumping. He was smiling and giggling, oblivious to any danger. Sam was ten paces behind him, laughing and chasing after his little brother but then he looked up and screamed out hysterically. A mass of cowbirds swooped up and away in unison out over the trees.

The boys sprinted into the middle of the field where a horseman charged out and grabbed Charlie by his tussled white hair and hurled him effortlessly up onto his mount with the little boy yelling for his brother and biting and kicking as Sam began angling away for the woods. Their mother watched helplessly as another rider closed in on her older son and bludgeoned him with his warclub.

The savages swarmed from the hills toward the cabin where the women and children scrambled helplessly as Sally barred the door and rushed the other children under the beds. They came riding headlong into the yard on painted ponies and all of them waving shields, lances, clubs, bows and whooping and howling and their faces drawn up with greasepaint and their eyes feral and crazed. The big war chief was the first to arrive. When he cleared the front yard pickets he dismounted and took his battleaxe and crushed the head of the snarling sheepdog and his comrades were making for the pens where they began to let loose the livestock and slaughter the goats and pigs. He burst through the door and gave out a whoop and the others came rushing in reeking like wild animals and glistening with sweat in the burning light of the early setting sun.

When Sally first looked at him tears came pouring out of her eyes. A cold chill spread over her face and bled through her body. He was much larger than the other warriors and his eyelids were painted white and his coiffure was parted with a greasy mixture of paint and buffalo dung. She timidly extended her small white hands in a desperate gesture of welcome and he shoved her aside and stepped to the table where he picked up an opened bottle of milk and began to gulp it down.

Please, take whatever you need, she said, as he reached over and grabbed the family bible. The good book was swallowed up by his gigantic hands. He opened it, touching the pages, feeling its heft. His face became inquisitive, as if he somehow sensed its spiritual nature. She began to sob as she motioned at their meager belongings. He glared at her. His eyes were dark, intense, evil. He surveyed the room. The house was chilled by a north wind seeping through the cracks in the walls and dust swirled.

The sister Sarah was only eighteen and when she appeared from hiding with a shotgun she was slapped down with a backhand. Wilma was on her knees praying and her little girl began to wail from beneath the bed. He reached down for the gun. He had in his other hand a knife dripping with blood and he pressed Sarah against the wall and placed it at her throat and pressed firmly at an angle, drawing out a thin line of seeping red. Sally Terry was trembling uncontrollably and at this she commenced to pray under her breath. Her left eye was already swelling shut and now another warrior struck her all out in the stomach and she dropped to her knees groaning and sobbing and cradling her abdomen.

The leader stepped toward the other room and she was able to gather herself, rising for a chair that she flung in desperation into his back, the chair splintering into a pile of sticks. He turned and drew his bow and shot her with an arrow that lodged in her left side and pierced below her right breast. She slumped over, whimpering. Outside through the window in the fading light she could see the chaos of the savages and she could see her little boys strapped to the back of the warhorses.

The raiders had been at the property barely five minutes. The women and children were hauled outside weeping and the old mule seesawed about the yard heehawing with an arrow jabbed in its eye. The raiders circled the grounds herding horses and starting fires. Two younger braves were hassling over the old man's scalp and they were stretching the skin and scraping the bloodied tissue and others were stripping mattresses or hauling away heaps of bedding and clothes and jumbles of other random paraphernalia. At once the left side of the cabin engulfed in flames and the last of the heathens appeared from within schlepping a sidesaddle over his shoulder and a box of money and rifle under his arms.

Somehow Sally was still alive, flames now billowing about the house. She crawled to the window and wiped the blood from her eyes and watched her family and friends being hauled away. By the time the leader reappeared she had passed out in the bloody mess of mud. He leaned over, studying her. Then he slashed her breasts three times. Blood began to trickle upon her soft white skin. He was breathing quietly and he slowly grabbed the arrow embedded in her side. He jerked it back and forth. She lay soundlessly on the floor. He stroked the side of her face with the back of his bloodied hand and then gathered up a fistful of her long brown hair at the back of her head. He grabbed his knife with his other hand and made an incision around her mane from her forehead to the back of her neck and he flipped her over face down and placed his foot on her shoulder and resheathed his knife and knelt and ripped her hair off back to front with both hands, lifting the pelt to eye level and watching it drip, flicking it lightly with his middle finger as if he was examining some scientific specimen. Then he walked calmly out the door.

In a few minutes some miracle brought her back to the edge of consciousness and she slowly arose to watch him ride away and join the savages disappearing into the hills. She emerged from the burning home and stumbled warily out into the yard. There were feathers floating listlessly in the glare of the late afternoon sun. She was completely alone and she tried to doctor herself up as she shuffled away from the fires. She limped along slowly, shambling sideways and grunting, gripping the arrow shaft near her breast with one hand to try and minimize the pain. With her other hand she cradled her belly and the baby that was no longer alive in her womb. She stumbled on, spilling blood. She had not gone forth twenty minutes down the trail before her husband came riding upon her.

RL Terry rode upon his burning home, his eyes shifting about to scan the hills, revolver raised slightly, and he watched the flames cave in the roof as billows of black smoke rose into the high blue sky. Sally! he yelled. Sam! Charlie! No signs of life. He could see other columns of smoke in the hills and out there all about the country his terrified neighbors were scrambling for the hidden cover of the ravines and caves that fed into the hillsides surrounding the river valley. He followed a trail of blood in the trampled grass toward the ranch house of Clint Small. A tunnel of ancient oaks that led to an open field of oats and here he could see in the distance through the smoky haze as if he were in some evil dream a wounded form like an apparition and he nudged the horse into a gallop and called out. Sally! he called. Hold up… wait for me!

As he approached the specter he came face-to-face with all of the horrors that could ever linger over a man. Sally! he called out again. Oh my god. She was like the walking dead and she was blubbering incoherently and the blood from her bare skull seeped forth globbing up frayed strands of hair and dripping into her eyes and onto her shredded blouse. He dismounted and put his arms around her. There was nothing he could say.

They made their way slowly with RL holding her up and the horse following. The trail led through a dark grove of oaks and soon they came upon a wide pasture. All about the surrounding hills they could hear the pandemonium of the aborigines. The sharp crack of rifles and men shouting. Women screaming, a baby wailing, death cries. The broken harmony of these random terrors echoing faintly beyond the ridges. Now the sun was behind them beaming from the hills and they were still two hundred yards from the house when a group of raiders appeared in silhouette upon the ridge.

RL watched them loping down the slope and into the pasture toward them and he tried to hurry them along. Come on honey, he said, you're gonna be alright. She had stopped moving her feet and RL was lifting and dragging her along in irregular, desperate heaves. Suddenly the horse took an arrow and it reared and squealed and he could hear other arrows whistling overhead. He knew he wasnt going to make it and he knelt her down gently and rose up and grabbed the reins of the bewildered beast and with his knife punched three short jabs into the horse's neck. Blood spewed. The horse screamed and reared and RL dropped his knife and took hold of the reins now with both hands and reared back and yanked the mare to the ground before them. He pulled his wife and he nudged them up against the horse, still kicking and squirming as it bled out. He reached out for a large round rock of perhaps ten pounds and whispered into the horse's ear and then crushed its skull in a flurry of violent blows. As the horse shuddered and fell limp he leaned his chin into its pulsing flesh and drew a bead with his revolver. He squinched his eye and honed in on the nearest galloping horseman. He reckoned high. The raiders were riding hard a few hundred yards out, six, seven of them, and they were yapping sharply like a pack of coyotes. He squeezed the trigger but did not feel or hear the blast ring out and as the smoke of the forty-five began to dissipate he saw the lead rider buckle over dangling from his mount. As he took aim again he could hear the drum of their hooves pounding into the earth and then the riders reined up. Silence filled the valley. They were attempting to take the wounded rider from his pony when in the periphery to his right he caught sight of a lone rider dashing out from the far side of the field.

It was Charles Goodnight and he had been riding from ranch to ranch warning the neighbors. Goodnight drew his pistol. Get to the house! he yelled. Get her in the house!

Now the sun had dropped behind the hills. Goodnight began to fire into the savages who had regrouped at the edge of the field and there were more pouring over a hill from the south, shadows riding up and over the ridge shaped against the evening light. Five shots rang out in succession like the methodic clang of a church bell calling for the disciples. He was aiming at their forms and daring them to ride in as RL arose to haul his wife toward the door of the Small's jacal home. RL leaned into her ear as they made for the porch. Honey, hang in there now, he whispered. It's gonna be alright. The indians whirled in the pasture and raised their bows. Goodnight sat his horse in front of the Terry's as a shield and he drew his rifle from its scabbard and started letting off rounds as he slowly backed toward the front yard. Clint Small had opened the door and was firing into the field. RL carried her through the doorway amidst a fusillade of gunfire. She was unconscious again.

Goodnight dismounted and scrambled inside. Clint, we need ever weapon you got, he said. He looked at RL. I'm sorry, he said. I'm sorry about all this.

Small headed for the back rooms calling for his son. Ed! he yelled, go fetch the ammo box.

RL was trying to catch his breath. How many are out there?

I dont know. They're all over. A hunnerd. Maybe more.

Goodnight spat and wiped his brow with his forearm and looked out from a window. They were trying to collect themselves.

Clint, what about the Warren boys?

Already off to McKavett, ridin for help.

They had rushed Sally into the back room where children were jammed under the beds and a slew of women were huddled in terror. Ed Small was bringing armfuls of guns and cartridge belts to either side of the front door and window, two old percussion five shooters and a Mississippi rifle that first saw action in the Mexican War, an even older, massive .44 cap and ball, a .36 caliber Paterson with a twelve-inch barrel, several newer second model Colt revolvers.

The walls surrounding the residence were framed by timbers plastered with mud and they saw to their arms and positioned themselves aside the window and door of this blockhouse to await the ambush.

From this new purview the ball of the sun now sat directly across the pasture opposite them. They whispered in low voices to one another. What are you thinking?

I dont know.

I caint see for the goddamn sun.

I know it.

It'll be down shortly. We just need to hold em off until dark.

Then they watched them appear, some mounted and some afoot, scattering madly about the property in their primal bowlegged scamper, a few carrying picks and mattocks appropriated from the barn. Goodnight saw a shadow and let off a shot blindly into the sunlight. The defenders were shielding their eyes from the glare, faces crinkled like prunes, stealing quick glances out into the bedlam. Soon they began to hear the thumping in the walls as the savages with the barn tools commenced digging out the pickets which formed the house.

The roof of the home was made of split logs and bramble from the cedar breaks and the savages may have meant to set the brush afire. RL left the window and moved to the north wall of the house and began to punch out loopholes in the mud creases and fire randomly at any sign of movement. The Small boy knelt by Goodnight watching his expressions and handed him a loaded double-barrel shotgun and Goodnight raised his left hand to block the sun and steadied the shotgun awkwardly with the other arm and let off a blast into the yard. He had not seen him crossing but an indian fell stumbling forward bleeding. RL shot a warrior in the face at close range and Goodnight fired again at a cluster scurrying behind a tree like a covey of flustered quail. Goodnight cursed quietly under his breath and the boy handed him up a loaded six shooter and RL reloaded his pistol and they raised the barrels and fired again. They each had an angle on a wounded brave crawling for the cover of the well and their shots laid him out dead in the dust. The home was filled with the haze of the smoke and then it became silent. They heard a warrior somewhere out in the pasture blowing a bugle.

Get on over here, RL.

What?

The window.

RL ducked down and scurried over and they surveyed the battlefield.

The raiders seemed to be humbled by these calamities and Goodnight pressed another Minie ball past the muzzle rifling and let off another shot as the raiders scrambled to gather themselves and flee back into the hills, carrying their dead and wounded away, their forms slowly growing dimmer in the dusk and their ireful yelps and the distant clamor of hooves echoing into the dying light.

They watched them go. It was a full minute before anyone spoke. Goodnight shook his head. I'm so sorry, RL, he said. He looked deep into his eyes, shaking his head. Damnit RL, he whispered. I'm so damn sorry.

RL sat there, staring out the window.

Goodnight looked to the back of the house where the women and children were hiding and he looked at RL again. He had no words. Clint Small walked over and put a hand on RL's shoulder and tried to make eye contact but it was a lost cause. He looked toward the back of the house and called to his son.

Ed, light us some lamps.

After a while RL walked to the back where the children lay huddled on the dirt floor whimpering with their eyes closed. A half-grown girl knelt beside Sally Terry singing a hymn quietly as tears ran down her face. Sally was heaving and vomiting blood and that shredded layer of skin atop her head was dribbling up in a puddled sheen of blood and pus. He laid down beside her and held her in his arms and an hour later he was still lying beside her and holding her when she passed.

2

— ★ —

Recollections of a Plainsman

The Goodnight Ranch House, Texas Panhandle
November 3, 1926

He sits up from his bed where he has been dying and rustles himself into consciousness. He begins to wheeze and cough up blood, spits it up into a trash can. There is bright sunshine, crispness of a fall afternoon, the creaking of an old house. He stands and moves sleepily toward the door, gimping into the hallway, feeling the pain of the ninety years in his bones. He shuffles across the wooden floor and slowly enters the breakfast room.

In the kitchen he pauses to get his bearings, pours coffee, and steps into a den brightened by natural light. He approaches his beloved old rocker by the screen door, the window view into the west pasture. Cool breeze blowing in the dusty dry odor of the plains.

He leans back into the creaking chair and sighs deeply. Beside the fireplace a young writer sits with a pad and pen, he smiles warmly, his eyes intensely studying the great presence of the old man.

Hours pass in a symphony of reminisces, as if he is pouring out his soul before the Lord. The writer soaks it all in and fills up his journal, looking up as the old man inhales a cigar, seeing his gray eyes. Swigs of black coffee, the pains of old age. His joys. And regrets.

He has been wandering the Staked Plains of Texas all summer in search of its secrets. Old timers, hanging on as relics of the past, their tales fading away forever. I was born for this, he thinks. The old man is larger than life to him. He sits slouched over, breathing heavily, slurping the coffee, glazed eyes reaching back deep into all that his life has been.

The writer avoids asking questions and only listens. Pauses in the stories leave powerful silence, the ticking of the grandfather clock, scribble of pen on paper, windgusts upon the ranch house. At times he is overcome by powerful emotions and finds himself fighting back the impulse of tears.

Goddamn, Haley! the rancher blurts out, slapping his thigh, breaking the poignancy of those moments.

In the hallway a young woman leans her head into the doorway, a caretaker checking in.

He raises his grizzled face with its piercing glare toward her. The writer puts down his pen, smiles, and begins to share stories from his own youth. Working cattle on the Pecos for his father, the rugged honor of the cowboys and the nuances of the horses that carried them.

And then the old rancher begins again, tugging the curious soul of the young writer deeper into the crevices of his mind, where the fleetingness of time screams profanities about the transience of each and every moment.

The adventures the old man relates so beautifully from the porch affect the soul like gospel. He evangelizes from the shade of the gallery, the brisk plains winds whispering through. He fondly recalls the early days on the Keechi range, his first close friendships and a woman who entered his life and changed everything.

I've ridden seven hundred miles in nineteen days carrying twelve thousand dollars in gold, laying up during the day and riding beneath the stars all night to avoid the Comanche.

The advantage of being young and fearless. The preoccupation with making something of my life. His eyes gaze longingly upon the prairies he once so supremely controlled. When the writer leans forward, the old man's glare stiffens back in focus in anticipation of another question.

The writer flips his journal to a fresh page. Mr Goodnight, earlier you mentioned something to me about the bodies you discovered at the Palo Duro.

The old man looks down and closes his eyes. Peers up and out the window and sighs. Outside there is a deep redness in the west. His knee is jimmying up and down, knurled fingers thumbing his white goatee.

Well, I was in the process of establishing the ranch down in the gorge of the Palo Duro. I found em while scouting the country, planning how the place would be laid out. We were on the headwaters of the Red River, a thousand feet down from the Llano Estacado. I'd brought Mollie down, the Adairs too. We were finalizing the terms of our deal. I'd left them back at camp and I was out alone. When I stumbled upon the first one I covered my nose and started to sort through just what in the hell I was looking at. Was it an indian? Going on three years since Mackenzie ran em out of the canyon, their ancestral homelands.

The Comanche knew they were finished. They'd come to learn that the United States military would hunt them down no matter the cost. Their way of life revolved around the buffalo and the white man was hell-bent on hunting them to extinction. It was a time of apocalypse. There were wise ones of course that had accepted it all along. And there were those that had fought to the very end and finally submitted. Quanah Parker was somehow able to see past it all into his future. You see, I wasnt the only one venturing into that country with an eye on permanent settlement. There were other cowmen and surveying parties. New Mexican pastores, mustangers, horse rustlers. Still some renegade indians wandering from the reservations. And that's what I thought I saw. At first I didnt think much of it. I'd seen death on the prairie before.

Who were they?

No response. The old man looks down. Now by god Haley, I thought you were here to talk to me about the trail drives.

You know… yes sir you're right. I'm sorry.

In the afternoons he summons a miraculous energy for his age. The writer tactfully nudges the dialogue along, introducing whatever topic he feels might inspire expressive responses. Bright sunlight gleams into the study beaming over the old man's face, clearly illuminating his weathered skin, soulful eyes, the relics from his life and others he's gathered that decorate the room.

The young man explores the archives of his mind, absorbing his stories into his soul. When the conversation lulls he is patient and supremely observant. He wishes that he could record it all verbatim, that his brain could magically transpose it onto the paper by rote.

Sometimes at night the old man is unable to sleep, still drunk on the adrenaline of revealing his memories, of reliving all of his old adventures. Or when he does sleep he awakens to a terrible dream.

He could see the vultures swirling up on top of the Caprock. Once he made the rim he saw a mound of blackness a half mile away. Heads bobbing, pecking. Not buffalo. Gorging and picking. The screech of those on the fringes unable to get their fill.

He nudged his horse and trotted toward the stench. Soon the vultures began to scatter. Flapping their dark wings and hopping about. Singles flying up and circling. Groups of them bounding to nearby vantage points. The wind off the plain bore a rancid smell and he spat and put his nose in the crook of his arm. A shock to the senses. He scanned the country for sign. He regarded the sun, the clouds floating above. He thought he saw something else on a rise about a quarter mile out. The horse was jerking its head and stomping and he wheeled it around to observe the distant horizon beyond the trail he'd just rode.

He did not want it to be this way but he knew what this was. It wasnt just a case of him being a rider discovering the common occurrence of death on the plains. Often numb to the realities, irritated by its inconveniences. He would have asked himself, what in the hell happened here? He'd be curious, thinking, what random events must have led to this little dust up? During his forty years on earth he could not count the number of deaths he'd witnessed. Then he noticed the belongings that were still on and about the remains. The personal items that caught his eye. He could not believe it.

Later, after dragging them back down and placing them to rest in the rugged red dirt of the canyon, his thoughts turn back to the past, their happiest moments and their smiles. He was unable to sleep that night, tortured. No remedy or forgiveness. He knew those voices in his head would never go silent.

He was facing these painful realities and he imagined in his virility that he would overcome it all by moving on, by pouring himself fully into the rest of his life. As if turning away all of the things in his life that had brought him to this specific moment was something that could make the pain go away.

The historian would sit with his legs crossed, his pen dancing across the journal on his lap. He would observe closely, between breaks of conversation or eye contact, the walls and shelves of the room that had become such a shrine to the settlement of the Llano Estacado. A place so many others had been seeking access to, the old pioneers dying off, and with time marching on, such an urgency to capture the lore and document the old man's recollections.

This was the phase in his life he would look upon forever as the one he felt most alive. A second-hand Model T Ford and fifty dollars a month. Touring the High Plains back roads gathering the folklore of the fast-fading pioneers. He felt like a teenager again cowboying out in Winkler and Loving counties, constantly free and on the move, sleeping under the stars with no cares in all the world.

He was like a sponge, soaking it up, not forcing anything. He was an invited guest, for now, of the old plainsman and his caretaker, here in the big white ranch house the old man had built forty years ago at the Fort Worth and Denver railway station. And yet he was prepared to leave at any moment to not overstay his welcome.

For both the old man and the scholar the presence of the young woman was one of life's accidental, mysterious pleasures. She had a charm about her that seemed to bottle up her youthful spirit and sprinkle it about all who were blessed by her presence. Full figure, wavy brown hair. Her bright smile infectious, genuine, caring. She had arrived from Montana a month earlier to find the subject of her curiosity in poor health, sad, very much alone.

So this new lease on life, for a man just recently back from the lip of his grave and still recovering from the painful loss of his wife of fifty-six years, was something deeply spiritual, as if the hand of God had reached out to invoke all of his mercy.

The old ranch house had a spirit of its own, a sanctuary to the settling of the old west. Each room with its own secrets, its own ghosts, the soul of the old plainsman's life. And now its energy had been restored. A burgeoning historian deeply respectful of West Texas history. A young woman breathing new life into the old home. Cleaning, organizing, doing all of the little things that would allow him to live fully in these final years before he would pass.

She was completely devoted to his well-being, to make him comfortable. She laughed at his stories, ignored his profanities and surly tirades, and prodded here and there with insightful questions. She boldly had her eye on reforming his gruffness, of turning him toward the Lord.

Yet she was also becoming engrossed in the essence of the visiting historian's efforts, ever mindful to supplement his research while he was away, sitting with the old man for hours on end recording his recollections and using her skills as a former stenographer to help him communicate at a furious pace with the outside world. During breaks in the interview sessions the twenty-somethings would whisper observations to one another like excited school children.

Evetts, can you believe his energy? It's just incredible! His mind still so sharp!

Yes, I keep thinking that someone really needs to write an account of the colonel's life.

Why, it ought to be you!

I dont know. I wouldnt want to disrupt his zeal at this stage.

Well now, I dont think that would happen at all.

They became bonded by the cause. Asking questions, listening intently to every word. Kindred spirits, playing off one another and tactfully sprinkling a complimentary point or inquiry to drive the old plainsman on.

The writer had the country deep in his bones, raised by his father to be a cowman. As a boy he'd ridden his gray pony eighty miles to the Home Ranch on the Texas-New Mexico border to work cattle with the old cowhands. Riding long hours with the feel of a fresh cow horse beneath him. Sleeping under the stars, the summer heat and winter northers. The camaraderie around a good campfire on a brisk fall evening where his current subject's legendary exploits were frequent conversation.

All of these things running through his head, barely out of college and his entire life ahead of him. He scribbles furiously on the page attempting to capture it all, and he finishes his last notation and looks up from his notebook again, hungry for more.

Goodnight followed the slope up to the rise where he'd noticed something moving in the tall plains grass. It was a forty-strong wake of vultures consuming a body. He pulled his sidearm and approached cautiously. The big birds hissed and hopped, flapping their wings and strutting about clumsily. The dead man had been shot through his abdomen and he lay there reeking and bloated. Swarms of flies buzzing, thick, almost deafening.

He put his handkerchief over his nose and mouth and held his breath. He'd been trying to tell himself that there was no way it was possible but he knew it was him. He knew the man suffered a long time in that place before he passed. He thought of the time he came upon the mule that had been the only living thing that remained from the wagontrain that had been slaughtered by the Comanche warparty. Lying on its side, patiently, still attached to the breeching harness, its leg shattered. Old, worn out, wasted. Waiting to die. What it was thinking. Looking up, walleyed, terrified, waiting for him to pull his sidearm and put him out of his misery.

Over the previous month the office had become the heart of the home. His charming new house guest caring for him, healing his body and soul, making him feel young again. Talking with him in great length about his life that was, his life to come. A sitting parlor, a library. A wardroom, a den. Like a museum, a shrine to the old west, sprinkled with relics of the old rancher's life.

There was a rocker, a rolltop desk covered in letters, papers, invoices, legal documents, random notations, poems, scriptures. A pair of buffalo horns on the wall cradling his old Ranger rifle. One solid wall of books, shelves littered with fossils, arrow heads, Mexican coins, antler sheds, boar teeth. A framed photo of Oliver Loving, one of a buffalo named Old Sykes. Leaning against a magnificent grandfather clock was an 1863 Henry rifle.

The writer absorbed the history when he sat in the room, this cathedral to a time that would never be again. He embraced the importance of his task, feeling the weight of the responsibility to honor this man and his times. Ticking of the clock. *An hour, once it lodges in the queer element of the human spirit, may be stretched to fifty or a hundred times its clock length.*

With the sleuth of a detective, as if he must examine and preserve every particle perfectly, he began to peruse through the cluttered contents of the desk. He picked up a receipt handwritten on stationery. *To A.B.S. for the Bowie knife I found on Custer Battlefield in North Panhandle of Texas & Oklahoma (Battle of Washita, 11-27-1868).* Underneath, a tattered leather-bound book. He cradled it in his hands. *Decline and Fall of the Roman Empire.* The book was heavy, musty, its binding barely held together from water damage. And then, as if he were a young boy getting caught with his hand in the candy jar, he closed the book and checked the door, tiptoeing nervously, holding his breath, and listening intently for anyone that might disturb his worship.

He eased back into the desk chair, thinking of the history of the book, opening it fondly in honor of its life's journey. He flipped through the pages to get a feel for the contents, wondering why it was even there. What was its story? What wisdom did it behold? What struggles did the author go through in its creation? CHAPTER LI. *The Conquest of Persia, Syria, Egypt, Africa, and Spain, by the Arabs or Saracens.* The chapter subtitles, as in all important historical works, seemed to have such a seductive allure.

He thumbed through several passages, already deeply struck by the impermanence of time because of his immersion into the home of this aging pioneer. And now the poignancy of these referenced lives from a thousand years ago, an entire civilization that no longer existed.

The little ranch town of Goodnight, Texas, named in his honor, had been mostly deprived from an oil and gas boom for the last year that included a ten thousand-barrel-a-day bonanza just two counties to the north. Amarillo was forty miles up the highway, headquarters of the major oil companies. Closer by the town of Claude, county seat and primary cattle shipping point, whose Palace Hotel had once made it the epicenter of the region. All of these towns sprang up with the railroad in the late 1880s. This was the same time he bought one hundred and sixty sections of rangeland on the Salt Fork of the Red River and custom built their two-story ranch house. And so began the second half of his life. As the railroads expanded and the droughts of the late 1800s lifted, the new century brought impactful change. Barbed wire spread, industrialization brought improvements to stock farming, and the big ranches began to be broken up and sold for cents on the dollar. The nesters flooded into the High Plains. And even though he was getting on up in years he was as active and ornery as ever.

Another decade ran by. World War I. Eventually his peers began to die off. One or two at first, then it seemed there was news of another every month or so. Yet he and his wife of forty-plus years stayed very active and maintained their status as patriarchs of the community. They funded churches, founded a school, experimented in breeding. The old rancher had become a legend in his own time. There was a push in the region to document the pioneers and they entertained the endless stream of visitors clamoring to meet him and hear his tales, experience him in the flesh and blood.

But by now they had become very old. He fought health problems. He could not get around as well as he once did. His finances were out of sorts. The home had lost its life source during those last several years before the lady of the house died. She had become consumed by dementia and deteriorated steadily to the point where she struggled to bathe and dress and needed to be fed. In the end she was bedridden day and night, lying there staring into space with no expression, no recognition of him or those who cared for her.

Virtually every aspect of the handsome home had been tailored for her. Its Victorian style elegance. The handpicked lumber, ten-foot ceilings, etched stained glass windows. Five fireplaces with slate mantels, custom hardwood doors from Colorado, a large dining room for entertaining guests. The old man had no use for these things. But he needed her, and the fire that remained inside him began to dwindle when she died that April of 1926.

His broken spirit and the failure of his lungs sapped his energy and unleashed an onslaught of sickness upon his tired body. He came to be cared for haphazardly, by committee. Employees of the ranch, old friends, volunteers from the church. An aging housekeeper, herself incapacitated from failing health. Her son, raised from infancy by the old man and his wife, now the foreman. The house was cluttered and smelled of sickness and remedies. Consumed by rheumatism, he could not move. When he did shuffle up and about his lungs could not sustain him. So he sat, he lay in bed. He fought off depression for a good while by dictating letters and entertaining visitors who came by to get their piece of history, nostalgia, the life and times of this man they called Colonel. But he could not sleep. He was having stomach issues. He fought high fevers and fluid in his lungs for over a month. Coughing and cussing. He considered the poignancy of a man's life, beginning to end, and then what. He thought a lot about dying. Then one day another letter arrived from the young woman in Montana that by coincidence happened to share his name. A month later Corinne Goodnight appeared upon his doorstep.

She smiled warmly and gave him a lengthy, loving hug. The first thing she noticed was the odor. A mixture of menthol, eucalyptus oil, and camphor. Tobacco, buffalo meat, whiskey. In some rooms the wallpaper and rugs, even the pine floors, had been soaked for so long in cigar smoke it was as if the entire home had been recently transformed from an old English smoking room.

The first thing he noticed was her beauty. Yet he instantaneously felt her intelligence, her complete presence. She had been orphaned as a teenager. She had worked as a nurse and eventually became a telegraph operator for the Northern Pacific Railway, all the while raising her younger brother and paying for his education. She was twenty-five years old and pretty and she had made a special point to stop by on her way to Florida not only because of their surname but like so many others, her genuine fascination in his story.

Before supper that first night she was already tidying up the house, generally picking things up, dusting, thinking of what all she could do to help. What she might do if it was her own home. The next morning she cleaned the kitchen and bathrooms. She drove him into Clarendon for groceries, medicine, cleaning supplies. When he asked her to stay and help she could not bring herself to say no. By the time the budding field secretary from the Historical Society arrived for what was now his third visit the old man was starting to feel alive again and the house had regained some semblance of its old soul.

3

— ★ —

The Journal of J. Evetts Haley

Canyon, Texas
November 3, 1926 (9:37 PM)

The old man wasnt all that cordial *upon my arrival, cussing incessantly, spitting impressive amounts of tobacco, and gesturing something derogatory about writers. I followed him across the tidy ranch house yard onto the shady wrap-around porch of a deteriorating, white two-story home that must have been something forty years ago. You can picture what this headquarters was like back then. There is a bunkhouse with a mess hall for the hands, corrals, a barn, various other aged structures that need work, and a large wooden-wheel windmill providing water. Over the fence near the railroad is another windmill; when I asked his caretaker, Miss Corinne Goodnight, about the setup, she responded in a reverential tone: "he built that one for the travelers."*

To the north and east of the home are orchards of locust trees set in rows that, Miss Goodnight explained, are where the old man frequently walks, not just to reflect but given his broken-down body, a chance for him to try and exercise in the shade. All about the grounds are signs of his love of wildlife and the outdoors. There are pens, for instance, where over the years fowl and animals had been raised. Over the course of my visit he referenced various species of quail, pheasants, chaparral birds, white doves, curlews, and even carrier pigeons, among others. He'd had ranges set not only for the preservation of buffalo, but he'd experimented with Persian sheep, different types of deer, antelope, and elk. In confidence one afternoon Miss Goodnight said that in the months since her arrival she'd heard accounts of a fighting goat, cross-bred turkeys and hogs, a moose that sickened and died from the heat, and even a seven-horned Navajo sheep.

Each day, about mid-morning, Mr Goodnight settles in at his office where it is now his custom to dictate letters and reminisces, which Miss Goodnight takes by shorthand and reads back to him. Based on his feedback she may handwrite the revision or perhaps type several copies for sending off and archiving. In the afternoons the scenario repeats itself, or she reads newly received correspondences to him, and she patiently listens to his reactions and takes notes for follow up as needed. Occasionally, when he wants to think, she will escort him to the upstairs sleeping porch where he sits in the sun and looks out over the open prairies and the rugged folds of Mulberry Canyon. But when he becomes fatigued, Miss Goodnight asserts, confirming what one might expect from a ninety-one-year-old man, "It is so very important to allow him his rest and he often will lay down for a nap."

When he enters the office, wearing a white Sunday shirt hanging loosely with suspenders supporting a pair of massive trousers pulled well above the navel, there is a moment of speculative silence, a pause perhaps out of respect, perhaps of apprehension and the obligation to assess the mood of an old man who teeters on the brink of extreme gentleness and fierce agitation. His bowlegged walk is seesawed, and he commands his cane with a flair, stomping or pointing for emphasis. He still seems large, despite his shrunken hunch, and his great shock of white hair is usually disheveled and yet somehow a charming accent. His features are rough-hewn, accentuated by enormous ears and a stern, skinny-eyed stare, a fascinating veneer for a man who often shows such a wide range of interests combined with deep sincerity, compassion, and wisdom.

His speech is low and gravelly but with such depth and emphasis, feeling almost biblical and as if, possibly because of such extreme hoarseness, to come from someone who is intentionally modifying their voice for a certain effect. And yet his authenticity amazes me and there is very often a clever little twinkle in his eye, an energy about him—characteristic is the fast bouncing of his right knee, not a nervous habit but seemingly a trait that helps him focus and pull amazing details from the recesses of his memories. And of course he is ever so apt to wave that cane angrily and blurt out imaginative profanities. Most of his statements initially seem to stem from deep impatience, as if he would challenge any angle of dialogue, however with patience and persistence I'm able to bring out his extremely sensitive nature and profound curiosity. When he gets going, as in a recollection of old acquaintances such as Bose Ikard or Oliver Loving, or when expounding upon the fate of the Comanche, he adopts a heartfelt, dramatic tone; the images he relays from the long ago will bring a tear to the eye.

Or contrasted against his incredible ability to cuss: a salty diction birthed from the trail, educated by the likes of Jim Bridger, Kit Carson, Lucien Maxwell and influenced by Indian and Spanish slang. No matter the audience—preachers, women, children—all welcome beneficiaries. The authentic nature of his articulation stems not only from the vocal fatigue, the frequent coughing fits and throat clearing, but from the poetic blend of a strong southern accent (truly a Texan accent, not from the deep south), and inventive expletive phraseology. No matter the topic, serious or sanguine, his sentences are often linked by accents such as "sonofabitch," or some form of "goddamn," and various philosophical religious blasphemies. And yet the symphony in which it is issued never seems to give offense, as there is a lyrical purpose that results not in true profanity, but its very own vernacular of a time that will eventually be lost forever. I have never heard any man cuss more beautifully, in such varied ways, or with such eloquence.

But most of all, I am overwhelmed with the depth of his nature and strength of his character. The brusque exterior is simply a mask. Being in his presence has forced me to consider my own mortality and imagine, unthinkably, what I might be like if I am fortunate enough to experience what life has to offer for another sixty-five some-odd years. I'm not exactly sure yet how to make good use of these interview sessions but I sense something spiritual underway.

4

— ★ —

Recollections of a Plainsman

The Goodnight Ranch House
November 4, 1926

In the office the writer studies the collection of relics gathered on the fireplace mantle. An old JA-initialed iron brand, arrow points, metal trinkets, rare rock specimens. Early morning sunlight and he is alone in the room. He picks up a drafted letter recently dictated. Dear Mrs G.A. Brown… Underneath there is a battered old book. It is the bible the old man reclaimed when he discovered the bodies.

He picks up a notebook the nurse has been filling with annotations. He begins to slowly read and absorb details of her meticulous shorthand notes.

Just west of Fort Belknap was the furthest line of white settlement, from there only wide-open country inhabited by the Comanche and Kiowa all the way to the Rocky Mountains. Prairie country for two hundred miles. Excellent timber. Rough but watered well. Generally good grasses. The headwaters of the Red, Brazos, Colorado, and Conchos spring from the canyons that cut down out of the Staked Plains. El Llano Estacado. I could never be lonely on the plains.

The canyons were the badlands. Crazy geology. Gypsum-laced water. Bizarre and beautiful. The Palo Duro became my home. Quitaque to the south was the primary Comanchero trading point with the indians, for the cattle they stole from us in the settlements. They called another Las Lenguas, for all the traders and their foreign tongues. There is the valley of Casas Amarillas, with its Cañón del Rescate, or Rescue, for captives that were turned over in its recesses. Hiding places. Trading grounds. There is also Blanco Canyon, Quanah's favorite.

Up on the Caprock an ocean of grass. Infinite. No trees. Open horizon. Nothing to block the northers rolling in from the plains. There were no white men who knew that country. Maybe five thousand Comanche and Kiowa. It was a paradise. We called it, Comancheria.

I began to learn the secrets of this region as a scout during the war. Sam Houston had placed Sul Ross in command of the Texas Rangers out of Belknap. I felt like God had put me on this earth to be a part of that regiment.

As a young boy a fine old indian warrior named Caddo Jake regularly visited our homestead and he would show me the ways of the wilderness, which set me on my way to become a proper scout. Over the years I came to intimately understand the essential qualifications. Key skills, an infinite number of hardened, appreciable talents and many others that are more intangible but are critical to the art of plainscraft, and without which, can mean life or death for the command. I believe many of these are innate from the womb. In these notes it has been attempted to preserve the nature of these attributes.

First, he must not become flustered in any condition for his strong presence of mind sets the standard for the entire command. In emergencies instant decisions are required. He must be able to read into the soul of every man in the unit, from the most indifferent high-brow commanders to the working-class everyman to the cutthroat outlaws, and he must earn and maintain their full confidence.

He must be born with a compass and never need any help but his own to find his way. He should have perfect eyesight with the ability to see clearly in any sort of light, the finest of details from very far away. This must be combined with sound judgment, reading the developments of the country, understanding the paths of least resistance, and the decision-making prowess to confidently pick the routes that avoid danger. He must be able to recognize and understand any sort of sign to guide the way through dangerous, unchartered country with precision.

Finding water. Familiarity with every species of flora and fauna that can indicate hints of the way to satisfactory water. Grasses, shrubs, the behavior of wild animals and birds and whether they are going to or coming from water. Some birds need water every day, others do not. The dirt dauber, for instance, will have mud in its mouth when coming from water.

When observing tracks and other indian sign he must intimately understand the process that time imposes on Mother Nature. The effect of temperature, the sun, moisture, and such all play a role in judging how long ago a particular sign was left.

Haley looks up from the page when the old man re-enters the study muttering profanities under his breath. Energized from the coffee, he sits down, slowly sizes up his thoughts, and without provocation begins to talk with great authority.

Haley, I was telling you about the Comanche and Kiowa. They were fighting for their existence. There were a few renegade bands when I began scouting the Palo Duro but not many. Most all of em harried into the reservations by then. I've always had a bent to chase the golden dream. I'm one who takes pride in understanding the country, the people, the markets. They said the Comancheria was uninhabitable, that it couldnt be tamed by man. But I am a man who takes action when others sit back. Hellfire. Thirty thousand square miles of wide ass open grazing grass. Hardly any buffalo left and the indians were about done. So opportunities present themselves. I'd come to know the streams, canyons, and springs. I knew every trail on those Staked Plains, the secrets of those who came before that had never made it into a map, chart, or book.

So I knew what I was after when I first entered the Palo Duro in that spring of 1876. Goddamn, seems like yesterday but what it is now? Fifty years ago? Anyhow, before all of this the Comanche ran the Apache out and controlled it all to themselves. Oh, what was it Dot Babb called it? Bosom of the Comanche. Yes, that was it, Haley. Bosom of the Comanche.

Hell when I was a boy the Comanche wadnt worried about the white folks. They were more concerned with the meskins encroaching on their range and so they started raiding down there back in the thirties and forties. They'd get organized up here before summer was over. Bands from all over. Five hundred, a thousand. Rendezvous at Big Spring, cross the border down at the Big Bend, spend months at a time raising all kinds of hell on the meskins. Four hundred miles or more south of the border. A thousand miles from home. And a lot of em stayed for the winter, which aint all that bad of an idea considering how damn cold it gets up here. Imagine it. Treat yourself to a little ole wintertime raidin vacation down on the Bolson de Mapimi. Eighty degrees on a New Year's Day. Good range country. Plenty water.

And they'd do it up good. Burning entire villages, killing all the men, bringing back one helluva lot of livestock and as many of the womenfolk and children that were tough enough to survive the ride back. And all the hell they'd put em through on the way.

There was an ole boy at the Trail Drivers reunion a few years back in Santone. I forget his name. Said he saw some statistic that claimed in the state of Durango alone, said over five thousand meskins killed and something like a thousand captives taken.

Damn, that's just hard to believe. Going on seventy-five some-odd years ago now. And then they started to unleash that business on us Texans. But we fought back. And then eventually the cholera got em. By the time they'd been beaten they was maybe only a couple thousand of em left.

Yes sir, I'd had my eye on that country for a long time. Mustangers used to talk about the gorges that cut into the plains and all that good range country.

Hard to think back on it now. I suppose it's the way of things. Since the beginning. They ran off the Apache. Then we ran them off. Or go back even further. Hell, that old book on the Romans over there tells all about how they fumbled themselves up. Aint nothing lasts forever. It's bound to happen here. Our little ole U-S- of A has been here what, a hundred and fifty years? Comanche didnt have it much longer'n that. We're just barely started but it's bound to happen eventually. Pains me to think about what this world is coming to. Makes you wonder what traces of us'll be left behind. When I was riding into the Palo Duro to claim that range, into that beautiful chasm, all I kept thinking was, it's no longer theirs. I for some reason remember very damn distinctly thinking, they're gone. Forever.

There were still signs of them everywhere. That last battle. Metal arrow points and tinklers. Rusted nails and tack. Picket pins. Bridle bits and buckles. Black strands of hair from the squaws hacking their lice-ridden scalps off in grief from their world being turned upside down. Hell, I found enough of it to make cinches.

But chew on this just a little if you will. Think about the ones before them. And before them and before them. That ole boy you brought in here the other day, what was his name? The archaeologist?

Studer?

Yes, Studer. He was asking me about some of the stuff I have, stuff I've seen. Dugouts of the Comancheros. Old whiskey kegs hidden in the hills. Knickknacks from the battlefields. But hear me on this. He's been digging into a helluva lot more. Things that go way, way back. Folks been roaming this range for longer than we'll ever know and back when I was pushing into that canyon I didnt have any perspective whatsoever on that. But I damn sure do now.

Studer reminded me about a place called Rocky Dell. And I remembered very clearly that Martinez, my meskin guide, told me about it on that very first trip into the Palo Duro. You know, you and I ought to make a run up there one of these days.

That would be wonderful. I would love that.

Goodnight had grown very fond of the young cowboy historian. He was built spare and wiry and had the gait of a young man who'd spent a lot of time on horseback. Perhaps he saw in Haley a fellow cowman—a man bred for the winds and sun and alkali who lived strictly by his own code—and he felt a strong urge to help him.

Anyhow, said Goodnight, Studer says there's rock art in there from long before the Comanches. Prehistoric. Five hundred years. A thousand. Just think about how long folks have been using that place.

We took those things for granted back in our youth. Like a lot of things. Now I only remember fragments of it and it is all like a beautiful dream, those times. The days I was scouting for Obenchain, those years running herds up to Fort Sumner with Loving, it got to where I didnt need a compass. Didnt need food or sleep. I got along with Tafoya and those Comancheros because I knew the country like they did.

It took way too long before the goddamned military figured out they needed to listen to folks like us who truly knew those plains. The Great American Desert they called it. Comancheros, buffalo hunters, pastores. The early cow men who ventured into that unknown territory. Shitfire, that country was the enemy more than anything! Hard to think that toward the end there were maybe only a few thousand indians in that area. Yes sir, things sure turned against em once we figured out their ways, and all of that wild ass country they controlled. Figured out how they went to war. Us white folks were coming and there wadnt a goddamn thing they could do about it.

All hell broke loose the year before the war. We were on the far western edges of the frontier, you see. It may have even been Quanah's daddy who'd been stirring up all them bands to a raiding frenzy. Right around Thanksgiving. That massacre, I think about what that poor bastard Joe Sherman must have walked up on. His pregnant wife had been dragged along by her hair. Clothes ripped off, likely in front of the children as they were being hauled off. I mean, roughed up good. Damn likely she was gang raped, then one of em took the honors of ripping her mane off for the trophy. The others shot her full up of arrows and then rode off to let her die. Cold ass rain of late winter. Picture it. She drags herself outside and calls for help. Lays there overnight and her husband finds her the next mornin. Gives birth to a dead baby shortly thereafter. Little did I know then that it was in the cards for me to have my own experiences with a terrible indian depredation. More personal. You know, closer to the bone.

When I was a boy the Caddos in my neck of the woods didnt conduct themselves that way. Anyhow, I'd gotten word and headed out in the rain to warn the neighbors. Gather men to follow, make a fight. But there wadnt no way in hell of tracking em in that rain.

And that was about all it took to get folks to pack up and head back east. But there were those of us ready for a fight. We got organized. It was Jack Cureton's company near Belknap and Sul Ross and us Rangers. Camp Cooper sent troops. It was so very damn cold. There were reports of a Comanche camp up on the Pease River. I was designated as guide, riding out ahead scouting for sign. And wouldnt you know it, on the trail plain as day I found Mrs Sherman's bible. Just layin right there for the taking like God set it there with his very own hand. The indians had stolen it intending to use it as reinforcement in packing a shield but they'd dropped it in the chase.

Never ceases to amaze me. You never know what this ole world might have in store for you. Haley, you ever sit there and ask yourself, ask how those things that seem so trivial in the moment often have a way of turning out to be meaningful? Now listen to me, Haley. Mark that down because that right there is a fact of life.

The field secretary has the old bible opened up to Matthew 6:33 on his lap. A solemn silence in the room. Grandfather clock ticking peacefully. Late afternoon light of fall filters in through the windows.

What... he begins to ask, coming out of his concentration, but he is unable to complete his question before the old rancher begins again.

Haley, have you ever caught yourself thinking about how you're going to die?

Well...

I mean really thought about what's going to get you?

Well no, not really. I dont suppose I have.

No. No sir you have not. Not at your age.

The old man looked out the window into his past. He shook his head sadly.

When Mollie started acting a little off I didnt think all that much of it at first. But my goodness did she go downhill fast. Several times we'd have visitors, mothers with their little girls. You know, the ones who wore those bonnets. And Mollie, bless her heart, she'd get a hold of the bonnet from them, all sweet about it but real strange, and she'd smile and put it on her own self as if she was a little girl.

Really?

And then she'd refuse to give it back! It was damn embarrassing, and I'd have to walk the mother off and apologize and offer to pay her for it. Mollie, she just really began to lose her mental abilities and it was such a terrible thing. It made me think back to Cynthia Ann Parker for some reason. Quanah's mother. Such a slow and painful way to waste away. Helpless. A damned pitiful way to die.

And Loving. After they ambushed him and Wilson on the Pecos. Somehow the poor bastard made it to Fort Sumner alive but by the time I got there the rot in his arm had set in something awful. You see, he wouldnt let em cut it off until I got there. Had to be some little voice in his head, something inside him that knew he was done for. And that damned greenhorn doctor felt like he could put us off. Considered us Rebel sympathizers. Finally amputated the arm but Oliver's hunch was right. The rot set in again. He lay there dying. Twenty-two days.

Now, the Coe boys didnt have to suffer like that. They were left to hang from the end of a rope. That custom goes way back, as you know. Hell, back then it was entertainment. Gallows set up for all to see. Pass the bottle around and watch em drop and leave the corpse to hang for the sopilotes.

The things we do. Oliver wanted to be buried in Texas so I dragged his ass four hundred miles in his coffin back home to Weatherford. Packed in powdered charcoal and sealed in tin. Now that's one helluva funeral procession. Laid him to rest with fraternal honors.

The old man was rubbing his long white goatee, staring at the floor, thinking of that time in his life. Then he looked up, peering at the writer. Haley, he said, What do you want your coffin to be? Have you thought at all about where you'd like to be buried?

Why now, Mr Goodnight I dont…

What are they going to say at your funeral?

Haley studied him. The old man glared back in expectation of an answer but Haley did not answer.

Yes, we'll all have our time, said the colonel.

There was an old Kiowa chief. Named Satank. Sitting Bear they called him. They say that when the Rangers killed his boy he went out and tracked down the location of his son's body. Picked up the bones and carried em with him. You get older, you see, and you think about these sorts of things. And did you ever hear the story of one of those last Kiowa chiefs? Kicking Bird they called him. Apparently one of his own people, a rival, poisoned him. Poisoned him with a damned ole cup of coffee! Yep.

And then apparently somebody had the idea that he ought to be buried as a Christian. Now, imagine that!

Or the Blue Death. Quanah's mother used to tell him of how the cholera wiped out a whole helluva lot of their tribe before he was born. Shit yourself to death, he'd joke. I suppose there's some sense in keeping things light. Quanah was good at that.

Haley looked up from his note taking and sat up on the edge of his chair. You know, I've always wanted to know more about his mother.

Now hold on just a goddamned second, I want to finish this.

Why, of course.

They'd look to bury them up on a high point with a view. Dig out a pit as best they could, draw up the arms and legs with chords and throw em in. Cover it up with big rocks to keep the coyotes from digging em up. The architect, Sayles, he can tell you all about it. He's been finding em all over out here.

Or some would build a scaffold and lay the body up in a tree. Tie em up real good and tight. Now, I never understood the thinking there because how'd you keep the damn buzzards away.

Something seems to be caught in his throat and he coughs hard and then chokes it up and spits a foul yellow hunk of snot into the trash can and then begins coughing uncontrollably. The young woman hurries in from the hallway. Sweetie, she says. You must be very thirsty from all of that talking. Can I get you something to drink?

I'd love a cold glass of iced tea. And if you have a little lemon. But please dont doctor it. I dont like those little sprigs of mint you get from the garden.

She smiled warmly and turned for the kitchen. He was trying to remember where he'd placed his flask of bourbon.

Anyhow, you said something about Quanah's mother. She was packing up a meat camp with a bunch of other squaws. Of course, I didnt see what happened initially. Ross' boys were up ahead of us.

The old man pauses, sighs, spits another stream of brown dribble into the can.

Really no use in saying much more on that. There's good men and bad men, and they make different choices in the heat of battle. We rode through that sacked camp over the dead bodies. I haven't forgiven myself to this day. Of the few survivors there was a squaw that was wailing somethin awful. That was Quanah's mother. Had a baby girl with her.

Really? That must have been incredible to witness.

Behind the filth if you looked real close you could see the blond features.

Quanah wasnt in the camp?

No sir, I dont think a Comanche buck one was in their camp that day.

The old man bit down on his lower lip, shaking his head. Haley watched him.

Chickenshit Sul Ross, he said. Useless as tits on a boar hog. It came to be known as the Battle of Pease River, but I assure you it was no battle.

So how did it play out from there?

Why, they took her back to the permanent camp. And of course she kept trying to escape. Very distraught. Never did cheer up. Finally brought her Uncle Parker in to see about her and when she heard her name it triggered something, spurred her to talking.

The Parker raid was in '36?

That's about right, she'd been a full-blood Comanche for that long. Twenty-four years I think it was. She'd married a chief. Quanah's daddy. They took her back home and tried to make her live like a white woman again. Apparently she wouldnt have any of it. Deeply missed her old ways of life, her family. Then her little girl died and apparently she starved herself to death.

It is silent in the room save for the ticking of the clock and the scribbling of pen on paper. Haley looks up, his face pained. What a terrible, terrible tragedy, he says.

Well, we all have it coming to us one way or another. Hell, look at me right now. You know what they'd do to me if I was Comanche? See, we're all going to get to a point where things are just not the same. I know I'm due for it one day. Well, if I was an old Comanche who couldnt get along anymore, and if I had any family, they'd be all up in arms about the spirits taking over my body. Then I'd wander off to take a leak or whatever, piddle around, get caught up observing nature. Likely get disoriented, and then I'd wander back to camp to find them gone. My own damned family! That's a fact. They'd ride on, without me! But you see, Haley, I wouldnt let that happen. Because like those old bucks when I know the time is near, I'll wander off alone and find a quiet spot to die. And that'll be all there is to it.

Haley excuses himself to use the men's room, leaving the old man there in the room alone with his thoughts, his mind drifting back to the depths of the Palo Duro that day when he stood over the first body that he found. Just a mangled, stiffening corpse.

He played it out in his head. What his final thoughts must have been before he died. All of the signs pointed to it being a struggle. There was a long trail of trampled, blood-splotched grass stretching for perhaps a half mile. You could see where he'd lain at rest but then was disturbed by the carrion seekers of the prairie and then fought them off and crawled on. Matted patches of grass stained with dried blood. He lay where he finally succumbed to the blood loss.

He imagined it all. Shot through the shoulder. Unbelievable pain. He tied a tourniquet and plugged the hole with his kerchief but he wouldnt be able to truly stop the bleeding. Not dead yet but he was going to die and it would take a long time. Mind racing. He got up and started walking, stumbling along, seeing blank spots, stars. Then he collapsed. Hallucinating. In and out of consciousness and then finally out for good. The great plains sun rises all morning, hovering high, passing into the afternoon with the vultures swirling and searching for scent. He comes to, briefly. He sees the light above the plains brightening with the sunset, suffering, fighting death as the great ball of fire dies into the horizon, and as he passes out again in the dusk the animals of the night come out and then all is dark.

A few hours later he opens his eyes to a pack of gray wolves sniffing and snarling all around him. He flails his arms wildly, slapping one on the muzzle and jumping to his feet, yelling in rage, intense pain shooting through his shoulder and his head. They back off, growling and snapping and barking. He throws rocks and forces them back, scattering into the darkness. A lone, haunting howl, then the eerie harmony of a chorus howl. The wolves around him, those in the distance, dropping in and out of the chorus for several melodic minutes. His horse is gone and he sets out on foot, infused by the jolt of adrenaline. They trail him as he moves slowly into the night, drawing close now and again only to fall back and scatter as another rock is hurled their way. An hour after midnight they finally pull back for good, slinking off into the side canyons of the Caprock to hunt some other prey. Then he lies down to sleep and he dreams but in the morning when the sun rises over the plains again and there is birdsong of the new day he does not wake up.

When Haley returns he sits down and looks at his papers. He is tired from trying to pull it all in, his fatigue and carelessness no match for this hierophant of the High Plains. Of all the fascinating topics they have covered he has become enchanted by this one recurring theme that seems to lie so deep and dark inside his subject. He rolls his pencil between his thumb and fingers and contemplates his approach. Outside the golden-red fire of the dying sun, the room somber and dark. He had thought it over when he stepped away and there was something that just did not add up. He raises the topic one last time. Mr Goodnight, he says. The bodies you found in the Palo Duro…

The old man looks up with a glare, wanting to release more of everything that is inside his mind, his soul, but not this topic. He inhales deeply, spits a wad of tobacco into the spittoon at his feet. Syrupy brown spittle in his long gray goatee. Now, by god Haley… Then he begins to unleash a stream of profanities at Haley more eloquent and beautiful than any man has ever heard.

5

— ★ —

Carried Away

The warparty was mounted and riding hard to the west leaving behind them in the ravaged valley of the San Saba a purgatory of fire and blood and smoke and the yellowed haze of traildust rising in the fading sun from the remuda of stolen horses they drove before them. Sam rode pillion behind the chieftain, holding on and gazing back at the shrinking image of his home aflame in the declining light. He was cut up and bleeding and he'd been secured by a rawhide strap to the torso of his captor and he held his breath for the feral odor. Blood was streaming down the side of his face from a chunk of his blond hair that was missing and as he jostled along he could hear the fading roar of the fires growing quiet as they ascended the draws riding up through the tangled maze of oak forests that would lead them to the plains. He saw the half moon rising with the spires of smoke and his ears filled with the whir of the wind, the beat of his heart, the rhythmic huffing of the warponies and their hooves pounding into the prairie.

These horsemen were Kiowas and they were led by a man known as Satanta. Some were members of the Koitsenko warrior society and among them were a pair of sergeants-at-arms who wielded fox pelt handled serrated quirts as insignias of office and their purpose was to rally this ambitious assemblage of young fighters, each ornamented in their own tailor-made costumes of war. Naked to the waist, smelling of earth and livestock and body odor, each half of their faces and torsos painted up in opposing clay paints and adorned with necklaces of beads and shells, breastplates of pipestone, the teeth of boars and bears. They wore headdresses of hawk or crow feathers from which long braided hair flowed with tinkling bits of metal. They carried bows and warclubs and had been provisioned with three-band muskets from Comanchero traders who themselves had been outfitted purposefully by the Union army and they had personalized these firearms with metal tacks and charms and the dangling dried-up trigger fingers they'd procured as hallowed souvenirs of war from their Tejano enemies.

They rode into the burning afterglow of dusk, the early night stars gleaming, herding the remuda and their seven white captives onward into the pale orange twilight through the rock-strewn prairies and over the hills along the trails up into the sprawling plains. Charlie had been hauled away by a newly appointed war chief named Mamanti who had risen to prominence as a shaman. He possessed the gift of prophecy of which he procured from the screech owl and in his medicine bag was a puppet of cured owlskin. Perhaps he saw the young boy as a future warrior, a pupil in the Rabbit Warrior Society who would come to know life much as had he, and he observed his nature carefully as he rode.

Riding along after sunset in the slow change of twilight before total darkness the captives began to come to terms with their fate and it brought on in them a new sort of terror. Stripped of their clothing with their pale white flesh exposed in the cold spring night they were shredded by the brush and bleeding and bruised and their backsides were blistering up from the endless rubbing of sweating horse flesh.

Charlie bobbed along with the motion of the horse, chin to his chest and his eyes closed. His head was throbbing and he was having trouble breathing, fighting back his tears with desperate little choking whimpers. His nose had been bleeding and he could taste the iron in his mouth. Wilma and her infant daughter were being led beside him followed by riders who carried the sobbing Duncan girl and the Mills sisters and their babies and as these innocent nurslings wailed uncontrollably the tears began to stream down Charlie's cheeks, soft and swollen and red.

When the noise from the babies and their mothers had become unbearable Satanta called for a halt. He sent scouts to cover their backtrails and he trotted over irritably to see about the commotion from his captives. Wilma was holding her daughter closely, consoling her with loving whispers but she began to bawl all the louder. Wilma placed her hand over the girl's mouth to muffle her cries but he wrestled the baby girl from her and as he rode briskly away he turned it up by the ankles and swung the child and bashed its head into a nearby oak. The little body became limp and he tossed it into the brush. The skull had exploded into a mass of shelled brain matter and he wiped his eyes and brushed down his arm and swabbed his hands on the sweatsoaked horse and grabbed the reins and turned to ride back toward Wilma. He stared her down and then turned his glare to the other captives. His face was blood-splattered and glistening in the moonlight. He looked at his warriors and then he turned the horse and rode out into the darkness. Wilma had let out a long, desperate wail and was now bawling and blubbering hopelessly her prayers to God.

They went on through the night. The brothers kept quiet and looked on one another as if to read the other's thoughts and twice that night they made eye contact and they were very afraid. Two hours before sunrise they came upon the shallow canyon of the Concho River. They halted and Satanta ordered the herdsmen to tend the livestock and see to the captives. They were pulled from the horses and goaded through the brush to an old rock trail that ran down a narrow precipice through a maze of prickly pear into a sheltered stretch of canyon walls covered in the art of the ancients and here they were made to sit down, flopping to the cave floor in exhaustion while a small fire was built before them.

As the firelight flickered and began to take hold of the rock shelter they could make out the images sketched upon the stone walls. Tracings of birds and suns, handprints and horses. Human figures clasping hands in ritual. Atop the bluff the clatter of footsteps and the low mumbles of the savages and out over the canyon the whinny of a mare from the remuda that had failed hovered eerily in the crisp night air. Sam looked about, studying the paintings. Fading tones of red and black in a rectangular design with two looming crosses. A beheaded priest gazing back at him in wonder from the stone wall. Times of war and peace. Seasons of good harvests and bad. The Kiowas filed into the shelter carrying chunks of horse meat and huddled around the fire with their hostages. A foul and depraved looking warrior with a clouded eye hauled Wilma off outside the cave. Soon the shaman appeared and approached the fire and stood before the brothers. He was a short man who wore his hair braided to the waist on one side and cropped tight on the other. He took a slurp from the mess in his hands and tossed the bloody entrails to each of the boys and then began speaking in a slow staccato lingo, some sort of sermon or invocation perhaps to honor the gift of the meal or invite them into their uncertain future.

With darkness RL and Goodnight stumbled about in the moonlight digging the grave in the rocky soil that would hold RL's wife and unborn child. He had washed her face and changed her bloodsoaked clothes and wrapped her up in her favorite blanket. He tended to her as best he could but it was not the woman he knew looking up at him with those lost eyes. He kissed her forehead and brushed his hand down over her eyelids. The only emotion he showed was the tearing up of his eyes when he began to shovel the earth on top of her lifeless form. They piled stones and built a small fire atop the grave and as it began to flare up they bowed their heads and prayed: In the full enjoyment of that love which constrained her to leave all for Christ and heathen souls Lo, we have left all and followed thee. Amen, they said, and Goodnight left RL alone in the deepest loneliness a man could know.

In the long hours that followed the neighbors came riding up out of the darkness, at first in ones and twos and then in handfuls. They looked beaten. These men were the patriarchs of the few dozen families remaining on the frontier and one look into the void behind their eyes revealed the darkness in their souls. Their homes and families violated, most all of the livestock stolen.

Jasper Milton and J.C. Winston, two stockmen on the lower Clear Creek, were the first to arrive. They were followed by George Cochran, Felton Sandifer, and a slew of other ranchers from the Las Moras draw and not long after the men from Celery and Fields Creek came straggling in. And so this posse assembled solemnly at the Small house and in the dim lamplight they milled about organizing their weapons and gear and swapping tales of the tragedies at hand.

Goodnight took stock of them and called for council. Dressed a notch above rags, their tanned faces sullen, framed by bandanas and flat-brimmed hats sat back, all decked out for battle with their big bandoliers, slings of Sharps rifles, cross-draw holsters cradling stag handled Colts and their weathered hands nervously toying with matching bowieknives they seemed ready to face Satan's army.

Gardner Barnes was the last to arrive, his place to the west on Dry Creek the first to get hit. They hit the McMurtry home too, he said. Bill was gone for Santone. The red bastards trampled his stepgirl Jane Ellen and then lanced her.

Goodnight was trying to formulate the plan. Pat Harkins is headed to Camp Verde to rally Sansom and his men, he said. But the ranchers were still lost in the shock of it all.

They came out of nowheres, said Barnes. I had a few hunnert cows just newly branded and theys all gone. Ever one of em. I aint never seen so many damned indians. Came down over Rocky Creek and worked the north side of the river. I imagin theys a goin to cross and head down the Llano.

I had three hunnert head, said Milton. Jasper had at least that.

It's the damndest thing I ever seen in my life.

How many of em you think?

Hell if I know. It's like they's a thousand damned wild ass injins out there.

Goodnight took a deep breath and paused to gather his thoughts and allow for questions like one used to dealing with others who looked to him for command. He made eye contact with RL and he looked back out over the search party again.

Listen up now, they've already done split up at the Kemp ranch, he said. And I guarantee some are ridin like hell down the Llano.

He spat. The men were nodding to one another as if to reassure themselves.

Them injins dont know who they're dealin with, called one.

They wont be expectin a fight, said another.

RL raised his eyes from the floor and spoke up. Listen fellas, I'd appreciate it if we could follow the trails headin west on account of there bein a better chance of tracking down my boys.

RL! Milton called. They took your boys?

He nodded solemnly.

What give you to think theys the ones ridin west?

That's the way they was headed. After we fended em off.

The ranchers began to mill about and there were murmurs.

Goodnight's face clouded and he held up his hand. Alright now, we best get goin soon and match their pace so we dont lose the trail. They're goin to set the prairie afire, scatter like quail, use ever trick in the book to throw us off. Let's get on with it.

He turned and headed outside toward his horse. They followed and began to saddle the horses and pack as much as they could fit into the saddlebags.

Goodnight was the first to mount up. This is goin to be one helluva hard ass ride, he said. He nudged his horse and led them down the trail toward the river, cursing quietly to himself. He looked back, irritated. Think on it now, he said. If you aint up for it then by all means, go on back home. No time to care for the weak-minded.

Before daybreak a bloodless solitude consumes the land. The early coolness of the air rising from the river and the warm glow of the moon and the hoot of the owl with yellow eyes glaring warily from the dark abyss. Along the trails the deer have begun to feed. The air is damp and smells of earth. A dull shine looms in the east. Chirping all about in the early light are the crickets in the trees. All of the men riding anxiously await the sunsight amidst this tranquil twilight chorus.

As they rode up from the river valley the new sun was rising and the day became blessed with light. The grass was tall and wet and gleaming in the sun and the sprawling hills that stretched for miles before them were covered in oaks. Two young bucks in velvet that had been grazing raised up watching dumbly with their muzzles dripping as they passed.

They came upon the remnants of a burned-out ranch at midmorning, the wispy smoke of waning fires wafted across the pastures and loomed above the home like some mystical death blanket. There were bloated forms scattered about the field. A bloodhound came limping toward them panting nervously and as it approached they could see that it was missing an eye. The dog was whining mournfully and it turned back and trotted for the home.

They went slowly through the field. The horses' ears were flicking back and forth. They rode beside a sheep that had been gored and all about the field others of the flock lay bloated in the morning sun. They crossed an old acequia and a small patch of newly planted corn and they entered a dirt yard shaded by a great pecan and they dismounted around the well.

The searchers looked about. A lone juvenile guinea sat atop a post screeching angrily and there were cackling hens strutting about restlessly. The dog was ambling around anxiously with its head down, whimpering, and it seemed to be trying to lead them toward the front door of the house. The posse spread out to look for sign. Goodnight walked toward the porch among the fowl, the back of his hand to his nose. A dull snarl of flies suffused the yard.

RL walked toward the rising sun hovering over the stock pen on the east side of the house. Pigs slain in the mud. He studied the house. He was thinking about what must have transpired at his home and he was thinking that they should get going.

Goodnight was climbing the steps to the open front door when he heard a cry from inside. He stopped. When he waved RL over the voice called out again and as he stepped inside he could hear moaning and he could hear the scraping of a boot across the wood floor. They looked about. Sunlight through a shattered window. An overturned table, the chairs smashed to splinters. Beyond they could see a man in a pool of blood lying propped against the kitchen wall. They walked over and looked at him. They were only twelve or so miles from home and they knew of this house and the man Beal who owned it but this wasnt him.

Sitting there waiting to die, his eyes were closed but he was breathing a belabored wheeze. A bloody spittle dribbled from the side of his mouth. He'd been shot through the right shoulder and scalped and he could not talk for the savages cutting his tongue out. His left ankle was strangely bent at a right angle. Then he glared wildly about cockeyed and some sort of sound emanated from him as he gestured at RL's holster.

RL leaned to Goodnight and whispered. You know him?

Never seen the man.

Me neither.

Two other members of the search party walked in but Goodnight waved them away.

What do you think? said RL.

Goodnight bit his lip and sat there for a long time looking at the man. I know what I'd do, he said under his breath and he turned and walked out. RL bent down and touched the man's leg. You're gonna be alright pardner, he said. The man closed his eyes again and he seemed to be drifting off.

Goodnight returned directly and handed RL a rusted old snub-nosed sheriff's model peacemaker and he turned and walked back out. It's loaded, he said. Let's go.

RL stood there a long while looking at him, watching to see if his chest was moving. Then he cocked the gun and sat it on the floor beside the man. A cat crouched in the corner yowled at him as he walked away.

Outside the searchers had mounted up and as they rode out on the trail upcountry they could hear the groans of the dying man and he seemed to be mumbling some sort of hymn with much passion and faith. They set the horses at a trot and no words were spoken and before long the melody seemed to wane and then a shot rang out flat and dead. RL reined up. He looked down and closed his eyes. The others held up and looked back in wonder and then Goodnight came trotting back toward the house, annoyed. Come on, he grumbled. We best bury the ole boy. Poor bastard's been there for who knows how long, and you'd think he'd of waited a while to let us get going.

In the early light the sounds of crying children awaken the brothers. The hurried rustle of warriors breaking camp and the whinny of horses and the mournful song of doves calling for the sun. Beyond the bluffs the horizon burns a deep red. Fog looms over the valley and there is no wind. Their long journey has begun. Bound to fresh mounts the dust-covered captives ride along wearily, the blood from their wounds caked black. None of them know whether or not they will survive the day.

When they rode out from the camp the dead mare was gone and the fires had been covered up. Sam's hands were unbound and he was mounted on an old dun mare and Charlie was sat behind him. Dorothy Mills' little girl had been crying and she leaned back and sobbed *Momma go home, Momma go home* as they passed.

They struggled all morning through a rolling hill country, the pitiful shrieking wails of the Mills girl piercing into their ears and echoing across the valleys like a dying rabbit. The toddler was bawling wildly and Dorothy leaned over humming lullabies and songs of Jesus. The brothers would look away and close their eyes. The Kiowas pushed them on. The toddler girl fussed and bawled all the louder, her dainty arms flailing wildly in a fit. Satanta rode alongside them and scowled into Dorothy's eyes and this made her scream out sobbing with rage. He leaned over and snatched the girl from her arms and trotted off into the brush and when he came back a minute later he was splattered with blood and empty handed.

Dorothy shrieked and began to flail wildly at the man who sat before her. A struggle ensued and two other Kiowas rode up to subdue her and Satanta directed them to take her away. Charlie looked up at his brother as if he'd know what to do but Sam just sat there staring out blankly like a boy who had lost his sight or had been afflicted in a seizure of absence. Tears streaming down his tender and dirty cheeks, dripping softly onto his mother's scalp. He watched them riding off, her screams fading into the distance as they hauled her away. When they were gone he turned to Charlie.

Are you okay?

Charlie didnt say anything. His eye was swelling and turning purple.

Is your eye okay?

Kind of.

We have to be tough.

I know.

Sam wiped his eyes with the back of his hands. We'll be okay, he said. You have to stop crying.

Okay.

Dont cry. I promise. It's going to be alright.

Okay.

Late that morning they reached the Colorado. They sat with the horses fanned out atop a ridge surveying the turbulent brown waters that roiled down from the desert plains to the west. Two deer broke from the grass and bounded away and the warparty dismounted to lead the weary horses down the bank into a foaming pool where they dunked their muzzles and rolled leisurely in the shallow bars of the cool brown waters.

Satanta knew that every second mattered and he studied the rising river and called two of his men aside and they rode out for council. He pointed to the south and they turned to watch the backtrack and then it seemed as if they were talking about the women who were sobbing in hysterics. Then he turned and pointed across the river somewhere beyond to the north. The warriors followed his eyes and nodded. Sam was watching them, imagine what he was thinking. Satanta had caught the boy's gaze out of the corner of his eye and now he was glaring back at him. He mumbled something to his men and they turned their eyes toward the boy.

When they returned the McBride woman was hauled away screaming. She was praying to God and pleading to them for mercy and they could hear her squealing and babbling hysterically as they disappeared over a ridge into the willow bracken.

Charlie's lower lip was out and his eyes welled again with tears. Wilma watched him from her mount. There were dark bruises swelling below his eyes and his nose was runny with blood and snot and a wet stain seeped slowly from beneath him and with the breeze there was a foul smell of horse sweat and urine. He nudged his brother.

What are they doing? he said.

Sam was silent, biting his lower lip. They could hear the slapping and the screaming from the brush. Charlie looked at Wilma.

Honey, dont listen, she whispered.

He looked down and closed his eyes.

We're going to be okay.

But why? Why are they doing this? Tears were streaming down his cheeks.

I dont know. Just keep quiet and everything will be alright.

Are they going to kill her too?

Wilma didnt answer. She was shaking and she began to weep and to calm herself she called on the word of God and then she began to quietly sing a hymn.

Sam looked out across the river and studied the desert scrub beyond. Mrs McBride wasnt screaming anymore and now he could hear the low roar of the wind, the thumping of his heart. He turned and looked back to the south toward their home. He was trying to be strong and he had wiped the tears from his eyes for the Kiowas to receive him well. Dad will be coming for us soon, he told himself.

The medicine man appeared from the brush. Eyes slit, caressing his doll of owlskin and mumbling some sort of prayer. He made eye contact with Sam but the boy looked away. In the surrounding prairies herds of bison grazed in the meadows and on the plateau across the river a lone buck deer stood sniffing the wind and the breeze off the water cooled his blistered skin. He blinked and looked at the unflawed sun and then looked out on all that wild country to the west. Cloud-shaped shadows sweeping smooth and silent across the prairie like phantom wagontrains drifting and drifting to the ends of the earth. The executioners in the brush had returned with the gristled scalp of their victim. When Sam turned back he saw Satanta on his horse atop the ridge, squinting inquisitively, studying the owl prophet.

Two hours later they happened upon a band of Comanches under the direction of the young war chief known as Quanah. They were raiders like themselves stealing horses and captives from the Texans and while there were only a dozen of them their remuda may have doubled the size of the Kiowas. They sat shirtless atop their painted ponies and gazed upon the Kiowas with their haggard and bloodshot eyes, proud and cocksure and yet they looked as though they had not slept in a week.

They wore their long hair braided with shining bits of silver and beads and some had pierced ears and some with battlescars outlined in paint and they were armed with battleaxes and bows and all carried elaborately decorated war shields with images of divine themes that had appeared to them in visions.

Satanta and his men regarded these accomplices and their plunder with envious curiosity. The Comanches strutted about with their heads back, ogling the one remaining white woman. Satanta traded token pleasantries with Quanah and then he paraded Wilma around proudly for this lustful posse. Sam watched Quanah, a larger man with lighter skin who cradled a battle spear as he trotted among the gathering to size up the scene. He rode alongside the brothers and stopped to weigh the older boy's countenance. He caught Sam's eye and he smiled, as if he knew what others could not. Tejanito, he said, squinching his eyes. Then he touched up his horse and took one last look at Wilma before muttering some crude parlance as he led his men back out on the trail west into the sun.

They watched them go. Satanta called out to them but they did not turn back, riding out and growing smaller with the trampled dust of the remuda billowing up a crimson stain that seeped up slowly through the noonday heat.

In the afternoon they began to ascend a range of low broken hills of red scrabbled badlands and forests of honey mesquite blooming in fragrant blossoms of creamy white. The medicine man rode in the lead wielding a sacred wand composed of a screech owl head mounted upon a piece of wood and Charlie sat before him. His lower half was numb and he bobbed along listlessly with a sour smell about him as if he'd been riding in his own excrement. The captives were rawlegged and backsore, covered in bruises and cuts and delirious from hunger and lack of sleep, their pale skin flaming red beneath the relentless sun.

They rode all afternoon with Satanta at the rear of the command. Now and again he called a halt to rest the horses. He would dismount and walk out to scan their backtrail for pursuers, the scouts laying with their ears to the ground listening to the earth. He felt the wind and smelled the air. He looked at the sky and eyed the sun and he studied the southern horizons as if he had another way of seeing. The rivers from the plains flowing to the sea. He knew somewhere in that country forty miles back the Texans were riding toward them.

By now there was a quarter moon in the twilight sky and they rode on into the darkness with the remuda scattered across the starlit prairie, driving them on through the night into the pale light of early morning, the horses stammering, the captives bobbing along asleep in the saddle.

In the morning they came upon a broad valley watered by seepsprings and they halted to rest below a ridge of rugged red buttes sprinkled with mesquite and juniper. The captives were made to dismount, stumbling numbly to the ground, barely able to walk. Satanta pulled Sam out separately and led him away staggering out into the pasture where there was a clearing in the prairie grass that he'd spotted from atop his horse. It was an orphaned calf curled up bellowing madly.

Satanta raised his brow and pointed at his stomach and then he gestured toward the yearling as if Sam would know what to do. He mumbled something under his breath. Sam was weak from the ride and had not eaten in two days and when he stepped toward the calf it jumped to its feet and bounded away. Satanta yelled some command. Sam took off after it, darting about, a jolt of adrenaline spurring him on and he quick and graceful as a swallow, catching up and diving headlong for its hindlegs tumbling the animal over helplessly.

Satanta followed on behind him and he jumped down and seized the calf in a headlock as it bawled out feebly with Sam leaning his weight into its flank. Satanta was talking in Kiowa as he unsheathed his bowieknife and cut the baby cow's throat wide open to the neckbone. Its panicked bawl drowned out in a gargle of blood and its hooves kicked frantically as he pulled back and plunged the blade back into the depths of its stomach. He set the knife aside and reached up into the guts with both hands. He brought up a handful of the abomasum and stuffed it in his mouth and began slurping up the soured milk like a ravenous dog. He swallowed and sighed with satisfaction. Smell of vitals and fecal matter. He looked at the boy. He reached out with his bloody hands and motioned for the boy to indulge and when Sam turned and ran he scrambled up and tackled him and dragged him back, grabbing the back of his head and forcing the boy's face into the guts of the calf. Sam yowled out, squirming about and struggling to raise up for a breath. Then Satanta pulled his head back up and with his other hand grabbed a handful of the insides and smeared them all over Sam's face, forcing globs of it into his mouth.

Techaro! he said.

When Sam began to gag Satanta squeezed his nose and forced him to swallow the warm guts down his throat. He was blinking helplessly and his arms flailed about and he began to choke and puke up the sloppy mush. He fell back, gasping for air. Satanta dug back inside with his knife and cut out a kidney soaked in warm blood and he handed it over to the boy.

Techaro! he commanded, pointing angrily at the dripping glob of warm meat.

Sam stared back, huffing, fighting tears.

Techaro!

Sam stuffed it into his mouth and gulped hard, water pouring from his eyes as he tried to keep it down but it came spewing back out and he caught it with both hands and shoved it back in his mouth. He closed his eyes and swallowed hard, smacking his lips and then spitting the metallic aftertaste into the dust. Perhaps the blood had settled his stomach for he was able to keep it down. Satanta smiled and handed the boy another chunk. Sam slurped it into his mouth. He did not really chew it, he just held his breath and sucked it down his throat and then he rose up on his knees and wiped his face with the back of his hand.

They crossed the Clear Fork riding north with the sun shining high over a long range of low rolling hills glowing green from recent spring rains. Now the weight of the journey seemed to be burdening even the Kiowas and every soul in this ragged regiment rode along solemnly with their thoughts. No one spoke. All day they rode toward a pair of flat-topped mesas that stood as sentinels over the prairie in the distance, herds of antelope bunched for miles moving north and watching them warily as they passed.

They rode that night under a sky black and starlit watching the silent flares of the meteors. A silver river of stars arched above. The horses and cattle spread out across the prairie before them, their dust rising in the moonlight and the outriders mending the flanks of the herd with elegance and ease. Charlie tottered along asleep in the saddle and in his jostled slumber he dreamed of his mother and she was caressing his hair and smiling at him lovingly.

They waded a shallow ford of the Double Mountain Fork of the Brazos with a line of storms building in the east. Two hours before daybreak. The remuda had crossed ahead of them and the smell of wet horses lingered in the breeze. The dripping ponies trudged along snorting and stamping and the lightning flickered soundlessly as they rode single file up a narrow trail out of the quiet river valley. They rode into the dawn. Before long the eastern sky came alive in a translucent glow and the pair of solemn mountains that had served as their guide appeared in the first gray light.

Satanta escorted the hostages away from the herd and they ascended a slender trail of switchbacks, stepping the horses over the uppermost promontory one by one until they had lined out to worship the birth of the new day. There was a steady breeze and the early morning air was dry and cool. Farther along the ridge out alone stood the medicine man, arms outspread to welcome the sun. He waved a rawhide rattle in a circle about his head and he raised his other hand and mimed the owlskin puppet and then he began chanting rhythmically. Charlie had been made to ride with Wilma and he sat before her like some angelic offering to the Great Spirit. He was shivering cold and he snuggled back against her as the horizon came alive burning red and hot and then the great ball of the sun rose up from the rim of the earth illuminating his angelic face and he looked up at her. Wide eyes watering, his hair glowing white, he turned his head and hid his face against her breast and she put her face into his frazzled blond hair wisping in the breeze and she kissed him.

The posse had made sixteen miles into the prairie country riding hard and taking short breaks to let the horses pace themselves and to study the tracks of the remuda. Vultures were turning in the sun and cruising the thermals in search of carrion and the ranchers rode under a high blue sky filled with their cruising forms. Goodnight rode out in front and they followed the contour of the hoofprints, single riders branching off, groups of herders and loose animals trampling the ground in random directions. The party they followed had ridden all through the night without stopping and Goodnight could tell by the depth of the prints that they were six, maybe seven hours ahead of them.

They watched for smoke or dust rising out on the horizon and halted every few miles when the views allowed them to glass the country for moving forms. They saw nothing but open country. By noon Goodnight rode off alone to sort out the trail of a lone horseman and in a clearing he stumbled upon a small, soiled form like an abandoned birth from some wild beast. He dismounted and studied it. Good God, he said under his breath. It was the mutilated body of Sarah Mill's four-year-old daughter and she had been left cold and stiff lying face down with the flesh of her naked scalp flopping randomly in the breeze. When the others rode up they sat their horses silently or mumbled whispers to themselves in their rage. Among the volunteers was a young man named Swaggart who was well respected among the settlers as an apprentice preacher and at this scene his boyish face became ghostly white and he leaned to the side of his mount and vomited.

RL walked up and circled the remains, thinking of his boys. He walked to the edge of the clearing and sucked his breath and let it out slowly as he adjusted his holster and looked toward the sun. A warm spring day. Barely a breeze. They went to work burying the girl and the boy parson said a few words in her honor and then the searchers mounted up and rode on.

They rode into the heat of the afternoon following the tracks and sorting out their mysteries and they reckoned the route of the savages due north headed for the Colorado. They followed the trail for another hour and they could tell by the castoff remnants of gear and food and shreds of clothing and from the partially eaten foal left to rot in the sun that the raiders had passed before them. Goodnight periodically called for halts and they took council. We best make up some ground, he said. RL rode out alone looking out from under his hat into the heatshimmer and the vastness of the country ahead. There was a pair of crows rushing a hawk, croaking and cawing and flapping their shining black wings about. Goodnight called out to him but he kept on. Before long the trail led them to the remains of an abandoned camp where a foul smell of decay arose from a swarm of buzzing flies in the brush. The horse whimpered softly and flared its nostrils. They could see a dark cloud of insects swarming and the trampled path was matted with blood and torn clothing and a lock of yellow hair. A Mexican named Augustine who worked for Jim Duncan was the first to dismount and approach the scene.

It was the remains of the Duncan girl and she was sprawled out dead in a scraggle of matted grass and rocks splattered with blood. He called for his boss. The flies were moving about the mass of entrails and there were slivers of brain visible through her small, cracked skull and the body was bound in a position that suggested the heathens had tortured the girl. When Duncan walked up he was seized by a ringing in his ears and he began to scream madly. He picked up a rock and hurled it wildly and he dropped to his knees over her sobbing amidst the mass of flies. He knelt down and spoke to her, caressing what was left of her blood-stiffened hair. When he set off south on the trail back home RL watched him cradling his daughter, their forms swaying with the gait of the horse, the head and legs of the dead girl dangling on either side of her father. He watched them a long time. Duncan was singing to her, his voice fading as they slowly became smaller in the heat haze of the hills to the south until they passed over a distant ridge and were seen no more.

All afternoon they rode the tracks of the heathen galloping north from out of the hill country. The heat had weakened them. A ruthless sun burned their flesh, sweat pouring down their sunburned faces and soaking their clothes in a sponge of sweat and grime like the horses they rode upon. They rode into an open plains country of tall grass and gentle valleys, past slopes of sotol and lechuguilla and small herds of bison feeding idly among the pastures. Here with the shadows growing long behind them the trail weaved through a forest of purple sage and out along the ridgelines of the weathered limestone cliffs overlooking a rugged desert valley scrubland where far below lay the gently flowing waters of the Concho.

Goodnight sat his horse and the searchers lined up abreast of him looking out over the valley, the color of the sky sucked up by the long, open views in the west. High clouds were building into the sinking sun and a breeze kicked up that cooled them. A mile away over the river they could see a swirling vortex of dark birds in a frenzy. Goodnight spat and took off his hat and wiped his brow. He sighed and looked at RL to gauge his recognition but RL said nothing and he urged his horse forward and they followed.

As they descended the plain toward the river RL could make out through the willows the bobbing forms of the buzzards battling over flesh. He veered off and studied the ground more closely. Tracks of horses. Tracks of men. He went on cutting for sign and before long he could hear the scavenger birds screaming and hissing. He stopped and listened and then dismounted. The tug and pull and slurp of the viscera. He slowly followed the tracks. He studied them very closely but they were not his boys. When he ducked through a thick line of willows and came into the clearing there was an eruption of noise and an explosion of feathers. The awkward, black birds flapped the air and settled back down. They huddled and bobbed and glared back at the intruder who had interrupted the feast.

There was an eyeless woman propped up against a boulder. Horrendous smell. Jesus, he whispered. He called back to the posse. A few of the searchers appeared from the trail and dismounted and crowded around and stood in silence. Her throat was slashed and there were gashes all over her body and she had been scalped. The body was naked and her pregnant form was held up by a spear that pierced through her shoulder. Signs of premature labor. They stood in silence. Beyond that was another naked female corpse laid out on its back. She had been lanced and gutted and scalped. Blood everywhere. She was reeking and difficult to recognize, the flesh from her face and arms and thighs picked away. Her insides slurped clean.

RL tilted his hat back and sighed. The rest of the search party arrived. Goodnight said nothing and turned back to fetch his spade and called to the boy preacher to prepare a blessing. They dug a shallow pit in a dry creek bed and dragged the bodies in the grave and covered them up with the sandy red loam and river rocks. The preacher winced when the first clumps of soil splattered over the bodies and they all stood solemnly with heads bowed to receive the simple eulogy before recruiting themselves once more for the journey ahead.

The Kiowas refused to stop. Their endurance and capacity for hardship was superhuman. They feared the Texas Rangers. Satanta proudly carried the badge of the Koitsenko order and the spotted antelope sash he wore over his shoulder identified him as a great warrior and this drove him no end. The following morning when they crossed the gypsum-laced waters of the Salt Fork and halted to water the horses he scanned their backtrail with much concern. They drove twenty miles that morning and drank the bitter creek waters from skin bags and rode north into the shimmering heat, a hot southerly wind pushing them deeper into the badlands.

When they halted he rode out alone looking far to the south where he saw a thin line of dust wafting faintly above the plain. Or he thought he saw it. He called for the Owl Prophet and they dismounted. They talked for a long time, gesturing, and watching the country with their hands held flat atop their eyes to block the sun, turning back now and again to assess the state of the remuda and the captives.

Wilma and the brothers looked on and the warriors guarding them leaned from their mounts with their necks craned out the better to pick up any subtle nuances of the council. The wind had died and in that bedraggled huddle of man and beast the stench of the sweating Kiowas blended with the soapy smell of lathered horses. They covered their noses and Charlie squinched his face up to fend off the bright sun and rubbed the corner of his eye where an ulcer had begun to fester.

Charlie, honey, be careful with your eye, said Wilma.

It hurts real bad.

I know sweetie, but try not to rub it.

Okay.

Sam was scanning the wasted countryside. He balled his hands up into fists and rubbed the corner of his eyes with his knuckles and took a deep breath. Charlie was trying to get his attention.

Sam, do you know where we are?

No, not really.

Who are these people?

I dont think they're people, Charlie.

What are they then?

They're indians.

What kind of indians are they?

Sam's eyes darted about furtively at their captors. I dont know. Comanche, I guess.

Are they going to kill us?

I dont know.

What do you think they're going to do with us?

Take us to their home, I guess.

Where?

I dont know.

They sat there quietly watching Satanta mount up and ride back toward them. The other Kiowas had been watching the brothers, listening to the sounds of their voices, studying their expressions and wondering what they were saying.

Charlie, said Sam.

What?

Dont cry. Dont say anything. Dont fight back.

Okay. I wont.

Do you understand?

Yes.

All afternoon they struggled through the crimson wastelands of the Croton Breaks where there was no soil nor flora save for the random clump of cholla. It did not take long for the gypsum water they had been drinking to take hold. They cramped in the saddle and the Kiowas chuckled to one another until the stench from their loose bowels became such a nuisance they could no longer ride on.

They made camp on a sandy bank of the Tongue River where beavers had gnawed up the woodlands and damned the shallow stream into a series of pools lined out for a half mile along the valley floor. When they dismounted the captives were allowed to walk freely and they wandered deliriously down to the water. The sandy soil was mudded up in quicksand and they stumbled in numbly, lunged and fell, crawled clumsily into the water. Wilma squirmed through the silt toward Charlie. She slipped and splashed down face forward into the muck. He had fallen and was fighting to keep his head above the water. Wilma flailed about to reach him as he called out and Sam had sprung up to help.

The Kiowas began to howl and giggle like tickled children. They slapped their legs. Their cackles echoed down the valley and they approached the edge of the water and looked upon the captives, sarcastically joking among themselves.

Aim Koe Bah! yelled Satanta.

The Kiowas demurred and subdued their antics. They snickered to one another and took to their tasks in a muttering of chuckles and slang. Satanta turned to the captives.

Bay Haw!

Wilma pulled herself up. Sam took her hand to brace himself and she leaned back and he bent out reaching for his brother. Charlie stuck his hand out and they dragged him upright from out of the water. They were as helpless as newborn fawns abandoned by their mother and while they were conscious and had a pulse the odds of them surviving another few days did not seem in their favor.

After dark the fires crackled in the dusk and Sam slipped out alone from the bustle of the camp as the Kiowas settled in to roast a deer. He stepped carefully and set off along a path of trampled grass and disappeared into a tangle of cattails that defined the river's margins where he shed his frazzled britches and entered the pool and slowly lowered his aching body into the cold water. He held his breath and dropped his head under the water and lingered there for a long while until he raised his eyes above the waterline and felt the breeze cool him. He watched the shadows of the Kiowas flickering about in the firelight. He lowered his mouth into the water and began to drink. He did this leisurely for a long time as he looked up at the moon and he thought about slipping away to try and make his way back home.

Then it hit him. What would be the use in trying to find your way back home on foot? he thought. Then he remembered he no longer had a home. Well, there might be a chance of running into someone out there looking for us. Someone who could help.

He dipped below the water again and came back up. He could hear them talking, a strange clucking guttural of conversation. Cricketsong in the brush. Beyond the lonesome wail of the prairie wolves out over the canyon.

If you were really able to sneak away from this what are you going to do when the wolves come after you?

He lay back, floating. I'd hide, he said to himself out loud. I'd throw rocks at em.

He saw more stars than he'd ever seen. The river trickled along around him and the frogs were chirping. He did his best to wash himself with his hands and he blew the dust and the allergens from his nose. He drank. After a while he rose and swam his way down the far side of the bank. Pondering his escape route. The river winding its way all the nights and days back toward home. No way to make any ground on foot. So Sam, how are you gonna get yourself a pony?

But you cant leave your little brother alone with the indians.

You better decide. You better just get back over there as quick as you can and pray to God they haven't noticed.

The moonlight reflected off the water. He kept his eye on the campfires as he swam back across the pool of the river. Probably gonna die anyway, he said.

No I'm not.

When he ambled out of the water the breeze hit him full on and he was cold but it was the best he'd felt in a while. He pulled up his pants and as he walked from the darkness toward the light of the fire he saw Satanta watching him. The big man rose and called him over and he seemed to be smiling. Sam came to the fire wet and dripping, looking about for his brother and Wilma but they were not there. Satanta took hold of him roughly and two warriors emerged from the shadows with a buffalo hair rope and somewhere beyond the firelight he thought he could hear Wilma pleading for mercy. Terrible screams like a sick cat yowling and he heard a loud slap and then he heard a desperate moaning and blubbering.

A young warrior lunged out at Sam and he skipped up as they tried to hobble him but the rope caught his ankle on the upswing and flipped him face down in the hard desert dust. He curled up gasping for breath. Satanta kicked him and he rolled over on his back. Two others swarmed down and a rope was tied around his neck and his feet were bound and his hands were secured behind his back. Wilma had been brought back from the brush weeping and in bad shape. Both of her eyes were swollen and she was bleeding from the mouth and now one of the defilers back-handed her upside the head and she dropped like a rock to the ground and lay clutching the side of her head. Satanta pointed the way with a lighted torch and Sam was hauled off to a clearing where two posts had been driven deep into the soft river sand and the Kiowas cinched his feet a foot up the post and they constructed a contraption of cordage that raised the boy's torso up horizontally and here he was expertly secured, suspended face down to the ground. He'd been bound so that even his slightest movements caused the chords to squeeze into his flesh and he closed his eyes and gritted his teeth with tears dripping into the dust and he dangled there swinging slowly in the firelight.

Satanta walked around and knelt down so that he could better see the boy. He lifted Sam's chin. Tejanito, he said.

Sam opened his eyes. He was terrified. He strained as he spoke. Please, he pleaded. Please let me…

Khoat!

Please, he gasped. Please.

Satanta patted him on the head gently like a caring father. He looked into his eyes and pursed his lips and put his finger to his mouth as if to quiet the boy. Khoat, he whispered.

He stepped back and a man came out from the far side of the fire and he and Satanta spoke and the man nodded and then set out up into the canyon and after a while he returned with a gourd of whiskey he'd procured from a cache hidden by the Comanchero traders. They sat by the fire watching the boy and passing the gourd and in their haggard state it did not take long for the inebriant to take hold. In his struggles Sam cried out and they gathered around to poke and prod him and they berated him and swore at him in their drunken stoneage slurs. This lasted well into the night and not long after the last of them stumbled off to make his bed a man came back from the dark shuffling along with a large stone for which to place upon the boy's back. It was in this position that Sam would awake the following morning.

In the evening the searchers stopped to water the horses at the river and let them recover in the fertile grasses of the flood plain. RL and Goodnight searched for signs of the raiding party and followed the tracks back up the canyon into the shelter of painted rocks. Recent fires and foot tracks scattered about in the dust of this ancient way station and they stepped slowly among what remained of the flesh and bones of the roasted mare. It was near dark and RL lit a lantern to better light their way. They reckoned the setting. Goodnight bent down to test the textures of the sand. Along the flickering walls they read the arcane journals of the primitives. Something caught RL's eye. Look here, he said. A scene of two crossed lances and two flowing scalps and another of a woman drawn horizontally. He was drawn to one the likeness of the devil.

An hour after dark they were mounted up and riding again. They followed the trace of the Concho by starlight and when the moon came up behind them they could make out the trail of the remuda spread out a half mile wide before them. Goodnight halted to survey the country. Broken ranges of mesas now visible in the moonlight. Faint traces of cool air rising from the river. The dippers high above in the night sky circling the polestar like riders on a Ferris wheel.

He dismounted and walked out examining the tracks that he figured were a day old and had been joined by another party thirty riders strong. He squatted down and grabbed a handful of sand and smelled it and felt its moisture and he tossed it aside and traced the trail of the tracks with his eyes until it disappeared into the darkness. We'll be gettin on into unknown country now, he said. He knew they'd been losing ground to the warparty but he kept it to himself. RL sat his horse beside him. They watched the sheetlightning flashing silently in the west.

How far out are they? said RL.

Hard to know for sure.

They've hardly stopped.

Nor have we.

Well…

Dont worry. We'll find em.

They turned to the north and pushed on through the night. The horses were hot and lathered and in their labors became sympathetic figures to their riders but the searchers trailed no spare mounts. Along about midnight they waded the muddy waters of the Colorado and they hazed them up beyond onto the plains skirting the edge of the river valley until the sun began to rise behind them in the east, their shadows long before them like divining rods luring them onward toward whatever destinies were at hand.

Here recent rains had enlivened the prairie and their way took them through seas of lush meadows, steam in the valleys, coveys of quail flushing in the crisp spring air. The jaded horses swishing through the tall wet grasses and the sprawling clumps of nopal. In the box canyons draining the prairie lay buckshot rocks holding pools of fresh water. The trail of the savages had become more difficult to follow and they halted to regroup and to recruit the horses. They hiked down to replenish the canteens and they rested and drank in silence. When the last of the searchers remounted Goodnight and RL conferred among themselves and then they pushed on.

Within the hour they passed by the lonely rock buildings of old Fort Chadbourne, eerily quiet and abandoned save for perhaps a small patrol out on escort of the Butterfield stage. They rode out along a row of deserted gardens and through long-dead crops of maize and sunflowers and through the remains of a makeshift horse track now filled with clumpings of horseweed. High above in the quiet sky thousands of migrating hawks soared together in upwardly spiraling kettles and a herd of mustangs rumbled away over the rocky hills as they passed. A strong southerly wind nudged them onward into a more open country and with the high noon heat their pace slowed, scudding clouds passing along with them, and three hours later they could still see the glistening stone walls of the fort on the treeless expanse fifteen miles behind them.

They slogged along all afternoon ascending the low rolling plains, passing now and again through rain showers rolling up from the desert to the southwest. By evening a mild front had blown through. They camped at the base of a notched mesa and woke under a gibbous moon in the middle of night and went on and rode along a trail littered with the bloated forms of cattle that had been arrowed or lanced. In the morning they took siesta at a headwater draw of the Clear Fork of the Brazos, spring-water glistening in the sun under a thicket of chittamwood trees. They watered the horses and sat in the shade for ten minutes and went on.

They had climbed up and out of the rocky north slope through a tangle of agarita and catclaw and into a clearing with good views to the west when something caught RL's eye. He reached into his saddlebag for his field glasses and scanned slowly over the grasslands that rolled up toward the friable rims of the high plains. He could see the mound-shaped swells of bluestem swaying in the gentle breeze and a vast mesquite savannah broken only by dry creek draws lined with groves of cottonwoods. Randomly sprinkled all about their purview were sandstone mesas looming like lost ships in a boundless grass sea.

The posse ambled up and they regarded the signs before them. Far out in the grassy gorges they could make out trampled pastures that framed a half-acre section charred by wildfire ignited by a sprawling old mesquite tree that had been the victim of lightning but there was something else and Goodnight turned to RL.

Look yonder, he said.

Yep, I see it.

They've been workin horses out there.

They damn sure have.

It took them a half hour to descend the plain. They were walking the horses along slowly and studying the tracks that vanished into the burning field only to reappear on the far side where the signs led them to the dismembered carcass of a chestnut mare. The riders reined up and surrounded the dead horse.

Goodnight grinned. Gentlemens, he said. Our fine redskin amigos found em some grazing mustangs and decided to kill em a fresh mare.

RL sat his horse looking at the mesas. He spat. We've followed em a hundred miles and the sumbitches have hardly stopped.

I reckon they wont hold that meat for long.

From there they made their way down a long juniper draw and concealed themselves below the crest of a ridge above which beheld views of the pasturage the herdsmen roamed. They dismounted and hobbled the horses and perched themselves at the rim. RL glassed the terrain slowly. Herding the valley was a small group of Comanche riders. He watched them. They were staking out a herd of horses and they doubled the Texans in number. They trotted and swerved at a leisurely pace and talked amongst one another. He lowered the glasses and sat watching them leisurely ride on. He did not think these riders had anything to do with his boys but that did not matter.

The party crouched back down the ridge to begin collecting themselves for the charge. The horses had their heads down and were grazing on clumps of grama sprouting up through the rocks. The ranchers were going through their saddlebags and readying their arms while Goodnight addressed them.

Boys, this is what we've been ridin for. When we get down on em it's got to be all out. Gutshoot the horses so we can get them afoot.

Swaggart looked nervous and he was kicking the dirt with this boot. But Charlie, it aint them, he said. It's just a group of kids herding horses.

I dont give a goddamn.

No one else spoke up.

Now listen, he said. When they scatter keep aim on the rider nearest you. And if you caint kill the red nigger you're after you damn sure better wound em.

They nodded and looked at one another as if to confirm an agreement. They waited another ten minutes to rest the horses. Swaggart was assigned to keep watch out over the herders but they were afoot and talking casually among themselves as the mustangs fed around them. When he came back with this news they mounted up. The ranchers were patting the necks of the horses and whispering encouragements and flights of doves were riding the breeze from out of the sun. When the wind laid they could hear the Comanches calling out jovially to one another. The vigilantes lined up abreast and looked to Goodnight. He nudged his rifle into its sheath and drew his pistol. He looked about the men and he looked at RL and then he jabbed his heels into his horse and took off.

As they galloped down into the coulee the herd of mustangs bolted in every direction kicking up full speed out into the reaches of the canyon. A covey of quail flushed in a big burst of feathers from the thick grass. RL shot first at a young brave who had been caught off balance and he was knocked down and trampled and then shot again. At this the Texans all commenced firing and they lined out to ride down the nearest mounted opponent as told, shouting curses and the pistols blasting in a fusillade of gunfire, the ranchers unloading every round in their chambers upon the young herdsmen who began to fall maimed or dead as the pistolsmoke rose and the scattering mustang herd pounded away into the recesses of the valley.

RL deftly peeled his horse away to chase two newly mounted runners. They were ducking low with their faces in the necks of the horses. He closed the gap in an instant and as they split up he dropped them easily with two successive shots. When he swung back around he saw Goodnight running down a single rider and firing point blank at the back of his head. The other ranchers were milling and circling among the bodies and letting off rounds at the last floundering survivors and those already dead and soon the echoes died and a strange silence settled over the canyon.

Each of the Texans were checking their startled horses, bobbing atop their mounts with the smoking revolvers held high, looking at one another and scanning the surrounding prairie for remainders. Nothing moved and they were all dead save one. The late sun was bearing down on the prairie, the ripe seed heads of the blue grama grass swaying in the breeze. Goodnight sidestepped his horse and leaned to his right, straining for a better view of something he thought he saw up ahead among the boulders.

The mesa, RL! The mesa!

RL holstered his gun and drew the other and kicked the horse into a jog toward the base of a lone red butte, eyeing his angle. Then he broke into a run. Sound of a lone horseman galloping across the prairie. Seconds after RL disappeared behind the formation a shot rang out across the canyon. The posse trotted out to see about him. Goodnight was the first on the scene and RL looked up at him with wild eyes. He was knelt down over the dead warrior and he'd pulled his knife.

What do you aim to do with that little ole thing, said Goodnight.

RL was breathing hard and he looked at his knife and he looked up at Goodnight.

What?

Here, use this. Goodnight handed him his skinning knife. RL studied it.

Come on now, he said. Get on with it. It wont be long before dark.

RL stood up and grabbed the knife and knelt down and gripped the lice-infested mane and passed the silver blade about its skull and tore away the scalp.

He came walking back leading the horse with one hand and holding the dripping slice of hair in the other. The only sound was a light wind and the scruffling of the ranchers pilfering the dead for souvenirs of battle. He laid the pelt out on a boulder and sat down and took a deep breath to collect himself. Swaggart had his horse lamed in the skirmish and Goodnight pointed his pistol to its temple and put it out of its misery. RL watched him. Goodnight was visibly disturbed at the fate of the horse but he spat and composed himself and began directing the young preacher on the merits of the available mounts left riderless by the dead herdsmen.

It seemed the dawn would never come. Sam was released from his bonds when the Kiowas returned from watching the sunrise. He looked harried and senseless and was fighting the will to go on. He was stiff and sore and covered in scrapes and scabs. They nudged him to rise but he lay on the ground without moving. Satanta shouted at him and drew his pistol. Sam dragged himself up to his knees. One of the Kiowas strung a bow and fitted an arrow and drew back at point-blank range and Sam pushed himself up wobbling on his feet. Another man walked up leading a pony and two others hefted him up on the horse and he flopped forward like a dead thing into its mane and held on. The others mounted up and they rode out watching the sunrise from the scrubland plains to the east.

The rugged canyon country was silent and blue. The remuda stolen from the Texans had been harried off for trade by other herdsmen and now Satanta drove them on less urgently. The Tejanos would not pursue them so far into the depths of their homelands. When he rode up alongside Wilma he smiled at her lustfully. The brothers watched him. Her fair skin and green eyes or perhaps her will to survive seemed to arouse something in him. He led them north all that day through the cragged breaks that bled from the Caprock looming in the west. Now on the fifth day of their journey the captives were filthy and frazzled and weakened by their hunger and they made for a pitiful portrait as they tottered along.

Late that day they entered a broken canyon country that stretched before them in a tangled maze to the foot of the high plains. The sandstone hoodoos to the west stood like prayerful fingers reaching up to the heavens in worship and the sinking sun burned a pale yellow glow over a herd of grazing bison munching peacefully in the prairie grass. The billowing cottonball thunderheads mushroomed slowly in the afternoon heat. High above the escarpment a sharp crack of lightning flashed across the sky to the north and a line of pronghorns herded along warily in the waning thunder.

Satanta saw something moving in the grass and he sat tall on his horse and looked out over the plain. He rode over and came upon two newborn antelope nestled among a thick patch of bluestem. He circled them and dismounted. They squirmed and looked up at him timidly with innocent eyes. He called back for another man and they gathered them up and carried them back to the main party of riders and handed them to the brothers. Satanta nodded as if to confirm some understanding and he seemed to smile when the boys cradled them like little dolls. When they rode out the brothers looked back as a pronghorn doe appeared from the brush. The little fawns squirmed in their arms. It was the mother and she stood there with her head up in curiosity, childless, watching them as they rode away.

That night they made camp in a grove of cottonwoods at the mouth of a rock shelter where a seep of water dripped like a time clock into the hardpacked earth and in the gray light the Kiowas piled up a stack of kindling surrounded by a ring of river rocks. The brothers had been sat down alongside the firepit and they cradled the two foundling fawns in their lap. The medicine man was rattling a small gourd filled with mesquite beans and pebbles and chanting out in a low mumble some cryptic doxology while his attendants furiously rubbed a set of notched sotol sticks that soon began to smoke with friction. The brothers watched the flames take hold and the canyon wall came alive in the firelight. Wilma leaned and whispered to them.

Why did they pick up those cute little things? she said.

The fawns looked about timidly and they were each curled up and snuggled into the boys like stuffed play toys. Satanta walked up and looked over the boys and urged them up to stand before the fire with their pets and pointed at the flames. He shoved Sam closer to the fire and shouted an order. Sam stood there, confused. Charlie called out to his brother.

Sam, no! Dont do it!

The command was repeated again and Sam looked down at the fawn squirming in his hands and he looked back up. Then he tossed the fawn into the fire. It flailed about in the blue flames and screamed like a young child. Charlie yelled at him but Sam reached down and yanked the other animal out of his arms and tossed it directly on top of its sibling. The fawns squirmed in the fire. Satanta used a sotol stalk to hold them over the flames like burning logs. Already they could smell the hair singeing, the fawns' legs kicking in spasm and squealing death cries as their eyes bulged out in the flames with the bones and flesh broiling and popping and crackling in the heat.

When Satanta pulled them out of the fire they were still squirming. He crushed their heads with a heavy rock. They were laid out to cool on a sort of makeshift tablestone and soon the Kiowas gathered around like hungry apes and pulled the legs apart and picked through the meat and bones as if they were devouring a turkey. It had been almost a week since the captives had digested anything of substance. Someone tossed a leg to the brothers and they voraciously chewed through what was left of the hair and skin and as they picked the meat off the bone it came off easily and was not burned.

They sat there feasting in the flaring light of the fire, silent save for the smacking of lips and the slurping of grease. Wilma sat back removed from this banquet. Sam took a nice hunk of meat from the fawn's hindquarter and handed it over to her. After they'd eaten the Kiowas began to mill about the camp and other small fires were constructed around which the savages began to settle themselves in for the evening. Satanta kept a wary eye on his camp, studying the captives as they curled up alongside one another by the fire and tried to sleep.

An hour later and the moon was up and the embers of the fire smoldered warmly and the hostages were still awake. They lay there huddled together with Wilma between the two boys. Sam was staring at the half moon with its radiant halo dulling the surrounding stars. His eyes were slits but he was studying the Kiowas talking among one another in the shadows of the fire. Charlie whispered something. Wilma turned on her side and put her arm over him and told him that it would be alright. We should pray, she said. Then she began to pray and the brothers whispered the words along with her.

Now I lay me down to sleep. I pray the Lord my soul to keep. Angels guard me through the night and wake me with the morning light. God bless Mommy and Daddy. Grandma and Grandpa. Hank and Blue. God bless everybody in the whole world. Make me a good, good boy. Amen.

Amen, they murmured, and then they fell into slumber. But Wilma could not sleep. She knew that at any moment she would be hauled off by the younger warriors, splayed out under the moonlight in a canyon grotto, the brothers awakened by her pitiful pleas echoing from the darkness of the valley where the savages would take their turns without discretion or compassion or conscience any more than a pack of wolves. An hour later she was pulled away. The boys woke to her hideous squeals coming from the brush and they lay covering their ears and after a while there was a slap and a last pained grunt and then silence. She had become numb. She had trained her mind to wander. She thought of herself in a different place. She thought of escape.

Charlie fidgeted about, rolled over, sniffling and coughing and tears welling in his eyes. He prodded his brother.

Sam, what's happening to her?

I dont know.

Is she going to be okay?

Dont listen. Just try and sleep.

Charlie lay with his face in his arms, covering his ears, terrified.

It's going to be okay.

They'd been dozing in and out of sleep for the next hour when Wilma crawled back beside the fire. She lay down between them and tucked her hands under her armpits and curled up in a ball on her side facing Sam.

He was pretending to be asleep. She closed her eyes and when she opened them a little while later Sam was looking at her. She was crying and her eyes glistened in the moonlight. He reached out and placed his hand on her shoulder.

Are you okay?

Yes.

She wiped the tears from her eyes and took a deep breath.

Listen to me, she whispered. I'm getting out of here. Tomorrow night.

Sam didnt say anything.

When we tend the horses, we're going to tie that dun mare out away from the camp. I want you to go with me.

Sam was picturing it and thinking of the pony he'd choose.

Wilma was pulling at a tiny clump of desert grass with her free hand and she let the stems drop and then she picked them up again. She watched him to gauge his reaction.

Sam was watching the tears stream down her face. I dont know, he said.

She looked at the Kiowas asleep on their blankets. Look at them now. We can slip away while they sleep.

But… but what about Charlie?

Wilma started to answer but stopped herself and she raised up and looked down at Charlie. His mouth was open and he was breathing deeply. He twitched in a dream, sweet little boy.

We cant leave him, said Sam.

But Sam, I dont think he can…

Yes he can.

He'll hold us back. Our only chance is to slip out and ride for help. I cant go alone.

I cant leave my brother alone.

It's our only chance.

He'll never make it by himself.

Yes he can.

Tears welled up in Sam's eyes. You can go on if you want to, he said. I understand.

You've got to come with me. I need you.

I'm not going unless he comes with us.

We cant risk it.

Sam lay there, thinking.

We'll ride through the river so they cant track us. We'll return with your father and the Rangers.

Sam watched her and she closed her eyes and then rolled over. They said no more. He looked at the swarm stars shimmering back at him, drifting ever so slowly. A puff of wind stirred the grass and cooled them and then it was gone. He rolled over and then back again and finally settled on his side nudged up against her. Her back was turned to him and her eyes were open again. Then she could hear him sleeping.

When they rode out that morning a sharp wind blew cool and dust churned the horizon and the early sunlight shimmered in and out of a steady line of slow-moving clouds dancing across the canyon country that fed from the Llanos like some godlike beacon peering down from the heavens as if to seek something that needed to be saved. Hint of moisture in the air. Sam was watching the rim of the western escarpment where a dark cloudbank was building on the horizon and he knew the weather was about to change.

They rode down into the broader reaches of the Palo Duro and the warm light of early morning began to burn the distant walls in a kaleidoscope of yellow and red and orange. They reached the valley floor at noon and waded a sandy-braided stream on the rise, sheets of rainfall on the Caprock looming silent and dark and fat dollops of cold rain now blowing down slantwise in the windgusts to the north. The Kiowas nudged their mounts forward with the mutterings of thunder and raindrops sprinkled the dust, peppering the rider's faces and the slick coats of the horses and as they rode the sweet smell of rain on the prairie consumed them.

They took shelter from the storm under a long grove of cottonwoods and within the hour the norther had passed and the sun came beaming upon a steaming and dripping land. Sam slouched on the horse and looked long out upon this scene with his hollow eyes. Shivering, exhausted. The sky lay pure and blue and a cool dry wind hissed down upon them from the plains. The horses splashed fetlock through the mud and water stood in little pools all about the desert glistening ripples of silver in the blustery gusts of wind. He took in the scenery as if it was all a dream. He kept a mindful eye on his brother. He thought long and hard about Wilma's plan of escape.

They set camp that afternoon on the sand-laden floors among a series of narrow slot canyons that dropped from the rims of the northern escarpment. The captives led the horses out to graze and began to gather water and collect brush for the fires. Bands of sunlight filtered into the canyon through the breaks in the fast-moving clouds and their footsteps crunched softly as they talked among themselves.

When Charlie sauntered off a ways Wilma pulled Sam aside to confer alone and she outlined her thoughts about the route back to their home and urged him to flee with her in the night. He was torn. She told him that everything was going to be alright and to get hydrated because he'd need it to sustain himself on the long journey. They knelt down by the water and drank and they whispered logistics and drank some more and after a while Charlie returned to join them. Sam arose and placed his feet in the cool stream and stared back toward the way home. They stayed there for a long time without talking and perhaps Sam was thinking about what might happen if they were caught. But what were their chances if they escaped?

Late that evening it was clear and cool and they were curled up beside the fire unable to sleep. Wilma studied the stars and listened and waited. One of the Kiowas walked to the brush and pulled his breechclout aside and pissed and went back to bed. An hour passed. When the fires finally faded and all was quiet Wilma nudged Sam and they began to carefully crawl away from the camp. Sam stopped and rose to his feet looking back at Charlie. He was curled up on his side in a deep sleep. His mouth was open and there was drool on his cheek. Sam watched him, thinking. There was no wind and the dark night seemed hollow as if every insignificant noise would echo in the void. He whispered something to himself, then he turned and went on.

They crept along for short distances, crouching down, lying still and listening, crawling quietly, a few feet at a time. They did this for a long time until they had made their way to the horses. Wilma whispered to the stallion and put her breath to its nose as she bridled it with ease and then began to gently walk it back down canyon away from the camp. Sam slipped the hide thong bit into the mare's mouth but when she riled he instinctively let it go. He glanced back at Wilma and then back at the sleeping camp. Then he put his head down and his hands on his knees. Dang, he whispered. Now what.

He set off on foot looking back toward the camp, tiptoeing to a safe distance and then breaking into a trot. When he caught up with her she looked back at him and he was crying.

What happened? she whispered.

He didnt answer. He looked back toward the camp. He sniffled and wiped his eyes.

Sam, go back and get the mare.

He just stood there. He bent down and grabbed a handful of grass and let it drop. He looked back at her.

We're going to be okay, she said. I promise.

She was looking back up the canyon over his head toward the camp. Shadows moving. Probably the flickering of the fire. So quiet on a starlit night. When she looked back at him he was stooped down with his arms out and hands clasped together. She bent her left leg and placed her foot in his cupped hands and lightly grabbed the mane and pulled herself up as he lifted. He kept looking back at the camp.

Go on without me, he said.

No. I cant go alone.

Yes you can.

No.

Now Wilma was crying. She wiped her eyes and looked out over the country, the gradual and glistening contour of the stream flowing in the moonlight. Sam stepped back. He was wary of the remuda following. There was a gust of wind and rustling in the camp and he thought he heard a voice. He began to slowly walk backward and he told her to be careful and she told him to be strong. She nudged the horse around and started it on a walk down the streambed but she heard something and looked back. She could see something rising far behind him from the camp and then the boy turned and hurried back. She said something under her breath as if to address him directly. Then she pulled the bridle and put her heels in the horse and started it at a trot delicately across the sand until they became small and then smaller in the lonely desert darkness until they dissolved forever into the night.

The searchers wandered the depths of the Comancheria for five more days relentlessly pursuing signs of the warparty that held RL's boys. They followed the trails through the eroded clay scabland country and they crossed the Double Mountain and Salt Forks of the Brazos and they scoured diverging trails west and split their party for sojourns among the endless mazes of red rock cliffs. They crossed the White River one morning under a blanket of fog and flogged the horses through sloughs of muddy red clay that bubbled and oozed down the arroyos of the Caprock breaks. As the morning sun burned through the haze they stopped for council. They were lost in a country they did not know. The posse was starved and beaten, the horses all but ruined. They were facing the reality that there was nothing for them to do but turn back for home.

They made their way to a narrow gorge of the river in Blanco Canyon and camped near the cool spring waters of Silver Falls, a place that RL would someday see again. He walked out alone with a flask of whiskey to a high ridge to think it all over. Long views of the rimrock cliffs and the white mudstone beds and the broken grasslands of the high plains and somewhere in the two hundred thousand square miles that surrounded them were his two boys. He did not know if he would ever see them again. He was crying and he lowered his face into his hands and then he looked up to the heavens and called out to God. Where are you? he said. Are you out there? And if you are, can you tell me… why?

He stood there alone for a long time watching the burning sun and he sipped from his flask and thought about his dead wife and he thought about his boys. It was my job to keep you safe, he said. I'll make it right. I promise.

He watched the last light of the sun and let the whiskey dull his pain. He was coming to terms with the fact that for now it was time to move on, and he held the flask out to salud the evening redness and he listened for the word of God and drained it.

In the morning they were drifting south following the phantom trails of the heathen to nowhere. RL rode at the rear of the column watching the riders slumped ahead of him and the long open country before them. The wasted horses swishing through the dry grass and sagebrush. In the broken flats of the canyon mouth miniature forests of spined cholla. They rode over rock strewn pastures into fields of wildflowers where the sweet smelling javelina bush filled the air like perfume. The butterflies fluttered daintily in the bright afternoon sunlight and RL caught one in his palm and cradled it like a precious jewel and urged it on and as he watched it flutter away the miracle of its journey seemed to touch him. They rode through a narrow gulch where the agaritas were fruited up in berries and they crossed a springfed valley at sundown where coveys of scaled quail were bursting from the brush and soaring into the sun, vanishing from sight like ghosts, running recklessly through the shortgrass and melting away into the prairie. They rode into a scrabbled desert flat, the famished ponies wheezing in the still, hot air, and in the hazy light as the boy preacher's horse leaned down for a nip of bunchgrass a seven-foot diamondback snake rattled up out of the scree where it had been coiled and sprung up at him with needlepointed fangs bared.

The horse screamed and Swaggart reached for the pommel as the animal reared back in hysteria. The nearest man was Goodnight and as he unsheathed his shotgun his horse stomped and broke into a nervous little bucking action and he was trying to rein it, jabbing his bootheels and hollering, when the snakebit horse turned at him rearing and kicking its front legs in a panic. Swaggart was thrown from his mount. He was airborne for a good three seconds and he landed hard near the rattler with a loud thud and the horse broke into a full sprint with Swaggart's hand entangled in the rope tied to the saddlehorn. Goodnight blasted the snake into a splattering mush of shredded skin and guts and blood and Swaggart dangling behind his running horse looked up at him bug-eyed with mouth agape and arms and legs sprawled out like some crazed victim in a medieval torture rite. All about the prairie a pandemonium of hollering and the bucking of horses trying to throw their mounts to the desert floor. Goodnight spurred his horse into a run alongside the defector pony as it ran off dragging Swaggart through a tangle of briarpatch and he swiped for the rope with a whiff of his knife only to lose his bearings and fall to the desert floor cussing and tumbling. The horse ran on, hauling the howling Swaggart in tow with the sound of his body being dragged through the rabble and cactus, bouncing off boulders, his wails mingling with the pounding of the hooves reverberating across the prairie. Someone fired a rifle and it blew up the dust ahead of the hysterical beast. Another shot rang out and the horse leapt a ridge, first the horse vanishing and then in midair its hostage falling from sight down into the arroyo in a cloud of dust.

The searchers scrambled to gather themselves as the horse galloped away. Goodnight remounted and took off following the dragmarks and soon the others were loping along a weaving trail of torn clothes and blood and trampled brush. They rode two miles before they came upon the pile of gore.

They reined up alongside one another, wincing at the scene. Swaggart's corpse was mutilated beyond recognition. Nearby the horse was spinning slowly in a tight circle with its swollen head held low. It had its nostrils flared and its lips pulled back and was rhythmically clapping its teeth as if this strange ceremony might somehow separate it from the rope that trailed along dangling the severed arm of its former rider.

Goodnight waved the men away and dismounted. He cocked his pistol and walked up to the horse and put the gun to its head and fired. Already the men were scratching out a shallow grave in the dirt. They pushed Swaggart's body in and cut the rope from the horse and threw it and Swaggart's arm into the earth and covered it up. They dragged the horse away. Then the posse circled around and stood about the grave with their heads down. Someone said a short prayer and they said amen and then they mounted up and set out to the south talking fondly of the honorable character and faith of the dead boy parson.

For the next two days they saw no indians nor signs of them and they passed no other riders. They were now on the tenth day of the scout and at noon they began to come upon a rangeland parched from drought, overgrazed and burned by the sun and littered with the bloated carcasses of bison decaying in the heat. They halted and looked out upon the dry valleys before them where dead bison lay like crops of pumpkins ripe and full in the fields and all that afternoon and through the night and all the day following they traveled to the southeast under dark clouds of swirling buzzards, a stretch of forty miles where the starved creatures lay as far as the eye could see in any direction. Thousands of bison had perished here and the searchers made their way among the swarming flies and carcasses with their eyeholes of hatching larvae and they raised their kerchiefs to their faces to fend off the stench.

It was late that afternoon before they came upon a clearing in the carnage where the numbers of dead bison seemed to wane. They could see a small rise of dust to the southwest. By evening an outfit of cattlemen came riding upon them out of the setting sun. Twelve men riding saddle mules and leading horses surrounding a bois d'arc supply wagon. The cowboys joined them by the campfire that night and swapped accounts of the trail over a pot of boiling prairie dogs.

It was John Chisum and a passel of hands coming back from the Pecos country and they'd been riding five hundred miles with eight thousand dollars in gold returning from the Bosque Redondo range in New Mexico and they gave details of the route up the Pecos to Fort Sumner and they spoke of driving the herd across the godforsaken desert and killing newborn calves that had dropped in the night and cattle drowning in the Pecos and the Comancheros and cattle thieves but by god it looked as though it might all end up being worth it after all, on account of them selling their beeves for sixteen cents a pound to the government contractors.

Charlie, RL, I'll tell you what! It's shore great to see you again, said Chisum. It's so damn nice to see some familiar faces back on the home range.

Goodnight nodded. Likewise, John. I imagine you're all pretty tired out.

Well, yes. But there aint much time to rest you see, because we need to round us up another big herd and make a drive back up there before winter. I got my boys up there tendin our business and somebody's got to get some beeves up there as soon as is goddamn possible. We been ridin two weeks traveling forty miles a night to avoid ambush and this last stretch was forty-eight hours with no rest ridin from the Horsehead. Now acourse we had to work our way out of a little run-in with the injuns. And then there was a cattletrain straggling along that ignored my warnings. Shit-all stupid sumbitches. Hell, I'd bet good money those poor bastards ended up getting slaughtered at the Castle Gap. You talk about askin for it. But we pushed on and damned if we werent about starved and who do you suppose we saw rambling along out there on that trail? That's right, ole Honey Allen. Haulin a wagonload of pecans. Can you believe that? He told us Jack Cureton and a pack train of gold hunters were somewhere along the trail. Cureton told him they was another wagontrain that had been besieged by the savages for three days near the pass in the ruins of the Butterfield Stage. It's been a helluva trip, boys. One helluva trip.

The Butterfield Stage, someone said.

Now it was time for the men from the San Saba to tell their own tales, such exchanges of manly encounters somehow raising the spirits of used up men otherwise how could they possibly hold their sanity? And as they listened closely to Goodnight's account of the tragedy upon the San Saba valley they looked at RL with heartfelt concern like men who'd been exposed to similar circumstances, faced kindred regrets. There was the uncomfortable silence that often occurs among those who are not sure of how to handle an interaction with someone who has suffered a great tragedy. Chisum listened patiently and he waited to speak and when he spoke he spoke for them all and he was sincere and considerate in the doing.

The company nodded their heads. RL made his appreciation known. He eyed Goodnight and then he rose to stoke the fire and the stars flickered and a meteor flared silently and was gone. Soon the fire had smoldered down, the wind was empty. The flies had found them and covered their cups and plates and they cleaned up the camp and settled onto their bedrolls and looked out at the stars. The talk turned to buffalo. Good grass on the Concho side and the herds never moved over to feed, someone said. Imagine that. All of em. Dead.

Well, it dont matter anyhow, said Goodnight. One day they'll all be hunted up and there wont be a buffalo one.

They all nodded to themselves. Goodnight shifted his head on his saddle and closed his eyes and pulled his hat over his face. The coyotes were yapping in the prairie all around them. Imagine what it was like long ago, he said. When there was no man.

Sam lay awake most of the night listening to the fragile and aimless wanderings of his mind. In his restless sleep he dreamt of Wilma riding away and when he rose up to face the dawn he was thinking about her out there all alone in the darkness. When the Kiowas discovered that she was gone Satanta sent three men out to track her and he glared at the boys with dark eyes. It should not have taken long to ride her down but it was almost noon when the scouts returned and they did not have her with them.

The Kiowas took council and called the brothers before them. Satanta palmed a ball-headed warclub made of maple and shifted his grip slightly so that the iron spike would not be received directly and he approached Sam with his arm reared back and swung with full force into his kidney and then he tossed the weapon to his nearest lieutenant.

Sam dropped to the ground doubled over, clutching at his side and grunting and gasping for breath. Satanta yelled at him and nudged him over with his foot. Someone tossed him a coil of rope and he seized the boy and slung him up against a hackberry tree and bound him to its warty bark. Charlie had been fighting back tears and at this he began to whimper and sob. Tears were streaming down his face and now one of the Kiowas slapped the little boy full across the cheek and he dropped and rolled over in the dust with his hands to his bloodied nose.

Satanta pulled his pistol and directed his lieutenants to stack a pile of brush at Sam's feet and a man scooped up a handful of coals from the fire and placed them just right and he waved his hand back and forth and blew it up into a whirl of flames and then stood back watching the results of his work. Sam fought the tears welling up in his eyes and he looked down at his brother with the fire crackling and smoldering hot in a shroud of black smoke. He was thinking about his father.

Go on! he screamed. Kill me!

Satanta stepped closer and smiled. He began to speak slowly in Kiowa.

Sam unleashed a wild and long and horrible wail. Just do it! he screamed.

Sam! yelled Charlie. No!

Some of the Kiowas had pulled their bows. Charlie could smell the tinge of Sam's leg hairs burning and when they made eye contact he began to crawl across the ground toward him.

Charlie, no! shouted Sam.

A man stepped forward to hold him back but Satanta waved him away and Charlie lunged out trying to save his big brother by throwing dirt on the brushpile. He was bawling and choking and blowing helplessly at the flames of the fire.

Satanta shoved the boy back with his foot and leaned up into Sam nose-to-nose. He was gripping his scalping knife and he slowly tilted his head as if to make a better assessment of his subject.

Do it! screamed Sam, and then he sucked up a mouthful of spit and hocked it into the face of his tormentor.

At first the chief's face clouded but then he slowly broke into a wide smile. He looked down and wiped his face and glanced back at his men before turning back swiftly with a vicious whir of his knife, slashing the boy's torso from his shoulder to his hip.

Sam commenced to scream hysterically. He'd lost all fear. He was kicking his feet about in fury and wiggling and trying to squirm loose from the rope that bound him, blood streaming down his torso. Charlie scrambled back up and came running headlong into the chief's legs but he was kicked back again and two men subdued him and held him down with a pistol to his head. Sam tried to calm himself down, huffing for breath, tears streaming. Please, he said. Please.

Satanta studied him. The rope had begun to come loose and Satanta reached down and untied the main knot and Sam wiggled free and collapsed to the dirt. He pushed himself up and wiped his eyes and spat. The man pulled the pistol away from Charlie's head. Some of the Kiowas were chuckling.

Thank you, cried Sam, sobbing.

It wasnt long before they were mounted up and riding out. They looked pitiful beyond all description. Charlie's eyes were swollen and red and he still could not catch his breath and he tried to say something to Sam about Wilma but Sam did not respond, bobbing along like a corpse, caked in dirt and scabs and staring out at the country like he was looking out a window that wasnt there. Satanta herded them on. By early afternoon they had begun to reach the outskirts of the main camp.

The sun was lurking behind a heavy line of scudding clouds when they rode upon a promontory with long views of the rugged river valley running north. A big wind blew down from the plains and pushed the clouds to the southeast and all at once in the bottoms along the winding banks of the Canadian the village came alive in the sun. Rows of tipis lined out for miles like figurines in a diorama. Strands of pecans and cottonwoods with their early spring leaves glowing green aligned with perfect symmetry the glistening water and in the nearby pastures a thousand or more horses stood grazing in the high grasses and for miles about the distant plains herds of bison were moving slowly along the skyline, their shaggy coats shining in the sun.

The brothers gazed in awe at the scene that lay before them. Down in the dale the swales of grass swayed with the breeze like silent wands conducting nature's mystic promenade. A lone bald eagle soared with its wings outstretched across the valley, dipping, rising, its white head glowing like a beacon in the crisp sunlit air, and between the scattered lodges they could see the tribesmen moving about like miniature stick people in their perfect little pocket of paradise. Satanta led them down. The boy captives herded along, pulled further from their origins into an alien culture of strange and mythical wonder.

They were led down a cliffside trail lined with junipers and boulders bedecked with etchings of human figures and they rode through a forest of soapberry and elms and down a steep precipice into the broad canyon floor. Grama grass pastures sprinkled with sandsage and daisies and basketflowers and groups of young braves reining up their horses to whoop out at them in welcome and attend respectfully the arrival of the immortal warriors and their tattered spoils of war. When the horses smelled the water from the lazy flowing stream they snorted and whinnied and they sensed the spirit of the larger herd, stepping smartly and flaring their nostrils in a pleasurable ritual of arrival. The air smelled of cedar and tobacco and cooked meat and the news of the warparty's arrival had begun to spread through the camp like a long-awaited blessing.

They were swarmed about like deities, prancing the horses slowly through the early rows of lodges in a celebratory buzz of jeers and shouts and laughter. Satanta and his returning hero warriors surveyed the scene stoically, nodding, smiling, waving at family members and admirers, driving the battered boy captives proudly through the camp under a light haze of smoke wafting slowly in the sun.

Little indian boys ran alongside them, shouting out and pointing their toy bows and arrows in play. They passed old men taking the sun who waved and nodded at them sagely, attended by weathered old squaws bent double with bare, shriveled paps. Young women carrying babies in crude, wooden carriers and others cutting firewood or scraping hides, sweat dripping from their haggard and empty faces. Brass buckets over smoldering fires, strips of drying meat hanging from sticks. They saw little girls kneeling in the grass with their faceless dolls singing or talking sweetly and they saw makers of saddlery and packs of yapping camp dogs and gamblers shooting dice for hides and knives.

They led them toward the center of the village and around a ceremonial bonfire roaring with energy, the black smoke swirling into the cobalt sky in a gesture to the spirits where they could see the severed and stinking heads of two white hunters impaled on stalks of sotol, the empty eye holes stuffed with river pebbles upon which painted rock eyes stared back in stonedead gaze, oblivious to the buzz of flies that swarmed about their shriveled and dripping flesh reeking in the heat.

They were dragged down from the horses and paraded through the crowds where throngs of wide-eyed young girls clamored forth to stroke their soft, blond hair. Villagers of all ages, of every shape and size, and even former captives who had been assimilated into the tribe cleared the way and watched as the brothers were herded through another long row of tipis to a buffalo hide lodge guarded by two juvenile warriors who shoved them inside as the heathen horde surrounded from all sides to taunt and jeer.

Inside it was dark and the faint hum of silence gave them solace against the raucous din of the villagers. The smell of leather and dirt and smoke and embers crackling softly. Their eyes adjusted to the low light and the blurred form of a shadow arose from across a smoldering cookfire. Someone came forward, a face illuminated by the glowing flames. Lighter eyes like theirs. Outside a dog fight broke out. The fevered yelp of scolded curs and men shouting. A muttered curse, a squeal, followed by silence.

Hello, a voice called. It was another boy captive like themselves. He was tall and dressed as an indian and when he stepped nearer they could see he had hopeful, green eyes. He was trying to place them. I seen you somewheres before, he said.

The brothers looked at one another. Sam tilted his head and cocked his eye, studying the other boy. He was trying to place him and then it hit him.

We's hunted with you and your daddy before, he said.

The kid thought for a moment, eyes wider, and then he began to nod slowly in recognition.

Yeah, that's right, he said. That's right. You all dont look so good. Are you okay?

Sam did not answer. A strange thought occurred to him. He stared at the fire deep in thought and then he looked back up. Say, that's not your daddy's head out there on that stick is it?

6

— ★ —

Early Days with the Kiowas

They were talking about what all they'd been through when the old medicine woman stepped inside to look them over. They looked horrible. They were starved and cut up and bloodied with swollen red eyes and they were caked in dust and the parts of their bodies that were not sliced and scabbed with scratches and cuts were welted up in bug bites and bruises all tender and painful to the touch.

The old crone said something in Kiowa and honed her eyes in on Sam. She approached him and stood before him, looking him over up and down. She reached and took hold of his hands and began to carefully explore their details. Sam held his hands out limply and he watched her milky eyes. The old woman turned his palms and felt them. She let his left hand drop and turned her focus to the right, slowly running both of her hands the length of his arm up to his shoulder and back down to his hand where she commenced to finger and read them like some ancient Chinese palmist. She had a slight smile and she seemed to be impressed. She put his hand close to her face, reading each finger, each nail. She studied the length of his fingers and bent them to and fro, tracing the tips of her nails across the length of his palm making mental notes of the shape and size. Then she carefully read the lines in the palm of his hand. Sam leaned forward the better to accommodate her in her readings when suddenly the woman gasped and let the hand drop and stood back looking at him with her jaw down as if she had just been visited by a dark spirit.

The captives stood wild-eyed and the old woman skinnied her glare at the boy, studying him, and then she reached out and took hold of his head, gently massaging his scalp as she meticulously examined the contours of his skull with the tips of her fingers. When the woman let go of him Sam stumbled back and put his hands to his head and Charlie rushed toward him to see about him. The other boy captive held his hands out before his face, looking at the lines and wondering what story they might foretell. The woman muttered something to herself and turned and rushed for the hide door. As she stepped outside of the lodge Sam called out to her but she did not return and they sat there in silence.

What was that all about? said Sam.

No answer.

Charlie rubbed his eyes and he sniffled up a big snot bubble that had emerged from his bloodied nose. The two older boys stood there looking at their hands and then Charlie did the same. They were alone for a while, wondering, whispering among themselves. Tell me your name again? said Sam.

Name's Billy.

I'm Sam. This is Charlie.

Billy looked them over. Sam and Charlie, he said. So you never saw what happened to your folks?

Not really. We were pretty far from the house when they got us and alls we saw was our granddad sprawled out on the ground shot up with arrows.

Well, I'll tell ya what happened to us was, my pa and Mr Johnson had ridden out to track a deer. It was me and David and we'd ate some lunch and were just sittin around waitin on em. We thought we heard some hollerin and we walked out and that's when we saw em ridin with the injins behind em. Whoopin and hootin and hollerin. I aint ever forget that. We turnt and made a run for it and before we knowed it them injins swarmed us down in the creek and it didnt take two seconds fer it to be done with. It all happened so's fast I's didnt really see what all happened to everone else. I tried to run but got knockt down. Knockt me out cold.

Next thing I knowed I's bein hault off on some injin harse. And I looked back and saw one of em scalpin my daddy.

How long have you been in here?

Since day afore yesterday.

Did they feed you?

Just some meat, that's all. Raw meat. Some injin women came in and cleant me up. They seemed nice enough.

They sat around the fire for a long time wondering what was going to happen next. Billy told them how they handed him off to another band of horsemen. Switching mounts and riding all night without stopping. He wiped a bloodied tear from his eye where a blood vessel had burst. I think we's goin to be alright, he said.

How do you know?

Well, they's another kid in here like us. I talked to him. He told me.

Who is it?

You can tell he's white like us. Older. Didnt catch his name. Seems he's been with the injins awhile.

Sam thought it over. He rubbed his head and looked at Charlie, now curled up in a ball and passed out sound asleep.

They laid back on pallets of hide robes, napping off and on and talking about what might happen. They could tell someone stood watch at the door. Now and again someone would poke their head inside to check on them.

These people. Billy, do you know what kind of indians they are? said Sam.

I guess they's Comanch.

Well, I'm gonna kill that big chief that killed our momma and hauled us off.

I know how you feel.

Sam sat there, biting his lip, stewing things over. Two women brought them baskets of dried meats and turnips. There were berries and nuts and fruits. Several gourds of fresh water. They watched the boys gorge themselves, smiling at them and whispering and giggling to one another. They could have been sisters. A third woman entered with a bushel of smuggled sweetbreads followed by two younger women carrying breechclouts and woven blankets and wagonboards of ointments and other supplies such as the roots of the yucca as well as an assortment of leaves harvested from local plants. A Kiowa boy came in with an armful of firewood. The medicine woman did not return. When they were finished eating the women scrubbed and bathed and doctored them with all of these varying supplies and then left them alone as the night settled in and they lay down and slept peacefully by the fire.

In the morning the boys emerged from the lodge into the sunrise and rubbed their eyes and looked about the village scene with sleepy curiosity. They were stiff and sore and they scratched their heads and squinted through the bright light, stretching their arms and legs and yawning out the kinks. The sun burned through a thin line of fog that lay like a gray wool blanket over the camp and the Kiowa women shuffled about their early morning chores.

After they had been fed and had their wounds doctored again they were taken to a lodge that served as a sort of supply house and they were ordered about the camp assisting the women in their chores. The woman in charge was an old heavyset squaw with three teeth and she cursed them through the village with their armfuls of provisions limping along among all of the stares and shouts and jeers. At the doors of the bison hide tipis were hungover men lounging, idly observing the labor of the women. In the afternoon the brothers sat in the shade of a cottonwood and rested and watched the little indian boys run around and play.

Sam, why did Aunt Wilma leave us?

To ride for help.

Does she know the way?

I dont know.

Do you think Daddy is looking for us?

Yes, of course he is.

How's he going to know where we're at?

He's with the other ranch men and they're following the trail.

A group of Kiowa women lingered nearby, listening intently to every word, fascinated with their speech and manner of interaction.

But if Daddy gets here they're going to kill him.

No. No they wont.

I wonder when he'll get here.

Dont think about it.

I know, said Charlie, his voice rising with an edge of irritation.

It's going to be okay. I promise.

But Sam, we've always been good, always said our prayers.

I know.

Then why did God do this?

I dont know, Charlie. He was shaking his head slowly. I dont know.

They watched the far side of the camp. There was a crowd assembling to welcome the arrival of some Comanches who were escorting a caravan of Mexican traders. Shouts and smiles and laughter. Women and kids running forward to help unload all of the trade goods.

After a while the old squaw came back waving her arms and slurring orders at them. Other women came along nodding and making gestures with their hands as if to reinforce the master's intent. Aim ahn, vamanos, they called. The boy captives rose and set out toward the gathering. They could hear shouts and laughter and the villagers were emerging from their lodges and hurrying over to see about the new arrivals. They shuffled along with the crowds and stood tiptoe to watch the proceedings. The lead rider dismounted and embraced an older chief who'd stepped forth to welcome them. He turned and gestured at the packmules and all of the goods they brought for barter. The Mexican traders were red-eyed and slurping from bottles of tiswin. Small boys and girls were running up to the Comanches with outstretched hands begging for curios and candies.

When the old chief warded them off they stood back smiling sheepishly. The merchants unpacked their loads. The crowd circled in closer, necks craned, watching the tarps being unfurled and ogling all of the goods that were laid out before them. Clear skies and high sunshine on a windless afternoon, tailor-made for a makeshift plains indians trade day, the simple and spontaneous surprises that are the pleasures of life.

They were visited by the older white captive, a German kid from the Pedernales River. This boy had been abducted fourteen months prior when he was sent by his father to look for some stray cattle and a raiding party snuck up on him and whisked him away as he walked along a deserted road six miles south of Fredericksburg. He lingered around the entrance to the tipi in his warrior garb and admirably considerate, keeping watch outside for threatening visitors, and in the afternoon in broken english accentuated by a heavy german accent he'd tell them of his early days in captivity and just how it was that he'd come to be an apprentice warrior. He'd been ridden upon in broad daylight on a sweltering summer day and he told them how he took off running and when the leader reached out to club him he dashed and darted as he ran and he was able to dodge a few of the riders until he tripped and flipped over headfirst and rolled back up just as another rider jumped from his mount on top of him and that was when the real fun started, him yelling and kicking and scratching and in this melee he took a beating but not without getting a good hold of that long black hair and pulling as hard as he could, biting a chunk of an arm and kicking the warrior, who he'd since become close to, so hard in the groin that he let go and doubled over grunting in agony. He told proudly of how it took the group of them to subdue him, and how they slung him into a rock fence and dazed him and tore his clothes off and soon had him bound upon the back of a mustang headed northwest and they passed the Keyser ranch and rode on stealing horses from the ranches and crossed the Llano where they lay up to rest but kept him hobbled and made no fire nor ate a bite of food and in a few hours were up and running again, scattering this way and that and they rode for six days straight without hardly stopping, the trip almost killing him, and all he thought was these men could not possibly be human. That was then. But look at him now, he was one of them.

I kebt zinking I vanded to die, said the kid, poot Quanah vouldn't let me. Effery now und zen he'd do zomething to help me. By zee fourth day I vas fery zick. Taken vith ze fever, mein legs vere zo zore und raw from riding pareback. Zey'd chust laugh at me. I dont know if I'd made it if it veren't for him. He rode me out to ein cornfield und bicked out zome husks, zen poiled zem up in vader und made me drink zee proth to break mein fever. Und zen mein leg vas lame und zey vanted to kill me off. He vouldn't allow it. Ve'd ride ein horze till it fell from hexhauszion. He'd chump off, sblit it oben und grab ein gut. Three, four feet of it. Throw it offer his schoulter und mount us pack up und schare zee raw slurp vith me as ve rode.

The brothers sat crosslegged across the fire from him chewing hard on strips of dried bison meat. Sam studied him.

What's your name? he said.

Zey call me Asewaynah.

Ase. Way. Nah, said Charlie.

What does it mean? said Sam.

It's ein long sdory, said the kid.

The brothers watched him. Charlie rubbed his eyes and scratched his scraggly blond hair. The kid's eyes were thoughtful and he rubbed the palms of his hands together as he thought about how to tell them.

Mein barents named me Rutolph, he said.

Sam pulled another long strip of jerky and asked questions as he gnawed. The kid told them of those first few months with the Comanche and they listened and queried him all the more.

I'll neffer forget ven I zaw mein first pooffalo. Chust pefore ve reached zee main fillage, he said. It vas all like ein dream. I could tell how happee zee var barty vas, py zeir smiles. I'd hardly zeen zem smile. Zey yelled out und kicked zee horzes into ein kallop. Efferyone in zee camp hoobed und hollerd und vistled back. Zey came svarming out to meet us. I vas ruschéd py ein group of old squavs und zey zet apout boking und brodting me, giffing me ein hard time. Zee next night zey but on ein big celeprazion.

Sam nodded and took it all in. The older boy was hard to understand but they were getting used to the pace of his speech. He looked at Charlie as if to reassure him and looked back at the boy, studying him closely from head to toe and back again.

So how long have you been here, Rudolph?

I dont know. I'fe lost track of zee time.

Well, what all have you been doing?

The kid smiled at them. Vadeffer zey vanded. I figured out vat zey liked. Learned real guick to like raw meat. It vas like zey vere tesding me.

Lots of hard chores. If I mezed up zey vould peat me. It vas like tordure at first. Early on I mized mein home und family. I tried not to let on zough. Vrestled, raced, fought vith zee other poys. Learned to help zem kather zee food. Fisch, catch turtles, ven food vas scarce. Early on I vas bretty much ein slaffe to zee man zat ovned me, Plack Crow. Tented to his horzes. Kathered vood, cleant his veabons, scrabed hites. Vasched him. Bicked zee lice off of him, vateffer. Zoze first few months it vas fery hard. I vas fery down. I tried to escabe once und I zought zey vere koing to kill me. Poot it all changed ven he pekan to train me to ride und fight like ein injian. Now if ve're not making veabons or hunding or preaking horzes ve do vadeffer ve bleaze. I eat vateffer und veneffer I vant und I sleep in mein ovn tebee und ve run horze races und svim und play ball und haffe schooding contests. Last month ven zee moon vas right zey took me raiting for horzes und vu von't belieffe it put ve snuck up on mein old home und I vatched mein own family koing apout zeir buziness. Zey joked about killing zem. I chust blayed along. Ve schtole ein slew of horzes from mein old neighpors. I'd of neffer zought it put I haffe no dezire to ko pack now to zat vay of life.

Sam was staring at his outfit, fascinated by the way he was dressed. He was admiring his necklace of mescal seeds and all of the enchanting gewgaws that dangled about it. Hey, what all do you have tied up inside that bundle on your necklace? he said.

In those early nights they dream of home. They will never again hear the morning bible readings of their mother. *Psalm 74:16. Yours is the day, Yours also is the night; You have prepared the light and the sun.* The sweet, loving nature of her voice reading scripture, teaching them. Finches flitting about singing in the sunshine. All of the adventures in the surrounding hillsides that lie in wait. The Sunday supper over, their chores complete, two curious boys set free into the wilds to play and explore.

A month later and their wounds have mostly healed. They move with the village to a sheltered canyon a three-day trek to the south. The lodges broken down, dragged along, reassembled. In the mornings they are hauled out onto the plains with the women to process the bison kills. They pin out the hides and scrape them and they work all day under the sweltering summer sun taking direction by hand gestures and grunts. They sleep in the lodge of the sister of one of the tribesmen who carried them away and they lie awake at night thinking of escape but they are afraid. With the passing of June Charlie begins his sixth year. He is a beautiful child. Bright, green eyes, smooth tan skin. He is pure even though his blond hair is now soiled up in dirt and grease to disguise his Anglo features. His eyes glow with an innocent intelligence and he follows his brother and he watches the villagers and he wonders, listening to the strangeness of their feral speech. They gather wood, they fetch water. They watch the storm clouds in the west that always build. Far away thunderheads, dark skies, funnel clouds on the distant horizons.

On a sweltering afternoon Sam is thrown violently from a green-broke two-year-old pony. Held back from a full run the horse bucks and jumps wildly. The boy sails through the air and slams into the rocks on his tailbone. Knocked out cold. When he comes to he cannot move.

He lies on a robe in a lodge in and out of consciousness for days while the medicine woman tries to revive him. She faces east singing songs or sitting quietly in meditation, waiting, praying to whatever spirits or enlightenments she has the pulse of. A small wiry woman with Mongol eyes and a sage-like smile. Some of the villagers want to leave him behind so that he does not hold them back but the woman appeals to the elders and attends to him until one morning he opens his eyes with the daybreak and looks for the light. He has come back.

Now a different kind of journey has begun to unfold. Each day that passes takes them further from their origins and the images of their past begin to fade, fleeting and then forgotten, as if only yesterday played out years ago in some long-lost dream. The world flows on. They are growing. Arms, legs, feet. The subtle changes to their faces, their voices. Blond hair darkened by bear grease and dirt and dung. They walk barefoot in breechclouts. Shirtless, with their calloused hands and feet. Seasons change. The spring grass grows green, the war parties come and go. Each day they watch the great sun rise and they gaze back to the southern horizons watching for the father that never comes.

They are in constant movement, working, moving with the village from place to place as they follow the herds, wandering west over the treeless expanses of the lonesome plains. They trudge through the shinnery sands of the western Caprock breaks. The wind blows sand in their eyes and grit in their teeth. The wolves howl at the moon all night from out in the darkness. They work all day and into the last of the light and as the sun slips down they settle in by the fires to observe the rise of a faint halfmoon, snacking on morsels of raw meat as a deer is butchered, now craving the flavor of the gallbladder bile sprinkled on their meal. Cliffswallow nests in the sandstone overhangs. Bands of wild horses grazing near the watered and timbered draws. The country has a raw edge to it and the eternal wind blows a gale from the canyon rims in the distance. They move west through the rugged desert plains, roaming for weeks on the fringes of the Pecos valley. They see mixed-blood fur traders accompanied by a delegate from the indian agency at Fort Sumner and they bring goods into the camp to barter for captives like themselves but the boys are hidden away and protected from those wary eyes.

Another month goes by, the father still has not come. With each day that passes they become more like The People and with these horse barbarians in the dry heat of the endless indian summer they descend into the depths of the Sabinoso wilderness for the great trade council that has been called by the Comanche elders.

They were standing before a row of tipis that had been lined out above the floodline of the creek. The distant buzz of drunken revelry echoed out over the valley. The Kiowas had been sharing the kegs of whiskey they'd bartered for with the Hispano traders and they'd been drinking heavily for two days running. Charlie came up from the creek hauling an armful of newly filled waterbags. He looked at Sam. His arms were held out and he was studying all of the strange garb he'd been adorned in. He wore a necklace of beads and the women had painted his face up in cryptic designs. Charlie reached out and touched him.

Sam, those beads are kind of neat, he said.

Sam reached down and scratched at the skin beneath his brass anklets and shook his leg. I guess so, he said.

What are they for? Charlie looked up at him and waited for an answer.

I'm not sure.

I kinda like em.

It seems like they're dressing me up for something.

Yeah.

Charlie touched the beads and rolled them around in his fingers to feel the texture and observe the bright colors. He looked at the women. They're nice, he said.

I know.

A lot more indians have been coming into camp today.

Yeah.

Sam?

He didnt answer. He was watching the women as if he'd not want them to hear. He looked out toward the far side of the camp.

Look, Charlie, let's just go along with whatever they make us do and not make a huge fuss about anything. Do you understand?

Sam, I know. Stop saying that.

All at once there was a roar of angry female voices, a handful of Kiowa women ranting at one another over some comment or misunderstanding. The brothers watched them hash it out. Beyond them they could see a large crowd gathering and there seemed to be some sort of commotion with the arrival of a new band of Comanches. Sam was standing on top of an old cottonwood log watching the proceedings when Satanta appeared. He was red-eyed and a little drunk and there was a handler with him carrying a sack of Mexican coins and they grinned and observed the boy closely and whispered to one another before calling him over.

They called out to Sam but he did not understand them and they waved him to follow through a long row of lodges and in the distance he could hear the big roar of the crowd cheering on two horsemen racing neck and neck toward a finish line surrounded by animated tribesmen. Charlie ran along behind them with the women and their dogs and a growing assemblage of halfnaked children who straggled behind skipping and grinning in curiosity, shouting playfully, some throwing rocks or dirt, the collection of them reeking of smoke and animal dung and body odor. They converged around Sam and Satanta in his inebriation cursed and shooed them away, herding the boy along through a scattering of hut clusters and into the bustling fairgrounds.

Now the trade meet was on the verge of degenerating into a drunken fandango. The horse race finished, the revelers whooping and shouting out strange sobriquets at one another. They saw a caravan of disheveled New Mexican merchants with high pointed sombreros spreading their wares, sipping from jugs, doing their best to maintain some manner of comportment perhaps to better position the value of their goods or just to keep the more ill-mannered drunkards at bay. Someone noticed Satanta and his cortege parading Sam into the grounds. Other heads began to turn and the Owl Prophet interrupted his processional to turn with his followers and observe the entrance of the big war chief and his white boy captive.

They began to gather around, forming a sort of makeshift amphitheater and showering Sam with a chorus of curses and whistles and jeers. The Comanchero merchants cheered for him. Tejanito! they called. Vamanos, Tejanito!

He looked around. Across from them another mob of villagers entered the arena escorting a bigboned captive boy, a Mexican, and as they ushered him forth into the ring Satanta said something to Sam and took off the boy's beaded necklace and nudged him forward to face his opponent. He had never seen the boy before.

The crowd yelled all the louder, anxious for the proceedings to begin. Sam turned to face the kid, sensing the size and strength of his body. Massive shoulders, hunched over. He looked like a muskox. Sam caught a fleeting glance into those wild eyes but he quickly looked away. Sam scanned the arena nervously, all eyes fixed upon him, and he was very scared and he looked back at Satanta for some hint of direction. What do I do? he said.

Just then a middle-aged Kiowa man, shirtless and inebriated, stepped into the arena and made a short speech, gesturing like an evangelist at each of the competitors and then at the crowd as if to formally initiate the proceedings. As he left the arena he shouted and waved his hands upward three times to fever the patrons and the crowd roared wildly.

The big kid took a few steps forward and stopped. He flung back his long hair with a toss of his head. Sam began a slow backwards shuffle but the kid rushed wildly across the battleground and pounced on him like a mountain cat and slammed him down into the hardpan dust with all the weight of his body. He smelled earthy like a greased and gutted duck bloating in the sun. Sam was breathless. The kid threw a flurry of fierce punches and then jumped up and began kicking him hard. The crowd roared. Sam came up gasping desperately for air and when he tried to stand up everything went silent. He fell back and rolled over in the dirt blinking, blood pouring from his nose as he tried to get up again. Then he rose up stumbling toward his attacker with the crowd jeering and took two wobbly steps before falling face first into the dust.

Charlie had worked his way through the crowd and stood hunched between two women where he could see the Mexican kid standing in the middle of the arena, grunting and gesturing with his hands and daring Sam to get up and fight. Sam! he called to his brother, but when Sam just lay there the kid came charging again. He dove headlong and gathered Sam into his immense arms and they rolled about in a ball of dust and scratched and clawed and spit and punched until the kid came out on top again, now pummeling Sam like some primitive punching bag. Blood was pouring from Sam's nose. He was like a limp and lifeless animal, no longer able to defend himself. His eyes were now almost completely swollen shut and he was close to blacking out and he twitched convulsively with each successive blow as the surrounding horde bristled to a fevered pitch. Finally Satanta stampeded into the arena to break up the fight.

He knelt and cradled the boy's head to study him but Sam jerked in a spasm and coughed up a mouthful of blood and phlegm and then he spit out a tooth. Satanta waved for the handlers. A passel of squaws came running to assist. They all knelt down around him. Someone wiped the blood from his mouth but it quickly filled again. When they carried him away through the crowds most believed he was dead.

In the days to follow Sam was set up in a lodge that served as a sort of infirmary where his brother and several young squaws took turns attending to him, bringing him meals and doctoring his wounds.

He mostly slept and when he was awake he was so sore he could barely move, lying motionless in a haze, eyes black, face and lips swollen. He spoke with a lisp and his ribs ached and it was painful to breathe. From time to time the healer would visit to check on him and bring him medicines from the earth. He drank a lot of water. He needed help to stand up and hobble out to relieve himself and it was a week before he stopped urinating blood and another week before he was able to lift his left arm again.

He was rustled from his rest one afternoon by the German boy captive. I'll pe leaffing in zee morning, he said. I vanted to check on vu.

Where are you going?

Zomeveres zouth.

South?

Ya. Ya. Zouth. How are vu?

I'm better. I thought that kid was going to kill me.

Vell, zat's vy I vant to giffe vu ein little hadffice.

Advice?

Lisden, zere's koing to pe ein big council in tvo veeks on zee vesdern preaks. All zee tripes. Effen bigger zan pefore.

Sam nodded.

Zere's ein kood chance zey'll haffe vu fight akain. Zat kid is beeg put he cant moffe zat vell. Vu can peat him.

Sam just sat there.

Listen, ven he charges vu chust need to drop dovn guick. Like ein cat. Drop dovn right at zee last zecond like zis.

He squatted low and imitated the move. Sam sat up, watching him.

Zen grab him right here. He pointed at his groin. Grab him right here vith all vu'fe kot. He mocked the motion, his face contorted. Uze all of your schtrength, he said.

Sam smiled. He looked like a raccoon with the black rings around his eyes but there was life in them again.

Zink apout it. He is koing to beg und scream like ein little squaw poot vadeffer vu do dont let go. Chust hold tight und vait. Vu'll know ven zee time is right. Ven vu let go he is koing to raize up. Slovly. He'll pe stunnd for ein sblit zecond. Und zat is ven vu need to hit him as hard as vu can right here, in zee noze. Zen keep koing. Pound him. Pound into him vith all vu'fe kot. Und dont let up undil zey bull vu off him.

Sam was trying to picture it and he giggled. He was smiling and rocking his head up and down in agreement. You really think that will work?

I know it vill vork.

They talked it through. Charlie came in with a basket of jerky. He was surprised to see Sam up and smiling and it made him feel good. Asewaynah poked his head outside and then stepped back in and knelt down facing Sam.

Get yourzelf vell, he said. Quanah vill pe vatching.

The boy captives had been traveling west with the Kiowas for ten days when they entered the trading camp deep in the recesses of the Cañón Largo. Here an important council was assembling, a diverse conglomeration of brownskinned plains rovers meeting to discuss potential alliances against the Texans in an extended binge of trading and drinking and gambling.

There was a contingency of Apache chiefs from the western mountains paying exorbitant prices for kegs of whiskey with horses and cattle stolen from Texas ranches. Mescaleros. Chiricahuas, Mimbreños, Lipans. Infamous inebriates already in the early stages of drunkeness and looking for action. They eyed the Kiowas warily and made wry comments to one another about the white brothers and their potential value in ransom.

A large crowd had gathered and Sam stayed close to the Kiowa woman who directed their activities. He kept a low profile, watching for anyone who might seem to be looking to trade for captives. Charlie followed along. They saw the Comanchero caravans with their tradewares spread out for show, the owners cautiously bartering while also regarding the brothers surreptitiously. They saw Asewaynah with Quanah and the Quahadis sashaying about the scene perusing the goods for sale. In their crude carretas or spread out upon the handwoven blankets and rugs of the Navajo the traders presented a wild assortment of goods. The much sought-after sweetbreads. Sacks of sugar, flour, coffee, tobacco, beans, corn. Onions and peppers. Gourds and beans. They sold knives and guns and ammunition procured from the military authorities in New Mexico and God knows where. Tomahawks and lances, iron or steel arrow spikes ready-made. They had clothing and calico and piles of cloth to make more. They had trinkets and beads and paint, all essentials to the boudoir of the plains indians. All of this and more was bandied about amidst a great frenzy of intemperance where many things are contested. Sam is pitted against Apaches in footraces and he is strapped on the winning pony in a hotly contested horse race and they witness numerous games of dice and cards where substantial fortunes change hands time and again.

On the afternoon of the fourth day he was gussied up to fight again. He was led to the entrance of another makeshift fighting arena and here he had more at stake than he could ever know. The wagers had been placed, the ring was surrounded by a horde of drunken Llaneros. The air smelled of cookfires and sweat and cornbrewed alcohol and you could see the smokehaze rising above the crowd in the late day sun. He took a deep breath and stepped forward. There was sharp gravel and pads of trampled prickly pear strewn about the fighting grounds and his eyes scanned the crowds nervously for the emergence of his opponent. The big Mexican kid was being escorted forward and he stepped proudly into the ring. The kid was rocking from side to side and glaring at him like an angry bull. He flicked his long black hair and spat into the dust. He rubbed his fist in the palm of his opposing hand. He was slowly mouthing some threat that no one could hear.

Sam took a few steps forward. They stood there staring at one another with the crowd shouting them on for what seemed like an eternity and when Sam gestured with a nod of his chin the kid came charging hard. He would remember what happened next, always in a slow hypnotic motion as if time itself was near ceasing, every day of his life until the very end.

He stood his ground until the kid was right upon him and then, catlike, he dropped down quick and grabbed ahold of his attacker's privates with all he had. He let out a primal scream. The momentum carried the kid over his head and he pushed up out of his squat and went airborne tumbling over and landing in a thud, clamping down his deathgrip on the kid's genitalia. They were like that for a few seconds, the kid bawling out like some crazed mule, Sam squeezing down and twisting all the harder as he whispered into his ear.

You had enough of that yet? I think you want a little more, dont you?

The kid was trying to use his weight, rolling, flailing his legs, and some may have thought that Sam was losing his leverage but he grunted and dug in with his knees and began jabbing the full force of his body and now doubling up on his grip and trying to rip the boy's manhood completely off. A hysteria swept through the bewildered crowd as the boys squirmed about in the dust of the ring, feet thrashing about wildly. The Mexican kid seemed to be begging for mercy in some strange babble and Sam squeezed tight for a long while, waiting, until he finally let go. The kid fell limp in a sort of shock, sucking for air, and before he could gain his bearings Sam jumped him and began pounding away at his face in a furious flurry of fists. The kid pulled his arms up and rolled up like a pill-bug, a shell of his former self so helpless in that swelling pool of blood.

Meanwhile a faction of Comancheros began shouting at the Mexican kid as if to rally him and at this he tried to scramble up but Sam clamped his arms around the kid's neck and jerked and then bared down in a steady choke hold. The kid kept trying to squirm out but Sam clenched his teeth and squeezed down harder, jerking and jerking the kid's head into the ground. He spat on him and screamed out and the spectators roared their approval at the carnage, watching to see how this would end. A shot rang out, whoops and hollers. He was holding back tears and talking into the kid's ear in a crazed whisperslobber when suddenly he was struck by some feral instinct and he bit down like a rabid dog, twisting his head and gnashing his teeth and with a fierce yank of his head he pulled back up with a bloody mouthful of ear. He spat it out. The kid reached for the mangled gash in the side of his head and he was thrashing about and shrieking and Sam just kept on slamming the boy's head into the hard-packed dust of the arena. What women there were in the crowd had commenced wailing, sank to their knees, stood with their jaws dropped and their hands atop their heads.

By now an air of absolute chaos and confusion had overcome the patrons. One woman, perhaps the adopted mother of the boy, broke through the crowd and rushed into the arena, and she was crying out and trying to push her way through the masses but there were others who were trying to hold her back. Sam released the kid and rose up and looked about. His eyes ran the circle of patrons and he looked for his brother. He wiped the blood from his eyes and face with both hands and he spat and turned and began walking away in a huff. The crowd fell into a murmur and strained their necks the better to see the gladiator boy captive. A few rowdy patrons called out, Tejanito! Tejanito!

As he left the battleground he was swarmed by a throng of villagers. Asewaynah made his way through, followed by Quanah, the handsomely dressed young Quahadi chieftain who was smiling ear to ear.

Mein friend, said Asewaynah, vu did kood. He smiled and patted him on the shoulder and they walked on.

Later that evening Quanah with a contingency of his followers mingled among a row of lodges awaiting the evening's festivities to begin. He wore large brass hoops from his ears and he was ogling the squaws lewdly as they went about their chores ordering the brothers around. Sam was watching Quanah. When their eyes met Quanah gave a slight nod of his head and he smiled slyly. Then he turned and said something to the man next to him and they started nodding.

That night Asewaynah pulled Sam from his lodge and they stood in the moonlight discussing his future.

Quanah vants to help vu, he said.

He does?

Ja. He's kot ein zoft sbot for us cabdiffes.

Really?

His ovn mother vas taken py zee Comanche as ein child. I zink he's koing to trade one of his favorite horzes to Zatanta for vu. If it all vorks out vu'll pe coming vith us tomorrow.

But what about my brother?

I dont know. He chust zaid zat any poy zat could take ein chunk of ear off ein enemy vith his teeth vas meant to pe ein Guahadi.

I'm not leaving without my brother.

I hunderstand. Dont vorry, I vil talk to him apout your prother.

But the next morning when the Quahadis rode out Charlie was not with them. Sam was on a fresh pony, turned slightly in the saddle, holding back tears. He looked back at his little brother running desperately behind them and crying out. The squaws held him back. They rode out away from the village on the trail to the Pecos, the sun rising behind them, their shadows long before them. When they reached the ridge that would take them out of sight forever he looked back one last time. The breeze fell silent and he could hear the voice of his brother in the far away distance, the little boy now small on the prairie with his arms flailing as the women fought to hold him back.

7

— ★ —

The Searcher

In those first nights of sleep back home RL succumbed to nightmares. He tossed and turned. He would awake screaming out and he was covered in sweat with his eyes bulging in fits of rage. He was wrought with regret and his head was spinning and his mind was like an endless tornado of confusion and evil so bent on revenge. He took to drinking. He could hardly function at all. The booze that he consumed numbed his pain and brought some comfort to him and he huddled in bed for hours on end as if it would all go away and his body became frail and weak and his eyes lost and empty of life.

He sat holding the cardboard flyer that would be circulated in the towns and cities of Texas and surrounding territories. Tears streaming, his face quivering, head slowly turning from side to side.

Taken from my ranch by the Comanches, in San Saba valley, Menard County, Texas, on Sunday, April 15, 1866, my son SAMUEL HADEN TERRY, aged eleven years, blond hair, hazel eyes and fair complexion; also, my younger son, CHARLES WARREN TERRY, aged five, blond hair, blue eyes, fair complexion. All Indian agents or traders, or any person having an opportunity, are requested to rescue the above-named children; and delivering them to me or notifying me of their whereabouts, will be liberally remunerated. New Mexico, Oklahoma, and Mexican papers please copy. April 26. —RL TERRY

He gazed at the photo. Boys, he said out loud, I'll search for you until I'm dead. He kept thinking back to the days when he would play and wrestle with them, laying in the grass holding them in his arms, out of breath and laughing. Three summers and a thousand years ago. He would hold them and observe them discovering the world, admiring the joy in their eyes and beyond them the skies so blue, clouds moving, trees swaying, and in those beautiful moments he would think deeply about how he just wanted to soak it all in and not ever forget that joy because he knew it would not last forever. He listened to their voices. The innocence, the laughter.

On the sixth day he was up and moving about in a state of semi-sobriety. He inquired of others how long he'd wait before giving up all hope but no one had a clue, did not know what to say to him.

On the morning of his thirty-second birthday he placed a bouquet of hand-picked bluebonnets on his wife's grave and he rode out on the road for San Antonio. He carried with him a bible that he could not bring himself to read and in that book he stuffed the letters that he'd written. When he arrived at the military headquarters it was the fifth of May and already ninety-nine degrees in the shade and unbearably muggy. He stood before the brevet major general surrounded by indifferent soldiers and they read his letter. Soon the officers in charge of the frontier scouting parties were given orders to search for the boys and two days later the account was reported in the *Daily Herald*. He offered them what little money he had but they raised their hands in denial and just looked at him sullenly.

As a courtesy the general sent him to a German businessman named Menger who was sympathetic to his cause. He was put up for no charge at Menger's new hotel and the German counseled him on various courses of action. His fellow countrymen on the Texas borderlands had also been bereft of children by bands of savages. They drank together and RL shared his knowledge of the cattle business, nostalgic for the opportunities ahead if he could somehow move on. Menger's attorney helped him draft a letter to the governor of Texas and accompanied it with his own introduction.

And then he disappeared altogether and no one saw nor heard hide nor hair of him for weeks. A broken man lost in the mire totally incapable of getting his mind on track to establish any sort of direction. Sitting crosslegged in a cave one hundred feet above a trickling creek with his finger wavering over the trigger of the pistol he held to his head and the first lone star of sunset twinkling in the western sky he finally got control of his thoughts enough to think of his wife and boys and this inspired him to commit to a path, to pay tribute to them. He made his way back into San Antonio, for the time being a revitalized man. And yet the search for his boys was in the hands of federal bureaucrats and this pained him no end. He received conflicting counsel as to how to go about his search. No one really seemed to care.

Months passed. He'd received no word from the authorities and he'd been drinking heavily again. Wandering through the quiet adobe town one evening at sunset in a whiskey haze he saw children playing in the plaza and he sat on a bench and watched the evening light fade. A mariachi in a wide sombrero came beside him and started playing. From a whitewashed building a horn player appeared and soon fiddlers arrived followed by cheerful Mexican families with laughing children. At first no one seemed to notice him but as the crowds gathered to enjoy the music little boys and girls approached him in their curiosity. When a young boy about Charlie's age asked him if he wanted a piece of candy he stood up smiling ruefully and said no thank you and walked away, eyes welling with tears.

Time moved on. In a gaminghouse he caught a run of luck playing poker and was able to forget his plight for an evening. He was near blackout drunk when he lost it all to three kings and with his last two dollars he bought a drink and a room for a light-skinned whore from Chihuahua who wore her hair up behind her ears like his beautiful dead wife. If the woman wondered why he could not perform she must have passed it off on whiskey dick as opposed to some personal demon.

Those that dared to be close to him tried to talk some sense into him. He'd been sleeping in the streets. He'd point his revolver and warn them away. After one particularly bad incident things became heated and one of John Chisum's foremen, a larger man, lost patience and cold-cocked him out of his misery. Then Chisum ordered three men to escort him on his horse two days and two nights back to his home without stopping. He suffered a month from the black vomit, old blood from ulcers and yellow fever. He constantly fought his spirituality. By now his pleas for help had been up and down the chain of command but in truth the authorities could only publicize the boys' disappearance. The Commissioner of Indian Affairs in Washington had received word from the Texas secretary of state and he in turn contacted the Indian Office's superintendent in Lawrence, Kansas who contacted the indian agent at Fort Sill. All that came of this was a circular in frontier papers and so at the urging of the authorities in San Antonio he wrote to President Andrew Johnson and then began to form a plan to take control of his own destiny. Time was now working like hell to heal his wounds and while it was in his genes to delve in drink and become consumed by his depressive nature he seemed to be honing his emotions into action, as if he finally understood that while all had seemed lost he had in fact begun his most important journey.

He truly sensed things turning for the better when a rider from the headquarters of the Fifth Military District in Austin passed through with news of a boy captive located in Mexico. He rode back to San Antonio where he learned both the consulate and district clerk on the border had commissioned a trader with one hundred and fifty dollars in gold to ransom the boy. Two weeks later a large crowd gathered on a Sunday morning to witness the arrival of the stagecoach that carried the recovered boy captive. The young man was indeed about the same age as Sam but it was not him. He observed the onlookers surrounding the poor child like a caged animal and he saw the boy in complete shock from the setting and he could not comprehend the wild and savage look of him and this broke his heart even more. This false alarm sent him back home dejected once again, but by now he was more regularly reading his bible, praying all the while for the strength to carry on and then miraculously a vision in his mind became totally and completely clear. He was home all of two days before he rode out for the indian country alone. Several in his circles asked him if they could accompany him on the journey but he wouldnt hear of it.

He was six months on the trail wandering as far north as the Kiowa-Comanche agency at Fort Sill and as far west as the Apache reservations in New Mexico and Arizona. He heard rumors of captives everywhere but he had no luck chasing the leads. In the teeth of winter he made a run to Fort Smith, Arkansas to pick up five hundred dollars from a great uncle to fund his search and he followed the rumors out west into the fringes of the Texas frontier where in the spring of 1867 he began to pour himself into a new career as a scout protecting the wagon roads and hunting for indian raiding parties out of the newly formed Fort Concho. He would not forget. He would never give up. He was committed to moving on.

8

— ★ —

The Keechi Range

The Goodnight Ranch House
November 11, 1926

The Spanish colonial system, despite the best efforts of explorers such as Coronado and De Soto, struggled miserably for over three hundred years in their attempts to colonize the Great Plains. From 1548 to the end of the Spanish-Mexican regime every attempt to penetrate the mysteries of the Llano Estacado ended in failure. For centuries this vast domain was controlled exclusively by the Comanche. It came to be called, Comancheria. And then after Texas' independence in 1836 the frontier began to expand westward into its fringes, with the United States government establishing strategic military forts and relentlessly promoting Manifest Destiny. Rugged pioneer families like the Parkers were willing to risk everything in pursuit of land, freedom, and their religion. These restless settlers are made up of homesteaders born from the soil, from Tennessee, Kentucky, Virginia, Illinois, spurred by the frenzy of chasing the promises of virgin land in the new Texas republic.

When they travel by covered wagon across the Mississippi toward Missouri and Arkansas, across the Red River and into the Dallas trading post at the Trinity on their way to the southern prairie country, they bring their families, hauling their faulty weapons and farm tools and followed by dogs and small children riding bareback who gaze in wonder at the shaggy-headed bison. Eventually they reach the fertile valleys and bends of the Brazos, a range where there are very few homesteads but a utopia of unspoiled sage and mesquite grass protected by forests of post oak and blackjack. It is a dangerous time, these tentacles of civilization bleeding out into an untamed indian frontier. The emigrants establish permanent camps in the valley of the Keechi, plant cotton and corn and then build crude log cabins, where they sit at tables on dirt floors eating supper, contemplating how to tame the great herds of longhorn cattle that roam the countryside. It would not take long for the depredations to begin.

Not a week passes by without a rumor of an indian raid. The newspapers report them in dramatic detail and letters are written to the legislature of Texas pleading for protection. The appeals pile up in bureaucratic delay and there are many debates and the controversial policies around frontier defense languish amidst a whirlwind of pleas into Washington. The east coast editors, rejecting the frontier outcries for more protection, hide behind their veils of education and superiority.

...that peculiar and unnatural and unjust warfare, which in disguise of frontier defense the settlers have for years past waged against the indians.

The gory details and deep pain and loss are finally understood from the distance of the modest state house on Capitol Square in Austin. In the 1850s the Federal Government began to establish a line of frontier posts—Fort Belknap, Fort Chadbourne, Camp Cooper. Also at that time the Texas Legislature authorized the creation of several indian reservations. Meanwhile there were settlers taking the matter of the indian problem into their own hands, forming local militias and running scouting parties to defend their homes. Still, any lulls in depredations were temporary and the brave or foolish souls that continued to push west inevitably faced the wrath of the natives.

The undersigned citizens of Parker, Palo Pinto, and other contiguous frontier counties would respectfully represent, that, in these counties, there are not left more than twenty-five hundred families... That since the disbanding of the militia the depredations and barbarities have increased, and, within the last four months, many of our most enterprising citizens have been butchered, and thousands of horses and cattle driven off, and that without some timely

> *remedy, these depredations and atrocities must inevitably become more extensive and alarming.*

When Sam Houston, former President of the Republic of Texas, was elected governor in 1859, the indian raiding was worse than ever. By the 1860s when the Civil War broke out the frontier line was receding rapidly.

For five years during the war the untended herds multiplied tenfold and became wilder. By 1866 the difficult period of Reconstruction began, and the vast ranges of ungrazed prairies now became an arena of conflict between the carpetbaggers, cow thieves, and cowmen. The Comanche and their Kiowa brothers made the most of the chaos.

In the wallpapered office the ancient plainsman thoughtfully burns the days. Like the old indian chiefs sitting, smoking, whose weathered bones come alive with their memories, their failing eyes brighten, with arms gesturing and toothless smiles, laughing and reliving the adventures of old. It was only yesterday. Those wondrous days in Palo Pinto County. The formative years when he was burgeoning into manhood. J Evetts Haley sits at the rolltop desk, scribbling it all down, riding alongside him as if it were all a dream.

In the summer of 1856 we had begun scouting the ranges of central Texas in search of the finest grass country. All over really. The mouth of the San Saba, all of the fertile land west of Waco and the virgin lands west of the settlements at Belknap.

We were ambitious, had an eye on going into business for ourselves. We set out west exploring for bigger ranges. Found good country near the old Spanish fort on the San Saba. I even had an eye at one point to venture all the way to California until I ran into my brother-in-law, Alfred Lane, who talked us out of it. He convinced me we were right where we ought to be. Wes Sheek, my stepbrother, was my partner at the time and I'd grown close to him in those years. Then there was his brother-in-law,

Claiborn Varner, who contracted us to take his herds on shares for ten years. Four hundred some-odd head, mostly cows. We'd get every fourth calf in pay. This was in Somervell County a few miles from the Brazos. Made for a good winter range in the bend of that river and even though we worked like slaves we felt like kings in that two room cabin we'd built with our own hands. Always looking for game, fishing the creek. Hunted black bears with Sheek's bitch hound. Beautiful country and nothing to worry about but taking care of ourselves and the cows. Nothing to the west of us for six hundred miles to the Rocky Mountains but untouched grass prairies. And of course, indians.

The Spanish Conquistadors were the first to tempt those treeless expanses. What must they have been thinking? What must they have seen? Random indian villages scattered about the emptiness of the plains, rumors of prosperous cities of five thousand inhabitants, whispers of gold. The Spanish journals of the sixteenth century speculate on the mysteries of those unexplored plains. There were rumors of a great unknown city, Gran Quivira, blessed with wealth and splendor. Yet in the three hundred years following Coronado's expeditions the Texas plains were hardly visited by white men.

In the 1800s a few explorers from the United States began to search for the source of the Red River. Major Stephen H. Long in 1820. Fonda in 1823. Gregg in 1839. The Pope and Marcy expeditions in 1854. All daring to venture past the 100th meridian. The region had become the domain of the Comanche and the hazards were many.

And here we came along, a rugged bunch of pioneers looking for cheap land to farm and ranch. We came with very little, some with nothing at all. We gathered at Sunday services and prayed for those who died, for ourselves and our neighbors who were struggling to better our conditions. We needed each other to survive. We brought our rickety wagons into the virgin lands and moved up the river valleys into the Western Cross Timbers. Out on the military road the village of Weatherford sprang up. New log homes with heavy rock chimneys scattered all about on the trails northwest a day's ride from Black Springs. In ten years I would be in love with the town's schoolteacher and depart from there for the western cattle trails, a grown man whose destiny was fully determined.

By the spring of 1858 we were pretty well settled and the cows were taking to the range along the Keechi. We picked out a spot up on a hill that overlooked the valley rolling down to the river. Began cutting logs and built a cabin. Moved our folks to the place. There wasnt much of a market and we werent branding all that many cows at that stage anyway. This was when Oliver's influence really began to take hold, when he shared so much about running cattle, his vision, and he had that store on the Belknap road. Freighting seemed like the most logical thing to do while we were waiting on the herd to grow. The rail lines had made it from Houston to Bryan by then. I'd make that two hundred mile run back and forth with two dozen head dragging one big ole wagon full of provisions. Salt, sugar, syrup, flour, whiskey. Then Sheek got married and became distracted with family life. Pretty much left me all to myself and I ended up having to go back and devote all my time to handling the Varner herd.

In the evenings after long days working cows we'd sit on Oliver's porch and contemplate the times. Mainly a bunch of us young fellas. Oliver's boy, William, was about my age. Another was Bill Wilson. And there was a fella named RL Terry I'd gotten to know well on the freighting runs to and from Brenham. The talk was always about the markets for our cattle. Loving was trailing herds back east into Louisiana and up north across the Red River and all the way into Illinois. We talked about the gold seekers in California, Colorado, and their need for Texas beef. He was older, wiser, always seemed to be talking progressively about how things would be playing out in the future. Things really began to sink in for me in those days.

I think it was 1859 when the settlers had finally had enough of the reservation indians slipping out and raising all kinds of hell on the region. There were the Brazos and Clear Fork reservations. An agent named Neighbors who felt like he could take care of em and make em right. Give em things. Feed em. Preach to em. But hell, these were wild Comanches. They'd been roaming free, the most marvelous horsemen I've seen in my life. We were frontier stock. German. Irish-Scot. The feeling back then was that the only good indian was a dead indian and I had come to embrace that way of thinking. So many of our neighbors were getting stolen from, murdered, their children hauled away.

The frontier had no chance in hell of peace. Mass chaos is what it was. 1857. 1858. 1859. All of our range. Jack, Young, Parker counties. Palo Pinto County. Really all the way through the war, the list of murders goes on and on. We did our best to fight back, defend all of the women and children. The old folks. Looking back on it now it was heroic how the people suffered and endured hardships in those times.

I remember the spring of 1859 when they hit the Cameron place. Slaughtered the father and son out in the field and then went to the house and killed Mrs Cameron outside. Then just up the creek they killed and scalped Mr Mason and his wife. Hauled off four of the children. Slit the throat of another. I've mentioned Old Man Lynn, who was the granddaddy. What must he have been thinking when he walked upon that scene three days later? Six mutilated bodies. Found his grandchild crawling around in its mother's blood in the cow pen. The blood of his daughter.

You see, in the mid-fifties things had generally been pretty quiet for a few years and then all hell broke loose. And the next year, fall of 1860, the Comanches made another big raid on the Brown ranch. Took their horses and killed Mr Brown, cut him up, cut his nose off. Then I caught wind that they ran through the Sherman house and I rode out trying to warn the other neighbors, and that's when I came across Old Man Lynn. Just settin there before the fire roasting a scalp on a long-forked stick. He had that thing salted with the hair tucked up inside, grease oozing out of it, and he just looked back at me and said good morning like it was just another day. Then he turned back to roasting that scalp.

Back then it seemed as though all we did was worry about how to defend the frontier. I just could not bring myself to be a staunch supporter of secession. And by the time the war started with all that was going on it made the most sense for me to stay in Texas and help fight to protect our land and our homes.

1861. Just before Christmas. The Frontier Regiment was organized, ten companies of indian fighting men. The Texas Rangers were back in business again. The plan was to set up a line of defense from the Red River all the way down to Mexico. Run scouting expeditions nonstop out into the prairie country to harass the indians. In our territory we had two camps, a hundred some-odd men under Jack Cureton, one on the Trinity and the other at Belknap.

One day in the summer of 1862 about twenty-five of us headed northwest on scout into the Quitaque country. We turned south at the Pease, near the headwaters of the Big Wichita, and found a small camp of Kiowas drying buffalo meat.

Out there the eastern edge of the Llano Estacado crumbles into a rugged line of escarpments. The headwaters of our rivers drain from those canyons. The Red, the Wichita, the Brazos, the Colorado, down to the three Conchos to the south. Good country in certain places, though the gyp water would tear your guts apart and much of those badlands were void of game and timber. These canyons were where the indians took shelter. It had barely seen white eyes and could be hell on a regiment unless a guide really knew his business. For two hundred miles back to the east ran open shortgrass prairie all the way to the settlements. To the west up atop the escarpment an endless sea of plains for another hundred miles and the trails to the Comanchero markets in New Mexico. This was a country that had been controlled for centuries by the Comanche and Kiowa warriors.

We approach from the south and come over the plateau at full gallop. The Kiowas jump on their mounts bareback and ride for the canyon to the north. Jim Tackett and I lead the charge across the flat. We ride within shooting range of two of them just before the cover of the breaks. They swing around and duck down the far side of their mounts, readying to sling arrows from underneath their horses' necks. I was riding all out holding my Colt in one hand and letting off shots with as much aim as I could muster. It sure felt like some of that lead found its way into their flesh. The indians ride on but in the melee one of them drops his shield.

That night in camp I open up the double fold of buffalo hide to see what had been used for padding. I find that thick old book you see over there, the one on the history of Rome.

It's been told that the Spanish traders and hunters named the region for the markers placed out to show the way along the lone, dry-season route through that great grass desert. *Los Llanos Estacados.* Someone decided to name the plains after the rivers that drain them. *Los Llanos del Agua Corriente. Los Llanos del Casas Amarillas.* I like to think about those Spaniards, some old Spanish conquistador, clanking along in a suit of armor in the sweltering heat of a summer day, perhaps easing his suffering with romantic designations. *Los Brazos de Dios. Sierrita de la Cruz.* The indians used those names in their feral spanish dialect. *Punta de Agua, Ojo Bravo, Rito Blanco.*

And so us Rangers hunting that unexplored prairie for indians became versed in those names like a set of biblical principles in Sunday school. Our aim was to learn that country, absorb it into our souls like them. We were becoming one with a place where only a few others before us had dared to tempt. Aside from the Comancheros and Ciboleros who traded with the Comanche, hardly another soul. As the plains grass grew with the seasons the indians rode and hunted wherever they found game. And they mutilated most every other human that got in their way. The land was theirs, seems like since the beginning of time.

Comancheria. *Nmn Sookobit. Comanche land.* The domain of the wild horse indians for one hundred and fifty years. Powered by extreme violence. Scenes of death. Scenes like a young man being picked to the bone by a swarm of vultures. A dying man in a sandy wash drags his maimed body hopelessly toward the rocks and madly fights off the pack of lobo wolves who've come to feed on him.

Haley looked at Corinne. The old man's voice was drifting off into a whisper. She was watching him closely. Haley could read her thoughts. What is he talking about?

The privileges of youth have ways of lavishing the soul with such naive intentions, deceiving us in ways we have no way of understanding. On the one hand there is no fear and we are willing to face down anything to please the ego. On the other there is our lack of experience, for there is no way of perceiving in the moment what we will deeply understand when we look back.

Yes indeed, when I was young there were things I was missing, subtle details I overlooked. There was that one night in the early days when I thought I might fall in love. I was fooled. Then later on when I met Mary Ann Dyer it was as if I was struck by a bolt of lightning.

But it was during the war as I was tending the Keechi herds around Black Springs that I truly began to understand my future. In those years I came to know the indian country and their ways intimately. Oliver Loving was like a father, he was the one who helped round me out as a man.

We were watching our herds grow beyond what our range could hold. We were debating the military reports of the trail from Pope's Crossing up to Fort Sumner. We were hearing the rumors in 1865 of the Patterson and Wylie herds trailing that route. I was restless. Perhaps a bit selfish. There was money to be made and I was tired of waiting.

A decade passes in a flash and you find yourself looking back and wondering how it is gone. In the middle 1850s we were all getting to know each other, know ourselves. Aside from being partners with Sheek my two closest acquaintances were RL Terry and AM Dyer. Each of them would introduce a woman into my life.

Our world centered around the undomesticated longhorned cows that were breeding like rabbits all over the country. Some Southern stock but fused with the mean Spanish blood that would attack a horseman, tree a man on foot. Mestenas, we called em. Small but wild as hell and spikehorned. And boy did we get to know one another through all of those long days of work. Running goods up and down the Brazos. On weeklong cow hunts, riding with light rations in our saddlewallets, sleeping under the stars, occasionally sipping fine Kentucky bourbon and philosophizing. When you work all day and night and hardly sleep, you need respite, and when the occasion called for it we looked to let loose a little.

I remember the Fourth of July in 1856 fell on a Friday. A camp meeting had sprung up for the holiday weekend. Preachers of every denomination. Baptist, Church of Christ, Methodist, Presbyterian. They were set up to hold forth and such, bring sinners into the kingdom. Folks in from all over, staying with friends and family, camping out. All sorts of folks. Proselytes. A lot of them there for worship but also plenty of raucous, hard-drinking fools in the mood to celebrate.

RL Terry showed up that night with a young woman he knew from the San Saba valley. He'd been drinking pretty heavy but was hiding it well. She may have even had a few sips herself.

Gentlemens, he said proudly, I'd like to introduce you to Miss Sally Johnson.

I noticed her figure, her smile, her silky blonde hair, but more than anything I beheld that twinkle in her eyes, those large pupils framed in a mosaic of hazel. I thought I was in love, but perhaps instead I was being tempted by some unknown force, one that would come to haunt me for the rest of my life.

The services were over and the sun had almost set, that sacred time of day. RL went to a wagon and came back with a brown jug of whiskey and a handful of tin cups. He liked his drink. Lubed him up to play cards and he was good. I dont think he ever put himself in harm's way from drink, but he would damn sure test the waters and he always seemed to have a keen way of toeing the line without stepping over. Like he was a little bit smarter than everyone else and knew just when to pull back. He knew we had not expected him to bring a woman and he poured us all a round with a shit-eating grin on his face. She was looking at me as she leaned back and took a big swig.

Only the good Lord must have known what she was thinking. All I knew how to do was work, had no clue what to say to a woman, wasnt really all that good at holding my liquor. My father passed when I was five and my mother ended up marrying a preacher. I was reserved at certain times socially, and with certain things, had a long way to go in learning the ways of a man. But curiosity can get the better of you. I guess you could say that evening I was like a little lamb lost out on the prairie, as embarrassing as that is to say.

After dark the gathering became more festive. We all made the rounds to visit and every passel of folks seemed to be passing around a bottle or a jug, laughing, carrying on in conversation. It was getting late and the moon was climbing high. I was watching her from afar.

Guitar and banjo picking filled the air. Some singing. I was drinking more than I should've been. I walked off toward our wagon near a big grove of oaks, away from the noise, needing to gather myself a little. But she had followed me, Sally Johnson. She slipped from the congregation like a cat and stalked gracefully into my presence.

She had a smell about her that I will never forget. There was a knot in my stomach, a tightness in my throat. She whispered something, and the awkwardness made me look beyond her into the crowds. I distinctly remember the sound of guitar and the glow of small campfires spread all about. The random pale light of lanterns, the shadows of everyone enjoying the evening. And all around us in those fringes of darkness there were fireflies dancing, flickering about on that hot summer night.

No, I didnt fall in love that night, but I sure took another step toward becoming a man. You can say what you want, that night was meant to be. I had no control over it. When you're touched by God, no matter good or bad, you feel something deep down in your soul.

With her many persuasions she entices him; with her flattering lips she seduces him. Suddenly he follows her as an ox goes to the slaughter, or as one in fetters to the discipline of a fool, until an arrow pierces through his liver; as a bird hastens to the snare, so he does not know that it will cost him his life. (Proverbs 7:21-23)

But by the end of summer she had become Mrs RL Terry and lured her new husband back to the San Saba valley. The following April she gave birth to a baby boy. Apparently RL wanted to name the first son in honor of me, but Sally won out and they named him Samuel.

RL was a close friend. He and Bill Wilson were the most reliable cowpunchers. Married life seemed to keep RL focused and his wages kept rising as we worked. He and Sally had another boy they did name after me, little Charlie, and RL was a loyal father to those boys, the oldest one with him at every step as soon as he could walk.

As the years rolled by I became like an uncle, a godfather of sorts to the oldest boy. Certain things about him that reminded me so much of myself when I was young. Passionately fond of animals, learned all about horses and could ride well, extremely inquisitive. Always wanting to hunt and fish. I had such fond memories of folks like John Poole and Jane Hagerman when I was a boy. Folks who inspired me in my youth. I saw myself in that role.

It was strange, the boy seemed to have an uncanny resemblance to me and over the years as he grew up it gnawed on me. Maybe it was just the things he liked, his expressions. Had a way of looking at things, the way he looked at me. He seemed to observe you so closely you couldnt help but be fond of him. As I watched Sam grow up I always wondered what it was about him. And so I did everything I could to have a positive influence on how RL was raising him.

The handful of times I saw Sally it was cordial. She was gracious and always made a point of saying how much her sons got out of being around me.

Present me with a problem and I'll figure out a solution. Give me a pile of seasoned bois d'arc and I will build you a chuckbox, complete with iron axles, a fold-down cooking table with a built-in sourdough jar. Back then on the Keechi range everything revolved around the trail. I'd take Mollie back home and sit with Oliver discussing the hazards of the Butterfield Trail. Camp Cooper, Phantom Hill, Chadbourne, the Conchos, and on out through a hundred miles of waterless desert to the Castle Mountains and the Horsehead Crossing on the Pecos.

The military authorities at the Bosque Redondo reservation near Fort Sumner, New Mexico are advertising for the need for beef on the hoof to feed the Navajos. It is being reported that Mr Loving and Mr Goodnight, of Black Springs, are planning to heroically pioneer a trail of several thousand

> *longhorned cattle along the old emigrant road and up the Pecos, taking roundance of the Indian Territory.*

That is how the newspapers worded their account of current developments. But the real stories buried under the actual history never have the chance to see the light of day. The adventures and the dramas and the secrets behind the men, their paths through this great journey of life, get lost over time and the newspapers and historical records can never come close to capturing the true essence of a man's existence.

The photographer's gallery in Weatherford is wallpapered in sheets of silver-plated copper. The likenesses of stoic volunteer soldiers commemorating their service, their departure for war, leaving mementos for loved ones. Like them my hair was combed, I was well-dressed. Like them I understood that I was facing unknown adventures. Why is it impossible when you are young to grasp the enormity of your entire life being ahead of you?

I stepped outside onto the boardwalk with Oliver. Mollie was waiting there along with RL and he had Sam with him. We all started walking in the sunshine back to the home that Mollie kept.

Mollie kept looking back and forth alternately at me, RL, and the boy. She was picking up on something. She was observant like that. But none of us were paying much attention. We had other things on our mind.

Her and I fell back aways a little, walking along, and she leaned over and whispered. I'll tell you what, that good lookin boy really has taken a liking to you.

He's a good boy.

And he sure takes after you, dont you think? Were you really that good looking when you were a boy? she said flirtatiously.

My mind was elsewhere. I was thinking about heading west.

9

— ★ —

The Indianization of Sam Terry

Pahvotaivo stepped forward in the dark for a better view inside the silent houses of the settlers. He could see the dim light of the candles, the kerosene lanterns, and he looked at Asewaynah and boasted that he was going to get their horses. Quanah watched over the scene, saw him looking at Isatai'i, who put his hand up and whispered for them to not go any farther.

Then he took off, out through the shadows of his old neighbor's yard, slipping into the darkness of the stable, a stone's throw from the San Saba. A sliver of slanted moonlight, the flash of it on his browned skin could hardly have hinted of his Anglo-Saxon roots. If he had lingered in the light Quanah would have been taken back to his former pubescent self in breechclout and leggings as an apprentice warrior seeking prestige among his peers. To them that one minute felt like an eternity before he finally came striding out of the barn with the first horse. But Pahvo wanted more. He was thinking only of what they would all say when he finished taking every last steed on the property.

Isatai'i, holding Asewaynah back, was walking slowly over to Quanah, mumbling epithets to himself, scanning the home for signs of life, anything rustling. Pahvo led the horse within range, tossed the rope to Asewaynah and turned back for the barn. Then he looked back at them grinning.

They heard him giggle. He vanished into the barn again. They could hear the animals inside getting skittish. One of the horses snorted. Asewaynah looked out over the property like a protective brother and he saw a lamp come on and then a dog barked.

Pahvo was grateful to him. He was one of the main reasons he was able to get by those first few months in captivity. Most of his time in the early days had been spent serving as a menial to the squaws. All winter it seemed his sole purpose in life was to collect firewood and water, scrape buffalo hides, try and make sense of the strange guttural sounds that somehow formed words. The other boys would carouse about the camp while he worked, ignore him or take pleasure in poking fun at him, but Asewaynah from the very first day always made a point to be helpful. The best thing he did was teach him the language.

He was the oldest son. Samuel Haden Terry, now Pahvotaivo. Pahvo. He and his little brother were the only male progeny that had the chance to carry the Terry name forward, a lineage that somehow weaved and wound its way back to the fringes of European royalty. There was that type of blood inside him. But now he was a young slave laborer in a roving band of horse warriors.

He'd been abducted by the Kiowa and traded to the Comanche. He was given the name of 'White Boy.' On the third day of his third month in captivity he turned twelve and not long after Asewaynah and the other boys finally began to encourage him to break away from the work of the women. It was when a raiding party returned from the Double Mountains of the Brazos. Isatai'i's nephew had been killed by the Texans, his mother enraged in grief. Pahvo was gathering water when she came running at him with a large butcher knife like a demon possessed, determined to take out her revenge on someone with white blood.

Quanah was only eighteen but had been steadily ascending in status, leading a restless gang of young raiders assembled from a random contingent of bands. Penatakas, Kotsotekas, some Kiowas and even Cheyennes. There was a handful of Mexican and Texan captives who'd been rapidly assimilated into their horse culture. Trained to become one with the horse, drilled in the art of war. They launched horse and cattle stealing expeditions from the canyons below the high plains, carrying their bows and arrows, shields adorned with spiritual insignia, personal trinkets paying tribute to the spirits. They had no concept of fear.

> *War is the pattern of life. The love of the fight. The zest for plunder and glory. Horses and cattle. Revenge. Honor in war is the basis of rank and social status in Comanche society. The pressure of the whites on their homelands only enhances these themes.*

It was claimed that some three hundred thousand head of cattle were stolen from the Texas frontier in the years following the War Between the States. They herded them back to the Llano canyons and traded them to the New Mexicans for blankets, tobacco, whiskey, trinkets. These young warriors collected horses to build their wealth. They thought nothing of murder and took scalps to count coup. It was a bonus when they carried away a young captive who was tough enough to assimilate into their culture. Another body that might help preserve their dwindling population.

Pahvo, after being trained in the ways of a Comanche warrior, after riding bareback sunup to sundown, would sleep restfully as the events of his day replayed through his subconscious. Now and again the image of his brother, or father, only fleeting, then back to the wrestling match earlier that day where his foe had got the better of him, with a cheap shot no less, and yet he'd let it go. Why did he let that go? He'd learn from that. Next time it would be different. And with sunrise the training would start all over again.

Before the men awoke, the boys roamed the camp in gangs looking for mischief, hunting the countryside for rabbits, bugs, and birds, or making weapons. A large rock placed into the fire would become very hot, causing the flint to pop off in small thin pieces. These were picked up with a split-ended stick, doused with drips of cold water, which allowed them to begin more easily chipping at the edges. A four-foot stone could produce hundreds of arrow points.

Most hours of the day were spent on horseback practicing in drill, riding at full speed and picking up small objects or racing other young warriors in open fields in tight quarters. The most important stunt involved the simulation of a rescue of a comrade on the ground in prostrate, riding in full gallop and leaning down in unison to sweep him up and carrying him to safety.

But Pahvo was not quite ready to venture out with the raiding parties and serve as an apprentice scout. This was when Quanah followed the direction of Mow-way and led his band of Little Horses not only into Texas, but also into the eastern portions of the New Mexico Territory stealing horses from the Navajos at Bosque Redondo. All throughout the spring of 1867 this went on, the military authorities growing evermore wary of the Comanche's growing trade with the New Mexican traders.

Meanwhile white traders were enticed with rewards to venture out in search of the captives, carrying ransoms. The captives had no way of knowing this. Pahvo's father had been hounding the New Mexico Superintendent of Indian Affairs with letters. In May an agent named Labadi visited their lodges demanding an end to the raiding and the return of the captives. The Comanches demurred arrogantly. Pahvo and the other boy captives had been sent away to herd horses in a nearby canyon. Not one of them thought of escape.

This was during Reconstruction, a time of total chaos on the frontier. Demilitarization of the South. The local militias had vanished. Congress was consumed by war debt and the United States military was undergoing rapid downsizing. It was believed by the civilized in the East, unbelievably, that the indian wars were the fault of white men. The mantra of peace began to take hold. It was obviously an ideal time to be an ambitious teenage Comanche warrior emboldened to wage war throughout the frontier... to hold back the advance of western civilization.

On his first war pony, on the ride south from the Caprock canyonlands, Pahvo rode in the rear alongside Asewaynah while Quanah and Isatai'i rode at the head of the column. His feisty little mare was painted with carefully chosen symbols. Circles around the eyes and nostrils to foster vision and smell, thunder strips on the horse's legs to please the gods of war.

The days leading up to the departure were filled with the making of medicine. The night before the pipe was passed, plans were discussed, stories told. Back in February when there was an early run of warm weather and a full moon Quanah led the first raid of the season, a quick ride into the Edwards Plateau to set up a base camp for a series of onslaughts upon the Texan ranches. They returned to the village into the teeth of a strong norther with a large herd of horses and a few scalps, celebrating with fires roaring and the wind swirling snow flurries and when the south wind returned five days later he took that same band with a few extra riders and headed back into the settlements again. That was the pattern in the early months of 1867 and Pahvo enviously watched them return triumphantly each time.

By the firelight in camp Quanah talked at length about the route planned, the hills and valleys and water holes, the areas of difficult terrain they would traverse. He was detailing the protocol of the horse-stealing raids to the young Pahvo as if he was his own flesh and blood. Himself orphaned as a boy and then ostracized as a half-breed, Quanah persevered with his physical gifts, his intelligence, his grit. He was stronger, more competitive, and half-a-head taller than most boys his age and he had an edge to him that projected upon others so that they understood he had nothing to lose. In time the elder chiefs took notice and his peers began to follow him. There were twelve raiders under his leadership in this warparty. Isatai'i and his medicine, a few close friends he grew up with, younger braves and Mexican and Texan captives, many of them under the age of sixteen. When they were not breaking horses or hunting or making weapons they lounged around the camp gambling or goading one another into games of hijinks or playing practical jokes on the elders.

But each evening they would sit around the fire, where they would listen to the old men long into the night and then the next morning continue training all day until sunset where the evening ceremonies resumed again with tales of brave adventures and warnings of the hated white man.

On a bitter cold day when I was twelve moons the Rangers came riding, killing everything. Women, mules, dogs. The men were away. Mother had been taken. My little brother and I rode away alone, following the three-day old trail of the band for one hundred miles back to the main camp, pursued by the Rangers night and day.

To Pahvo it sounded like the greatest adventure he'd ever been told. He was also learning to despise the whites.

Quanah's boyhood mentor and close friend was an aspiring holy man named Isatai'i who nurtured the spirits and looked after Quanah. He was his spiritual advisor. He was a few years older and the bond they had formed over the years combined with their collective mettle made them a powerful combination. Each landmark they passed heading south was pointed out in detail by Quanah. *Over there is a clear spring that flows from the depths of that canyon.* The expectation upon first time raiders like Pahvo was that they would absorb those nuances of the country into their souls. Quanah was everything he wanted to become, Pahvo thought to himself. If he was facing certain death it would not faze him in the least and his way of dealing with others was confident, carefree, respectful, and yet you could tell he was not someone anyone cared to challenge. Eighteen years old, muscular arms. He just looked better than the others. They had seen him charge his horse fearlessly at a massive bison and shoot an arrow entirely through the bull while riding full speed. He did not back down when challenged by the older chiefs in the village. He had been planning with Isatai'i, the medicine man, how to amass more horse wealth than any of their people.

No one said much on the ride down to the settlements yet the evenings in camp were rife with tales of procuring the spirit powers and how that medicine influenced the success of their adventures. Quanah had a way of putting everyone at ease and bringing out the most of the situation. He would hold court around the fire, smirking and chewing on a chunk of tobacco, posing some random scenario for one of his disciples. Boy captives, seasoned warriors or indifferent peers. As if it were all a game. They felt a strong connection to him. He had a way of bringing out the joy in everything they stood for. The fact that he was able to rise to prominence as an orphaned half-breed infuriated some but was never a surprise to anyone. Enemies, friends, elders, admirers, anyone that ever found themselves in his presence. His Comanche father a respected chief, his Anglo mother from ambitious Scot-Irish frontiersmen, descendants of Celtic warriors who spent their lives fighting Viking hordes and Roman armies. He trusted deeply in his bear medicine, and he believed his puha would carry him through any situation. He, like Pahvo, was only a boy when he was first faced with a great adversity, fleeing with his little brother from a posse of Texas Rangers after their camp had been routed on the Pease River, just the two of them on the run, heroically, day and night for a hundred miles across the rugged prairies to the Comanche village in the Wichita Mountains.

They roasted a deer and then passed the pipe, going over the logistics of the horse stealing mission. Quanah always made a point to pull Asewaynah and Pahvo aside. They nodded as he spoke, worshipped him. They would do anything to please him.

Quanah spoke slowly and with conviction and he watched closely for what was behind their eyes and he paused often to gauge their understanding. Asewaynah would translate certain things for Pahvo. Quanah told them how much he believed in them. Trust one another like brothers. He wanted them out a half day's ride scouting the country. They went over their system of signals. He described the location near a bend in the Llano where they would establish a temporary base camp. Then they would scour the country and report back. If the results were favorable they would finalize their plan of attack. By then the full moon would have passed. Isatai'i had not predicted rain. The time is right. Be confident in your skills. Trust your horse. Never abandon one another.

Quanah was referring to the first time in his youth he earned recognition as a warrior. He had turned back in the face of enemy fire and rescued a fallen comrade by reaching down and swooping him up onto his horse, riding away unscathed. He was preaching that strictly held religious belief that to abandon a fellow warrior in the field to be left for torture, mutilation, and scalping, was the highest disgrace.

Samuel Pahvotaivo Terry had been accepted into a new family and he would never look back. Not even a year removed from being carried away from his dying mother on the back of a Kiowa warhorse and already an apprentice warrior being trained under the tutelage of a half-breed Comanche war leader, destined one day to be appointed as principal chief of the entire Comanche nation. Sam had no control over the circumstances that had led to this fate, whatever mystery in the universe that turned his life upside down. Not even a teenager, he had spent these last three months of his captivity with young warriors being schooled in the art of war. Now as he entered these early stages of manhood, even though his real father was wandering the plains in search of him, there was some instinct inside of him that kept him in the moment, some innate understanding that moving forward, refusing to look back, was his only path.

When they were with the larger camp there were three other white captives, one Mexican, and another ten Comanches among the young boy warriors. They would be led into the fields and ordered by the medicine man to observe their surroundings and pay their respects to the Great Spirit. He would gather his horse, mount up and talk to it, while the others joked to one another. He was getting better with their language and took joy in their fun. He nudged the pony into a trot and felt the fresh breeze on his skin, smelled the fragrance of the grass and the flowers, just letting the wind blow through his long and dirty hair. *N nakaaka puuku.* He repeated the enunciation under his breath in his new Comanche accent to persuade the horse. *N nakaaka puuku.* He rode back toward the mingling horsemen who were lining their mounts up alongside one another, looked about the group and felt the eyes of the medicine man studying him. He liked that he was being noticed. He needed that. He sat up tall on the pony and led it beside Asewaynah. They smirked at one another and Pahvo nodded toward the four posts set two hundred yards in the distance, decorated as their target with two long red sashes that flapped with the wind. There were two strips of buffalo hide stretched across about eight feet apart. He looked over and caught the gaze of Quanah again. He waited for the gun to be fired. When he kicked the horse with his heels it took off and it felt like he'd been thrown back but then it was just the whir of the breeze in his ears and the rhythm of horse hooves. He was the first to the marker by a half-length. He jumped the horse with all four feet between the two strips and reversed back and in another leap cleared the barrier and took off back toward the starting point. It wasnt even close. The Comanche men were grinning and shouting sarcasms at the stragglers.

They circled around a very jovial Quanah who was roasting a young deer over a mid-day buffet and expounding upon the most colorful details related to the adventures of his earlier youth. That afternoon they were tested on their ability to lean from their mounts in full stride and shoot arrows from beneath the horse's neck as they supported themselves with only a leg hooked over the animal's back. They were using loops of rope plaited into the horse's mane in order to slip it overhead and under the outside arm for support. Pahvo was the best at using his free hands to sling arrows accurately at the target and he showed off by picking up several heavy chunks of wood that were sprinkled about the training grounds. He took pleasure in their surprise that a white boy could outperform their own flesh and blood.

He had come from a family where work ethic was strictly emphasized and he was always tasked with labor intensive chores. Clearing the fields and building rock walls. Then those fields needed to be plowed and the crops planted. Twelve-hour days under the Texas sun tending to the livestock and helping his family get by. Every now and then a bible verse might be read to him but there was no school, no friends, no entertainment. He only had two sets of ragged clothes and he rarely wore shoes. He was constantly being hounded to help make soap, milk cows, wash clothes, gather firewood and haul water. If his father was gone for an extended period they would run out of food. He would work all day and be fed pigweed or mush in the evenings. Then he would get up before sunrise and do it all over again. But now he was with a group of like-minded young men all about his age and they did pretty much anything they wanted when they were not working with the horses or hunting.

The day before he turned thirteen he was allowed to go on his first raid with the Quahadis. This budding war chief who had gambled recklessly for the boy captive and then used his winnings to buy him from the Kiowas pulled him away from the fire and walked with his arm around his shoulder. The peculiar witch doctor, Isatai'i, escorted him over to a special tipi reserved for ceremony, handed him back the medicine shield he had been painting with designs, and proceeded to lead him through several detailed rituals to assist him in the accumulation of his spirit medicine. He did not need to remind the boy of the significance of the shield's adornments. Two horse tails, two scalps, a handful of bear teeth.

Upon leaving the tent Isatai'i was smiling and patting him on the back in a congratulatory gesture. Quanah was there to depart his wisdom and confidence, that countenance that had been consistent all along as he had been considering the possibilities for the boy. Tejanito! he beamed. Pahvo thought he heard Quanah giving Isatai'i a hard time, making an off-colored remark to his close friend about the value of his medicines. Quanah put his arm around Pahvo again and was walking him back to the bustle of the camp. Pahvo was warm with pride and felt some tinges of anxiety. He was listening to Quanah describe the preparatory proceedings they would undergo the following day.

Now he was one of them, transforming from boy to man into their cult of plains warfare. He had a new family, barely a year from being hauled away from his own, as if the murder of his mother never happened, a string of events willed by God, his natural path.

In the morning the war shields of the raiding party were hung on racks before the tipi doors to absorb the medicine of the sun. The day would be spent in preparation and Pahvo had seen the routine before. He had been learning, as he did all things, by observation, but now he was a participant in the rituals.

Along with Asewaynah and Pahvo, the only boy captives permitted on this mission, there were ten other warriors who made up the raiding party. The horses were attended to, their equipage organized, each of the warriors taking care to ornament themselves with paint and all of their various cherished curios of war. Late in the afternoon alone in his lodge Quanah began to drum and soon the other raiders arrived and joined him in the songs of war. At sunset Quanah led the warparty on a parade through the village. They rode single file with Pahvo in the rear, mumbling the parts of the songs he was unsure of.

With darkness the entire village had gathered around the bonfire and commenced to celebrate. Quanah gave a short ceremonial and while he made reference to the necessity of the raid it was more of an impetus to rile the crowd into an evening of revelry. The camp had become a carnival, the rhythm of drums and music filled the air. The warparty converged around the fire, singing and dancing in a raucous brotherhood of war, their tribesmen converging upon them and urging them on with shouts and gestures. Rattles and gourds were passed around along with jugs of Comanchero whiskey and the celebrated warriors found themselves surrounded by singing children and pretty young maidens. Old drunken warriors would stop the drummers to interrupt the festivities with nostalgic tales of their youth and as they finished narrating details of some great coup of yesteryear a mingling of war whoops would begin and orchestrate into rousing ovation. Then the drums and dancing began again. Meanwhile Quanah had slipped away from the scene earlier and without ceremony. He had predesignated their gathering place outside the village. The crowd began to clear and Pahvo saw Asewaynah sneak away with one of the young squaws they had both taken an interest in, sliding off into the shadows. Pahvo returned alone to his lodge for his horses and equipment.

He looked over his accoutrements and reflected. He did not get the girl this time but it did not matter. He was excited, inspired, in his element. He was loving everything about his new life as a Comanche. At midnight they would gather at the rendezvous and his first adventures as a raider would begin.

He is with his father in Fredericksburg seven months after being recovered from the reservation when he tells him about that first raid with the Comanche and the skirmish with the Rangers that won him acclaim. They had been on the road for a week and had stolen a large herd of horses from the settlement of Viejo Creek. The Rangers were on their trail. A party of seventeen hardened men armed with .36 caliber cap and ball six-shot revolvers that had declared open season on the plains indians. An unsanctioned, restless regiment scouting out from Fort Mason. May 1867. He was riding scout near the Llano late that afternoon with Asewaynah exploring the ranches along the river valley in search of horses for Quanah. They had been up since dawn working out and back from the main party and had ridden forty miles. He recalled how they had come upon a lone rancher working a fence and when they rushed him he scrambled away on foot but they just let him run and took his big bay mule. They had talked over the merits of riding him down. It was two hours before sunset but they were exhausted. He was only going to run home and hide. They let him go and turned back to ride for the camp.

But an hour later they had watered their horses in a clear bend of the Llano and began to climb up out of the valley when the mule stopped dead in its tracks. It forced them to acknowledge the view. The river winding its way along through the rolling oak-covered hills and the cleared, rock-lined fields of the German farmers and the low sun had a way of framing all that country in a peaceful light. And then they spotted something. A faint cloud of dust rising in the slanted sunlight. It was a party of horsemen crashing through the brush and rocks in hot pursuit of their trail.

They rode hard for the staging camp where Quanah questioned them sternly about the details of what had happened and why and what exactly they had seen. His eyes said something about his concern over their report of the riders. The posse was very close and would not stop. It meant they would need to quickly round up the remuda, leaving many scattered behind, and it would be difficult to outrun the Texans with all of their loot.

They were on the road two days and nights with little food or sleep. Quanah would split them up to conceal the trail. Amidst the chaos Pahvo and Asewaynah found themselves alone with a pair Lipans who had joined the raiding party, seemingly on a more western route, sidetracked from the main group of Quahadis. It was every man for himself. At the end of the fourth day they thought they had left the posse behind. They carelessly butchered and roasted a mustang that night and slept well.

But the Rangers had pushed on through the night and rode upon them with the sunrise. He could still picture the scene vividly in his mind. Slow, like in a dream. He heard the first shot and he heard the bullet smack one of the Lipan's horses and then he saw him buck heavily with the shot. Everyone was shouting. The Lipan took off on foot and was soon picked up by his comrade and he lost sight of them over a ridge with a handful of riders in pursuit. They had all scattered in different directions and Asewaynah was nowhere to be found. Somehow there was only one rider following him but he seemed to have an angle on him. Pahvo was weaving his mount back and forth and was able to deflect several bullets with his shield until his horse took a shot and stumbled. He distinctly remembered that he did not feel the impact of his body slamming into the dirt. But there was something wrong with his leg and when the weight of the injured horse pinned him into the earth he was breathless and sucking for air. For some reason he remembered the sweet smell of the horse, the blood and dirt and sweat and the raspy, guttural death groans as it fell limp over him

The Ranger walked up calmly with his gun drawn. He surveyed his surroundings. The man had a squinch about his eyes, something seemed off. He was confused. Ordinarily he would have been shooting without even thinking. He knelt down for a closer look. He was looking into the eyes of a filthy white boy laying there like a wounded animal. Then he rose up and set off at a trot calling out to his comrades.

Pahvo could hear them hollering at one another. He would just need to wriggle free and crawl to another place. The voices became frenzied and more distant, and then he heard a series of gunshots. He was finally able to shimmy his legs free and he scrambled downhill through the tall grass, but then he thought better of that and began moving back uphill toward another ridge. They would be expecting him to flee down the drainage. After a while three men came riding in search of him. He had found a swale on the other side of the ridge and he lay there silently, listening to them hunt for him for the better part of an hour. By some miracle they did not find him and eventually they moved on.

He got up slowly and began walking, hovering low behind the cover of the grass and mesquite bush. When he arrived back at his dead horse all of his gear had been taken. He was all alone and afoot, walking with great difficulty, with no food or weapons. He limped to the northwest. He found both Lipans splayed out dead in the grass. Stiffening, they had been scalped and large sections of their skin had been peeled away. Red, raw flesh drying into massive, oozing scabs. It could have been him in their place. He stood there staring, respectful to death in passing, aware of his breath and his beating heart in the silence, and then he surveyed the lonely country and began to collect himself.

He started walking again. It was still early in the day and very bright with the sun shining. Blue sky and waving grass. He stopped and looked back toward the settlements. A fleeting thought entered his mind. If there was a time to go back to his old life it was now. He was at a crossroads. There was something about it that triggered a memory of his father. Or it could have been the way the Texans talked, that distinctive drawl that he had just heard for the first time in a long while. A silent voice in his head, from way back. Son, I'm raisin you to be a man. It aint like this ole world is gonna be waitin on you hand and foot. I know you're young but listen to me. There's gonna come a day, or days, where you'll make that choice. To sink or swim. You'll know you need to dig deep. You've only got one enemy, and that is yourself. Listen to me, son. If I do one thing right in this life it's to get you to consider that.

The long journey back to the main village almost killed him and it would take him months to fully recover from the ordeal. He pretended that he was being observed by the elder warriors, and put one foot in front of the other, one step at a time all through the day and through the night, thinking about what Quanah and the others would say about him if he could survive this ordeal. The calories from the lizards and grasshoppers sustained him. He followed the course of the dry creek beds until he found water. To protect his leg he took it slow and rested often. He would sit in the shade and, with meticulous detail, carefully prick the long, sharp spines of the nopales. With the pad smooth he could sink his teeth into the firm outer flesh, suck up the moisture, and chew the raw pad for its nourishments. It felt like the right thing to do. The problem was that he could not see the quills, the microscopic needles that soon lodged in the roof of his mouth and throat.

Doubled over on his knees, choking, trying to get air through his lungs. Of all the ordeals he had overcome this one felt the most like death. He made his way to a spring at the base of a small canyon and lay in a bed of ferns. He knew he had to wait it out. It was two days before he was on the move again.

That evening he could see a group of riders on a distant ridge perhaps twenty miles to the north. Just a fleeting glimpse, but it was something. Or maybe he did not really see it. At dark he came upon a fresh trail and followed it through the night under the moonlight. The night air was dry and cool and there were no fires to be seen from atop the ridges. He found that his respite had helped him heal enough to press on. The swelling down in his knee. The ulcers in his mouth scarring over. He urged himself on. Another day and night passed and when the sun was fully up the following morning he could see the Caprock looming in the distance.

By noon he saw another rider approaching. He tried to conceal himself in a stand of junipers to assess any potential danger but he could not make out the nature of the mount. He chewed on a stem of ryegrass and gazed out over the country. Then he saw the rider ahead of him. A little speck out in the immensity of the landscape. The rider disappeared in a depression and then reappeared again. He realized he'd already been spotted and there was little use in hiding and he began to think through his options for defending himself without any weapons. He stumbled weakly from his hiding place and walked out with his arms held high and in a short time he could see that the rider was one of his own. He waved his arms in peace and when he walked up the horseman had reined up and sat staring in bewilderment at his approach.

Pahvo looked like hell. He was disheveled and dirty and had a crazed look in his eyes and he had taken to chewing off his fingernails for his nerves or perhaps nourishment and the tips of each finger were red and raw and caked in scabs. His savior's eyes were cautious as he tried to get a read on him and they stared strangely at one another in silence as if neither one of them could quite get a handle on if what appeared before them was reality or in fact some sort of bizarre dream. It was Ki-do-seet, the Mexican boy captive he had beaten in the fight in his first days of captivity. Pahvo walked up to the horse and held out his hand and the boy leaned down and helped him up on the back side of the horse.

Ki-do-seet unslung a deerskin pouch from around his neck and untied the lip of it and handed it back for him to drink. Pahvo drank and they rode for the north watching the Caprock. An hour before dark they saw the camp up ahead of them. The scout on watch recognized them. He realized Pahvo's condition and he turned and ran his horse back to warn the village. The horse they rode perked up and trotted on and soon they heard shouts and saw their people coming out to greet them. Ki-do-seet held the horse steady and when they rode up the tribesmen fanned out in a long half circle curiously watching their approach.

The villagers looked troubled. The women were weary and red-eyed and bloody about the face and arms and they had hacked their hair and gashed themselves with obsidian to honor their grief and their wounds were blistered and oozing with blood and pus. Quanah's countenance was that of a humbled man, troubled by the failure of this raid and their medicine and yet he was pleased at the surprise arrival before him for he knew that Pahvo's survival would lift the spirits of the dignified band of warriors that stood so solemn and proud to welcome the boy's return. They helped him down off the horse and held him up to support his weight and they gathered closely to embrace him and shower him with encouragements. Every now and then someone would admiringly call his name and everyone was smiling for there was joy in the village again.

Pahvo had been given up for dead. Two members of the warparty did not return and Asewaynah and several others came back wounded. The Rangers had ridden relentlessly, scouring the plains for any sign and every trail and had forced the warparty to abandon the herds and flee for their lives. They had recaptured three-fourths of the stolen horses and drove them back to Mason and Llano County to be delivered to their rightful owners. And yet the Quahadis had no way of knowing the Rangers' spoils in war. They'd procured the weapons and shields and sacred trinkets of the fallen warriors and had taken pleasure in the mutilation. Fingers and ears, arm skin for coin purses or saddle ornaments. The scrotums for tobacco pouches.

The adrenaline rush upon his arrival sustained him for a time. He was taken to a lodge and made comfortable and here he told of his ordeals. His knee was swollen and bruised and it was elevated on a roll of leather hide. He was dehydrated and starving and he told them the pain all throughout his body was as if he'd been visited by the devil ghost. He was shivering. The eagle doctor was summoned and this old woman in her healings gave him sneezeweed and prickly ash and she fanned him with crow feathers to ward off the evil spirits. He went to sleep for a long time. When he awoke she was still there and she knew that he was not well and so she applied peyote tea to his face and sang to him and then placed a cow horn to his knee and began sucking deeply to draw out the sickness. Then she chewed up a handful of milkweed and placed it in the palms of her hand and began massaging it into his knee.

He was set up in a tent on a bed of buffalo robes for ten days while the sister of Quanah's wife cared for him. She treated his leg, she brought him food. A beautiful young woman with smooth skin, flowing hair, the soulful eyes of a saint. By the time he healed he had been struck by those first pubescent pangs of lust and she lay beside him and talked with him deep into the night until they were lost in themselves. When her mother called for her she left and then he dreamed about her.

Then one night she snuck back in and some of those dreams came true. Lying in the dark, groping awkwardly, she seemed to take the lead. Strange, tingling sensations and the erotic smells and tastes of the opposite sex. The feel of soft, smooth skin in youth. The warmth between her thighs. When she touched him there whatever feelings of shyness he had vanished in a rush of blood and breath and semen. When they finished they lay back breathing deeply with relief in that silence and when she giggled he just lay back smiling and they began to process what had just happened to them.

In time he was up and about gimping through the camp and he knew, everyone knew, there were so many things different about him. He had become taller and stronger, his features maturing nicely. He was lean and athletic with the muscles in his arms and shoulders and chest now more prominent and so different from the softer forms of his Comanche brethren.

A month later his limp was gone and as he worked a herd of mustangs out in the pastures he saw a group of wagons carrying trade goods but he was wary of their eyes on him as they trotted their horses into the village. He kept his distance from them and hung about the fringes of camp watching these men go about their business. No one said anything particular that might indicate the nature of their mission. And yet he seemed to have some sixth sense they were looking for someone like him and after breakfast the following morning Quanah came and told him there was someone that wanted to talk to him. He gestured toward the man and looked at his apprentice as if he did not have the option to say no.

In his confusion Pahvo talked back in an arrogant tone that few boys his age might use toward a mentor but Quanah patted his shoulder fondly and said that he should talk to just this one man, and to open his heart and free his mind.

It was late in the afternoon when he was made acquainted with Lowndes Jones, indian trader, guide, a man of many interests and dialects. He was a sincere, ascetic looking man known in some circles as El Indio and he had long white hair framed by a rugged face and he sized up the boy with soulful, gray eyes that had seen many things. He was old and disheveled and with a coat too small his long, brown arms protruded clumsily from the sleeves and on his left wrist he wore a sterling cuff bracelet etched in intricate patterns that was presented to him as a token of goodwill by the Comanche. He looked about the camp to assess the eyes that were on him and he expertly blew a thick string of snot from his right nostril before he looked up and smiled warmly at the boy.

He spoke in comanche and he asked his name and he asked him how he was.

At first Pahvo did not say anything, perhaps he was thinking about how old the man before him was. He sat up just a bit. Pahvotaivo, he said, but he said no more.

The old trader smiled. Then he spoke in english. What name did your mother and father give you?

Pahvo looked away. He had not heard his native language in such a long while. When he answered he spoke the name very slowly. David. Johnson.

Well David, I've been asked to check on you and see how you've been doing.

Pahvo thought about how to say it. What words to use. When it came to him he said it slowly, awkwardly. By… who?

The indian agent. At Fort Sill.

Pahvo stared back.

Have you thought about the fact that your father is looking for you?

No.

Well, of course he is.

Jones looked at him. He was trying to picture what all the boy had been through. Son, I'm here to help you, he said. Do you want to go back home?

Pahvo glared back. The old trader repeated the question in comanche and then again slowly in english.

Pahvo stood up and shifted his legs. He looked away. He seemed to struggle to form his words. Who… who are you?

I'm just an old man, he said.

He smiled as if he knew things that most did not and they sat there silently, looking at one another.

I guess you could say that I'm a traveler. A seeker, a watcher of the seasons. And I have a business trading goods out here.

This is… my home… n… now, said Pahvo.

The old frontiersman smiled. No one knows what you've been through. Only you know. But I understand.

The boy sat back down.

Just listen to me, said Jones. I figured we could just talk.

He took his bracelet off and rubbed it with his thumbs and put it back on again. Hear me, he said. Just you and me. I want you to think about what your family has been through.

He leaned forward and patted him on the shoulder.

The boy slunk back.

I'm trying to help you.

I dont n… need. Need. Any help. I dont need any help.

Jones persisted.

He spoke deeply in the cool shade of the cottonwoods. He took his time, speaking in comanche and in a slow, drawn-out english that he accented with Comanche phrases to emphasize his points.

You were born, he said, into this world. Chosen by God. It's not like you had a choice. Life is cruel. You had no control whatsoever over the circumstances of which you were born into and there is a randomness to events that we can never understand. Stay with me now. I know you are young. In this life we are presented with scenarios. Adversities. Opportunities. Choices. Think about what all's brought you to this place? In the past there were times that it surely didnt seem like you had any options. And yet there were in fact options and you chose them, innately, and now here you sit before me as a fellow traveler. A survivor. I can tell with one look into your eyes that you are ready to receive this. You are at that age when it is important to be taught these things. That's not the case for everyone. What is your faith? What do you believe in?

Pahvo sat there uneasily. He had been carrying a small flat rock with him as a talisman and he was rubbing it restlessly in his hands. Are you some kind of pre… pre… preacher, he said?

Jones looked down and winced, he rubbed his eyes. Why do you think I have been placed before you, in this place? At this time? On this day?

They stared at one another. Jones looked deep into his eyes, studying the countenance of the kid.

Think about this, said Jones. On a trail drive, when there's thousands of cattle trampling through the grass, what saves the eggs of the quail in their nests?

The kid stared back. Long silence. Jones put in a fresh chaw of tobacco and spat. You see, there's some things about the cosmos that you just caint explain.

Pahvo looked up and he seemed to be nodding.

Ah hell, said Jones. I suppose I'm mainly talkin at myself. But as I said before, if you want me to get you out of this place I can help.

Nothing, said Pahvo.

What's that, son?

There is nothing… for me… in my old home.

Flesh and blood, said Jones. Look at me. How much Comanche blood runs through your veins? Have you thought about what these people did to you and your family?

They didnt do it.

I see, said Jones.

It's not like that with them.

Jones stood up. He adjusted his arms inside his coat and took the bracelet off and massaged the portion of his wrist where it had worn his skin.

Well, I suppose there's something spiritual in how you've so easily accepted your fate.

He stepped forward. He smiled and patted the boy's shoulder. I better get going, he said. Those fellas are watching us. They seem uneasy we're still talking.

He stood up and adjusted his britches. I dont know about you but I dont like it when someone's eyein me, he whispered.

Pahvo watched him go. The old trader gimped off slowly, shoulders hunched, and then he stopped as if he might have turned back to say something but he did not and then he set off walking again.

In a few days the band was on the move southward. A young woman had given birth to an ill-formed infant and had abandoned the child on the outskirts of camp like a butcher discarding entrails. As they set out along the trail they could hear the weakling wailing in the distance. The mother in her sorrow turned to go back but the medicine woman spoke to her in her infinite wisdom and then they went on with the tribe, leaving the child on the plains to die.

In the evening bivouacs Pahvo spent his time smoking with the medicine man preparing for his great quest to obtain power from the spirits. Isatai'i examined the boy's new shield closely and held it over the fire and shook it. The horse tails and hawk feathers ruffled about.

He asked him if there was enough cushion inside to absorb the bullets of the Tejanos. Pahvo looked at him. He punched each side of it several times with his knuckles. He handed it up to the kid and told him that he would have directions for him in the morning. Pahvo took the shield and walked formally and with much respect in a wide circle around the fire before arriving back in front of his donor. Then he thanked him and walked off into the dark for his tipi.

That night the girl crawled into his lodge again and they lay there in the dark while she told him about what their lives would be like if they could be together as they became older. He just lay there and let her talk in whisper. She had rolled on her side to face him and she put her nose to his cheek and touched him. When they were finished the girl kissed him and slipped out from under the robe, tiptoeing from the tent and leaving him alone in the darkness.

When the band moved out the following day Isatai'i rode up alongside and told him that he'd seen the vision for the design of Pahvo's shield and the time had come for them to choose an artist. He also handed him a thick, leather-bound book that he had received in trade from the Kiowas and he told him that he should use it to reinforce the inside padding of the shield. It was a bible and he held it in the palms of his hands and studied it carefully for a good while until suddenly an image crept into his head. He saw his mother sitting in the sun leading a bible study on that Sunday morning before he and his brother were abducted, her hair waving in a light breeze, the very same bible he was now holding cradled in her hands.

He looked up, riding in silence with his thoughts, and he nudged his horse off the better to ride alone. He surveyed the country and he briefly raised his eyes toward the heavens and then he looked back down and stopped the horse and opened the book. It had been marked to Philippians 4:13 and he was looking at the string of letters that made up the words and it was difficult for him to make it out for he had not seen the written word on paper in four hundred and twenty-two days. But then he noticed his mother's handwritten notes in the margins.

He touched the thin, worn page with his calloused fingers and slid them slowly over where she had placed her private notations of faith. He could not understand it but he sensed something more. He sat there looking at it and then he closed the book and rode on with his head down. All the mysteries of the universe right there in his hands. No way to make sense of the flood of thoughts and emotions flowing through his head. All the life that was behind him and all of it that was ahead. He sat there for a while thinking about all of those things as his tribesmen kept riding on and then he looked up and saw them slewing away from him, gliding gracefully across the plains in the flawless sun like a flowing river. He closed the book and chucked up the horse and kicked it into a run.

They rode south for three more days descending from the high plains and they pushed further into the headwaters of the Conchos. On a high mesa overlooking the broad desert watershed they shared a meal of bear meat and honey while a warm summer wind fanned the flames of their fires. Pahvo sat on a boulder stirring a dish of cinnabar he held for the shield painter and the medicine man gave instructions as the artist prepared to work.

On a makeshift easel of wagonboard he lined out his ochre pigments and arranged them from light to dark and opened a beaded pouch from which he pulled a handful of horsehair brushes. Pahvo unlaced the straps atop the shield and removed the frame and rummaged through the inside of the leather to clear more space. Then he wedged his mother's bible into the center so that it was surrounded by padding and replaced the frame and sewed the edge up tight with the rawhide thongs.

When he had it cinched up good and tight he strapped it to his forearm and felt its weight and beat the face of it with the inside of his fist and held it out before him and tested it. It felt good. He took it off and turned it clockwise and one by one studied the adornments that embellished the circumference. Feathers of birds and raptors. Tinklets of broken mirrorglass. Bear claws and strips of bright red cloth. Some skin from the tail of a mountain lion and strings of pearls from the Concho River. He slid the strap over his head and slipped it on his shoulder and down his waist and then he simulated the pull of a bowstring as it hung against his hip. It felt like a natural part of his body.

The artist had been listening intently to Isatai'i's conceptual vision for the shield and now beside the fire he unfurled a holy robe on the ground and centered the shield and arranged the paints and brushes around it. In his hand he held a battered Joseph Dixon pencil and he began to sketch out the design of a cosmogram that would properly capture the medicine of the celestial spirits. He was deliberate in his art and there was no doubt or tremor in his ever-steady hand. When he was done he picked up a brush and wet it with his tongue and dipped the paint.

He painted a concentric circle to represent the sun in yellow and red and turquoise pigments and he centered this with a beaming orange orb, accentuated by a series of black lines that angled toward it from the outer edges. The artist is not just a simple composer of images, but a chronicler of the times and an enabler of the spirit world. He searches in his art for the truth, whether it be motifs of shamanic journeys to the otherworld or altered states of consciousness or to invoke the supernatural protection of his subjects from injury in battle.

He added to his masterpiece a triangle shaded in black, a red four-pointed star of the summer solstice sunrise, and lastly, a grizzly bear floating, its feet with exaggerated claws, reaching devoutly for the sun. All of this the artisan painted cleanly and with precision, a two-dimensional cosmos, the Great Spirit's own view of everything under the sun.

The vision seeker and his mentor watched him. With his last brush-stroke he rose from his knees and said something to himself and he smiled as he inspected his work and then he bent down to pick it up, admiring his work, and then he carefully placed it aside to take the wind and dry.

They gathered around the piece and admired its singular beauty and they took turns caressing it, lightly fondling the consecrated talismans that dangled from its fringes. Then Isatai'i placed a hand on each of their shoulders and he seemed genuinely pleased with their accomplishment, ever prideful in his medicine and much satisfied that the transfer of his vision was now complete.

That summer with the rising of the grass the Texas cowmen began gathering cattle and shaping their herds for the westbound trails. Quanah and his warriors would not hold back. They rode west into the depths of the Chihuahuan desert and all along that great gypsum plain they raided relentlessly for months plundering the Butterfield Stage line. A handful of overland mail coaches carrying passengers and letters along the twenty-eight hundred mile route from St. Louis to San Francisco. Wagontrains of goldseekers slaughtered or wounded and left to die in the desert. In the middle of July they stampeded two thousand head of cattle in an outfit ran by Jim Burleson on the Pecos River and two weeks later as they descended from the spurs of the Guadalupes they rode down upon two men on saddle horses riding north across the plains for the letting of the beef contracts at Santa Fe. A desperate encounter ensued in which the cattleman Oliver Loving was shot and wounded and left under siege three days and nights before he was able to slip into the river and escape under the moonlight.

In the fall they were in the Kansas territory camped along the banks of the Medicine Lodge Creek, a spiritual site of the Plains tribes and the designated gathering place for the great council with the United States Indian Peace Commission. Over a fortnight upwards of five thousand tribesmen turned out with general indifference and loitered about solely for the purpose of receiving the widely advertised gifts promised by the white men.

When the Quahadis arrived Satanta was giving an oration on behalf of the entire indian population and through the infinite rows of soldiers and tribesmen Pahvo tried to make sense of all that he saw and heard. He thought back to that fateful day so long ago when the big Kiowa chief and his band hauled him and his brother on horseback away from his burning home. Where was his brother now? He could picture him that day. He could see the blood and the tears and the terror in Charlie's eyes. He could also very clearly see his mother's bloodied and dripping scalp dangling from his hands. But he could not remember his own fear. Just his anger, his rage. Some innate desire to fight, to survive. To be strong for his brother. That day there was no time to stop and think. Just his instincts had carried him through, he thought, and he was proud of that.

He lingered on the fringes of the proceedings as the sun set and more speeches were said. Then with great fanfare the commissioners unveiled the treaty to end all treaties and the consenting chiefs lined up one by one for the touching of the pen. All of their traditional tribal lands to be exchanged for millions of acres on the reservation complete with houses and barns, schools and tools, all in the spirit of learning the ways of the sedentary Anglo farmer. Signatures were stamped and the bystanders who had been waiting patiently for the proffered gifts were rewarded handsomely.

But the Quahadi chiefs did not sign. In the evening when he and Asewaynah returned to the camp the aguardiente was flowing and Quanah was indignantly rummaging through the gifts. He distributed the tobacco and food and trinkets and tossed aside most of the cooking utensils and all of the tattered Civil War uniforms that had been issued to them. Pahvo took it all in as he sat by the fire. The talk that night was about all of the nonsense that had just ensued. They also talked about the mild weather. There was still time to raid the Tejano ranches for horses before winter set in.

He never saw his brother again. He'd kept growing and then he grew some more and he was in every mustang roundup and buffalo hunt, every raid and ceremony. A cocksure teen with his entire life ahead of him and that fearless edge that comes with having nothing to lose. Dozing in and out of sleep on a frigid January night with his pelvis rubbing on the bison robe he slept upon and an erection pulsing pleasurably between his legs he was interrupted by an older squaw and introduced to the particular beauties of a mature woman and shown different amorous techniques to perform. He lay with his lover gasping in the tent where the warm embers of the fire smoldered and glowed. She leaned on her side facing him and placed her hand on his chest. In a few minutes he fell asleep.

Soon the arctic northers came sweeping down upon the plains. He spent long days and nights huddled in his robes, tending the fires, waiting for the snow to stop and the return of the south winds. Appearing from his lodge one morning at sunrise with the front lifting he saw a figure hobbling off in the distance and he put on his boots and ran out to help. A old blind man in a breechclout sat himself crosslegged in the ice and he raised his head up from the noise of Pahvo's approach. In his right hand he held a Confederate Bowie knife and on his left knee he held the other hand out, palm open. The man sensed that something was there and he looked up briefly with those hazy eyes and he smelled the cold air. Pahvo stood to the side in silence, still, watching. When the man began his death chant and sliced his wrists for them to bleed out Pahvo turned without speaking and quietly retraced his steps back to the camp through the snow.

He took his first scalp when he and Asewaynah surprised an Overland water hauler running barrels from the Mustang Ponds to the Staked

Plains mail station. He had it dangling from his shield the next week when he was recruited to ride under a head chief by the name of Paru-acoom and it gave him confidence when they crossed the Llano in a heavy snow and rode for the Cedar Mountains to slaughter the helpless settlers of Legion Valley. There was no longer any question about his ability to withstand the rigorous life of a warrior.

He stole livestock all through the spring and summer months and he could not get enough. He plundered the Hill Country ranches and the cattle trails of the Pecos and the scattered camps of the Navajo in New Mexico Territory. Each time they returned they were celebrated as heroes. He did not back down from any confrontation. He became accepted among the tribe as someone who, despite his youth, had the potential to make the most of his thaumaturgic powers. By now he'd collected a handful of scalps and a small remuda, the foundations of Comanche wealth. He was another year older. In his medicine bag he carried a vial of herbs for healing, a raven's tailwing, some sweetgrass, an assortment of bird claws. He also carried things more specific to his history. Talismans that fostered his powers. The deer tail from his first bow kill. The snout gristle of a large javelina sow that had attacked him in defense of her young.

With his green eyes and lighter complexion it was easy for those who did not know him to shun him for his Anglo blood but it made no difference to him, anything they thought or said or did, he was his own authentic self. The homelands of his adopted family were being overrun by those of his native race and his fate had cruelly trapped him between these two opposing cultures, one fighting for its existence, the other taking over the western world. Yet somehow to him the hardships of his universe were of little consequence and although it was accepted that someone in his plight would be conflicted or give up hope or die he just took it all in, even persevered, as if all of the forces in the cosmos had conspired to make it so.

Son, you're tellin me that you were in the raid on Legion Valley?

Yes. Yes I was. I remember the bitter cold, the sunset that evening.

It was a massacre.

You understand I rode as a scout?

RL looked through him.

I was always the first one to sneak in and stake out a ranch, start taking the horses. It was all women and children. I thought we'd get the livestock and ride on for the next ranch.

It was a massacre.

Yes. There were a few bad indians with us and it got out of hand when one of the women tried to fight back. Quanah would not have approved. My job was to run the horses. It made no sense to haul off a bunch of hysterical women and their small children.

What happened afterwards?

We didnt make it far that first night. Too cold. The women were beside themselves and them and the kids were giving us all kinds of trouble. I was assigned to tend the herds. They wanted to kill Temple Friend so I took him and he rode behind me. He reminded me of Charlie. We rode hard for several days. Didnt have any troubles. No one on our trail. No Rangers. The only other thing that stands out was when we made the Buffalo Gap we saw the strangest thing. It was a line of mules in harness pulling a wagon, riders lined out in front and behind. Just cowboys riding with their saddlebags. No other stock. We were studying the wagon, wondering what was inside. The cold front was clearing and when the sun came out what looked like a big tin casket bouncing along on the inside of the wagon reflected back at us in the sunlight. I still dont know what that was about.

RL just sat there stone-faced, looking at him. Son, that was Oliver Loving's funeral procession, he said. You dont remember him but you knew him when you were little.

Sam is sitting on the couch in the living room talking with RL. An attractive young schoolteacher who'd been hired to serve as a tutor brings them coffee, the soft hollow between her breasts heaving from her low-cut blouse, which is a sense of pride, and it is a secret pleasure when she catches them sneaking glimpses. She holds her position bent down with the tray and looks into his handsome eyes.

Samuel, we should start your lessons soon, she says.

The young man looks up into her eyes, his expression matching the subconscious flirtations. Yes ma'am, he says.

As she leaves the room he swigs the coffee and clears his throat with his hand over his mouth in the proper manner he is becoming re-assimilated to. He looks at RL who is grinning and shaking his head slowly as he watches her exit the room.

There was an unusually beautiful Kiowa squaw, said Sam, and she was married to a head chief they called Satank, who had several other wives. She had been sold to him against her will and made to give up her true love. One day he discovered that she had been unfaithful and he punished her by disfiguring her nose. I saw her once, nose burned off. She was older but you could still see her beauty.

Nose burnt off?

Yes, to the bone. No skin, just both nostrils wide open. No I notice that whenever I see an attractive woman that image still creeps into my head.

Son, there's something I've been meanin to ask you.

What?

At what point was it exactly that you decided you was going to live as a savage? Like a wild damned animal?

No. It's not like that.

Well…

You dont understand.

I just caint get my head around it.

Sam glanced off across the prairie for a long while as they sat in silence before he looked back at RL again. Think about it, he said. When they hauled us off we were swept along into their world. As young as I was I picked up early that they had no tolerance for weakness. When they hauled us away we rode for days, hardly stopping, the only food was a chunk of horse meat from a foal that had failed. Or the guts of a calf. They tested us at every turn. I had to learn to eat like them. Slaved all over the camp. Racing, fighting. They'd put you inside a circle with just a shield for protection, throwing rocks from every angle to try and knock you out. Herding mustangs, we were the first to be thrown on top of those wild ponies, to try and start to wear them down to be broken. They observed us closely. How we rode. How afraid we were. How much pain we could take. They were practical. They were engaged. Engaged in us, in the land, their faith.

That meant something. If they noticed any potential they knew it was in their interest to foster that. And besides, it was war. I've seen what a party of Rangers can do to a village whose warriors were away on a hunt, where only the women and children were left in the camp to face the wrath of a bunch of outlaws wearing badges. What those soldiers did to us on the North Fork. It was a slaughter. There's bad men. *Wild animals,* as you say, in every tribe. Comanche. Mexican. Kiowa. Texan.

RL had his elbows on his knees and his hands clasped. He was staring at the floor. Sam kept talking.

I was too young to understand it then but I know now that it's not in my nature to dwell on the past. Once I got over the shock of what was happening I started to see their world more clearly. Started to see my future. I was tested. I fought to survive. Early on I could sense their reactions, things they liked in me. Little glimpses of respect.

RL looked away, across the room.

As much bad luck as it was that day when the Kiowas rode upon our home I see now looking back over those ten years all of the good luck. And what say did I have in it? Quanah bringing me in, looking over me. I'd think about how you had things set up for us. You were always gone or working. It seems like from the time I could walk all I did was work. It was easy to forget about my old life. I was able to just move on.

RL nodded. He looked at the floor and sighed and turned his head toward the far side of the room. The grandfather clock chimed the quarter hour.

Quanah took me in. I began to learn their ways. Every day was an adventure. There were other boys my age. Other men that I looked up to. I had friends for the first time. I was working with horses, learning to hunt, being taught to understand nature. Things that felt natural, that I was good at. I stood out and was recognized. I felt special. I had never felt such joy before. I guess I figured out I didnt want my life to be like it was where I came from.

RL sat there looking at him. A measured silence before he spoke. Is that right? he said.

You see, Quanah was like a father to me. When I wasnt allowed to ride down with him into Mexico that fall there was a void in my life. I realized how much I needed that type of a presence. He motivated me. I had this growing sense of purpose.

We were camped near the Guadalupes late that summer when it truly became clear. I was seeking a vision. I bathed early in that cold creek and set out for the tallest peak. Carried only my robe, some flint, my tobacco and pipe.

I stopped only to smoke and pray. When I reached the summit I was very weak from fasting. I sat facing south and listened to the wind. Salt flats. Desert. The streaking colors of the setting sun. I slept facing east until the sun rose over the land. Later, on the fourth night up there, I felt the spirit like never before and then I heard a voice.

RL took off his hat and wiped his brow with the back of his sleeve. He put the hat upside down on the coffee table and closed his eyes. He took a deep breath and ran his hand through his hair and then he opened his eyes again.

Son, what kind of voice did you hear?

Sam smiled, thinking back fondly. What I'm trying to tell you, he said, is that in those years there was this momentum, like a flowing river. I was swept along, as if I wasnt in control. There was no time to look back or question things. I was just in the moment. Going on instinct. I was going along with it all, doing whatever was before me or whatever I wanted to, like…

They heard a knock and the schoolteacher stepped inside the doorway. Mr Terry, Samuel, she said. I'm so sorry to interrupt but we really should get his lessons started.

He always looks back on that first raid. He slips the halter over the last horse. He feels the heat from its nostrils, smells the dust and grass and manure from the stall. They slip off into the moonlight, Asewaynah and the others heading north with the herds, but he stays behind with Quanah near Fort McKavett looking for more horses. Quanah stands beside him, describing the nuances of the cavalry horses, assessing the difficulty of the conditions. He knows that behind him Isatai'i lurks like a phantom listening and observing.

The scenario seems impossible. The sturdy picket fence surrounding a heavy-timbered stable, guarded by sentries outside on foot and another asleep inside, so he'll have to time his work well and avoid waking the other man as he cuts the dowels to remove enough posts to sneak the horses through. It is still and quiet in the night. He is coiling his rope neatly and fingering the plaited hairs of the bridle. He has no extra equipage about him and can move with stealth. He is anxious, looking over the various horses.

He listens to Quanah whisper. He is having difficulty making out the Comanche terms for the various horses he is describing. He follows Quanah's eyes and tries to make out the horseflesh he is eyeing. He watches a large reddish-brown stallion with white above its hocks and white spots on its face and belly.

Pahvo? Quanah calls to him quietly and nods toward the stallion. Pinto, he said.

Isatai'i steps forward and sticks out his fist and opens it palm up. There is a smooth, round ball from a buffalo's stomach and he hands it over to Pahvo. He is smoking a cigarette rolled in a cottonwood leaf and steps back into the shadows while chanting quietly.

Quanah places his hand on the boy's shoulder and points toward another animal. He seems to be absorbed in the nuances of the various horses, especially the sabino stallion. And he is intrigued by the precarious circumstances involved in stealing him. He mentions its hindquarters and talks admiringly of its demeanor and its combination of size and agility, which reminds him of a horse he once owned. He casually breaks into the story of how he stole the horse but then soon lost it in a wager. Nothing about the logistics of stealing the pinto stallion before them. Pahvo had been studying the pins on the top side of the corral that fastened the pickets together. Quanah has proven his faith in him by not mentioning the difficulty of the situation. He finishes the story contentedly, hands Pahvo a beaded, leather-fringed sheath and he tells him to trust the spirits, his puha. It holds a knife made solely of flint, colorfully banded with a serrated edge along its entire length. Then he steps back to watch Pahvo work. A sabino pinto stallion. He remembers working like a ghost in the dark for several hours to take it. He sawed off the pins and dug around the posts and removed the pickets. The snoring sentinel rustled some as he slipped out with the horse but he did not wake up.

10

— ★ —

The Goodnight-Loving Trail

There was, after the Civil War, no longer any legitimate cattle market along the Mississippi River to feed the Confederate forces. For the five years during the war prolific seasons had overrun the Texas ranches with cattle and yet very little had been sold. Opportunity. The late 1860s was a time when every Texas cowman with a sizable herd had an eye on heading north for market. And yet as early as the 1850s there is a history of ranchers venturing into the western fringes of Texas and holding large herds along the confluence of the Concho and Colorado Rivers. Virgin land, free grass, live water. They build log huts and pens and work to improve their ranches, not another neighbor for thirty miles or more. Men who are young, tireless, fearless, and in need of more pasture to expand their herds. Camp Colorado sprung up on the route between Fort Belknap and Fort Mason. There was money to be made.

When the cowhands trail herds from the Cross Timbers west into the fringes of Comancheria in search of new ranges they surround a team of big bay mules, equipment wagons pulled by teams of oxen, the chuck wagon, and they ride alongside the horse wranglers and admire the spare remuda, plodding along leisurely chomping up the tall grass, seeking respite from the lonely days on the trail. These are hard frontiersmen, many with troubled pasts, working sunup to sundown and taking their pay in gold and silver only when the stock is sold. It is a monotonous time. They ride for long hours in silence looking at the country. The cowboys arrive an hour before dark, go about the chores of setting camp and then take a plate of beef and beans from the cook before gathering around the fire where they eat their food in silence, gathering themselves after the day's journey. As the stars come out the stories begin.

Every conversation is about their adventures on the trail. A story is told of a herd taken to Little Rock and someone counters with one of the drives to Shreveport. Their tin cups are filled with rations of whiskey, the miraculous lubricant that spurs their conversations with new energy. The man speaking, it is assumed by all, speaks the absolute truth in his Texan drawl, as he experienced it his own self or had been informed by some trusted source.

I been told by a few ole boys in the know that the United States troops at Fort Bent had been paying the Comanche and Kiowa to cross the Red River and steal horses and cattle from the Texans…

There is inevitably some angle that involves a run-in with the hostile indians. *Last week the indians raided the Kemp and White homes on the old Jack Bailey place twenty miles down on the Keechi.* Not a week goes by without news of a depredation and yet there is that false intuition inside of a man that makes him think it will never happen to him. All men are dreamers and the rumors of the adventurers that came before them, the successes of their contemporaries, inspire them and spread across the prairies like wildfire.

Loving trailed a herd of fifteen hundred up north over the Red River toward the Arkansas and wintered at Pueblo. Sold his stock to the miners for gold but the war broke out and the Union authorities prevented him from coming back to Texas. I wonder if there's still money to be made in the mining region? What would the route be like if we trailed straight west and stayed south until we reached the Pecos and then drove them north? Is there any water to be had between the Middle Concho and the Pecos? What are the government subcontractors at Bosque Redondo paying for Texas cattle?

James Patterson, cattle rancher, driver, and merchant in Texas and New Mexico, had been posing these questions in the early 1860s. By 1864 John Chisum and his brothers began making the first forays into New Mexico trailing small herds and scouting the range. *Not only is there fine grass range and money in the mining region but the reservations and Army posts in Arizona and New Mexico need beef to feed the indians.*

It was in the mid-1860s when Oliver Loving and Charles Goodnight first began to shape their herds and put plans in place to trail that more western route. By 1866 the trail was no longer a secret among Texas ranchers and that vast and desolate country became one of the most well-traveled cattle trails of all time.

September 1926. Farm-to-Market Road 70. Gray County, Texas. They were driving to the ranch of TD Hobart in Charles Goodnight's brand-new Buick Town Brougham Sedan—the colonel and Corinne and Evetts Haley. The Hobart place was believed to be the location of the indian camp where Julia and Addie German were rescued in 1874 after being held in captivity by the Cheyennes and a reunion had been planned to commemorate their adventures and the history of those times.

Saturday. Sun shining and the windows down. The dry, warm Panhandle air of early fall fresh and clear flowing through the car and the big, 274 cubic inch inline-six engine humming. The handsome car was climbing a hill and they were bumping along.

Haley was driving and he looked over at the colonel and asked him about Hobart. They were cruising at thirty-five miles per hour and the old man's white shock of hair blew wildly with the wind. They were skirting the rugged edge of the Caprock and the rough gullies that fed down to the east and through the little window splattered with the yellowed guts of grasshoppers he could see the flat tableland grass plains stretching forever before them to the north.

TD Hobart is a good man, said the colonel. A Yankee, but a good man. He was fiddling with a section of plaited rawhide rope and gazing out the window studying the long views of the country. A man who felt good to be alive, felt in his soul all of the memories from the days gone by, the ever-running images of his life and times. All those years and the work and the adventures and the days. He started to talk about his early days on the trail. Corinne leaned forward from the back so she could hear and Haley as always listened with great attentiveness the better to ingest the spirit of the old man's words. Goodnight covered his mouth with his kerchief and cleared his lungs with a deep coughing fit and when he finished he began to talk loudly so they could hear him over the noise.

In 1866 we had our sights set on the western route along the old Butterfield mail route, going around the more hostile Kiowa and Comanche country and taking the Pecos up into the New Mexico Territory. Bosque Redondo. Fort Sumner, then on north up toward Denver.

I know you understand this, Haley. We were Texas cowmen through and through. Loving had taken a different route through the indian country up to Denver in 1860. And I'd been hearing about that trip and others. About the type of men required. Boy, we had us a crew, I'll tell you what. One-Armed Bill Wilson. Then Nigger Jim Fowler, who we assigned to kill the newborn calves. Bose Ikard, another former slave. God bless him, that fine man is still alive today. I owe him my life. Cross-eyed Nath Brauner, from Kentucky, who was our rattlesnake killer. We even had Clay Allison, the gunfighter, believe it or not. That man knew not to cross me. Let's see, who else? RL Terry didnt make that trip, bless his heart. He and one other ole boy had to back out on us at the last second.

The Butterfield Overland Stage Trail. Fairly well-known at the time but still dangerous, three hundred miles of it winding to the Pecos. As Oliver had been told, not a drop of water the last eighty miles. Some of the ugliest, driest, harshest country a man could step foot in. It ran from the headwaters of the Middle Concho into the lower portions of the Staked Plains through the Castle Mountains all the way to the Horsehead Crossing of the Pecos.

I had a used government wagon rebuilt with bois d'arc. Iron axles. Built-in can of tallow to use in greasing. On the back a chuckbox with a hinged lid that you could set down on a leg for the cook's worktable. It was hell findin cows. I couldnt hardly get a thousand head fit for the trail, as the outlaws and indians had run me out. Before we left we had to make a run toward Fort Worth for horses. Made the final preparations in Weatherford. Shitload of ammunition and foodstuff. Even got our pictures taken for posterity. And of course I spent some time with Mollie.

Haley looked in the rearview mirror. Corinne, he said, that chuckbox he mentioned. He invented it. They still use em today.

Corinne had leaned forward and was anxiously watching the old man's reaction. She reached up and placed her hand on his shoulder. Charles, what was the weather like that day? she said.

About like today. Hot as hell. Dry. I can picture the details along the map of that route as clear as if it all happened yesterday. Good grass country through Camp Cooper. Those chimneys at Fort Phantom Hill. We turned south around where Abilene is today. Buffalo Gap. Fort Chadbourne. Then that pretty country along the North Concho, north of where they built San Angelo.

And what about the indians? she asked. Werent they just everywhere then?

The old man turned and looked back, perhaps to better emphasize his point. We had us a good outfit, he said. Men who fought in the war. Hard, tough men. We knew one another's strengths. We were well armed and figured we knew how to handle ourselves if they decided to give us trouble.

Haley was looking in the mirror again to gauge her reaction and he had a huge grin. The colonel was feeling good.

Anyhow, we watered one last time at the Middle Concho. Centralia Draw. The ruts of the stagecoaches plain as day. Castle Gap and on to Horsehead Crossing. Those god-awful alkali plains in far West Texas. The Guadalupe Mountains looming in the west. The country out there dont pretty up until well north.

From the back seat Corinne spoke up. Oh Charles, honey, if we head to Arizona this winter we should really think about driving those roads. I'd love for you to take me on a tour.

The old man smiled. Corinne, that'd be real nice, he said. I'd like that very much.

We set out on the sixth day of June, eighteen of us and two thousand longhorns. Twelve yoke of oxen. I had joined Oliver's herd twenty-five miles southwest of Belknap. A lot of things running through my head, some strong emotions. Loving took charge of the drive and we pointed the herd west toward the Clear Fork of the Brazos. The start of a month-long journey.

We made fifteen miles that first day and settled in early. I'll never forget that first night around the camp. Everyone's energy, giddy like schoolgirls. The sun slipping away and the last flares of red in the west. We gathered around the campfire and sat in its warmth watching that magical change of evening light. Above us the first stars. There would be no moonrise for another two hours. We boiled us up a hot pot of strong black coffee. The cattle were munching on grass, a little edgy from the day's drive, all their bawling echoing in that still night air made me think of the indians. We ate supper and then talked about how good it felt to be out on the trail. It just made you feel alive.

Up at sunrise and lined out, riding for a big ole moon that was still high in the morning sky. Our best hands rode on either point and directed the herd per Oliver's instructions. Behind them the others rode to hold the herd in line and they'd shift positions throughout the day to mix up the duties. I rode eight or ten miles out ahead scouting the best route for signs of water and indian trouble, doubling back now and then to signal the pointers. That book in my bag there, Corinne. Hand that over would you please.

She handed it over. He read the title aloud.

The Log of a Cowboy. Okay, where is it? Yessir, right here. Ole Adam's does a helluva job puttin what it was like on paper.

He fingered the page and looked over the words, his eyes squinting. He began to read, his old chiseled voice deep with tone. Slow, thick, weathered.

There were about fifty or sixty big steers in the lead of our bunch, and after worrying them into a trot, we opened in their front with our six-shooters, shooting into the ground in their very faces, and were rewarded by having them turn tail and head the other way.

The old man paused, chuckling. It was the first time Haley had ever heard him show any inclination of humor. But then the colonel caught another extreme fit of coughing and he hocked up a mouthful of mucus out the window and then handed the book back to Corinne. Excuse me, he said. I'm sorry about that. Read this for us, little girl, would you please?

Why, of course. She adjusted her eyes to the bouncing of the car on the road and read the passage, dramatically, like a stage actress.

Taking advantage of the moment we jumped our horses on the retreating-leaders, and as fast as the rear cattle forged forward, easily turned them. Leaving Joe to turn the rear as they came up, I rode to the lead...

She paused, looking at the colonel as if to confirm she should keep on. He was smiling and nodding, urging her on. She kept reading.

... unfastening my slicker as I went, and on reaching the turned leaders, who were running on an angle from their former course, flaunted my "fish" in their faces until they reentered the rear guard of our string, and we soon had a mill going which kept them busy, and rested our horses. Once we had them milling, our trouble, as far as running was concerned, was over, for all two of us could hope to do was to let them exhaust themselves in this endless circle.

Goodnight was excited and he reached back for the book, closed it emphatically, and gestured with it as he made his next point. Now Haley, the main reason I'm readin this is if we ever write the book, we've got to give it the true flavor of things like that.

I would be honored to help you with that.

All these stories I go on about. We just might have something folks would be interested in. I like the way that's done. Void of fluff.

Yes, I completely agree.

Well, anyhow. I got sidetracked a little there. About that first trip. We made damn good time. At the headwaters of the Middle Concho we held up and kept the herd on water all day while we planned for the drive to the Horsehead. Centralia Draw lay before us. Then the Castle Mountains.

But there's no water out there for near a hundred miles. The old steers slurped away and we filled the water barrels and canteens. Pointed the herd into the setting sun and rode until midnight. The herd was already suffering from thirst and refused to bed down, milling about nervous as hell damn near that whole night and not a one of us slept, herding all night under that bright moon.

We ran out of water the next afternoon and rode them through the night and all the next day. That damned ole sun was brutal as hell. Liked to of killed us. No shade whatsoever and a heavy white haze from the alkali dust. Those animals suffered like hell. Horses haggard. Cattle crazed and bawling and moaning for water, looking like death walking with their eyes sunk deep in their sockets, tongues lolling up at the dust. Their ole ribs stuck out and their flanks all drawn up. Every now and then one would turn on you as if to fight and we knew at that point to just drop it out and leave it to its fate. At two in the morning on that third night we reached the Gap, still twelve miles from the river.

There was a cool, damp breeze that next morning and the herd could smell the water. Became crazed for it. We couldnt hardly hold em back and I was with the first half of the herd when they hauled ass rushing into the water, fillin up that river like a big ole nigger mammy in a bathtub.

Charles! Corinne leaned forward and touched his shoulder.

Oh Corinne. Hush now.

She sat back, embarrassed. Haley grinned at her through the rearview mirror, chuckling. The old man kept on.

There were half a thousand cattle blocking up the current, water halfway up the bank, and trying to drink as they swam. Took us ever bit of an hour to get em settled. There was some stragglers found an alkali pond as I was ridin back to help Loving, who'd been fightin like hell to hold the other half of the herd. I saw one after another drop in its tracks and die from that poison water.

Just then a gust of wind come up and they couldnt stand it any longer. Come a haulin straight-ass for a bend in the river where there was a cliff-side bank. Ever sorry damn cow pourin right ass over the edge and all our extra horses with em. Talk about all holy hell breakin loose. Shitload of em drowned. It just pains me no end to think about our losses that day.

The smart ones scrambling about to get their footing on the steep banks. But there was quicksand you see, and we had cows getting caught up in the muck.

We laid up for three goddamn days after that mess. Saved the ones we could. When we rode out there were still a hunnerd head bogged in the river, alive but stranded for dead. Damned pitiful. When we rode out to the north for New Mexico there were at least another several hunnerd laid out dead along the backtrail. I kept doing the math in my head. We still had some of the most terrible country a man could step foot in ahead of us. And we werent done with our losses yet for all the dropping of newborn calves. Ever mornin I give Fowler a six-shooter and he'd set out to put down the calfies that dropped overnight.

And it was just pure-ass luck to not have run into any indians on that two week stretch up to Bosque Redondo. Pope's Crossing to the west and up north across the Delaware and the Black. The Guadalupes towering over the desert floor, stronghold of the Mescaleros. We crossed back east and up by Comanche Springs and then through Bosque Grande on up to Fort Sumner. At that point there was this huge relief, each of us about to realize substantial profits for our efforts. The Navajos were starving and we were given eight cents a pound for the steers. We were elated. It felt too good to be true. In that perfect grazing country north of the fort we celebrated the Fourth of July, feasting on the best meal we'd had in a month. We sat in the shade and thought things through. What all we'd do different. Two days later Loving went north to deal our remaining stock and I headed out, with more gold than I could have ever imagined packed in my saddlebags, on the seven-hundred mile ride back to Texas.

I set out with three hands, each of us with saddle mules and provisions and trailing our fastest horses. Riding at night. I was worried the Comanche would sniff out our trail. A storm came up near the Guadalupes. Hard, hard rain. Wind, lightning. A big thunderboom scared the hell out of the mule carrying our gold and he tore ass like a streak of lightning and I took off after him. When I caught up I flung myself at him and snagged the pack rope and we wrassled like a pair of horny badgers but I got him settled. All our food was gone but the money was there. We rode on. Watered at the Pecos. Shot a few catfish. Made that long-ass ride back through the desert and then would you believe it, twenty miles from the Concho we thought we saw indians. But it was just old Rich Coffee with a wagonload of fresh watermelons and we sat in the shade of his outfit and swapped stories as we ate our fill.

We'd made about forty miles per night. All told I think it was seventeen days to Weatherford. I knew we could do it again, so I immediately began loading up for a second trip. I spent a little time with Mollie. Deposited our money, and God Almighty did word spread fast of our success. When we made it back to our range it seemed ever sumbitch with a herd of stock was scrambling to round up cows and head west. So I hired my hands again and got things in order. Took me just ten days and we were headed out again. Forty days later we arrived back at the Bosque Redondo.

August 1866. The Chisum herds were also setting out from Trickham and there were other small groups of ranchers with outfits, looking to sell Texas cattle at a premium to the government contractors at Sumner that winter. Looking for other northern markets in 1867 and 1868 and however long it might last. Not seeing a woman for a month. Losing entire herds to the damn Comanche up along the Pecos. Just us and the horses, riding mile after mile, all day every day, day after day after day. Stretches of unbelievable country. Some of the most beautiful places I've seen in my life but also some of the ugliest. We were Southerners and damn proud of it. Texans. Not a one of us scared to fight indians. Gradually we were settling the west. I grew to love those times. There is something about a man in his thirties. When you've lived enough to gain a little wisdom you develop an edge to your fearlessness. But nothing lasts forever.

No one believed the Comancheria could be settled. Like it was some mystical void, a waterless wasteland desert. Controlled supremely and ruthlessly by the indians, long before any white man stepped foot on the continent, a void within our nation that would remain impenetrable, despite the military treaties and peace policies and battles that were won. The rumors of those first explorers, the adventurers blazing those trails, consumed our thoughts and dreams. We were fascinated by the possibilities of settling those virgin lands, at all costs, despite what we might lose in the process. It was a place of unbelievable opportunity. We dared to venture into its depths. We abandoned all comforts to explore the uncharted lands named by the Spanish and others yet to be named. Cattle country and indians. East of the Sangre de Cristos running north to the valleys of the Cimarron and North Canadian rivers. Southward to the jagged, sandy steppes where the Pecos cuts into the western escarpment of the Edwards Plateau. The badlands on either side of those Staked Plains. I knew my life would center in and around those places that we would discover. All I cared about was consuming myself in this new phase of life.

The indians, the Comancheros, they also understood the opportunities before them. In those unsettled Texas ranges, untold millions of cattle. As all of us strung our herds out along the trails, the Comanche and Kiowa horse warriors swarmed down upon us with a vengeance, stealing our stock. Quanah wanted our horses but he discovered something else. He knew his path to wealth was in dealing the cattle he stole from us to the New Mexicans. Jose Tafoya and his boys knew the game, trading with Quanah and others for tens of thousands of cattle at the Quitaque. Our brands were the CV, the Circle W, the WES. Cattle. Horses. And white captives. It would take another ten years for it to all play out before it would be practical for me to slip across those invisible borders and settle that vast cow country once and for all.

Early spring 1867. We had wintered in dugouts set into the bluffs of the Pecos. Forty miles below Sumner. Me and Loving. The Patterson brothers had a camp. RL Terry, who'd been bringing the Chisum herds to share in some of our contracts. Frank Willburn. We were delivering monthly herds up to the reservation and to Santa Fe. James Foster took our remaining stock up north to summer on the Capulin Vega and we set out back for Texas.

We leave Bosque Redondo on March 28. Loving and I both dead set on making heavier drives, learning from our earlier mistakes. Just a few of our best saddle and work stock. We had an old rascal named Farrar and a fella named Willburn. RL Terry made that return trip back with us.

After our drives in '66 the indians had been lingering all up and down the Pecos. They'd stolen the Adams herds. Some of Chisum's cattle he had contracted to us. It's just hard to put into words the number of conflicts in those days.

Once we crossed back into Texas we had several close calls with small raiding parties but we were able to fend em off. Snuck out of our camp at dark to slip through Castle Gap and avoid an ambush the next morning. Suffering terribly in the desert heat that next day. You never knew what you were going to come across in the desert. We watched a long line of dust from way out and after a while we could see a large herd of cattle. Them boys, I tried to warn them. You know, you can tell a man of the danger that faces him but you caint save him from stupidity. That outfit pushed on past us along the route we'd come from and was ambushed by the Comanche at the Gap, losing their entire herd. Wagons burned. Men killed. But our outfit, luck was on our side that trip and we continued unscathed on the backtrail to the Keechi. I tell you what. Those days were wild as hell. It just never ceases to amaze me what we all went through to settle this country.

That first trip in '67 was doomed. We'd gathered our cows early that summer and headed out, and on the second night out the Comanche came ridin down at us and stampeded the herd. I found out later from Quanah that it was him and bunch of his young bucks. In his early days when he was first makin a name for himself as a warrior.

RL and I trailed the lost cattle north toward their old range on the Elm Creek Ranch. Recovered them about four hours later and turned back and brought them into camp around midnight. After conferring with Loving I laid down for some rest. Threw my buffalo robe down and collapsed into sleep. There must have been something watching over me that night. Hell, I look back on my life, the force of fate as it wove itself into things. I sure appreciate those things now. I was sleeping like a baby that night. The edge of my buffalo robe had curled up in the high grass about a foot off the ground when just at daybreak damned if those Comanche didnt come at us again. Real close call. I would have been hit for sure if it wadnt for that robe flopped up and blocking their arrows like a shield.

Then, on another night there come a big storm with the wind and rain so bad all we could see was the flash of electricity on the horses' ears. I took hold of mine's but didnt feel a thing. All that trip the cattle were so shot they'd stampede each night and run till they couldnt run no more. You talk about a trip that was cursed by the devil his ownself right from the start. We lost another couple hundred head at the Pecos. Indians all about the country.

Then it got to be late July and Loving was worried about the Santa Fe contracts due in August. He was a hard-headed old cuss at times and wouldnt listen to a damn thing I had to say. Didnt want to hear it. Or maybe I didnt do a good enough job convincing him. And that was when he and Bill Wilson set out ahead of us and came under siege on the other side of the Black River. He died at Sumner on September 25, 1867. I told myself when they set out that I ought to be the one riding out ahead to meet those contracts. I couldnt stop thinking about that when we buried him. I've always been haunted by that.

February 1868, we gather every piece of metal at Fort Sumner and solder them into a big tin casket, all shiny. We'd of course already buried Loving but we dug his ass up and put his wooden casket inside, packed it with powdered charcoal, sealed the lid and then boxed it up with new lumber. Put him in a wagon and set out to take him home, on that long, rugged journey back to Texas.

Pretty much the whole of 1868 and 1869 I was on the trail between southern New Mexico and Wyoming, the longest stay four days in Denver. We set up a headquarters at Sumner and received the Chisum herds there to be trailed further north. RL Terry oversaw the delivery of those herds.

My memories of those years, they're just flashes. Let me think. I asked Mollie to be my bride in the spring of '68? No it was '69. I was in Weatherford settling up with the Loving's. I acquired the ranch up in Colorado on the Arkansas in the winter of '69. Went back and got her and we married in Kentucky in the summer of 1870. Bless her heart. Took her on a boat to St. Louis, then by rail to Abilene, Kansas, back when it was one rough ass town. Took the stage four hundred miles across the plains to southern Colorado. Stayed at the old Drovers Hotel in Pueblo and that was when we woke up the next morning with the two Coe brothers swinging from the telegraph post out front.

RL Terry was in and out of the picture all those years. After he lost his family I did what I could to help him. Gave him the best advice I could. Loaned him money. He didnt make the first trip in '66, of course, after what happened that horrible day of the big raid near Menard. But he worked for me and Loving in those early days on the trail. Rode with me to find Loving at Sumner and was with me when we stumbled upon Wilson in the cave and rode with us in Loving's funeral cavalcade back to Weatherford. And he worked for Chisum. In fact he helped me tolerate that sonofabitch. Things got sideways once when I took RL to task over delivering us stolen stock. But he spent a lot of years around Concho, freighting and helping with the build out of the fort. Lord, I know now I should've been much more sympathetic to his cause. But I had moved on by then. I poured myself into converting that ranch up in Colorado into what I thought was Mollie and I's 'forever home'. I was done with Texas, or so I thought. That lasted six years. In the meantime RL kept on searching for his boys. He joined the Fourth Cavalry out of Concho as a scout for Mackenzie and began fighting the indians, looking for his boys all the while. Hell, he even came through Fort Sumner in the summer of '72 when he was serving as a scout for Mackenzie.

Anyhow, after we made it to Sumner in '67, when Loving was on his deathbed, word spread about the indian agent at Santa Fe. Labadi was his name. He was headed to the Panhandle with a small contingency of civilians to trade with the Comanche for captives. RL went along hoping to locate his boys. I dont think they discovered much. Years later, on another scout, he located another white captive named Rudolph Fischer. Full-ass Comanche in buckskin. Dirty, long black matted hair and dark like an indian from two years in the sun. That kid wouldnt have anything to do with him. So RL definitely knew there were captives that had assimilated as indians but despite all his troubles, somehow no signs of the Terry boys ever surfaced.

It is so damned difficult to move on with life when you have things hanging over you. The time just slips away. There are those little tidbits of memory but you find yourself wondering, where did all the details go?

My sole purpose in those days, the first half of the '70s, was to settle that range along the Arkansas. Meanwhile RL was searching for his boys, trying to move on with his life. And there was about to be a war of extermination waged upon the Comanche and Kiowa. I spent those years ditching that valley for irrigation, growing corn, an apple orchard, breeding cattle. Had all sorts of business interests in Pueblo. We were newlyweds with our whole lives ahead of us. Had all sorts of so-called 'friends' and that brought a lot of joy to Molly.

That word, 'friend.' There was a time when I'd admitted RL into the innermost chambers of my heart. But life plays out and things happen that cant be taken back. Some known, some unknown. There's always a level of randomness involved and there's that little devil of a voice that tries to convince you it aint your fault.

Corinne leans forward, intrigued but confused, taps him on the shoulder, trying to catch his eyes for meaning. Why Charles, just what exactly happened to the Terrys?

Goodnight took a big breath and fiddled with his beard, sighed and shook his head slowly. The self-indulgence of our youth, he said. Excuse me for saying that, y'all are just babies, but learn from me. Please. The temptations to structure your days around all the selfish things that drive you when you are young. On the one hand you need to eat, make a living, and there's your sense of pride. On the other side of that though is your inability to see other viewpoints, that little voice pushing you to seek instant gratification at all costs.

As we age those things soften. Or they ought to. The realities of the world start to add up. It's when we're young that we lack perspective, make mistakes, make choices that will mean things to us in the future that in that moment seem trivial. Some things turn out. But you think back and find yourself laughing. Or cringing as you think of how you handled yourself.

Back then we thought we were bulletproof. We lived in the moment. We'd never grow old. We thought we knew everything and had no regard for what it all might mean if we were lucky enough to live to be as old as I am now. We didnt study the verses.

Remember also your Creator in the days of your youth, before the evil days come and the years draw near of which you will say, 'I have no pleasure in them.'—Ecclesiastes 12:1

Somehow RL didnt catch the finer details of what transpired between Sally Johnson and me on that hot summer night in 1856 when we were celebrating the Fourth. We were on the San Saba range working cows all that summer. He pursued her, every chance he got, but boy she was the kind of gal to relish all attention.

There's youthful lust, and it can feel like love. And then there's true love. I came to learn that when Mollie Dyer stayed a few nights as a guest of my mother at the Sheek Tavern. That was later that fall when I happened to be visiting my folks in Black Springs. She had just turned seventeen. A pretty feisty young gal but mature beyond her years. I couldnt stop thinking about her. That was how RL felt about Miss Sally Johnson.

Sally Johnson. Good Lord, she was something. The power of a woman who is aware of what she can do to a man. She'd say little things. Look at you just right. Move certain ways. Whether due to some specific intention or for the sheer pleasure of it. Did it to me. Did it to others. I know she took hold of RL from the way he was acting. She was sure as hell bent on finding a man. I knew his feelings for her but I cant deny that time and again that summer she was able to draw me in like a helpless child. That was the beginning, a woman who had issues.

I began to say no to her when I met Mollie, which of course enraged her. It became heated one night and she caught me by surprise with a swipe of her nails and it drew blood. I suppose she could have had real feelings for me. But then it became a game of jealousy, which was good for RL even though he had no clue. I didnt care. He didnt know. There's not a lot of men that have savvy for the ways of a woman. They get that first little taste and begin to ignore the deeper realities. I'd not expected him to fall that deep under her spell, but I went on assuming there was something there that was meant to be. Give her credit. She eventually grew out of that phase and most definitely did not deserve what happened to her a decade later.

We went on with our lives and eventually she let it go for good and committed to RL, and I of course, spent as much time as I could courting Mollie, who was teaching school in Black Springs and then Weatherford, while also raising her brothers. We went about our business tending cows and freighting and from time-to-time there was cause for us to get together with the Terrys. Sally seemed like a different woman, although now and again I'd catch her with a distant look like she'd been struck by some poignant thought. RL and I took the oldest boy, Sam, hunting or let him tag along while we worked the range. Told him stories of the cowboys and indians. We were all doing just fine despite the hardships in those days but things took a pretty drastic turn when the war broke out and from then on it was constant chaos. Hell even more so after the war, as I've said.

We were gathering our herds early in the spring of 1866. I was making final preparations and RL had set out for Menard to gather more cows and await our arrival before we'd planned to head out on that first big drive west, taking roundance of the indian country as I mentioned earlier. Five days later when I rode into the San Saba range the entire country was afire. Ranch houses engulfed in flames. Indians everwhere. The Terry home had been raided, both boys hauled off with some of the other women and children.

I rode up and saw RL and Sally out in the field on the ground behind his downed horse. Out in front of the Small house. The whooping and yapping of those damned indians. Arrows whistling. Evidently RL had hit one of them as there was a buck brave that had buckled over injured from his mount and they were scurrying about in a frenzy.

I tore off toward em firing my pistol as they regrouped. Sally looked dead to me when I rode upon them. Pregnant, scalped and bloodied, an arrow sticking out of her. There were more riders appearing from the hills and I sat my horse in front of the Terrys and held off their charges as RL dragged her into the house. And that's what was in the cards for Mrs Sally Terry. She hung on a little into the night and died in RL's arms. We buried her the next morning before setting out to track the indians and save RL's boys.

I can still picture RL and Sally. And Sam. What joy they must have felt when he was born? He was a beautiful baby boy. It's funny how life can change so abruptly. A helpless infant transforms into a toddler and then the amazing innocence and curiosity of a little boy, dreaming, asking questions about ever little thing and then like that, overnight, they're on the cusp of being a young man.

A month before the Terry boys were taken, Sam was with us in Weatherford getting provisions. He was always helpful. His face was full of wonder and he was completely enamored with our coming adventures. I can still clearly picture this one look he had when he'd crinkle up his brows in concentration as he became consumed by whatever task was at hand. It made me think of how I was when I was a boy.

Over the years, and even more so now, I've found myself trying to answer why it had to play out that way. Life takes you in one direction and then that path is gone in a flash. Those boys didnt have no say in it. RL having to live with all that hanging over him. Common, hardworking man. Living and thinking and dreaming. I was, perhaps, a harder man then in those times, my thought bein it was all such a damn shame but there was nothing to do but move on. I was generally one to subdue emotion at all cost. I thought it best to move forward, keep my focus on the bigger picture.

But I had it all wrong. I should've been impacted differently. I should've done more. I helped RL put her in the ground and then we shoveled up the dirt and the rocks and piled the soil of the earth on top of her, and as much as I hate to say it, all the while I was thinking about my herds and the need to get on with taking them to market.

You give me five days and I'll gather a herd. Assemble the outfit and I will lead them from range to market, turn it over intact. Indians, outlaws, storms, floods, the lack of grass or water. There will always be trail trouble. I could ride without sleep from Bosque Grande due north across the Arkansas, through the divide to the Platte, swim the herd at Cow Creek and drive them on to Cheyenne. Then turn back through all of Colorado and down through New Mexico and do it all over again. That's the way it was for us cow people in those days. And Haley, I'll tell you what, I've been thinking about something. I've been meaning to tell you this. Now I sure appreciate everthing you're doing. More than you'll ever know. But I think I've a mind for the way you're thinking and I for damn sure dont want you to put it in the record that I was the first one on that trail.

There are records of at least two herds totaling 3,200 steers in the fall of 1865, known to be led by Robert K. Wylie and George T. Reynolds, on behalf of James Patterson, beef contractor at Fort Sumner, New Mexico…

Haley, it truly warms my heart to know that we have young men like you in our younger generations, others who have the interest and passion to put something down for the record about all of those incredible years. But as I said, the finer details of our memories can hardly ever be recalled. There are always those underlying secrets that, so far as the record goes, are lost forever.

That one night. In the humid heat of a late summer evening in Texas. You know how the big oaks come alive in that beautiful, mysterious symphony? It'll be silent and then the cicadas start to vibrate their tymbals and it becomes that bizarre, deafening chorus. I'll never forget that night. I had had all I could stand and our voices arose in the frustration and anger of departing lovers. Sally said things to me that I didnt think she had the capacity to say. I saw something inside of her I'd never seen, feelings that she did not seem capable of having. But I knew where my heart was. She had tears in her eyes. She grabbed my arm and placed a sealed envelope in my hand. *I ask only one thing. Just read this, please.* I took it and walked away.

11

— ★ —

Searching

Fall, 1869

RL Terry had been scouting the indian trails west and north of Fort Concho. He sat his horse at the junction of the Rio Conchos watching the pecans and the scattered mesquites and the tall dry grass prairie sway gently with the breeze. All to the south the prairie had been burned bare from recent grass fires. A dozen mallard flapped up from the water and whistled away and he stepped the horse along the course of the stream and eased his way into the dusty and sunbaked main street of Saint Angela.

Two large dogs came barking out to greet him but otherwise the village was lonesome and silent in the ice blue burnish of the flawless sky. Piles of broken lumber and trash and the ragged dugouts of the wayward settlers. The crisp clipclop of hooves in the hissing wind and now the soothing sounds of a banjo tune and laughter wafting faintly from the shanties and saloons.

Across the river at the newly formed post he dismounted and walked among the motley civilian crew of workmen. The German stonemasons directed the placement of soapstone blocks and hammered precisely at the heavy bricks into the forms of their artistic eye. Their countrymen—wood-cutters, lime-burners, saddlers, and the like mingled about on the grounds and cussed at one another in their heavy german tongue. The build out of the fort also relied upon a large regiment of black soldiers. The men worked tirelessly in the heat to the rhythm of their works songs as they lugged wheelbarrows of wet river sand and puddled the mud into molds of drying adobe bricks. Their soulful field hollers rising and falling into falsetto and urged on with shouts and affirmations all the better to feel the spirit, pass the time, or subtly insult the tempestuous Irish muleskinners that transported the hay and corn and timber across the grounds.

RL sauntered stiffly through this bustling construction site leading his horse and packmule toward the water wagons. The post surgeon had completed his morning rounds and RL watched him walking toward the only finished ward of the hospital building. Three days prior at Permanent Camp a wily old mule had bitten off the nip of RL's left middle finger and with it turning black from infection he was thinking about getting it attended to. Nearby a tent service had recently adjourned and when the chaplain recognized RL he eagerly approached him, holy book in hand.

Good morning Mr Terry. You just arrive back in town?

RL nodded. Mornin preacher, he said.

Well, I've been thinking about you.

Now that's awful nice of ya.

Yes. There's been more and more of talk of the reservation indians.

RL looked past him toward the center of the parade grounds. What sort of talk? he said.

Why, seems like every day I hear rumors of the white children they hold captive.

Yes.

You get any leads about your boys on your trip?

No sir.

Well, I'm awful sorry. But God willing, it's bound to eventually happen.

RL was looking back and forth impatiently at the chaplain and the other activities about the post. Tell me, he said, what's brewing over there at the adjutant's office?

Haven't you heard? It's Colonel Mackenzie. He arrived here a few days ago and everyone's on edge about his inspection.

RL cocked his eye and surveyed a group of military men assembling around the office. The chaplain was opening his bible and he started to say something but RL said excuse me and patted him on the shoulder and stepped around him and walked on.

A bell had been rung to alarm the post of the noontime mess hall where there was a big buffet lined out and attended to by the cooks. The meal consisted of platters of fresh game, potatoes, hominy, and bean soup. The troopers shuffled along silently with plates held out for equal rations. RL eased his way to the back to take his place in line but then he noticed the man he'd been looking for and set out to greet him.

The commander of the post was a man from Illinois named Gamble. He seemed a ball of nerves directing activities, the soldiers hauling wood and supplies and going about their various fatigue duties looking as busy as possible in order to impress Mackenzie and his men. His first lieutenant stood beside him taking notes. When at first RL approached they ignored him but he placed himself directly in front of Gamble and held out his hand and said hello. The captain sighed in irritation but shook his hand. Mr Terry, as you can see, we are extremely busy.

RL persisted until the captain felt compelled to have his assistant talk further with him and after he and RL stepped aside for a short exchange he waved Gamble back over for another council and then they set out across the grounds toward the officer's quarters, RL passionately gesturing with his hands and talking and the military men listening with great interest.

They walked down a long row of newly built stone buildings under a covered porch of milled juniper that gave relief from the sun. RL continued talking as they approached the adjutant's office, their boots clacking across the stone slab floors. The lieutenant opened the door without knocking and stood aside, first for the captain and then RL next behind. The men in the room stopped talking and looked up. Behind a large mesquite table surrounded by a handful of standing officers sat Ranald Slidell Mackenzie, Colonel of the 41st United States Infantry.

Captain Gamble, he said. Please tell me you have sufficient cause to interrupt us.

Well, yes sir. I need to introduce you to this man right here. I believe you'll want to hear what he has to say.

Is that so?

Yes sir. It seems he has information of the Rio Grande Hispanics who've been trading with the indians.

The Comancheros? Mackenzie narrowed his eyes and studied them.

Yes sir, said the captain. Seems to be very legitimate intel.

The colonel sighed, closed his eyes, slowly shook his head. With a slow sweep of his hand he reluctantly waved them in.

It better be, he said.

Two days later RL with four of the Fourth Calvary's best soldiers set out for the landmark known as Mushaway Peak at the head of the Colorado to search for the Comanchero traders. They each had an extra packmule with ten days' provisions and the cavalrymen were dressed as civilians, appearing more like horse thieves or foreigners on the lam from the law in order to avoid drawing the ire of the indians. For the purposes of buying back his boys RL had procured a magnificent paint horse to use in barter and in his packsaddle was a wide variety of items the indians might also consider in trade, as well as three hundred dollars in gold and silver coins, his shares of the most recent Chisum herd he'd delivered to Bosque Redondo.

They ventured to the foot of the Caprock in four days without incident and ascended the headwater valleys of the Colorado until they came upon a ledge with a distant view five hundred yards out of a Hispano encampment spread out in the shade of a massive pecan tree.

They could see a rafter of turkeys with their heads down pecking and scratching in the dirt. No other animals were grazing. There also appeared to be an assortment of lean-tos constructed of poles and animal hides but there was no one about. Then RL noticed something. He pulled up his field glasses and watched for a long time. Nothing moved. The riders dismounted and let the horses out to graze and then watched some more. RL left three of the men on watch and he and a soldier named Melville snuck into the camp as silent as if they were stalking game.

The sleeping man was sprawled back against the tree with an empty jug of aguardiente laying at his side. Trash everywhere. He was snoring. He was a deep coffee brown and dirty with a reeking stench of sweat and alcohol and other things and he was barechested and wore a pair of baggy breeches to the knee, shredded stockings, moccasin boots. There was a Spiller and Burr .36 caliber revolver laying on a leather bag by his left hand. RL carefully picked it up and released the cylinder. He stood and unloaded the bullets and placed them in his pocket and then he placed the pistol back near the man's hand. He took his hat off. There was a light breeze and it felt cool in the shade. He turned and surveyed the camp for signs of life. Just a songbird. He thought about his options.

When he knelt down and nudged the man to wake him he called him amigo. The man shrieked, jerked madly and bug-eyed out of his slumber as if from a bad dream, and as he did so he instinctively grabbed the gun at his side and drew it and cocked it and pointed it at RL. Cabrón, he said. His eyes were wide open. Black. Bloodshot sclera.

RL raised his hands innocently. Esta bien mi amigo, he said. The Mexican smiled wide. Big teeth stained brown with gaps. Si, esta bien, he said. Then he squeezed the trigger but when it just clicked his eyes softened like an innocent child. RL slowly shook his head. He took a deep breath and exhaled slowly through his nose. He reached to his holster and drew his gun and put the muzzle against the man's forehead and cocked it. He raised his eyebrows and tilted his head. Cuál es tu nombre? he said.

The Comanchero was a man named Polonio Ortiz who had been left in that place for the purpose of receiving a Quahadi raiding party delivering a herd of horses and cattle from the settlements. Now he'd been mounted on a large black mule with his hands bound in rawhide and made to come to terms with the fact that he would guide the searchers further into the eastern edge of the Staked Plains in search of the camp of the Kotsoteka chief known as Mow-way.

That evening by the fire he was released from his binds. By now the hostage had sobered up and as he slurped up a plate of beans he thanked them for sparing his life. RL said that it wasnt necessarily so. Ortiz appealed to him that he knew the indians well. He told them about the good roads with plenty of water that stretched all the way east across the Llanos. He drew maps in the sand with his finger and he spoke in detail of the routes and places of trade with the indians, enriching his tales with specific adventures of their commerce. Sí, sí. Yo se de los cautivos, he boasted. Mucho. Puedo ayudarle.

He studied the searchers through the firelight. RL rubbed his chin and squinted in deep consideration. Ortiz flubbed through his pockets for a small cigarillo and leaned to the fire to light it. The other men were kicking the dirt and generally lingering about casually but they kept a close watch on him.

Necesitas caballos, he said. He sucked on the cigarillo. Y mucho dinero.

RL sat quietly, slowly inserting bullets into his pistol. He wanted to see what was said next. Ortiz then reached in his shirt pocket and handed up a mangled piece of paper signed by a United States government indian agent.

Es no prollem, he said. Tengo papeles.

Papeles?

You know, how you say, pay… pay… papers. He spat and ran his filthy fingers back into the rear of his mouth to dig for a chunk of meat, nodding, and when he'd pulled it out he flicked it on the ground and looked at them and smiled.

RL studied the paper. Ortiz was smacking his lip now and nodding as if to assure him.

Sí, es okay my fren, he said. You have monies. You have caballos. Es posible we can get los cautivos.

When Ortiz fell asleep that night the searchers took turns on watch but he had no notions of escape. The night was clear and the stars were sparkling. After midnight a gibbous moon and Aldebaran rose in the east and RL watched them climb upward and soon it became too bright to sleep.

In the morning the sun fired the vermilion cliffs of the Caprock with a hot and glorious glow and they skirted the base of the escarpment's sheer walls following trails that Ortiz knew like the back of his hand. He led them deeper into the recesses of the sprawling canyon country and in the afternoon they began to pass through abandoned campsites, recent signs of cookfires and refuse spread along sheltered ledges. There were indian scouts at vantage points on the horizon watching over the prairie and Ortiz raised a friendly hand in greeting as they passed.

It was warm and the canyonlands glittered in the sun. They were moving north all that day and Ortiz watched for smoke but there was none and at dusk they came upon a narrow cut in a canyon wall where the air was cool and the trail fed to a trickling spring bubbling from the base of the cliffs. Here they dismounted and watered the animals and made camp.

The next morning Ortiz ascended a bluff that offered a better view of the country before them. RL watched him. He pulled a signal mirror from a beaded buckskin pouch around his neck and raised it overhead. Then he turned the glass in a measured pattern to flash the sun and then he sat his horse and looked out over the booming void and awaited a response. Then he did this again and after a while he looked back and waved the Americans on and when they arrived they could see a delegation of mounted indians riding to greet them.

They were an advance guard of Penatakas, six, eight of them. They were splendidly mounted and well-armed with rifles and revolvers, perhaps procured from Ortiz himself, and as they looked the riders over the trader uttered an introduction in comanche and then he turned and spat and looked back at RL and his escorts. The white men sat their horses abreast of one another and said nothing, rifles to their knees. The scouts sized them up. They were young men with long black hair braided to the waist and they had wary eyes and conferred with one another in low voices. Ortiz spoke to them in their language again.

They looked from one to the other and then one of them spoke.

Son Tejanos?

No. No son Tejanos, said Ortiz. The scouts looked the soldiers up and down, nodding skeptically. Then Ortiz nudged the searchers forward and walked the horse up beside them and they rode on to the north with the indians following closely to the rear.

Later that morning they came upon another contingent of horsemen and after a short council one of them turned to the east and raised a fragment of broken mirror wrapped with leather and angled it to the sun. All of the riders looked out, waiting, as far as they could see. Soon a return flash of light reflected on the horizon and then they all rode on and before long yet another group of mounted scouts appeared and after a short council Ortiz was granted permission to chaperon his contingency into the main camp of the Kotsotekas.

They rode into the camp at Cañón del Rescate, a slur of scrabbled crevasses lined with yellowing cottonwoods and juniper and sheltering a migrant assemblage of plains indians and Hispano traders. It was late in the day and above the Caprock rims the sky had grown dark. A warm southern wind and the smell of rain. A yellow pall of dust came over the village with a flash of sunlight and a handful of barking dogs announced their arrival. A string of packmules were being loaded with trade wares and a group of men were scurrying to cover and load several pounds of lead and powder ahead of the storm. Ortiz stood up on his mount to scan the premises and whistled loudly and soon another Mexican came walking over talking in slang.

They dismounted and greeted one another. Ortiz presented his associate formally and the searchers each in turn nodded and shook his hand, the man introducing himself by stating his full name slowly in a beautiful spanish accent. Jose. Piedad. Tafoya, he said. He was filthy and in the early stages of drink. Despite the heat he was wearing a utilitarian serape handwoven with intricate, Navajo designs and he smelled bad and was sweating profusely. He took off his sombrero and wiped his forehead. He spoke very rapidly, a slurred spanish of slang and epithets and when he was done he looked at them waiting for a response. The searchers stared back blankly. Como? he said. He raised his brow. Ortiz said something and nodded over to RL's saddlebags and as he spoke Tafoya squinched his eyes and pursed his lips out and began to nod slowly as if he'd been made to understand something important. He thought it through. Then he smacked a louse from the side of his head and plicked it betwixt his teeth as if he was nibbling on a chunk of pinole. He waved them on and turned. Pasale, he said.

He led them along the edge of the camp and they set the animals out to graze. A crack of lightning struck the mesa top and a rumble of thunder echoed down the canyon. Big, cold drops of rain began to fall sporadically. Here they were directed to a line of crude dugout shelters that appeared to be abandoned and once they were settled Tafoya escorted them to the entrance of an oversized lodge. He motioned for them to wait outside as he turned back the hide flap that concealed the interior and stepped inside.

Wafts of smoke emanated from the opening. A voice slurred out drunkenly and there was laughter. Just then another big gust of wind blew through the canyon and dollops of rain plunked the earth. Then it began to pour from the sky in sheets, blowing sideways. Large claps of thunder. Specks of hail peppered the searchers and they pulled their hats down low and hunkered. After a few minutes Tafoya reappeared and called for them and they stepped inside dripping, wiping their eyes and adjusting to the dim, smoke-hazed light.

The indians were seated around a small fire and others, perhaps servants, were barely visible behind them in the edge of the firelight. They were passing a long, thin pipe inlaid with pewter and they surveyed the white men and nodded and gestured for them to take seats. They'd entertained such searchers on many occasions and aside from any fiscal benefit they stood to gain, the simple diversion of their visit was satisfaction enough.

Tafoya said something in comanche and the indians looked at the white men and then RL spoke up. Appreciate you havin us, he said. They just looked at him.

Ortiz translated and the banter would have continued but the storm outside intensified. It was difficult to hear with the roar of the rain and the howling wind tested the lodgepole construction and when the smoke-flap became compromised water dripped down upon the smoldering coals. Smoke hissing. The men began to shuffle up off the sheepskin hides and they were muttering under their breaths, who knows what, and they gathered themselves, looking up cursedly to the roof of the tipi and glancing about uncomfortably at one another, inconvenienced, and listened to the wind moan, the deep rumbles of thunder over the canyons and the rain pelting the temporary hide shelter. They all stood there together, awkwardly, and listened to the storm. After a while it passed and they made their way outside.

Now RL was able to get a better look at them. The western sun had dropped below the clouds and shimmered the canyon in a golden yellow light. He knew which man was in charge from the way he carried himself and this man they called Mow-way that they had been looking for was admiring the sky and listening to the sounds of the waterfalls up in the rimrocks. He smiled to himself. He was heavyset and shirtless with a round chest and large, soft, middle-aged arms and he wore a tattered breechclout that was dressed up around the waist by a thick belt adorned in elk teeth that he'd procured from a Blackteeth ceremonial in his travels as a young man. Beside him barely to his shoulders stood a red-eyed Mescalero scout named Domingo whose face was painted with white circular designs and he, more so than the others, carried a sullen countenance toward the Americans. Aside from the handful of drunken chieftans that issued themselves from the tent was an older, distinguished looking Kiowa called Woman's Heart in his people's language, who upon taking a chill from the damp breeze proceeded to unfold a long robe made of lobo skin lined in red flannel and in a deliberate and dignified manner unfurl it and wrap it about his shoulders, taking care to brush down the human scalps that lined each side. The indians seemed fully satisfied there, inhaling deeply the heavy smell of wet juniper and settling themselves in the cooler air and the evening light.

The searchers wiped the mud from their boots in a patch of grass and RL called to Tafoya.

Que pasa con ellos? he said.

Not a one of the indians even acknowledged the white men at all save for the Apache and he was discrete in his observations, considering perhaps the satchel of coins nestled in RL's hands. He said something to Tafoya.

RL weighed the man's tone, a hint of a question that might have shed some insight into his thoughts. He leaned to Tafoya. Listen Jose, he said. You need to tell the little man he best stop eyein me.

The Apache sensed that RL was uneasy and at this he grinned wryly and stepped forward toward him. He reached and tapped the leather sheath that held RL's bowieknife and pulled back again. Cuchillo, he said. Cuchillo grande.

RL eyed him.

RL's escorts held their hands at their holsters.

Me gusta tu cuchillo, the man said.

It aint for sale.

When Ortiz stepped between them to intervene the Apache drew a pistol of his own and cocked it and pointed it at the face of the Hispano trader. Ortiz lifted his eyebrows and stepped back and raised his hands innocently but as the Apache let down the pistol he turned back and found himself staring into the barrels of RL's huge sidearm.

RL grinned and spat in the dirt. The others watched in silence. Then he lowered the pistol and placed it in his holster and nodded toward the larger chief. He called out to Tafoya.

Introducciones. Jose, how about we get back to some introducciones.

Tafoya smiled nervously and took off his sombrero. Sí, sí, he said. Sí, por supuesto.

Now the leader was stepping forward to put the Apache at ease and accept the formal acquaintances. He nodded at RL and placed his hand out awkwardly and Tafoya confirmed to RL the man's name and importance. RL reached out to firmly shake Mow-way's hand but when he grasped the large palm its limpness startled him. RL Terry, he said looking into his dark eyes. Then Tafoya began more lengthy introductions in comanche with a touch of spanish sprinkled in. When he was finished Mow-way rubbed his chin and nodded his considerations. The collective audience stood about in the dying sunlight listening with great attention, nodding. The big chief was rubbing his chin and sizing up the searcher.

El es Tejano, he said.

RL spoke up. Nope, he said. I'm from up there in them mountains.

Mow-way looked him up and down.

RL spat and looked the chief square in the eyes and in a slow, southern, and poorly accented twang he said, Cerca… de las… montañas.

Mow-way's eyes narrowed.

Colorado, said RL.

Mow-way glanced over the escorts and he seemed to roll his eyes before surveying his collective audience and when he turned back to RL he began to speak in in a slow staccato monotone. A deep, distinguished Comanche voice highlighted beautifully with emphatic utterances issued perhaps to better accentuate various key points. He detailed for the searchers some of the recent troubles of his people, his fist clenched and pounding the air in frustration over the lies of the Great Father, things said at the Medicine Lodge council that were, as Ortiz translated it, *no too much sweet like thee azucars but beeter like thee gourd*. He made clear his utter disdain for the encroachment of the Texans and he spoke of the blue coats, who in the previous winter had employed converging columns of cavalry along the Canadian River in an attempt to run him and all of his people to the ends of the earth. He'd been to the military fort in peace but was arrested, incarcerated, then shipped under guard to the reservation where a bald-headed white chief handed out gifts and meager rations of food and preached senselessly to him to pursue a sedentary life of farming and all the while pushing him to encourage his people to release their white captives. Tafoya translated all of this efficiently and with great objectivity and when he finished he stood at attention, sweating, his eyes shifting back and forth anxiously between the two men.

There was an uncomfortable silence but RL pulled something shiny from his vest pocket and stepped forward and respectfully handed it up to the big Comanche. Here, I'd like you to have this, he said.

Mow-way carefully examined the device, listening to the Mexican's translation and gently fingering its smooth texture. In his hands he held a 16s three-quarter plate State Street model pocket watch. It was gold-plated and had been meant as a wedding gift to RL from John Chisum and it featured steel parts and glistened beautifully in the last of the evening light. This timepiece was the seventy-fourth manufactured by the New York Watch Company out of Springfield, Massachusetts and there were less than three hundred in production. Mow-way was turning the watch over and over and he gently opened it up and placed it to his ear to listen to it ticking. His lieutenants began to gather around. RL studied his reaction and then Mow-way's wide mouth broke into a smile and his narrow eyes opened brightly in his pleasure.

Oh que hermosa es! said Tafoya. Someone let out a whistle. The surrounding indians softly whispered judgements to themselves or one another. Mow-way raised his hand to quiet the murmurs. RL reached out with his hand, asking for the watch and letting his eyes talk with an air of reverence and surprise. Mow-way handed it back.

Now look here, said RL.

He cradled it solemnly and wound it so that the minute hand was just right. He held it out, gesturing at the watch as a thing of life and then pointing at himself enthusiastically and also up toward the heavens. His audience looked up. Pink glow of a summer evening, dark storm clouds now looming to the south, a fierce flash of lightning followed by a long roll of ominous thunder. When the alarm sounded the chief jumped back and a great roar of surprise rang out and there was a smattering of whoops and hollers that died to a murmur of wonder and as all fell quiet, stunned by the enchanting spectacle, the alarm fell silent and a woman somewhere out beyond the fringes of the congregation who had thus far not had any part of the mystifying proceedings began to sing and chant in the way of a healer.

Mow-way nodded his head briskly, squinting respectfully in a sort of frown-smile and reaching out to take back possession of the watch. He turned to the interpreter and conferred orders and he and Tafoya walked to where a pile of canvas duffels had been spread out for display and Tafoya rummaged through the provisions and made clear they were intended as presents for the chief. They began to examine the goods. RL approached them with an armful of gifts and he urged Tafoya to communicate that in consideration of his goodwill he expected delivery of any captives being held in their camp.

Mow-way smiled. He looked at his men and then turned back to RL, sizing him up with those large, wise eyes. Then he presented his hand to RL and gave his compliments to the interpreter and waved them on toward his lodge to continue the proceedings.

Earlier that year Mow-way had been turned over to the new indian agent at Fort Sill as part of his incarceration. During his short stay he and the agent, a peaceful Quaker, had developed a mutually beneficial relationship. Their partnership involved the chief as a liaison to the various indian bands both inside and outside of the reservation and in consideration of this his comfort in residence and eventual release was assured in addition to an abundance of annuity goods being made available for him and his tribesmen. However, the agent also demanded details of any captives being held among the plains indians and while Mow-way was accommodating, they eventually fell into dispute over his refusal to deliver them to the agency.

Now in his lodge around the fire he and RL and the interpreter along with his most trusted chiefs finished their meals and Mow-way detailed for RL the stories of several white captives who had assimilated into their tribe. He told him flat out he was wasting his time. RL listened patiently. He claimed that anything could be had for a price. Mow-way told him that while true, based on what he'd seen it was simply not enough. RL spoke highly of the merits of the paint horse they'd brought in trade. At this one of the subchiefs spoke up. He asked Mow-way to consider allowing the visitors to at least talk with one of the captives in their camp. Mow-way nodded in agreement and then elaborated at length. Tafoya translated each point and nuance perfectly and when RL and his escorts walked across the village to settle in for the evening they had the chief's concession to make a captive available for council the following day. That night RL's mind was racing as he lay down to sleep and he must have felt some sense of hope yet he knew if he allowed himself to desire something too strongly he would invite the chance that his prayers would not be answered.

In the morning he was taken to a tent at the edge of camp where a long slice of horseflesh hung on a stick over a smoldering fire just outside the open hide door. He stepped inside and sat on a folded buffalo robe watching outside where the meat sizzled in the morning sun. No one explained who he would meet in that place. He sat there alone for a long time waiting but his only visitor was a woman that passed by to tend the meat. He listened to the noises outside and reflected upon his circumstances.

As he waited he began to whisper thoughts to himself quietly in rehearsal, thinking of his boys and fighting his emotions under the weight of all that he had been through. Within the hour he looked up and found a strapping young man at the door, the stick of horsemeat in hand, peeking inside curiously. He wore buckskin and emanated the stench of a wild animal. His muscles bulged from his outfit and from his waist dangled a sheath that held an Alibates flint knife and he also carried an urn of bark filled with kiln-dried corn that had been boiled and mashed. He handed the bowl of mush to RL and drove the stick of meat into the dirt and spoke an awkward, broken german-english greeting.

Haa… llo, he said.

RL stood up to greet him. Hello son. They looked at one another. Then RL gestured toward the robes on the ground and handed him back the bowl and they took their seats.

What's your name?

The young man didnt answer. He took out his knife and sliced off a thin chunk of meat.

Did they explain to you why I was here?

He tilted his head and his eyes seemed to show some recognition. A slight smile. He reached for the bowl and with the meat betwixt his fingers scooped up a helping of the corn. His mouth was full and he spoke as he was chewing hard on the meat. Asewaynah, he said.

Excuse me, son?

He gestured at his chest, corn and grease dripping from his hands. Name, Asewaynah.

I see, said RL. Ase. Way. Nah. He enunciated it back slowly as he had heard it but it came out awkwardly. He was studying him. In his mind he had envisioned a boy as a slave to the savages but this was no boy. He had long black hair and his complexion was dark from the soil and sun and there may have been slight signs of Christianity in his eyes if you caught an expression just right but he looked just like any other untamed teenage Comanche warrior.

Can you understand me, son?

The kid nodded. RL cut off a slice of the meat and dipped it in the bowl and commenced chewing. Son, what is your Christian name?

The kid eyed RL as he gnawed at the meat and then he looked away out into his distant past searching his memories and then RL asked him again.

Your name. What is your name?

He whispered awkwardly. Roo… Roo… dolph.

What was that? He noticed the german accent.

Roo… dolph. He said it slow, a little louder. Deep, strong voice.

RL just sat there. It took him awhile to respond.

Well I'll be damned. Rudolph. Rudolph Fischer. Why, your Gottlieb Fischer's boy.

The kid's eyes perked up. He looked at RL, studying him. This had caught him off guard but he thought for a moment and then nodded slowly.

The Fischer kid put the bowl to his face and slurped up the last of the corn and then he set it down and licked his fingers and wiped them on his roughhide shirt. RL leaned forward and spoke to him quietly but he wasnt sure if the kid could understand him. Excuse me, he said. I'll be right back.

He raised up and stepped outside into the sun and in a few minutes he returned with Tafoya, the better to facilitate the dialogue.

RL could tell that Rudolph Fischer and the Comanchero trader knew one another. He spoke at length, slowly and with much passion, making signs with his hands and miming out certain things to make himself understood. He told him that he worked for important people who had commissioned him to procure the release of young men like him and that he understood and was sorry for all the hardships he had been through and could help him, that he had met his father and that his true family missed him and loved him very much. He told him that he would surely die in this place and that he would not leave him for the bluecoats would wage war to the death and the people he lived with must succumb to the ways of the white man or be wiped from the face of the earth forever.

When RL was finished he sat back and took a breath. He studied the kid's indifferent face as Tafoya translated his message and when he was done Rudolph Fischer chuckled. Then he and the translator each broke into laughter as RL looked on.

You get that? RL studied the facial expressions and the tone of his voice as Fischer responded flatly and with ease in the Comanche tongue.

He looked at Tafoya. What did he say?

Tafoya sighed, looking upward, sheepishly. He was thinking about what and how to say it but he kept quiet.

Tell me what he said.

He say… He say you go, a casa.

What?

He say for you to go a casa.

A casa? Home?

Sí.

What for?

Porque heese Comanche padre and the other chiefs are there now, stealing mas caballos. Mas cautivos.

Fischer sat across from him gauging the dialogue, smirking.

What else? Qué mas?

He say he run from heese casa when los Comanches locay him. Now tres años con los Comanche. And, he has dos… He held up two fingers. Como se dice, esposas, in espanol?

Wife.

Sí. He has dos wifes. RL strained his eyes the better to see his indifferent face in the darker light of the tipi. This boy's full of it, he said to himself.

Oh, señor, said Tafoya. And he no want your help.

Does not want my help.

Tafoya was smiling. He say… you go a casa. He say… to grow mas caballos for heem to steal.

Hay otros cautivos?

This time Fischer responded. Sí, sí mucho, he said. His voice was deeper, as if to flaunt the news of their captive population. The spanish accent was beautiful.

RL guarded his heart. He took an old, crinkled photo from his vest pocket and looked at it and handed it over to Rudolph Fischer. It was a grainy, studio portrait of Sam and Charlie Terry taken in Fort Worth three months before they were abducted.

You recognize them boys there?

Fischer took the photo, studying it carefully.

Jose, ask him if he recognizes them boys there.

Tafoya did not understand. Como?

Conoces a esos… come se dice, boys.

Boys? Ah… chicos, he said. Sí, sí. Chicos. Then he asked Fischer if he knew of them.

Fischer held the photo as if it were a spirit and he looked at the brothers he'd first seen in the Kiowa camp on the breaks of the Canadian River almost two years prior to the very day. Then he looked up at Tafoya and then at RL and he tilted his head back and tightened his lips and crinkled his nose and began slowly shaking his head from side to side.

12

— ★ —

Moving On

When they rode out of the Kotsoteka camp it was first light. The changing leaves of the willows and soapberries and the snakeweed flowers in the slopes suffused the plains in an electric, yellowed haze and behind them atop the Caprock a norther was blowing in from the arctic like the devil's breath on ice.

Over the course of his councils RL had learned the Kiowas and Comanches were holding countless numbers of captives. He also sensed how quickly they became assimilated. He rode and stared long out over the big country before him. The sun rose alongside him but he was consumed by the darkness. Time had moved on, so much changed. The Terry boys dead or indianized. He rode on in silence watching the skies and if he sensed God he did not feel compelled to pray. He might live to look into the eyes of his boys again but his failures as a man were complete and no matter what was to follow he could not take any of it back.

They returned to Concho at noon of the third day and sat their horses atop a mesa that looked down at the fort, the lines of canvas tent quarters, the delta of prairie grasses and mesquite surrounded on all sides by the sparkling Concho rivers, the roads lined with german ox and mule trains and the surrounding fields of hay camps and the partially-built stone chimneys and the cistern and the voices of the government teamsters and negro soldiers echoing up the river valleys.

On the outskirts of the fort they came across a series of corrals holding herds of horses stricken by the epizootic. The hostlers worked in small teams among the weakened animals carefully studying for sign and moving the deathly into separate pens. Wheezing and whining incessantly, their eyes bulged strangely and the more pathetic victims emanated a foul smell from the enlarged ulcers that festered in their mouths.

About the bustling parade grounds was a motley collection of frontier society defying any description. Scots, Germans, Irishmen. Veterans of the war. Negro soldiers and laundresses and cooks. Mexicans hauling rock and masons and large crews of men sawing timber. Lime burners and saddlers. Tinners and carpenters and cowboys. The sun was high and warm and a light breeze blew up from the course of the surrounding streams. Everyone seemed to be out. The post surgeon, the chaplain, the tailor. Even the lawyer.

RL dismounted and thanked his escorts and handed them each a handful of gold coins in appreciation of their efforts and they sidled off to their ragged tent quarters to recover from their journey. He watched the mail carriages and westbound emigrants following their military escorts toward the Butterfield road and he walked across the plaza observing them. The week prior Comanche raiders intercepted the stage near Johnson's Station and killed and scalped the driver and set the carriage afire. The postmaster had been fastening the straps of the dispatch boxes and detailing important protocols and warnings and he wiped his brow and took a deep breath when he was done.

RL stepped forward. This stage headin west? he said.

Yes sir.

RL studied the horses.

When's the next one goin east?

Day after tomorrow.

He looked across the parade grounds. Where can a fella sit down and write some letters? he said.

Right yonder.

RL followed the man's gesture and scanned the garrison. The man was making notes on a bill of receipts and he spat in the dirt and told RL to look for a man named McCarthy who'd have everything he'd need.

He led his horse across the plaza along a line of pens and the slaughter corral. Here the assistant quartermaster, ever authoritative and diligent, surveyed the activity and barked orders at the soldiers who were working the beeves. Suddenly a gun fired and a cow bawled and a one hundred pound English bulldog sprang up savagely from out of nowhere and latched onto the muzzle of the wounded steer. RL stopped to watch. The handlers shouted encouragements and in a fit of slobber and flesh and blood the growling dog pulled the stunned animal down to the dirt where it gave a last desperate bawl and died. The soldiers cheered and went about dragging the beast over to the skinners. One of them threw a chunk of meat to the dog. RL shook his head and turned and walked on with the horse following.

When he entered the mailroom McCarthy wasnt there. He sat down at an open desk and opened a drawer and pulled out several pieces of paper. He placed them upright gently in his hands, stacked them perfectly and placed them on the desk before him. From another drawer he took a steel-nib dip pen and wet the tip with his tongue and shook it until he felt like it was in working order. He tried to write but he could not. He told himself that if he could just get the first sentence down the words would flow on from there. Then he hunched his shoulders up with a big breath and slowly exhaled and put the pen to paper and began to scribble out the first letter in a cryptic cowboy cursive jumbled with print.

The first letter he wrote was addressed to the newly appointed indian agent at Fort Sill. He detailed the location of the Kotsoteka camp where he encountered Rudolph Fischer and he described the details of his visit. He wrote how the boy did not seem a victim, was in fact fully indianized and now the perfect image of a savage Comanche warrior, completely content, generally irreverent, with an utterly confident gleam in his eye that defied all reasonable logic and that he had even claimed multiple wives and when told that he could be returned to his family he snickered and looked back with stone cold eyes. RL wrote that the Plains tribes were holding countless numbers of white captives who assimilated into their culture and it was of the utmost importance to recover them, else their precious souls would be lost to those savage ways of life forever.

Over the course of the next few weeks he drafted letters infused with passion from deep within his soul. He wrote to other parents of boy captives. He inquired from every reservation, every frontier trader, every state and federal official for news of his boys. He made known the intimate details of the Comanchero trade and he ridiculed the Peace Policy as one of humanity's greatest embarrassments.

He'd carried within him the past few years a great faith but now much of his hope was fading and he found himself on Christmas Eve in the overcrowded messroom of Barracks B with the post's entire population present, festive souls who may or may not have been interested in the Lord. Just a middle-aged man living out his life who finds himself considering all of the cherished things that he'd let slip through his fingers. Sitting in the front row before Reverend McFalls with a borrowed bible open in his hands and the stories of God coming into the world flowing through his ears he was seen as a sympathetic figure by the few who knew his story. They were told of baby Jesus wrapped in bands of cloth lying in a manger. The pastor said to have true faith, but to what they should profess in was not made clear. Then he preached of the devil with great fervor.

He spent the rest of that winter eighty miles east in a shack on Mukewater Creek that was no more than a trading post for the cowboys gathering herds of cattle for the Chisum ranch. In the spring he set out for New Mexico leading a handful of cowhands and a herd of seven hundred beeves contracted for delivery to Charles Goodnight. When he arrived a big snow was blowing in and his old partner greeted him with a handshake and a heartfelt hug. They sat around a blazing campfire while darkness set, exchanging the news and discussing their lives of late. They studied one another as they spoke, the powerful inner thoughts, the invisible currents, and they avoided talk of those early years and as the evening wore on they pondered their road ahead.

Two days later when he set out back to Texas his thoughts were heavy and filled with blackness. He would ride off alone and talk to himself out loud, testing his thoughts, his ideas. There was no use in taking stock in his fate compared to other men of his times and yet these are the things that consume a man when he knows time is running out on him. Each morning before he set out he'd sit there with his coffee steaming. Legs bowed, heels in the dirt, shoulders shrunk over, and he contemplated. Then he'd remind himself again that it was time to move on with it all.

When he returned to Concho a funeral was underway. The camp of Colonel Merriam had been swept away by floods. His wife and child, their nurse and three soldiers, washed out in a hail-laden deluge and drowned in the raging waters of the Middle Concho. The attendees stood under the sun in the mud listening to the hymns. When it was done they milled about solemnly, the sounds of the post's construction echoing across the prairie as they dispersed amongst the garrison to proceed with the day.

By now the build-out of the fort was proceeding at a frenetic pace and RL hired out to the firm of Adam and Wickes out of San Antonio for the purpose of transporting supplies to and from the settlements. His outfit was made up of ten wagons, a hundred mules, and all the weapons and camp equipment needed to haul freight all over the rugged trails of western Texas. Keeping himself busy seemed to subdue his periods of darkness but time and again there'd be news of some depredation that would trigger his vengeance.

He ran freight all that summer and through the fall. He drove every wagon road there was and he routed new ones. He tried to only think about the roads that lay before him. He may have garnered sympathy in some places as a victim of great tragedy yet misfortune was a given in those times and a man was expected to get on with life and not look back. There were rumors of certain boy captives but they were only rumors. He tried to make his life about his work. He kept the portrait of his boys they'd taken at the fair and he carried this photo with him inside his vest pocket. He would remember that beautiful Saturday in Fredericksburg that he and Sally spent with them. One of those magical, poignant scraps of life that slip through the fingertips like the waning moments of a bloodred sunset. She had them dressed nicely with their hair combed, handsome and smiling, eyes shining large and bright and overwhelmed in the thrill of all of the curiosities before them. That is what I will always remember the most about them, he thought. Those smiles. The innocent voice of a little boy, the inquisitive and loving eyes. The true joy of youth. Sally was so happy and she kept kissing and hugging him all day. I wish they were still here, he whispered.

He made three runs to the city of San Antonio and back following the military road and on each trip he made a point to seek out a parent of yet another child that had been abducted by the indians. He tracked down Gottlieb Fischer in Fredericksburg and the man's eyes welled up with tears when he made sense of RL's account of seeing his boy. He met Louis Korn at Fort Mason. His son, Adolph, hauled away while herding sheep at Castell on New Year's Day. At the trading station of Llano he met a Methodist circuit rider named Friend. This man's new mission was to scour every corner of the earth searching for his grandson, Temple, who'd been taken two years earlier in the massacre at Legion Valley. All of them showed signs of hope and it must have been therapeutic to share tales with kindred spirits yet if they asked God for his strength it was a lost cause for they were chasing ghosts, looking for needles in a haystack.

He turned thirty-five. His hair began to gray. He rarely stayed in a place more than one night. Every hay camp and corn field, every rock quarry and sawmill. Fort McKavett. Fort Griffin. Fort Richardson. Fort Sill. In the heat of the summer he hauled watermelons and cantaloupe, loads of salt from the flats near the Guadalupe Mountains. Hundreds and thousands of pounds of hay and wood. Flour and coffee, sugar and potatoes.

In time the weather began to change. Dust storms blew in from the plains and the first cool fronts of fall brought relief from the heat. He attended the wedding of a man who would die one week later at the hands of a small party of Comanches disguised as white men. Stuck full of arrows, scalped alive, left for dead in the desert with no horse and the soles of his feet shredded bare of skin. Then he attended the funeral.

Another month passed and the conditions of the post had become unbearable. Eight companies of men with poor facilities, bad food, polluted water. And the sickness was rampant—malaria, typhoid, gonorrhea, syphilis, dysentery. He was sent back to San Antonio for an emergency procurement of medical supplies that had been languishing at the Quartermaster's warehouse. Rochelle salt, castor oil, iodide of potassium. He crossed through the Hill Country in ten days without incident and arrived on the third of November on a cool, blustery day. Throughout the town were flyers posted and flyers blowing about the streets announcing the abduction of Herman Lehmann. RL picked one up and uncrinkled it gently like a valuable bank note and settled it rightwise in his hands.

Carried away by the indians. May sixteen. Green eyes. Fair complexioned and freckled. Now age eleven. He looked at the photo of the boy and then let it go, watching it float listlessly in the wind.

That evening he sat alone at a corner table in the bar of the Menger house. A cup of whiskey and his thoughts at the end of another day. The low hum of the patrons discussing life, death, the news of the world. Among the clientele were officers from Troop A of the Fourth Cavalry and RL had encountered them at the headquarters earlier that afternoon. They ordered pints and a man walked over and greeted RL. Mind if we move in on you, pardner?

Make yourself at home.

Name's Thompson. First Lieutenant. Just in from Galveston.

How do you do?

Several others pulled up chairs. A toast was given to their health and they touched glasses and sipped their drinks. The following morning they were to report for duty with orders to drive a half-hundred wild broncos that were designated for assignment to the cavalry regiments stationed at the western posts. They talked about how excited they were to be in Texas and RL gave them a report of the roads he had been traveling.

It's big, beautiful country, he said.

They nodded in the candlelight. RL, when you going back to Concho?

Well, we've about done cleaned out the big storehouse of medicines. I imagine I'll head out tomorrow. Or the day after.

What's that trip like?

It's pretty nice this time of year after some good rains in the fall. And the indians generally dont bother with the military road.

How many days?

With all your stock, I'd give it fifteen.

You ought to just come on with us, said Thompson. I'm sure Colonel Beaumont wont mind. The more the merrier. Hell, we ought to just make a party out of it.

How so?

Well, on account of us being on our honeymoons. Me and Carter. The second lieutenant. Married a month ago. Brung our wives with us.

Where's Carter?

They all grinned. One of the younger recruits spoke up.

Lucky bastard, he said. I bet him and his bride have been upstairs dorkin they brains out.

All of them broke into big smiles. Someone whistled. They started chuckling but soon their laughter died off as they stared wistfully up toward the ceiling of the bar with explicit images of honeymoon love-making running through their minds.

The following morning the spring wagon sat in front of the Menger with doors ajar and an accumulation of trunks lined out along the curb. The ambulance had been shipped to Galveston at the end of the war by the firm of Harkness and LaBarge and had been of service in Texas ever since. RL stood there looking at all of the luggage. A military man in uniform appeared from the lobby and greeted him good morning.

It was Robert G. Carter, a West Point graduate from Boston and the other bridegroom. He was under pressure to get loaded and going, the colonel and his troop of sixty men already out on the road ahead while his bride and the Thompson's casually finished breakfast inside the hotel. A young Mexican teamster attended the mules. At RL's urging he hustled over to begin loading the gear. Carter walked up to RL and extended his hand and introduced himself.

Avery much appreciate your help, he said.

Yes sir, Lieutenant. They said I needed to see about your trousseau.

Well, it's a few days behind us in delivery I'm afraid.

RL nodded. Carter gave word to the bellman to call for his companions and he and RL finished loading the last of the luggage. The teamster took his seat and adjusted the reins as the two wives and Thompson emerged from the hotel smiling and talking excitably of their journey ahead.

RL's outfit was already staged with the herd in a chaparral of mesquite at the head of the trail. As he and the lieutenants rode alongside the wagon the women inside peppered them with questions, talked incessantly, gossiped like schoolgirls of all the exotic sights before them on the way out of the city. The men answered them tersely, peered angrily, and then quickly re-immersed themselves into a deep dialogue that consumed them to the exclusion of all else.

By noon when they caught up with the larger caravan it was one of those delightful Texas days of fall with the sun shining warm and the blue skies crisp and clear and how could there be any worries in all the world? Out on the meadow in an ocean of grass and wildflowers where they paused to say blessings before dining on biscuits with bacon and honey and sandwiches of ham in a perfect prairie picnic before setting out again on the wedding tour of the Concho road.

13

— ★ —

Fort Concho

1869-70

The command arrived back at Fort Concho to complete the wedding tour after a twenty-day march. Early of a Sunday afternoon, the twentieth of November. They rode toward the edge of the windswept parade ground holding onto their hats and shielding their faces from the sleet of a strong Texas norther. Tumbleweeds rolled in from the prairie and bounced along and the officers and enlisted men huddled by fires emerged hospitably from the warmth of their crude tent quarters and walked briskly into the bitter cold to welcome the new arrivals.

The caravan stopped at the entrance to the plaza. A large crowd began to gather around the wagons, shouting greetings and grimacing from the bite of the cold and cussing the weather to one another. A man stepped forward to open the carriage door as the captain of Troop E walked around calling out orders for the horses and gesturing and pointing at the places he wished for his men to take action. The newlywed brides stepped out into the cold. On the fringes of the greeting party teams of negro cavalrymen stood tiptoe in the trampled grass with their eyes wide peering curiously through the crowd as they took handle of the horse herds. Colonel Beaumont hollered for them to get on with it so they could all get the hell out of the cold. This inspired a cheer and the newly arrived men began shaking hands and the gathering of greeters began to mill about and make themselves as helpful as they could. Their luggage was gathered up and sent off and they were pointed the way, walking hunched over into the cold on their way to the officers' quarters.

RL weaved through the gathering with the newlywed couples close behind and familiarized them with the layout of the post. A group of workers were puddling mud into molds to dry as adobe bricks and RL held them up by a pile of newly dried blocks to tell them more about the build-out of the post. Nearby a line of men pushed carts of quarried stone toward a building under construction where other men were busy dressing lumber. A group of workmen under the direction of the post surgeon were examining piles of soapstone stacked at the base of the old limestone oven.

What have we here? said Carter.

Well, we got to rebuild this bakery, said the doctor.

Carter looked around rubbing his hands together and then blowing on them to give them warmth. Awful lot of construction going on, he said.

Now aint that the truth.

RL looked at the brides and introduced the man. This is Doc Notson, he said.

Pleasure to meet you all. Welcome to our lovely little post on the Conchos.

The wind was howling and the women stood crossarmed and shivering. RL shouted to be heard over the wind. Tell me something Doc, he said. Have those corrals been worked on since I've been gone?

They all looked back to where he had gestured.

Well, yes. A little, said the doctor. May be hard to tell but I spose there's been some progress.

All of them looked about the post. Doc Notson was trying to get a glimpse of RL's hand. Mr Terry, he said. How is your finger doing since we nubbed the tip of it off?

RL held his hand up for all to see. Hell Doc, I dont even notice it. It's as good as new.

The women grimaced. Carter kept looking around the post as if to make some sense of the realities he and his new bride were now facing.

Mr Notson, have you heard by chance where Captain Webb intends for us to stay? said Carter.

I believe it's right yonder. The doctor pointed toward a framed hospital tent nestled against a stone chimney. He glanced at the women and he seemed apologetic. She's not quite finished I'm afraid.

Not finished.

No sir. Colonel Beaumont is pushing hard, but the truth is, you see, we're just having a hell of a time procuring supplies. One hell of a time.

Carter turned to gauge the reaction of his new bride. She was quivering from the cold or anger and he put his arm around her and whispered reassurances in her ear and while her eyes were watering from the icy wind he considered that she may in fact be crying.

They started a fire inside the primitive tent quarters and went about getting situated by hanging the gray military issued blankets on the sides of the tent to block the wind. The house was unfurnished save for a mattress and a box of groceries that sat on a shelf above the bed. Men filed in with camp chairs, a butter keg, a commissary box, a barrel to serve as a dressing table. Mrs Carter stayed behind to unload the rest of their things and RL escorted the lieutenants to the officers' quarters.

The commander of the post was a general in the Union Army from Tennessee named Gillem. He was issuing a fiery tongue lashing at the post quartermaster who was shifting nervously and wiping beads of sweat from his brow with the paperwork for all of his delinquent supply orders spread across the desk before them. Captain Webb stood off to the side listening. With the knock of the door the yelling stopped. Who is it? the commander called.

First Lieutenant Robert Carter, sir. Reporting for duty, sir.

There were told to come in. The lieutenants stepped in and saluted them. RL eased into the room behind him but lingered back. The captain raised his brows and looked them over. Give us just a moment, he said.

They stood at attendance. The general looked over the paperwork in silence. They could hear him breathing through his nose. He was gathering his thoughts. He nodded as if to satisfy what he'd said to himself and he shuffled and stacked the papers and set one in particular aside specifically for his signature. He spoke slowly in a firm but calm manner as he signed the paper.

Now, I'd like you to ensure that Mr Hicks adds three wagonfuls of sand from the Llano, he said. And I want you to make sure that he knows that the fifty thousand shingles signed for on this purchase order, and I expect cypress shingles, should be delivered *after* the other materials required to complete those additional quarters have been delivered.

Yes sir.

As the quartermaster left the general looked at the captain and sighed. They turned to the new men. The captain shook their hands and pointed for them to take seats and the general sat down and adjusted himself in his chair. He had a receding hairline and wore a bushy beard with specks of gray and his eyes had a gentleness about them.

Well, welcome to your new post, men.

Thank you, sir. It's good to finally be here.

We're pleased to have your service.

Yes sir. Thank you.

And who is this gentleman with you?

This is Mister…

Name's RL Terry, sir, he interrupted.

RL Terry. And what might the RL stand for?

Robert Lee.

The captain looked away squinty-eyed and puckered his mouth up as if he was trying to capture a long lost memory. He looked back at RL. Robert Lee, he said. He studied him for a moment and nodded and then he looked at Carter. Tell me, he said. Did Colonel Beaumont make it in okay?

Yes sir, he's well and he's attending to the new herd.

Good, good. That's good to hear. Now, tell me about your trip. I'm sure you enjoyed your time with Beaumont.

Yes sir. The weather held up nicely. Of course, until now. No real troubles. Well, we did have some drowned mules on the Guadalupe. That, and of course the remuda was wearing down pretty bad these past few days.

The captain interrupted. Sir, Lieutenant Carter is on his honeymoon, he said, grinning. Him and Lieutenant Thompson. They brought their wives with them.

Is that right? He said it slowly, surprised and excited. Quite a honeymoon!

Yessir. Carter smiled sheepishly and nodded.

Well, congratulations! You've had a long journey. Did you have any of that fine german beer in Fredericksburg in celebration?

Yes, as a matter of fact we did, sir. It was nice to sit in the sun and drink the cold Kolsch beer.

The captain was watching RL. RL was studying the general. Carter, said the captain. What's prompted you to bring Mr Terry in here with you today?

Well sir, I dont really know. I suppose it just played out that way.

Played out that way?

Yessir. You see, we've spent the last two weeks on the road with Mr Terry and we've gotten to know one another pretty well. And he's been so helpful. I should say extremely helpful. Knows this country intimately. Knows the indians. We couldnt have asked for a better guide.

I see.

But as far as him being here with me in this room, right now, it's just on account of him being kind enough to help out and go about getting us oriented.

The general nodded. He had been studying RL. He remembered now seeing him about the post. How long have you been in Texas, Mr Terry?

Most all my life.

I see, a true Texan.

Yes sir.

Where did you serve in the war?

During the war?

During the war.

I run scout for the Texas Rangers.

A scout, said the general. He looked over at Captain Webb. The captain and the general made eye contact as if they knew what the other was thinking.

Carter spoke up. Sir, actually, Mr Terry has extremely intimate knowledge of this country out here and knows a lot about the ways of the indians. And I also suppose it's worth you knowing that a tragedy befell Mr Terry after the war, he said. The indians raided his ranch. Murdered his wife and took his boys.

The general's face saddened and took a big breath through his nose and let it out slowly as he contemplated the tragic circumstances.

Well now, that story sounds familiar. Seems I've heard others at the post discussing this. I'm very sorry to hear about your losses, Mr Terry. Were they Comanches?

RL shifted uncomfortably in his seat. He looked at Carter and the captain and then back at the general. Likely, he said. Comanches and Kiowas.

I'm terribly sorry. And I take it you haven't gotten any word about your boys?

No sir.

But you've been searching.

It's been five years now.

God bless you, Mr Terry. I'm so very sorry. I just cannot imagine.

RL nodded in thanks. There was a measured moment of silence.

The general took a gentler tone. Well I suppose there's no question as to where you stand on the Peace Policy.

RL just looked at him. The general was nodding slowly to himself in thought and then he looked to all of them.

I'll tell you what gentlemen. Just when we think the one war is over another's begun.

The general paused to gather his thoughts. He was slowly tapping his pen on the desk. I must say, I have to admit. When I first came out here I was of a mind to let the Quakers try and convert the indians. All that rhetoric back east, made it sound like these indians down here were gentle people. Any savagery caused by some provocation of the white man. And then when I read the testimony about what happened at Sand Creek. Have you heard about that?

Yes sir. I believe so.

That's the most horrible thing I've ever heard. Our men shot down squaws. Blew the brains out of innocent little children. Fingers, ears, noses cut off. And this done by our very own United States soldiers. Over six hundred of them. Slaughtered a village of one hundred fifty. Most of them women and children. And the elderly.

RL and Carter sat silent. Captain Webb looked at the floor shaking his head.

The general placed a firm hand upon the desk. And the Medicine Lodge meetings. What on God's green earth sense does it make to ask an indian to agree to stop being an indian? To settle down like us white people. Try to farm. All so we could settle all this land. Hell, might as well call it their land. They've been here long enough. And then put the piss-poor worthless Office of Indian Affairs in charge of things. Why, they couldnt feed the indians if they tried! No sense whatsoever. They situated the more warlike Comanches with the more peaceful bands. Let them come and go on the reserves as they please and neglect to station troops at the agency to police it all. You tell me what in the world would you do if you were a Comanche?

His eyes scanned the men awaiting a response but there was none.

You'd raid and steal and kill and scalp and mutilate anyone that got in your way. Wouldnt you? That's what they did. What they're doing. The general pounded his fist into the desk. He seemed torn about the position he was in.

There's not a week that goes by that the Comanche are not raiding this very post for horses. Out there grazing in the grass right outside the damn fort. Would you believe that two weeks ago the wily bastards got away with thirty mules from the quartermaster's corral? Right in the smack damn middle of the post?

Oh my.

The general stood up and adjusted his britches and sat back down. What we all better realize, and realize real damn quick, is that we're up against a bunch of ruthless, savage warriors. They have no fear. Not one ounce. Are not afraid to die to defend their land, their honor. They roam around in bands. Eat raw meat. Have no government. Dont believe in God. We are dealing with a race of people who hate us and everything we stand for more than we could ever comprehend. Now, you tell me what good it does to sit back peacefully and allow them to impose their will?

He sat up straight and raised his voice. Makes zero damn sense! he said. All the ranchers out here are fleeing in droves back east toward the settlements.

There are hostile forces on three sides of the state of Texas. The Apaches to the west. The renegade Mexicans and the Kickapoos south of the Rio Grande. Kiowas and Comanches north of the Red River. Colonel Grierson allows them to draw their rations out of Fort Sill and steal his horses and then head out on the warpath to kill and scalp and take captives in Texas. Does not do a goddamn thing to punish or restrain them! And no wonder General Sherman is getting hell from the Texans who know good and well the reservation indians are at fault. He's going to wake up real quick. He better. Real damn quick.

As we speak there are mass meetings being held in every border town. Protests and petitions are being issued into Austin and Washington to call for the defense of the frontier. There's absolutely no doubt in my mind that the garrisons of the Texas posts will be organized for a major campaign against the indians. Our country's finest fighting men pushed to the front to deal with the problem. These savages will be brought under our control, disarmed, and made to raise corn, and our nation will be free once and for all from these barbaric bands of murderers that are inhibiting the settlement of this country.

The general was looking at Carter and then he turned to RL. RL was restless. Mr Terry, he said. You have my word. We are going to seek retribution for all the harms that have been done to good people like you. He turned to Carter. We have a job to do, he said. Then he rose up and walked around his desk to stand before them. It's just a matter of time. It may get worse before it gets better. But eventually Sherman will come to his senses and all holy hell will be unleashed upon these indians. All holy hell.

He placed his hand on RL's shoulder. And we will do everything we can to help you track down your boys, Mr Terry. Yes sir, you have my word that I will do everything in my power to ensure they are brought back home safely. Back where they belong with their father. Back to their native culture. The United States government is duty bound to make amends I believe for their suffering and yours. It's been five long years. But you cannot give up hope. Do not under any circumstances ever give up hope. I generally have a feeling about things and I have a feeling about you. I believe this world needs men like you, and for your type what wrongs there's been will be made right. You have my word. You understand?

I appreciate that, sir.

No need to thank me. No sir. It's my duty, something I take great pride in. To ensure that the finer men I encounter, men of character, are given every opportunity to make the most of themselves. That's for you as well Lieutenant Carter. Ask Captain Webb here. We've got no chance in hell to bring the indians under control if the leaders of our country cant wake up and put us in a position to succeed. What needs to be done can only be accomplished by men like you.

The general had a faint smile and he seemed proud of what he'd said. He nodded his head as if to acknowledge that all were in agreement. RL placed his palms on his thighs and pushed himself up impatiently. The others followed and they headed toward the door making small talk of the weather, the living arrangements, the abundant game that surrounded the countryside about the post.

Mr Terry, whereabouts do you call home around here?

Oh, I'll generally stay out at one of the cow camps. But I'm mostly on the road of late. And I spend some time over in Trickham.

I see.

General Gillem turned to Carter. Listen Lieutenant, he said. Once you all get settled, we need to see about getting you out on a hunt.

A hunt?

Why, of course. You've had a long trip. There's work to be done but you need to see this country.

Oh, that'd be nice. I'd love that.

It's going to be another long winter. We'll keep an eye on the weather and pick a nice, mild day after one of these cold fronts. Get your brides out and let them see the country. Relax a little. It's hell on a woman being out here.

Sir, what about the indians?

Ah hell, we'll set you up with Major Rendelbrock. Old Joe loves to get out and he'll take good care of you.

What sort of game have you been seeing in these parts?

Well, of course there's buffalo herds that number in the hundreds of thousands.

Yes, we saw them on the way in.

Droves and droves of wild turkey. And you cant hardly go five minutes without flushing a covey of quail.

Are those bobwhite quail, sir?

There's bobs, and we also have a blue quail out here on the fringes of the desert. Scaled feathers. Run like hell. Oh, and we also see quite a few prairie chickens.

Prairie chickens.

Captain Webb spoke up. Have either of you ever seen an antelope?

Antelope. No sir.

Yes. Called a pronghorn. Massive herds of them. About the size of a deer. Little bit like a buck goat, eyes like a sheep. Fastest damned animal you'll ever see.

The general slapped them each on the back and shook their hands. Captain Webb, he said, dont forget your due in Santone first of December.

Yes sir.

Take care of these men. Lieutenant Carter needs to be debriefed in full as he'll be in charge in your absence.

Yes sir. Will do.

Take care men.

When an early winter cold front looms on the plains of West Texas the air is warm and dry and it is pleasant for a hunt. The breezes blow steadily from the south and in the electric blue southern sky the sun slides low and shines bright like a heater placed to burn back the cold. Everyone knows there are things to get done before the weather turns again. It was just a day as this when the hunting party rode out west for the Twin Mountains discussing logistics and tending to their weapons like men preparing to go into battle. All along the Fort Stockton road the vast prairies were black with immense herds of buffalo.

It was just before noon on a Friday when the women of the garrison had settled in for a relaxing picnic social. They poured glasses of tea from a pitcher brewed in the sun and ate bowls of venison chili, talking spiritedly among themselves like old girlfriends who had not seen one another in a very long time. Nearby a toddler girl, the daughter of Mrs Stapp, entertained herself among a patch of winter wildflowers. She was a precious little thing with a bright and curious face and she had just learned to walk.

Cleta, what is that sweet little girl's name?

Her name is Hadley June.

Hadley June. Oh my word, that is so cute!

I know it. June was my great grandmother's name, and we thought Hadley was so darling.

Just look at her tromp around out there would you.

She is a handful, I'll tell you what. I cant keep up with her.

Other women had gathered around and they all had big smiles. The little girl had her toes pointed inward and was making ground away from them in a high-speed wobble and the women were giggling at her awkward gait.

Damn if you're gonna have to put a rope around that little gal.

The mother started walking into the parade ground. Hadley June! she yelled. Baby, get back over here. Come on now!

Cleta, put this lariat here around her waist and fasten it to that stake right yonder.

Where?

Right over there. By that old tree. Oh what do they call that out here, a mesquite?

Why, I caint go and up'n hobble her like a high-strung mule!

She broke into a jog. Jenny, cover up my bowl for the flies, would you.

When she came back the girl was whining and squirming like a greased piglet and when she slipped out of her mother's arms she toddled away again, giggling.

Where does she think she's going?

Cleta Stapp caught her up again and Hadley June slithered and squealed. She slipped the lariat around her daughter's waist and tightened it and then fastened the far end thirty feet away into the picket pin. She kissed the girl and set her out free to romp around and play to her heart's delight.

You really think she'll be okay like that?

Why of course she will. Look around. What in the world could possibly harm that girl out here?

General Gillem and Captain Webb noticed the little girl as they crossed the parade ground on the way back to the officer's quarters. They stopped and looked about for any signs of the mother or a sitter. The women were inside the canvas quarters washing dishes and preparing desserts and Hadley June sat in the yellowed grass studying a bouquet of handpicked wildflowers.

Would you look at that, said the captain. That poor little girl is out here all by her lonesome.

The wind was picking up and on the horizon to the southwest the sky was turning brown from the dust. They looked out on the country and they could see the bison herds grazing several miles from the post and between gusts of wind they could hear the random muffled gunshots of the hunting party in the distance. One of the women poked her head outside to check on the girl and the men waved out a hello and kept walking on.

Hadley June, are you havin fun? yelled the woman.

The girl looked up for the voice she did not recognize. She held up her handful of flowers in a show of pride.

Come on over here girl. Let's get you some food.

Hadley June sat there in the afternoon sun. The breeze was blowing her thin hair and she looked all around in wonder. A pair of crows soaring overhead cawing, the flag flapping steadily in the wind. Perhaps she felt something in the earth and her gaze extended out over the prairie where several thousand head of bison were breaking into a stampede toward the post in a craze of fright. They rumbled on, a dark mirage still barely visible to the eye floating faintly out there in the desert.

Within minutes the first of the herd had reached the edge of the parade ground, a great mass of thousand-pound bison bulls with black beards that tangled in knots and slobber and the younger small-shouldered bulls that followed blindly and raced one another head down and kicking their thin legs in a fury to keep pace and then the cows with the little humpbacked, lumbering calves bringing up the rear, their frantic bawls lost in the thunderous sound of the hooves pounding into the prairie. The parade ground began to rumble and shake. The women stepped outside to see about the commotion. Good God almighty! said Cleta Stapp.

Her daughter was toddling around clumsily again and now directly in the path of the herd's rapid approach, bobbing from one foot to the other like a little bowlegged cowboy. Hadley June had found another patch of wildflowers and could not hear the women screaming. She paused and looked back at the women and then tottered on. She tripped on a patch of grass and fell to her knees, babbling and drooling a string of spit into the dirt. Then she rose up again and stood alone tottering. She raised her hand as if to point at the herd and she was gibbering some nonsense and before she could make it any further she'd stretched the slack of the lariat out full and fell down again.

Now RL on an errand from Veck's store was approaching the parade ground with a cart of commissary goods, deep in thought, and when he heard a woman's scream and noticed the danger he dropped it cold and set off running headlong into the stampede to save the little girl, just reaching her at the last instant to pull the picket pin and draw the lariat and gather the child in his arms before hurdling up into the branches of the mesquite tree just as the first of the herd passed. He waved his arm and shouted as the buffalo diverged around the tree. Hadley June wailed. The buffaloes came pounding on and on and he clung to the branch like a hunted puma cat and he cradled the small and fragile girl in his arm. The mass of the herd passed within inches of the gnarled tree, three, four hundred of them, and ran on across the other side of the parade ground and rumbled on down the sloping plain toward the river, seemingly picking up speed. When the last of them passed RL slithered down. He covered the girl's head for the dust. The rumble of the hooves faded and passed on into the prairie and he said sweet things to her and she became quiet and at peace again as the women came running.

14

— ★ —

The Southern Column

Ranald Slidell Mackenzie had been at service on a Special Military Board in Washington when he was informed that he was being transferred to the command of the Fourth Cavalry at Fort Concho. When he arrived back in Texas in late February of 1871 he was met with an apathetic regiment of Civil War veterans whose sole purpose in life involved hunting the prairies and drinking and whoring across the river in Saint Angela. But he brought to bear an indomitable will and that along with the few capable officers who were loyal to him enabled him in just one month of intensive training to whip his five companies of cavalry into an efficient fighting force ready to take on all comers. His irascible reputation preceded him and everyone respected that he had the tacit support of President Grant. Every soldier under his command understood implicitly that while his discipline was based upon absolute fairness and justice he tolerated no insubordination, suffered no fools, accepted no compromise in the performance of duty. In his tidy new residence at the center of Officers' Row he invited his most trusted advisors in for a formal steak supper and after dessert Carter convinced RL to sit down and debrief the colonel on his experiences fighting the wild horse barbarians of the Texas badlands. The colonel complimented RL on his bravery in saving the Stapp girl and then got him to talking about the nuances of the guerilla warfare used by the mounted tribes. He listened carefully, he even took notes. He asked several very pointed questions and he explained that he was preparing recommendations for General Sherman, who would soon be expected on his annual inspection tour of the Texas posts. RL was able to include particulars and perspectives that only a man of his varied and tragic history could explain. Mackenzie asked if it was possible to take the fight to the indians on their own turf. RL told him that it was the only way. He said there was no doubt the reservation indians were responsible, perhaps along with the renegade Quahadis, for all of the recent depredations. Mackenzie asked him if he would be willing to help and after RL accepted his offer to serve as scout the colonel broke the news to all in attendance that he had earlier that very day received official orders to move the headquarters of the Fourth two hundred miles northeast to a small tributary of the West Fork of the Trinity River.

Two days later all five cavalry companies set out on the long march to Fort Richardson on the banks of the Keechi to prepare to deal with the indian problem more directly. They left the bustling parade ground at mid-morning with a long line of wagons and packmules, splashing across the shimmering waters of the Concho with barking dogs and the muleteers cussing and all eyes watching a line of dark storm clouds building on the horizon.

The glory of springtime in Texas. Cool mornings and warm afternoons. Songbirds chirping and the call of doves. Heavy rains with the fronts passing through and the oaks in molt and new leaves budding. Wildflowers and the endless plains glowing green in the newly grown grass and the creeks trickling cool and fresh. They crossed the Colorado and the Clear Fork. They saw the abandoned forts at Chadbourne and Phantom Hill. Cool, crisp evenings by the fire with wild turkeys baking in a dutch oven and the first stars coming out.

They crossed the plains for twelve days in all this splendor and rode down through the Brazos valley and led the command through old Fort Belknap and crossed the Salt Creek Prairie along that treacherous stretch of military road where they began to come upon abandoned ranches and the crude headboards marking the last resting place of those who'd been massacred at the hands of the savages. *Three negros killed by indians Jan. 3,*

1871. They murmured warnings and speculations among themselves and kept close watch on the distant hills.

It was early afternoon when they rode into the town of Jacksboro, the horses and mules trampling through the dusty main boulevard and the populace turning out en masse to witness the arrival of the Fourth. This town, like all the settlements along the Texas frontier, had been deserted during the war but was now abuzz with the presence of the military and the families who had fled the countryside for the protection of the post. News of the command's occupation of the fort had preceded them and the street was lined with citizens watching curiously as they passed, the town's councilmen decked out in their business suits and bowler hats and the ranchers and cattlemen in flat-brimmed Stetsons or Boss of the Plains styled hats with straight-sided crowns and creases that had been formed to signify some particular coterie. It took a long while for the entire regiment to pass. It was a windless day beneath a bright sun and the dust rose above the street before them. RL hung back from the procession and looked on the scene nostalgically thinking of how it was when he was familiar with this area as a younger man such a long time ago.

They began the process of settling into their new homes, spreading out like a mess of angry fire ants with their luggage and gear and rushing to claim any vacant quarters, the overflow picket huts littering the overcrowded post as if it were some Civil War refugee camp and all of Jacksboro's leading citizens scurrying about with baked goods and pats on the back and offers to help, these soldiers of fortune now welcomed so warmly into their little town with the dream of restoring everlasting peace to the wild Texas frontier.

In the middle of May a messenger arrived with the news that General Sherman was making his way toward Richardson and was expected any day. The four-star commander of the army and his inspector general and staff had been en route from San Antonio for several weeks and Mackenzie immediately dispatched Carter with a team of men to greet him and escort him into the post. He took fifteen men and a fresh set of mules and rode out at dawn along the Fort Griffin road with the mist rising in the warm morning sun. They reached Rock Station at noon that day and received the general and his cavalry escort very formally and with salutes. The general was cordial and very thankful for their hospitality but he declined the use of the mules or their escort and he rejected any consideration whatsoever that there might be hostile indians lurking in the hills. Take your time, Lieutenant, he said. Your horses look warm. Just kindly point us the way and we'll head on.

Are you sure, sir?

Yes, of course. We should get on our way. It looks like the weather is building.

They lunched on summer sausage with slices of pickles and cheese they loaded up and moved out briskly down the road. Carter and the troops watched them go. The horses clopped up the dust and the wagon jangled into motion and soon they'd ridden the road around a clump of oaks and disappeared from sight.

An hour later and Carter's command not fifteen minutes departed the Kiowas attacked the ten-wagon train of Henry Warren that happened to be rolling along on that very same stretch of road carrying corn and supplies for delivery to Fort Griffin. Wrong place, wrong time. Picking up the pace to beat the storm with the dark clouds building and happy to be ahead of schedule. The savages came riding down from the hills howling war cries and racing one another across the exposed plain to cut off the lead mules and count coup. From the timbered ridges around them Satanta blew his bugle and the Owl Prophet stood beside him with his eyes closed chanting rhythmically to the spirits.

They were upon the train before Warren could corral the wagons. The teamsters in the chaos leaped to the ground and scrambled to unfasten the leather sheaths that held their rifles and scurried for cover under the wagons. Gunfire began to ring out and echo across the open prairie and already three of the teamsters had been shot down in the first rush. A drove of arrows whistled through the wagons and more warriors came swarming from the woods, some mounted two to a horse and some sprinting afoot, and the white men lying prostrate fired a steady volley at any moving form that was visible. A few men panicked and made a run for the woods and were shot down with arrows or pistolfire and a when a single runner slipped through the volleys out into the woods he was pursued by a pair of horsemen and a bevy of squaws who came howling from a nearby bluff to cut him off.

The shooting from inside the breastworks seemed to come to a curious halt when the Kiowas began whirling their horses around the corral, yelping and yapping like a pack of jackal wolves and firing randomly under the wagons where the last defenders held out and as one apprentice warrior charged toward a wagon to claim it as loot a wounded man pulled back the canvas cover at the last moment and shot the young indian full on in the face. Satanta and his men converged upon the Texan in a crazed caterwaul of deathcries. They swarmed him and stood him up against a wagon wheel securing first his arms and then his legs with chains while the squaws lit up a bonfire at his feet.

By now Clint Small was the only teamster alive and he curled up in the dirt gripping his guns, listening to the man scream in agony as he was beaten and scalped. He could see other savages scurrying about the battlefield. They'd looted and torched the wagons and were hacking up the corpses and the medicine man stood like a priest before the fires reciting an invocation over the man now being burned alive. Small closed his eyes and contemplated the final decision he would ever have to make.

He caught them off guard when he scrambled up running at them out from under the wagon. Burn in hell you bastard red niggers! he yelled, and he walked toward them firing methodically with a revolver in each hand, shooting two dead and wounding a third and as the others began to swarm down upon him he looked up into the heavens widemouthed and jammed the barrel of the big Colt into the roof of his mouth and squeezed the trigger. His hand jerked back from the gun and the top of his head exploded into a great hunk of brains and showered the wagon cover behind him with a mass of bloodied skull and goop. The Kiowas stopped dead in their tracks. Small sunk to the dirt and lay cockeyed with his matter seeping from his head, splotching the prairie dust with the cruor forming up into little muddied dirtballs.

The Kiowas just stood there. They looked to one another. One of them called out from across the killing field. There were dark thunderclouds to the west and they could hear a mutter of far-flung thunder rolling down from the plains. Satanta ordered the loot to be gathered and the wagons burned and this was done quickly while the vultures came swooping overhead riding the downburst winds ahead of the storm. He turned and walked off to be alone. It had started to rain. He took a big breath and smelled the damp air and he paid his respects to the spirits as he studied another clump of the black scavenger birds hunching themselves downwind on a granite outcropping to wait out the storm.

General Sherman was welcomed into Fort Richardson at sunset. He was greeted formally and given a detailed tour of the facilities. A delegation of local citizens who had been given word of his impending arrival came forth to complain about the seriousness of the recent indian depredations and while he made himself cordially available as the perfect politician even these impassioned appeals from the common people fell upon his ears with skepticism. However later that night a man named Brazeal limped into the post and told the horrific story of the massacre of the Warren teamsters. A cold chill fell over the general, struck by the inexplicable notions of fate and destiny, taken aback that it could as well have been his caravan wasted by the savages and he envisioned himself, merely a wayward soul in a universal drama, bloating and stinking out there in the hot sun upon the Salt Creek prairie. When he was done with the formalities he stepped outside to be alone under the stars. He pondered it all, weighed his options, listened to his gut. He'd been wrong. He considered the potential consequences of taking drastic military action and when he returned to address his staff they began to outline plans for Colonel Mackenzie to march out immediately to the scene of the bloodbath to investigate and pursue the savages.

Four companies of cavalry were organized along with the post guides and Tonkawa scouts and they set out at sunrise in a driving rainstorm. Urgent letters were written and couriers sent out and the following day Sherman set out with a small infantry escort for the reservation at Fort Sill. When he arrived there three days later the Quaker agent in charge received the news of the corn train slaughter with much chagrin. He knew the belligerent Kiowas under his supervision were away from the fort.

The search party had meanwhile ridden out with great urgency along the military road. Sometime in the late afternoon the horses began to hold up and toss their heads and stamp. The soldiers reined back, stepping slowly and looking for sign, and it wasnt long before they came upon the scene of the massacre. They had been riding through the mud in heavy rains and now with a break in the storm the burning light of the dropping sun reflected sharply in the pools of water that dotted the battlefield. The teamsters were strewn about the corral of charred wagons bloating in the mud. Mackenzie nudged his horse forward and stood up tall surveying the scene. Dead mules, grain sacks slashed open and scattered about, piles of corn soaking in the water. At the edge of the corral he dismounted and stepped gingerly through the mud to study the victims.

It had begun to sprinkle again and the soldiers dismounted and sloshed among the dead teamsters in silence. Six of them lay gutted and scalped and two were missing fingers and toes and two had been beheaded. Perhaps they fought with great courage in the face of death but the number of arrows lodged in their swollen forms and the nature of their wounds indicated great suffering and none more than the poor soul who'd been chained up and set afire and now hung with his limbs drawn up in a contortion of ash and blackened bones, skeletal face fixed in a final rictus staring out with hollow eyes.

A week later Satanta and the other principal Kiowa chiefs who'd been responsible for leading the Warren raid appeared at the agency to draw rations and after being questioned by the indian agent boastfully claimed credit and described the depredations in enthusiastic and exhaustive detail. Shortly thereafter they were called to stand before General Sherman who made his own inquiries of them as they were discretely surrounded by a team of armed soldiers and by and by after being informed they were under arrest and would stand trial in Texas for murder they began to awkwardly adjust their story. Tensions rose and the scene became combative, sparking a tense melee where one warrior was killed and the chiefs were henceforth subdued, arrested, and thrown under guard in the post jail.

Mackenzie and his command arrived back at Fort Sill on the fourth of June and four days later loaded Satanta together with a chief named Big

Tree and an old Koitsenka warrior known as Satank into heavily guarded wagons and set out on the road for the Cache Creek crossing to deliver them to the civil authorities at Jacksboro for trial.

Bouncing along handcuffed and hobbled in irons with a line of mounted troops riding escort and two guards equipped with loaded carbines on either side of him Satank began to chant his death song as he slipped his blanket over his head and proceeded to wrangle himself free from the shackles around his wrists. But the troopers beside him had been up all night drinking and suffered in the morning heat and when the bitter old war chief threw the blanket from his shoulders and howled out some deranged bloodoath and lunged at them with his scalping knife they dove out of the wagon in panic. One of them was stabbed and dropped his rifle in the tussle and the old chief seized the carbine and raised the gun and cocked the hammer and took aim at the nearest soldier but when he squeezed the trigger the cartridge had jammed and he was left there helplessly fooling with the mechanism. The wagon halted. He stumbled forward, regaining his balance and as the chaos took hold men were shouting and ducking and scrambling for cover until at last a flurry of shots rang out and Satank slumped over limply covering a wound in his chest. The captain called out and the nearest soldiers rushed the wagon to gain control of the wounded chief. But Satank was like a spirit ghost and had somehow recovered himself, rising up wondrously and working the lever of the carbine. Another round of shots rang out. By now the other chiefs were looking to escape in the pandemonium and a teamster behind the wounded fugitive had rushed in to assist but was now the unfortunate victim of a stray bullet and the man sat his horse with blood oozing between his fingers where he clutched at the gunshot wound on his shoulder. Satank fell back to the floor of the wagon, blood bubbling from his chest. As the last flashes of life vanished from his eyes he could see the soldiers converging upon him. RL had been hanging back with a cautious eye on the other chiefs and as they began to nudge themselves off the backside of their wagon he rode up with a pistol in each hand and held them under guard.

An hour passed before the command was ready to move on. The two remaining Kiowa chiefs rode along in silence and as they passed their fallen brother they could better see the work of the Tonkawa scouts. Laid out for his roadside burial their comrade had been scalped and the subcutaneous tissue from his glistening skull had begun to shrivel like a prune in the Texas sun and he was staring up with lost eyes at his old companions as they passed along slowly before him.

In the following month RL found himself in an overflowing Jack County courthouse that was surrounded outside by an anxious horde of angry citizens, most of them armed and all of them listening breathlessly through the open windows to the proceedings inside. A cowboy jury of hardened frontiersmen with pistols strapped to their hips had been assembled and all rose to witness the entrance of the hated Kiowa chiefs. When the charges were read the interpreters on behalf of the prisoners plead not guilty and already there was such an outcry of shouts and catcalls and murmurs that the judge was pounding his gavel in an urgent call for quiet. RL sat wedged between the widows of two Warren teamsters while the defense counsel's speech was countered by the slurs and shouts of the impassioned court patrons. He kept a squinted eye on Satanta, who knows if he could somehow sense it. The man before him who'd led the raid upon his home and murdered his wife and stolen his boys. The chiefs sat sullenly with their heads down. General Mackenzie and the Fort Sill interpreter along with two of the surviving teamsters were brought to the witness stand for the prosecution and when it was done the jury retired to a far corner of the courtroom to quickly confirm their agreement. When the judge asked for the verdict the foreman stood up with his arms held out to fully embrace the congregation, pausing briefly for effect before he hollered at the top of his lungs for all to hear. We figger em guilty! he yelled, and everyone jumped up in triumph with their palms facing up toward the heavens as they broke into raucous cheers of celebration and joy.

15

— ★ —

Clarendon, Texas

Winter 1927

In the early days of the new year the colonel and Corinne move out of the old ranch home twenty miles east to the town of Clarendon and their days are busy getting things situated in their new home. In an effort to be more mindful and to commemorate the fresh start to the new year Corinne has resolved to keep a daily journal and whenever she finds some quiet time over the course of her busy days she settles in to listen to her inner voice and she notes the casual goings on of their days.

Jan 6: Busy getting things in order, G is pleased with so many windows.

Jan 7: To Goodnight on business, get things. Left his tobacco there on purpose!

The month passes quickly. There are trips back and forth to the old ranch home to gather more things and they motor to the town of Claude so the colonel can take his treatments from Mrs Newberry. His asthma is very bad but he is generally in good spirits, invigorated by the new woman in his life and the stimulation from his new environment. On those cold days when the fronts blow in and the temperature drops fifty degrees in a matter of hours and sleet and snow blanket the land they spend their days inside by the fire where she takes dictations to facilitate his various correspondences. She reads to him from last Sunday's *Amarillo Globe-News*. Letters from old acquaintances or from associates related to his business interests. They finish reading *Billy the Kid* and start the most recent book that has been sent to them, *Norfleet*, about the adventures of fellow West Texas rancher Jasper Norfleet. The colonel takes pleasure in these reminisces and he envisions how the stories of his life and times might be described in a book.

Corinne tries to stay true to her aspirations of keeping a journal but her entries are sporadic and short, just a few notes here and there, hardly anything at all. However one evening after they celebrate her birthday with a fine meal and a dessert of chocolate cake she has time to relax and she finds herself inspired to sit down and read from the Somerset Maugham book she picked up at the library. Before she goes to bed she makes a note about the day.

Jan 17: I'm twenty-six today, still an old maid though I've met a few fair gentry. Photo from Charles taken about twenty years ago.

The following day the colonel is sick from something he has eaten and she spends the morning attending to him before taking him to the doctor in the afternoon. They return home at sunset exhausted from the stress of his illness and they retire to bed early, awaking the following day to a beautiful morning, crisp and cold and clear.

Jan 19: Spend the day reading and writing, we enjoy the contentment and happiness we find here.

When the weather is nice the colonel prefers to bundle up and sit outside in the sunshine, closing his eyes and listening to the birds and thinking about his life and how the years have passed. He has a song in his head from one of the recent camp meetings. *Jesus, Lover of My Soul.* A long and lonesome tune. He thinks back to when the cowboys on the range would sing to the cattle and he thinks fondly of Old Blue, the beloved longhorn steer who endeared himself to the cowboys like a favorite pet, rising from his bed of grass under the stars and stretching out, shaking his head and taking in a big breath of the Texas air as if he was thankful to be alive. On these days Corinne sits at the breakfast table by the window, reading and dabbling in her journal, keeping an eye on the colonel as he soaks in the glory of the sun.

Jan 22: Usual bath morning, G does love cleanliness and is so appreciative of every little thing I do for his comfort, health, and happiness; asks me to comb his hair several times a day, he has such beautiful hair. First thing I noticed about him when I saw him.

The days fly by and by the last week of the month she is frustrated that she has been so neglectful of the journal. Oh my goodness, she says out loud to herself late one afternoon. Where does the time go? It's already the last day of January!

She sits down and lets out a big sigh as she looks out the window. The yard is covered by three inches of snow, glittering from the late flares of the evening sun. She opens the journal and flips the pages back, slowly, perusing her limited notations over the course of the month. Not one word written in over a week. She turns to the memorandum that marks the close of the month and begins to write.

The great teacher of life is life itself. We learn by the experiences of others. Their eves are sure guideposts to our own living to achievement, success, happiness. That is why autobiographies are so fascinating, because they contain the secrets of life, of power, fame and fortune. All great men have become great by studying the lives of others... footprints on the sands of time, the successful ones who went before them.

Then she closes the journal and walks down the hall to check in on him sleeping.

Inside by the fire they can see the cold gray clouds through the windows. There has been no sun in weeks. Every now and again a breeze will swirl, scuttling a scattering of dead leaves sometimes this way, sometimes that.

A tumbleweed rolls by running from the stiff plains breeze. The fire burns a low roar. Car wheels hum the pavement from down the way and the sound is growing louder, breaking the peaceful silence. Outside the wildlife is bedded down, dormant in the cold, wary to feed. Somewhere the songbirds are hidden, longing for the sun.

Even though Corinne has promised herself that she will spend time with her journal each day of the month she is continually distracted tending to the house and caring for the colonel. She only makes one entry in that first week of the month.

Feb 2: To Amarillo, splendid dinner at the KC Waffle House with Mr Nelson, Miss Hamner, Mrs McClellan, and Annie Nunn.

On Tuesday of the second week the colonel is feeling very bad and the home is once again consumed by stress. She turns to her bible. She prays. She tries to be mindful with the journal.

Feb 8: G has asthma bad. Eight years today since mother and sister passed away.

Feb 9: Have doctor twice today for G's asthma.

Feb 10: Does not feel much better. I'm so worried about him. He gets so discouraged.

She sits in the room with him as he sleeps and watches over him, his massive chest heaving in a deafening upwelling of snores. His large head of white, wavy hair matted against the pillow. His long nose curving down over the sunken upper lip, mouth is wide open, jutting chin curving up. The old heart ticks along and he dreams.

She is a woman of the west and at home on the High Plains. A native of Colorado who moved to Montana as a girl with her family. An orphan at age seventeen, left alone to raise her younger brother, who'd spent a month the previous summer working at the ranch for the colonel. She'd traveled across America. California. All over the west. Trips through the south. Alabama, Mississippi, Florida. Traveling for her job. Hard working, caring, a keen sense for business.

She watches him, rustling awake in sputtering gasps of air and then he settles comfortably back to sleep. She knows he is okay. She opens her journal.

Feb 11: Weather more settled today and G feels much better. Says to me repeatedly: never in my life have I wanted to live as much as I do now and I want to make money for you. Bless his dear heart, he has felt this way about life and me since the first day he ever saw me, even though he was then on the brink of eternity.

Feb 13: Enjoy some heart-to-heart talks about many things today. Past, present, and future. He tells me many things of interest about his married life. He is a man in a million. Seems my admiration and respect for him grows with each new day.

The colonel had asked Henry Taylor to arrange for the delivery of a big, beautiful bouquet of roses and a box of chocolate-covered strawberries to celebrate Valentine's Day. They arrive in the early afternoon when he has lain down for his nap. She walks from the door into the kitchen and opens the chocolates, savoring the first one in the first row. She tells herself that she will eat them in order, only one per day.

She pulls the scissors from the drawer and takes a hand-painted porcelain vase with elaborate floral designs and large gold handles and fills it half full with water. Smelling the roses, she smiles and clips the ends over the sink and places them carefully in the vase, arranging them just right, and she carries them through the kitchen and into the hallway.

The colonel opens his eyes when she comes in. A wide, joyous smile lights her face and she places them on the counter by the window where they shine splendidly in the sunlight. Then she turns to him as he awakens from his nap and gives him a sweet, soft kiss on his wrinkled forehead.

Look what I got for Valentine's Day! she beams.

Sweetheart, there's no reason for you to push yourself when you're not feeling well.

Corinne, now darlin, you need to stop your worrying. I'm just fine.

Well I'm not so sure about that.

The sunken-cheeked old man stares outside at the cold and the rain, continuously coughing, his body's desperate attempt to break up the thick mucus stuck inside his inflamed lungs. Haley rises from his note-taking and hands him a fresh kerchief. Red, hollowed eyes. Mouth like a sea urchin. He spits up a mouthful of gunk. Clears his throat. Begins talking. This is one of those times when the only thing that makes him feel alive is the sharing of his life's stories.

The long days gathering cattle for the trail. Oceans of tall prairie grasses, infinite heaven of blue skies, cattle spread all over the ranges there free for the taking. There were not many people in our half of Texas in those days.

After the war you could ride for days and hardly see a single soul, just you and the horse and unimaginable numbers of game. Endless herds of antelope and deer. I saw racks of horns back then as wide and high as you could hold your arms out. Thick, thick horns, too many points to count. Turkey, bear, mountain lion. Millions and millions of doves. The ceaseless whistle of quail. Coveys of em thirty or more flushing seemed like every time a horse put its foot down and my Lord, the marvelous sound of those birds flying off.

That spectacular country was our playground, our work, our home. Wide open and full of opportunities, all of our lives ahead of us. We shared our dreams with one another, RL Terry and I, of how to make life better. When we rode along or sat exhausted by the evening fire he'd paint the pictures in his mind for me. The home he'd build for his family, their education, the profits we could realize from the methods we'd use to manage our herds. He would talk about how lucky he was and how all of the hard work was for his wife and their boys.

We were in Fort Worth just before Christmas in 1865. Everyone is jovial and filled with the holiday spirit. Loading up on supplies, shopping for Christmas. Oliver and his boy are somewhere down the street. I'm walking with Mollie. Chilly outside with a light snow. The storefronts decorated and everyone feeling the holiday spirit. We run into RL and his family. His oldest boy Sam runs up to me first, grinning. RL and Sally walk up thereafter. She's holding the little brother and he is cute as can be. RL jokes, some offhanded remark about spending all of their money.

Mollie and Sally say hello and give one another a big hug. RL and I discuss the weather and the plans for heading home. There is the typical small talk and it turns to what the kids are asking Santa for Christmas. After a nice visit we say goodbye and go about wrapping up our business in town.

Mollie was the most observant person I've ever known. Why Charles, she says, Did you notice the mole on Samuel's neck? I stopped. Why no, I didnt. I'd never noticed it.

At the time I was mostly clean-shaven and just wore a goatee trimmed up nice and clean. She put her nose up to my neck real sweet and gave me a little peck right about here.

That boy has a mole just like yours right in the very same spot, right where I just kissed you.

I didnt think anything of it.

Early evening and the colonel is already in bed. It looks like he is sleeping soundly, said Corinne. She sat down at the kitchen table with Haley that evening with two glasses and a bottle of wine.

What do we have here?

This is from… Oh I cant pronounce the French. The Chateau Margaux in the Medoc region of Bordeaux. A cabernet sauvignon. Mrs Adair gave this to the Goodnights before prohibition.

Oh my goodness, what a nice surprise!

Yes, I know. Of course, Charles does not drink wine. A shame since it would do him some good. Poor old guy is just not doing very well. And now he refuses to take his medicines.

Haley opened the bottle and poured them each a glass and said a brief toast to celebrate the day and their evening together. They touched the glasses.

Well, it seems like you had another productive day.

Yes, I think so. Very productive, in fact.

What all did you talk about?

Well, he was telling me about the early ranching days up here, after the indians had been run out.

Evetts, can you believe his ability to recall things? I mean, he remembers it all in such vivid detail.

It's true. I sure hope I can have that sort of recall at his age.

He reels it off as if it had all just occurred yesterday.

Listen Corinne, I've been thinking. He's not going to be around much longer. We have to face it.

No. No he's not.

He's outlived them all. Just about all of the old timers that lived through it all are gone. His incredible story. Those times. His contributions. I've been thinking more and more about writing the history, somehow weaving it into the story of his life.

Corinne smiles warmly, reaches out and places her soft hands around the writer's wrist. Oh, Evetts, I think that would just absolutely be the best thing ever, she says. They finish the wine and make their way to the sofa by the fireplace. She lights a candle and pours them another glass as Haley places another log and stokes the fire. They sit down, warmed by the wine, the heat of the fire.

Think about what all he's seen, Haley says to Corinne. Ninety-one years. Born the day before the Alamo siege ended. Bareback all the way to Texas from Illinois when he was only nine. Family settled in the middle of nowhere.

They were much tougher back then.

Well.

Oh, Evetts.

I mean, he hunted with the Caddos as a kid. Was managing his own herds before twenty. And he guided for the Rangers and was with the command that found Cynthia Ann Parker. By thirty, he'd routed two thousand miles of cattle trails. By forty had built a ranch up in Colorado three hundred miles west of the nearest settlements. Then in 1876 he was the first into the Panhandle and by the age of forty-five controlled twenty million acres of that range.

I know it. I just cannot begin to imagine all the change he's seen.

Yes, it's incredible. Barbed wire. Railroads. The nesters invaded and transformed the ranges up here into farmland. Then automobiles. Oil. World War I. Airplanes. It's just so damned difficult to fathom.

And it needs to be documented for so many reasons. It must be.

But there's something else I keep wondering about. For a man who's seen so much, who's accomplished so much in his life, there seems to be some awfully deep pain. Have you noticed this Corinne, that he seems to carry a great burden?

Well, his burden is all the life that he's lived and now he's facing the end.

Of course. That's part of it. But think of the subtle things he keeps weaving into our discussions.

Like what?

The Keechi years. In the 1850s. Remember the fling with Sally Johnson?

Why Evetts, they were so young then.

They were young, yes, but dont you think that it was a little strange given his history with Mr Terry?

No, not really. He talks about so many of his old acquaintances.

At the Palo Duro. When they first got there. Those bodies he found.

I know you're hung up about that. He talks about it, yes. But it was, I think, just an odd way to start that new phase of their lives.

Maybe so. It was so long ago. He can be so sharp but still goes in and out at times. Who knows what is really going on in his mind.

They sit on the couch staring at the embers and listening to the hum of the fire. Haley is piecing things together.

My gut just tells me there's more to it.

Perhaps, but I think he's just very old and his ninety-one-year-old brain just takes him in different directions, she says, leaning over and squeezing Haley's thigh as if to reassure him or perhaps she is tired of the topic and wishes to shift the dynamics of their evening together.

Corrinne, you haven't been with us every single second of these conversations.

It's true, but...

I'm collectively thinking through everything I've heard.

That's fair, I suppose. But it goes both ways. I've sat with him quite a bit when you're not here.

True.

So, tell me more.

Well, in 1866 the Kiowas and Comanches made a great raid. Remember he's touched on it before with us but it was hard to follow him. He was gathering the herds, prepping for their first trip. And RL Terry was with him, away from his home and family when the indians raided their home. They murdered Mr Terry's wife and took his boys. Just a horrible, horrible story.

I know it. I just cannot imagine. I cannot believe that was only what, sixty or so years ago. It just wasnt that long ago.

Mr Terry got there first. And the colonel rode in a while later and there was a big fight. They fended em off. Then, after they buried Mrs Terry, they took the trail in pursuit of the indians. To find the boys. Find the others that were abducted and hauled off. They came upon the remains of several women and children but not the Terry boys. Then shortly thereafter the colonel up and left with Oliver Loving on their first trip. Meanwhile Mr Terry stayed behind trying to put his life back in order.

I just cant even begin to imagine what that must have been like, living in those times.

So there's great tragedy there. And it seems like there was more to the affair with Sally Johnson, or rather, Sally Terry, ten years earlier. Wasnt just a one-night deal. Of course, they all moved on when he and Mollie got together. He and RL stayed fairly close. And he talks about the oldest Terry boy an awful lot.

Yes, Samuel.

But that raid seems to have pushed the colonel away from Texas. When they started trailing, having some success, he kept on with it and stayed north. And I presume all the while Mr Terry was searching for his boys, trying to put his life back together. But at some point you have to move on, I suppose.

I dont know that I'd be able to.

I know he was delivering the Chisum herds to the colonel up in New Mexico. It's like Mr Goodnight ran away from it all. Only came to Texas on business. He's never said all that much about how Mr Terry was going about finding his boys. See, the colonel built that big ranch up in Colorado, married Mollie, and they stayed out of Texas all of those years during the indian wars. From what he's said it sounds like he was involved in all sorts of business, making good money.

Yes, it sounds as though they had quite a life up there.

But why didnt he and Mollie ever have kids?

I dont know. I do wonder about that.

He's never mentioned anything specific?

Well, he talks an awful lot about how much he wants to have a son of his own.

He does?

Yes. I think if he could have one thing in the world it would be a son to leave things to, to pass on his legacy.

Hmm. I suppose I understand that but, I mean…

Evetts, do you know anything else about what happened to the Terry boys?

No, I dont really know. I try not to press him too much.

When did RL Terry pass?

I'm not sure. Could still be alive for all I know. Corinne, I try not to pressure him. But you know, for an old plainsman with no education he sure has a knack of sprinkling in poignant philosophies. Like he's yearning for more dialogue, to explore things, and then when you dig for more he jumps all over you.

Yes, I know.

I dont know, maybe it's just me but it sure seems like there is some deep, deep pain inside that man.

Listen to me Evetts, I really feel like you are just overthinking it.

You're probably right. I'll regret this one day when I'm an old man.

Corinne smiled and whirled her glass by her nose and took a sip of the wine, letting it sit on her tongue and absorbing the flavors. Haley kept playing with the scenarios in his mind, almost as if he was talking to himself.

So the colonel was the first one to move into the homelands of the Comanche after they'd been beaten in the Palo Duro.

What's your point?

No point really, just pondering all of it. And he said Mr Terry joined the Fourth under Mackenzie. Scouting again. His boys hadnt been found so that's in the back of his mind. A lot of these old timers have been telling me what it was like in the early 1870s. Incredible history. All those years the colonel was having success in Colorado it was brutal warfare here in Texas. In '74 Mackenzie slaughtered over one thousand indian horses after he ran the Comanches and Kiowas out of the Palo Duro. That was the big blow but it took a few more years to settle things. The colonel watching it play out from afar. Then we killed off the buffalo and it wasnt long before the last of the wild indians poured into the reservation. My god, the history. It's fascinating. There's just so much more I'm curious about, I just cant get enough of it.

She leaned in closer to recapture his attention, to break Haley out of being lost in his thoughts. She was supportive. You're making progress, she said.

One day at a time. Those things will work themselves out. And you know I want to help.

Well, thank you. I'm sure going to need it. There's so much to do back in Austin and it's just not the same when I'm not here in person. There's not enough time with the deadlines on all of the papers that I have due. But you know how I've been approaching it. Keep him talking. It's good for him. With you taking dictations it'll be as if I was here. You can send me the letters and I will send back more questions, more topics to explore.

Yes of course, Evetts. You know I will. I just hope I start feeling better. I just have not been feeling well at all.

Are you still feeling nauseous?

Yes, it's very random. All this week. Maybe longer. I've even thrown up a few times.

He watched her sipping her wine in the firelight. During all their days together in the colonel's home she had become increasingly more charming to him even though he had questioned her true motivations from the beginning. Like him she was twenty-six years old and still single. What a pleasant surprise, he had thought when she first arrived, finding her very pretty. It wasnt long before they had grown to know one another, to appreciate one another more. At first just the light flirtations of a curious young man and woman. Then she had caught him once gazing at her as she worked in the kitchen, the colonel rambling too long again about something they had already been over, the perfect chance for him to take advantage of his clandestine view and observe her beauty. She had given him a look and then before long one thing led to another. He had not been able to subdue his natural urges, felt unbelievably guilty about it. One night after the colonel had gone to bed and they settled a foolish disagreement with an even more ill-advised romantic interlude, their anger fueling a particularly passionate bout of love making, he became too absorbed in the moment and by the time she realized he was still inside her it was too late. Corinne shoving him aside, expressing her shock at his negligence in a flurry of angry whispers.

Now he was staring deep into her eyes but his mind was lost in the passion of that old moment. I'm sure it will pass, he said. It's probably some sort of virus.

I hope so. It's been like this for well over a week now.

Feb 26: Meet Mr Nelson at Amarillo. Spent night with Nunn's, get G's oil certificates transferred from Paul. Take out stock in the Nunn Stubblefield Co. Agreement with Annie for 500 shares stock for her $250 note which was due Jan 1, 1927.

February Memorandum: Charles has handled men since 19 years of age (negroes first). "Goodnighting." Passion and sex theory, very good. All good and all bad things result of this power. G takes chiropractic treatments from Dr. Galloway since coming to Clarendon.

In early March they are in the First United Methodist Church of Clarendon and Haley is able to pick up the nature of the old man's conversation with Corinne from across the reception room. Aside from Goodnight being hard of hearing and speaking loudly, the writer has an uncanny knack for observation. He can grasp several conversations in parallel to the one he is engaged in, can pick up nuances and body language from angles that he seemingly has no viewpoint. It is the colonel's ninety-first birthday and he has just shared his wedding vows with the charming young woman who is his secretary and caretaker, who was born more than six decades after him. Cakes, tea, coffee. A small, private gathering of close friends to celebrate the occasion.

The jovial murmur about the room halts abruptly when the old man barks an order at his new bride. Well now goddamn Corinne, if you're sick go on to the ladies' room and get yourself in order! There is a lull in the murmur of the crowd and when the conversations pick up again Haley heads over to talk with Goodnight to make sure everything is okay.

When he arrives he sees Corinne trying to explain to her new husband more details about her condition. The old man leans down, cupped hand extended from his ear and his face is strained as he tries to make out her words. He puts his arm around her and she seems to be uncomfortable, frustrated that he cannot hear. She peeks at Haley and smiles shyly, embarrassed but thankful for his tactful interruption.

Goodnight glares at him. Well congratulations Haley, he says. You interrupted our very first argument as a married couple.

Oh Charles, dont be so dramatic, she says.

Haley gauges their expressions.

Excuse me gentlemen. I'll be right back, she says as she slips out of the room.

They watch her walk into the hallway.

Colonel, is she alright?

Oh, I think she's a little sick to her stomach.

I wonder if she's had too many sweets.

Well, I dont know about that. I guess this thing's been naggin her off and on for a while.

In the bathroom Corinne locks the door to the stall and lifts the lid of the toilet and begins to gag and then she throws up for several uncomfortable minutes. By now it has become routine. She knows when she is done, cleans herself up, and walks back down the hallway into the reception room worried that her face is pale and tired.

So how does it feel? Haley asks in congratulations to the newlyweds, To be officially tied at the knot?

I'll tell you what, it feels very damn good, said the colonel. I dont know that I've ever felt any better. This little lady has given me a completely new outlook on life.

He smiles and puts his arm around Corinne, looking at her lovingly.

She puts up with me, takes care of the house, feeds me. I never thought in a thousand years I'd have a second wife. Hell the way I'm feeling now I may live another twenty years.

He turns to Haley.

I suppose Quanah was right, he joked. The more squaws a man has to take care of him, the better.

They were smiling, looking around the room. Haley keeping an eye on Corinne's reaction. Tell me, Colonel, about what year was it when you first met Quanah Parker?

Oh, that would be, let's see, well I sure as hell met him informally back in the day out on the frontier. But formally, well it must have been sometime in the late seventies. He brought some of his cronies from the reservation. Into the Palo Duro to hunt buffalo.

But that was your range then.

Well, we were in the process of makin it that way.

Was it friendly?

A little tense at first, I'd say. A little tense. The buffalo were about hunted out by then. I told him kindly that we were many and well-armed but that he and his boys were welcome to make themselves at home. Essentially do as they pleased, and I allowed that they could take one beef a day to feed themselves.

And he agreed?

Well yes, of course he did.

Corinne perked up. Her eyebrows were high and her imagination was running, trying to picture that scene.

What was he like, Colonel? Evetts told me you got to know him some over the years.

Quanah Parker was a special man. A true leader. Not just as a warrior but on the reservation as the Comanche were forced to adapt to modern times. I've told you about his mother Cynthia Ann. My history with her and her story.

Yes, of course.

Any man with any savvy understood his presence. Burk Burnett, Ranald Mackenzie. Quanah got to where he ran the tribe's business up there on the reservation, negotiated for them to receive grass payments for grazing rights on their lands. He was one of a kind. Some called him, The Eagle. His heart gave out on him early, in 1911. He didnt make sixty.

As the afternoon winds down an hour later Haley watches the beautiful bride taking congratulations from the guests, smiling graciously, and tolerating all of the mundane questions about their future lives. She is pleasant and cordial, gracefully hiding her discomfort. He is the only one who knows that she is not herself.

Anyone who becomes acquainted with her story questions her intentions. She appeared from thin air, a stranger of meager means, endearing herself as a caretaker but now professing an undying love for the very famous, elderly plainsman. It was in private that she let her charms take hold of you. There is good in her heart. She has carried herself well, seemingly oblivious to the accusations and whispers. Something far beyond their control had brought their paths together in a common destination, in the home of the colonel.

He observes Corinne moving about uneasily, white as a ghost. He had been denying it to himself all along but now it has suddenly become very clear. The moodiness. The sickness. Why didnt he pick up on the signs earlier? She is pregnant.

16

— ★ —

The Scout for Kicking Bird

1871

As the heat of the Texas summer set in Colonel Mackenzie began to assemble additional companies of his cavalry, sending several of them to establish a base camp on Gilbert Creek from which to scout for the hostile Kiowas. There were also requisitions made to Whaley's Ranch at the mouth of the Big Wichita for wagonloads of corn and supplies. He spent long hours planning with his field adjutants and post scouts and with his knowledge of the country RL had become a credible informer to this staff. Also on his staff was a man named Lawton, the new quartermaster just transferred in from the Twenty-Fourth Infantry and well known for his ability to cut through red tape and get things done. Mackenzie's plans often had little regard for official policies and despite being reprimanded by his immediate superior for violating regulations he continued to push aggressively in preparation for an extensive campaign to search for the Kiowa village of Kicking Bird. When the planning was done he'd organized ten companies of cavalry into five battalions of fighting men. Busy at all hours of the day and night with little or no rest, he pushed himself relentlessly until he had ciphered the exact amount of hay required to feed the horses and mules, ordered old wagons repaired and new ones built, and calculated every last detail that might influence his chances for success in guerilla warfare against the Plains tribes.

On the twenty-eighth of July Mackenzie sent an advanced command out ahead with orders to establish a camp on the Little Wichita. Clouds of dust wafted faintly in the rising sun and the sweating horses snuffled and stepped smartly into the haze and a pack of dogs had lined out along the road in the shade of the oaks watching the long procession of soldiers. The prairies that lined the trail were burned up and bare of grass from drought and as Carter walked up alongisde the command the heatshimmer was beginning to refract an imaginary lake far out on the horizon and RL was staring thoughtfully at the orderly march of the cavalcade sipping his coffee in a slow slurp as if to not singe his tongue.

Buenos días lieutenant, said RL.

Good morning to you, said Carter.

These boys are headin out early.

Yes, they're going to span the bridge on the Wichita.

When do you think we'll head out?

I'd give it another four, five days.

They were watching the sky. A peregrine came lashing down from out of the rising sun and glided over them, circling, turning, its back and covert feathers gleaming in the sunlight like clusters of golden beryls. A harsh, exultant cry came drifting down from out the blue haze.

I sure love that, said RL.

Oh my, said Carter. That was beautiful.

Yes, indeed. Now look at that sky, would ya. Looks like another blistering hot day with no chance of rain.

Yes sir.

RL swallowed his coffee and looked up into the perfect blue of the morning. Now a pair of ravens were soaring out over the road with their caws echoing out over the parched prairie.

Not a drop since the middle of May, said RL. Not one damn drop.

Five days later Mackenzie with his staff and a team of escorts set out for the rendezvous point on the West Fork of the Trinity River to join up with the forward command. They took with them a contingency of Tonkawa scouts and they left at dusk, riding off into the darkness talking quietly among themselves and trotting the horses briskly into the silent prairie beneath an eternal kaleidoscope of twinkling stars.

They made good time under the bright moonlight and followed the trail across the rolling prairie and led the horses through forests of post oak along the northwest course of the river valley and slipped into bivouac an hour after midnight. When they arrived the command was fast asleep and the campfires glowed softly in the shadows of the trees. They quietly staked the animals out in the pasture to graze and as they rolled into their blankets they could hear the gentle roar of the fires, the horses munching peacefully, the lonely lobo wolves howling at the moon.

The rising sun found them lined out in a steady march across the prairie, a white-hot sky already burning their eyes, not a cloud on the horizon. The wagons creaking along and men cussing the heat and the unceasing whinny of horse and mule. There was no water to be found along the road and what little grass remained lay yellowed and wilted and the coalblack soil had been baked into a sooty maze of jagged crevices that would swallow the hoof of a horse. When they stopped to water at Buffalo Springs the holes were dried up and caked in mud, littered with the waste of decomposing cattle.

RL had taken to riding with the First Lieutenant of Troop F who was in charge of the Tonkawa scouts. His name was Peter Boehm and he was born and bred in the East but wore a much admired wide-brimmed sombrero in the style of a Texas vaquero. Perhaps he felt compassion for RL's tragic history or simply admired the man as an authentic Texan and seasoned scout, and he picked his brain to soak up the older man's knowledge.

I'd put my money that ole Kickin Bird's village is up on Rainy Mountain Creek, said RL.

Where abouts is that?

RL wiped the base of his gums with his pinky finger and flicked a wad of tobacco in the dirt. Up in them Wichita Mountains, he said. Hunnerd miles north of here.

RL, you know much about these Tonks?

Not much. Just some stories you hear now and again.

That ole boy McCord there. Lordy, what a character.

RL watched him ride. The breastplate of sandhill crane bones he wore bounced upon his chest with beads and trinkets jingling. He was lean and fit for an older man and his dark eyes bore the baleful countenance of many tragedies and yet he had attired himself in such a wild array of accoutrements he seemed more suited for a traveling vaudeville show. He wore a well-fitted paisley work shirt and dressed it up with a silk jacquard necktie but the checkered woman's apron he wore underneath protruded awkwardly below his holster and seemed to hinder his movement.

You speak any of that injin pidgin jargon, said Boehm?

Nope. Not a lick.

Me neither.

They watched the Tonks riding along.

I guess I'll be learnin it.

I guess so.

RL shook his head slowly. Say, who's the chief of those Tonk scouts?

Name's Henry.

Henry.

Yup. We been callin him Ole Henry.

You know when I was with the Rangers I'd hear the stories of em fighting alongside Rip Ford's boys back in the day against the Comanch.

Is that right?

Yep. And the word is those Comanch dont care for em one bit. On account of it got out that the Tonks had a hankerin for eatin human flesh.

Cannibals?

Yessir. Story I heard you see, was there was two Kiowa brothers had a run in with a band of Tonks. One of em was captured but the other got away. Well, when he got back to the village, told everyone of his ordeals, a band of warriors promptly headed back to that Tonk camp.

Is that right?

And they didnt like what they found.

What'd they find?

Them Tonks were cuttin up the brother and cookin him on the campfire.

Mhmm.

Yessir. And so word got around. And of course, they were then looked down upon even more than they were before. Then during the war the pro- Union tribes tracked em and caught the whole bunch of em in a big camp, asleep. Slaughtered damn near ever one of em.

Really…

And ever since then there just aint a whole helluva lot of em left.

RL was eyeing a Tonk squaw who had secretly slipped into the command of scouts against Mackenzie's stern orders to restrict women from the expedition. Boehm leaned and whispered to RL.

Well, now she sure is a fine-looking specimen.

The woman made eye contact with them and nodded austerely. She rode a light dun pony that she had striped with black paint to resemble a zebra. When she noticed RL admiring the tattooed lines about her face and neck and breasts she removed the thin cigarillo that dangled from her lips and smiled wide, bearing a great mouthful of large, white teeth, much like a horse's.

All that afternoon they watched for signs of water along the trail. The country seemed burned out running every direction to the horizon and it was almost dark before they found a spring giving life to an oasis of willow trees within sight of old Camp Wichita. They spread out in the shade in a rough bivouac and watered the horses and took turns filling their canteens and settled in to sleep under the stars.

The camp striker woke them where they lie sleeping among the tweeting morning birds and as the sun rose they were on the march again riding through the remains of the abandoned settlement of Henrietta. Two months before the wife and daughters of the peaceful Quaker Goodleck Koozer were violated by a Kiowa raiding party as he was made to watch and they were hauled off and he was bludgeoned with a warclub and scalped and left for the buzzards. His home and the ranches of his neighbors stood tattered and burned, lonely and empty in the whistling prairie breeze. Mackenzie pushed them on and by noon they came upon the trail of the advanced command and followed it all afternoon into a greener country of post oak belts and rolling prairies.

They caught up with Troop I that evening and made camp along the banks of the Little Wichita, the soldiers still busy at dusk with pickaxes and shovels building a freshly laid roadway of tree trunks secured with pins and lashes in order to span the steep banks of the ford. Mackenzie and his lieutenants were invited into the camp of Captain McLaughlin where they were debriefed on the planned route and served a supper of wild turkey and catfish and there was much talk of the indian campaign ahead.

In the morning they pulled the wagons over the makeshift bridge by hand and swam the horses and mules across the river. A wild and broken country, narrow trails through forests of mesquite and deep ravines cut by sandy creeks where the wagons bogged deep to the axles in the muddy red quicksand. In the afternoon clouds began to build and the earth seemed to seep with heat and when they came upon the main branch of the Wichita River a line of heavy summer thunderstorms moved in. Black skies and rolling thunder. The quartermaster worked his men to prepare the ford and the others lay up under their half-faced guttapercha tents, watching the rain and telling stories of all the big rains they'd seen in their days.

With darkness there was a break in the line of storms. The campfires blazed and popped and the air smelled of smoke and wet leather and the musk of damp gear and when the wind blew just right the occasional sweet-smelling waft of wet horses.

RL took his supper in the tent of a fellow camp guide and as they shared a plate of backstrap and beans the big rains picked up again and they reflected on their suffering. His name was Dozier and he'd been driven from his own ranch into Jacksboro by the indians, a veteran campaigner, and two years prior had survived a desperate fight with Kicking Bird's band in the nearby hills. He raised his cup in toast. Here's to killin injins and trackin down your boys, he said. His lips were dry and cut and dribbled with blood. He doused his drink with a corrective fluid of lime juice and brandy and he sucked the excrement in through his teeth, picking out the bison hairs one by one as he spoke.

Drink up, he said. There aint nothin better than a little buffalo piss after ten hours in the saddle.

Other toasts were said and after supper they had a little whiskey. Outside the frogs were chirping and beyond they could hear the lazy cicada-drone of a summer night. Within the hour RL turned in for bed and as the rain passed streaks of lightning flashed on, flaring the night sky bright as day. The supply wagons sloshed on through the flooded river all through the night and he lay listening.

They rode for the Red River valley the day following with the high grass swishing the haunches of the horses and in the distance wild bulls lounging in the shade of scattered oaks and in the early afternoon the riders, soaked to the core and drenched in sweat like they'd bathed in buckets of rain, rode down out of the rolling mesquite prairie through a lowland of deep red sands and into the camp of McLaughlin's advanced command resting along the banks of Gilbert Creek.

The command was organized into squadrons and two companies of infantry were detailed as guards for the wagontrain and supply camp. They set up tents in the shade of the cottonwoods and the Tonkawas rode west to hunt for game and when they returned a few hours later each of them had deer and turkey strapped to the backs of their ponies. There was a peaceful evening light with the sun sinking low, the horizon bloodred and the meat sizzling over simmering fires of red-hot mesquite coals. They ate quietly while being debriefed on the days ahead, ten troops of the Fourth Cavalry in the early stages of adventures into uncharted country, the younger recruits so hopeful and ambitious, yet so naive in the truths of life and war.

The following morning as they rode out for the crossing of the Red the packmules refused to line out along the trail. They bunched up anxiously into one another with their loads clanging and clattering in the quiet morning air and they bucked up kicking wildly in panic, scattering mess pans and camp kettles and sacks of rice and coffee and bags of beans in a crazed chorus of whinnied heehaws that set the men to cussing and the mules scattering every which way across the prairie. Mackenzie nudged his horse and stepped it sideways out of the fray. In the chaos of all that noise whatever he hollered out at the pack herd officer was understood by no one and his authority in that moment seemed much diminished. He sighed and dropped his head down low in disgust, biting hard on his lower lip, and then he gathered himself and headed off to help wrangle them back under control. Settling the animals and repacking the loads took them a full hour, strapping the sawbuck packsaddles firm and tight and as they rode out a white haze of flour still wafted over the prairie.

They straggled all day in the heat under a sadistic sun and there was no breeze to tender them relief. The men took to riding with wet bandanas or sponges under their hats and some wore goggles to ward off the sun's relentless glare. In the afternoon one man slumped over and dropped from his mount like a rock, crumpled up limp from sunstroke. An hour later another did much the same. These men were hauled along by travois and covered with wet blankets to cool them from the sun and they were dragged along slowly at the rear of the command bouncing and jostling at the mercy of the land.

Mackenzie called for an early halt and these men were laid out to recover in the shade and that evening with the sun going down a small party was detailed to transport them to Fort Sill. Little was said around the camp that evening. As the company spread out on the south side of the river and wandered toward the creek to bathe, three men slipped off into the timbered hills to the east never to be seen again, branded for life as deserters. The command settled in for the night at dusk and were snoring by dark. They had been asleep for only three hours when they were awoken by a wall of roaring fire.

RL was dreaming when something roused him. He opened his eyes and lay there and looked at the ceiling of the tent glowing orange like the sunrise of a new day. He was still breathing deeply in a relaxed slumber and the dream he was still so engaged in placed him very vividly in a time of his past before life had truly taken hold of him. He rose up dumbly and sat there gazing at the brilliant light wavering mystically through the tent canvas. Out on the prairie the long sedge grass was engulfed in flames and a tremendous wall of fire roared toward the camp in the brisk night breeze. What in the holy hell, he said. It was the shouting of men that finally woke him up for good.

He jumped up and rushed outside and looked about and a bugle sounded and others appeared from their tents muddled and milling about and they began to recognize the massive sheet of fire rolling toward them from the south. Men were scrambling for their gear and shouting and running for the horses and mules to prevent a stampede. By the time they were packed up and the cavalry had mounted their ponies and headed toward the sandy bottoms of the river the great fire was bearing down on them from close range, an ominous wall of leaping flames that rumbled on and roared into the starlit sky.

They could hear the grasshoppers and field mice blowing up in little firecracker pops and they could see the broomweed and the juniper shrubs combusting into huge orange balls of flame. Welcome to plains indian guerilla warfare. On the hunt for a roving band of Kiowas and they set the prairie afire while the command sleeps. The wagons creaked and moaned across the sands and the quartermaster with his steaming soliloquies of obscenities whipped them on. When RL got his things safely across the river he turned and looked back and caught his breath. The first of the supply wagons had bogged down in the wet river sand and as they sunk down the wagons behind veered around them, one at a time, losing momentum and getting stuck, the ankles of the mules sucked down into the muck and the constant *weehaws* and the crack of the whips now barely audible, as if they were being drawn back into the void of the fire, the entire wagontrain of the Fourth Cavalry now lined out side by side stranded in the river bed with big gusts of wind firing sparks and flames and fueling the blaze higher behind them.

The crazed animals came running. A pack of coyotes scurried out ahead of the fire splashing across the river. A deer here and there. Skunks, raccoons, porcupines, foxes. Soldiers scampered about hauling handfuls of gear. The cavalrymen were running back into the river to help with the wagons. They unhitched the mules and prodded them one by one to the north side of the river. The muleteers fastened ropes to the frameworks of the wagons and long lines of men were attempting to pull them from the quicksand and the soldiers on the bank frantically strung long lines of rope back to the wagons and re-hitched the mules, now standing on firm ground, and began to whip them into motion. Other groups of men stood knee deep in the mud pushing from behind like some crazed horde of army ants.

Slowly the wagons began to nudge up out of the sand, a few feet at a time, the fire raging into the breaks of the river smoldering in a hiss of cooking varmints and the pungent smell of burning animal skins. A long night. It was dawn before they pulled the last of the wagons up from the riverbed and they could see the buzzards and the hawks in the rising sun swooping down onto the blackened prairie to the south.

They gathered themselves and watched the sunrise, the river flowing on, glistening in that surreal fire-branded light of the new day. Then something miraculously appeared from out of the smoldering blackness on the far side of the river, limping along in agony until it collapsed at the water's edge. It was a lone buck antelope, seared beyond recognition and fighting for each breath. RL waded back into the river with pistol in hand. When he reached the animal its forelegs were scraping the wet sand. Eyes burned out, gurgling on its own blood. A line of men had gathered at the shore to watch him and he put the gun to its head and fired. The shot rang out. RL stood there staring at the animal. Someone called out to him but he did not look back.

All that morning they crossed a broad flat layered in sandhills and shrubbed up in forests of honey mesquite. In the afternoon they began to pass through the sprawling packed earth mounds of the prairie dog towns and they could hear atop their little bare dirt houses the short chopping yip calls of the sentinel dogs calling out in warning as others emerged to watch. There were desert vipers lying coiled in the hot sun and when a rider passed the prairie hummed in rattle. Enormous herds of buffalo were grazing upon the grasslands as they rode through the heat of the day and with the setting sun they saw the forms of burrowing owls that had emerged from their holes to hunt their prey in the cool of dusk.

That night they camped along the banks of West Cache Creek with rib roasts of buffalo larded with bacon roasting on the fires and they garnished their plates like gourmet chefs with salt and pepper, onions and biscuits, and medallions of backstrap cut from antelope and deer. When they rode out in the morning it was still and warm. They crossed the old Radziminski Trail and in the middle of the afternoon they reached the tree-lined banks of Otter Creek and acquainted themselves with the command of the Tenth Cavalry who had been awaiting their arrival there.

General Grierson was the man in charge of this mostly black regiment. He'd garnered acclaim during the war leading a successful incursion deep into the Confederacy as part of the Vicksburg Campaign and he had just arrived here two days ago for the cooperative expedition with Mackenzie and the Fourth. They were recovering from the hardships of their journey and there had been several men deathly ill from the vile water along with a small remuda of unserviceable animals. The regiment also included the two Fort Sill post interpreters who were well-informed of the Kiowa ongoings and there was talk of the village being located somewhere in the Wichita Mountains along a stream known as the Sweetwater. There was also much discussion that they would have with them a bevy of white captives.

Mackenzie disdained any man who went about his business with an air of false pretense and he was distrustful of Grierson despite his cordial nature. It took them the better part of a week to establish the supply camp. The officers of the two regiments held conferences and surveys of the surrounding country were made and they gathered themselves for the dangerous journey ahead.

Now three weeks into August and the two commands and their pack trains set out along divergent trails into the shinoak sandhills that led up the traces of the North Fork of the Red River. Late that morning a mounted courier that had been sent from the supply camp caught them up where they were dislodging a wagon bogged down in the sand. He had with him a sealed envelope and rode hastily into the command and dismounted and saluted before removing an official letter from his saddle bag and handing it to Mackenzie.

Mackenzie took the envelope and walked out alone atop a ridge with long views to the west. He opened the letter and up on that plateau it flapped furiously in the wind as if somehow it was not meant to be in his hands. A bank of clouds floated under the sun and a darkness fell over the land and a rogue gust of wind swirled up a whirl of red dust that consumed him in that silhouette. He read the letter twice, carefully. Then he crumpled it up indignantly and dropped it in disgust. He stood there for a long time. The breeze blew it on but after a while he walked over and picked it up and stuffed it in his field shirt and turned back.

It was a ten day march into the great gypsum plains hunting indians. Long ranges of marl and clays sprinkled with crystals of selenite. Large sandstone slabs looming tall and glistening in the sun as if they'd been balanced by the Gods on towering red columns of clay. Shores of dry streambeds frosted in gypsum, great handfuls of salt piled alongside their trail. They rode through acres of agate and jasper and chalcedony and masses of broken rock fields dotted with dwarf junipers and stunted mesquites. Their course was west of north. There was no breeze. The thermometer read one hundred eight in the shade. They mixed their canteens with citric acid and smeared their lips in camphor ice and they covered their faces in boneblack or wore goggles to deflect the glare. Mackenzie called a halt and he rode out from the head of the column to join the scouts where RL chartered course by taking bearings with an old prismatic compass. The colonel pointed west and RL flattened his hand slantwise a quarter angle to the north and then they looked back to take in the scene of the country and the command following before finishing their council and riding off into the badlands again.

Whah en da hell dey look'n fo? said a negro field cook from Troop C.

Oh Lawdy Gawd Jeesus I's aint agot a no damn notion! But I knows dem injuns sho nuff got sense nuff not to be en dis place.

Deys lost, dah's whah dey is.

By noon of the seventh day they began to come upon broad trails of trampled grass where the indian lodgepoles had rutted the ground with dragmarks and they rode through abandoned camps with burned out pits and the refuse of the nomadic tribes. Animal carcasses, piles of flintknappings and crushed beanpods, trinkets and tools broken and discarded. The Tonkawa scouts would ride out ahead, the command slogging along burned by the searing sun and pained by the back fever, cramping and grimacing from the effects of the vile water and making sudden and hurried halts to rush off into the brush, then back in the saddle again, shifting uneasily from the chafing.

That evening they camped along the banks of a foul-smelling stream amid swarms of horseflies as big as hummingbirds and they bathed where the buffalo had wallowed and when they emerged from the water in their skivvies the desert breeze dried them up in a thin sheen of gypsum crust.

The Tonkawas returned after dark placing the bivouac by the light of the fires. Mackenzie rose from his supper to look them over and greet them. They had made sixty miles that day and their ponies were wasted but the Tonkawas looked none the worse for wear. He sat with them and listened to the reports of their findings as they roasted the steaks of a fawn over their fire. When they were done he walked off and stood in the shadows alone with his thoughts, watching the new evening stars twinkling in the last light before dark. He took off his hat and let it fall to the grass and he dropped his face into his hands and rubbed his forehead and eyes for a long time before he looked back out upon the prairie. Somewhere out there beyond the ridges the coyotes had set up a wild sad clamor. This is my job, he said. I dont sleep and I'm in terrible pain. I hunt indians. This is my life. Then he sighed and picked up his hat and headed back to his tent to endure the long dark night.

They were lying shirtless atop their blankets snoring loudly when a band of Quahadi raiders crept upon the horse herd in the middle of the night. They'd been spying them from atop the bluffs the previous day, studying the wretched condition of the remuda as the command struggled on. A handful of young warriors snuck into the loose herds under the moonlight and scared the bejesus out of some grazing colts, two rearing at their lariats in play until one of them bucked up on his haunches and then broke for the creek like a thunderbolt.

Panic spread through the herd within seconds. They awoke to the rolling thunder of hooves and the wild yip yapping of the raiders rushing them on, the horses in full stride stampeding through the camp. The Tonkawas dashed off in pursuit. It was three hours before first light and the Dog Star was rising in the southeast. When they returned an hour later they had the bulk of the horses with them and they secured them with sidelines and then all laid down to sleep.

The next day they crossed the trail of a small party of indians. They could tell by the tracks it was four riders strong and they followed a thin trace of hoofpath through the sagebrush running uphill and as they crested the ridge they ran full on into a band of horsemen charging up toward them from the opposite side. Wild shouts and panicked curses. A greenhorn screamed like a schoolgirl frightened by a mouse. The indians wheeled around and fled. Boehm and his scouts set out in pursuit but when the riders glanced back and saw Old Henry waving a white rag the lead rider reined up and his comrades halted behind him. Henry called out to his men and something in the tone of his voice must have garnered their attention for they murmured among themselves and stepped their horses forward with discretion, clutching their weapons.

The raiders were just boys on a joy ride away from their village and the oldest might have been thirteen. They sat bareback, two of them on fillies and two of them on colts, and they were naked save for breechclouts and they carried hunting bows of osage and quivers of antelope skin slung across their sides, ornamented with buffalo hide and horse hairs or turkey beards and each of the weapons with patches of coyote fur to bring luck to the hunt.

Mackenzie came forward to question them but they stared back coldly and did not answer, trying their best to disguise their fear until suddenly the eldest of them wheeled his horse and whipped it into a run and then they all set off galloping to the north. He watched them go. The cursed letter he carried from Washington held certain orders that he kept solely to himself. The Tonkawas watched the departure warily, the forms of their enemies growing smaller. They shook their heads and muttered obscenities to themselves as the dust of the fleeing ponies rose slowly above the prairie.

They rode west that afternoon across the crater of an ancient volcano, scrabbled fields strewn with fossils from the old seas and scoria from the lava that once flowed there. The sun reflecting off the bedrock burned the hooves of the animals and in that bakeoven heat several of the weaker horses and mules began to fail and were left behind.

RL had been riding out ahead on scout and he surveyed the long ranges of igneous bluffs glistening in the sunlight with much attention. He rode over to confer with Boehm. He'd seen subtle movements in the hills, fleeting flashes upon the horizon. They rode back to debrief Mackenzie but he kept the command on the march, slogging across the prairie with his eyes casting furtive glances upon the emptiness about.

That evening they pushed farther into the wasted badland hills. In the early moonless night the stars swung slowly and shimmered in their endless cycle. They took to reckoning by the lodestar. The Tonkawas pushed on ahead into the darkness and RL and Dozier led separate patrols, fanning the riders out to cover wider ground and advancing them slowly afoot to scan the desert tracks for signs and then they would remount to ride back and give report to the lumbering command of wagons and mules that followed.

The wagons creaked and groaned along through mazes of cobbled trails and broken arroyos, the packmules scrabbling across the dull white pavements of gypsum. The quartermaster steadied his horse and called out orders to the drovers, halting them at a steep ravine to reroute them along a gentler egress, the men pushing them into a slide down the bank and beating them madly on to the upside of the slope. They whipped and cursed them onward through the blackness of the night but the trailers would ram up into the frightened lead mules and the entire conducta would bunch up and break into an earsplitting chorus of brays, bucking this way and that, the contents of their packs clattering and clanging and scattering all about the broken talus floor.

They repacked the panniers and drove them on through the night. Upward of one hundred mules strung out, lumbering over a dozen or more rugged ravines. At dawn the Tonkawas returned with news of fresh signs along the course of the North Fork an hour ahead and with daylight they halted to take their bearings. They bivouacked without food or water and the wasted animals lay down and rolled upon the ground groaning. They had made that night only seven miles.

They set forth in a burning dawn and high clouds slowly filled the sky and by noon a warm south wind heaved and hissed across the barren sunbaked plains. Crossing the rocky bluffs that afternoon they took signals from the scouts on the flanks who had spotted fresh trails of the indian hunting parties. They came upon another deserted campsite lined out along a dry creek where water had once pooled. Hundreds of buffalofish had gathered here to breed in the shallow waters and died, their bones strewn along the shores with the feathers of buzzards and eagles. Dozier whistled at RL and called him over to a sink of soft sand

and they knelt down and commenced to dig for a seep but it was dry.

Carter made his way across the wash and handed RL a canteen.

What do you think? he said.

I dont know.

The waterkegs seem hollow.

RL spat. He took a sip from his flasket and grimaced and handed it over to Dozier. I'll tell you what you ought to do, Carter, he said. Go tell them damn Tonks to find us some water.

Carter stared back. He turned and surveyed the command. Mackenzie had walked out onto a promontory and was studying a map that he'd spread out on the cracked prairie floor. He had Thompson with him scribbling in a notebook and another man was taking altitude by barometer.

Dozier, how far to agua pura? said Carter.

Dozier turned his weather eye. Well, If we can make good time I'd reckon another day's ride.

Carter looked up as if to consider their options or the weather but there was not a cloud in the sky. And I dont suppose there's any chance of rain? he said.

Dozier was chewing hard on a massive quid of tobacco but when the question was posed he stopped. He was scanning the sky with a squinched eye and reckoning the breeze and he seemed to be smelling the dry desert air with a sobered attention. He spat out his chew. Well, sir, I may not know nothin, he said, and then paused for effect. But I shore believe we's a goin to have us a turd float come evenin.

They went on scouting the west side of the North Fork without resting. They left a broad trampled trail across a vast mesquite plain into the early evening where in the distance they could see the fork of the river winding its course across the plain. Well after dark the pack train had still not come into the camp. They lit torches of dried grass as signal fires and waited and made speculations using various uncertain military and frontier theories and after a few hours a long line of mules slowly appeared from out of the darkness. A thin slice of moon was sinking over the western horizon. Lightning flared to the north and there was a long distant rumble of thunder. By midnight the wind howled and sheets of rain poured down upon them as they slept. The tent flies sagged under great buckets of water and the ridgepoles leaned and bent, trembled weakly, collapsed into heaps of wet canvas. They spent the better part of the next morning wringing out clothes and drying gear.

They set out in a steaming mist and soon the great sun burned away the clouds and baked the prairie again and in the afternoon they came upon a buffalo wallow that had filled with fresh runoff from the storm, the animals rushing into the clear pool and trampling it into a sloppy concoction of soupy mud, the riders trying to rein them back and beating them as they cursed out commands. When it had settled they dismounted and dipped their canteens in the mudpool and watched the murk slip slowly inside. Then they mouthed the canteens and sipped gingerly, just enough to wet their lips. This went on for a good while. Then they let the animals to water and set out again.

They scouted slowly along the course of the river. Signs of the indians everywhere. There were networks of fresh hunting trails and abandoned grass huts scattered across the valley. All day the high clouds floated above the plains and a hot wind whipped in from the south. They rode for miles and miles with herds of bison pressed along their flanks. They turned north and crossed the shallow river and at dusk a cougar came bounding out of the shore reeds and frightened the horses and the Tonkawas dashed off in pursuit.

Two days later they rode into the valley of the Sweetwater where it entered the Indian Territory, a boundary Mackenzie's classified orders forbid him to cross. He rode out ahead on the prairie and observed the scouts and they pointed out across the low-slung sandhills and the rolling grasslands and the winding river beyond where only eight miles downstream to the southeast were the late summer hunting camps of the Kiowas for which they sought. He fought the darkness inside that possessed his soul. He'd been forbidden to hunt them down. He dismounted and led the horse out alone to a place of vantage and stood there for a long while looking out over the country, as if the solitude might somehow appease him, and then he remounted and caught them up.

He led the command back to the southeast and in the days to follow they began to see in the distant hills to the north columns of smoke rising where the Kiowa scouts had signaled warning of their passing but by now the lieutenants knew they would not be going there. They descended from the plains back into the badlands again, a scrabbled gorge of conical mounds of every shape and color with gypsum water gurgling clear and cool from the scabrous points. The Tonkawas would head out along some random rocky path, stepping the horses gingerly through whatever food-stuffs or camp goods had been hastily abandoned on the trails, dismounting to put their ears to the ground or studying the sand for some faint trace of hoofprint.

They rode into camp at dusk with the news of their findings and they crouched around their fires grumbling sullenly among themselves. A fiery sun dropped low in the west highlighting the wild shades of outcroppings and along the red marl of the bluffs the shadows of their firelights flickered and danced and in the night wolves appeared out of the darkness to howl and slobber and snap their teeth like rabid werewolves lingering upon the fringes of the camp. As always, by the faint light of candle into the early hours of morning sat Mackenzie, sleepless and tormented. He walked his tent in circles and shuffled his maps on the crate before him and he leaned over, studying them deeply and nervously popping the stubs of his crippled fingers murmuring various philosophies and convictions to himself.

Mackenzie ignored his scouts' advice. His duty to follow orders as a soldier held true. He hardly spoke. Even though the intelligence regarding the location of the Kiowa camp was specific and believed true he knew it would be foolish to disobey orders. Two nights later when his lieutenants requested council to question his strategy he was indifferent. They crept into their tents and fell asleep in silent speculation and in the morning they rode out whispering various theories and rumors to one another.

The way back out of the badlands toward the supply camp led them through a rolling shortgrass country where grouse and bobwhite quail foraged and flushed. They rode for the Salt Fork and the country became broken again and there were many rugged ravines and they descended and ascended them repeatedly. Shrinking puddles of water lay stagnant along the beds of the creeks they followed, ringed by deposits of satin spar and pyrite. In three days they reached the Salt Fork. On the fourth they found Grierson's command again, living in luxury at the Otter Creek camp, lounging and smoking in the shade of a grove of cottonwoods. The captain in charge had been expecting them and he hurried out to the edge of the camp with a detail of men to greet them. Mackenzie looked them over from atop his horse and then he dismounted. The captain saluted him.

Captain Carpenter, said Mackenzie. Where's Colonel Grierson?

He's gone to Fort Sill, sir.

Fort Sill?

Yes sir, Fort Sill.

Mackenzie glared back. He slowly surveyed the scene about the camp with narrow hawk eyes. Carter, he said. Get the men lined out wherever you see fit.

Yes sir.

Mackenzie turned and started walking and he was shaking his head angrily and mumbling to himself when the captain called out to him. He was following along carrying a large envelope in his hand.

Excuse me sir. Colonel Grierson asked me to deliver this to you.

Mackenzie held up. The captain handed it over. The package was colorful and elaborately printed in flashy, morale building propaganda. Mackenzie held it in his hands and studied the artwork. It depicted a scene of the Battle of Mill Spring.

Thank you, Captain.

My pleasure. And one more thing sir.

Mackenzie stood there impatiently.

We've a fine camp set up for this evening. Over in the grove by the stream. I'd like to invite you and your lieutenants to dinner, sir.

He pointed the way. Mackenzie turned and surveyed the set up. Well Captain, now that's very kind of you, he said. Let us get settled and we'll see about that.

In the evening dinner was served at a long whiteclothed table set between two canvas wall tents and shaded by a spanking new tarpfly that had been stretched overhead. The sun had just set and there was the quiet light of dusk. A nice summer breeze was blowing. A paraffin lamp had been lit upon a side table and candles were lined out before them. They were seated in folding oak camp chairs with handwoven Danish corded seats while a leadwaiter and two attendants brought appetizers of grilled quail wrapped in bacon and plates of sweetbreads and they were served in courses great heapings of wild turkey and buffalo and catfish from the stream. Once they had eaten the talk turned to the indian campaign and they were served a prune pie dessert and after they had finished Carpenter excused himself and returned promptly with a set of tin cups and a decanter of Old Crow whiskey.

Mackenzie sat at the head of the table and he raised his cup and gave a toast to the prune pie and the captain's hospitality and also to President Grant and then he began to engage the captain in a seemingly casual series of compliments and inquiries that got the captain to talking as they sipped their drinks. Carpenter downed his whiskey and it warmed his soul and he began to reveal to the table details of their indian adventures, including some of which on Grierson's orders he was not at liberty to divulge. Carter poured him another drink and before long Carpenter confessed to them that they had in fact found the Kiowas. Mackenzie prodded the amenable captain, listening for subtle details that might confirm what he believed, that Grierson's true commission was solely to warn Kicking Bird of the Fourth's approach and perhaps even escort them into the reservation at Fort Sill. He watched the captain and in his soul he cursed the letter that he held with his orders, nodding, biting his tongue, mulling over the darkness of his thoughts and confirming the harsh reality he knew in his gut. His campaign was over and there was nothing to do but march the command back to Texas.

17

— ★ —

Blanco Canyon

Fall 1871

Three weeks later Mackenzie had the command assembled on the Clear Fork of the Brazos and he sent a detachment to scout a practicable route for the wagontrain. There were in the camp now six hundred men from ten companies of troops along with one hundred packmules grazing in the lush grasses along the banks of the river. Mackenzie kept his officers in preparatory meetings but otherwise left the bulk of the command at their leisure to rest for the journey ahead. Both Carter and RL had become trusted advisors in his planning and several times each day they would assemble around a long table that would be covered every inch in maps and papers. They drew lines and made lists, meticulous notations of every manner. They reviewed their strategies ad nauseam and studied the route that would lead them along the thirty-third parallel beyond the California and Paint Creeks and across the Double Mountain and Salt Forks of the Brazos.

The outriders returned on the third of October and a few hours later the command set out west along the military road, anxious and excited for the trails ahead, singing a spirited tune of an old regimental song. RL rode out ahead of the command with Boehm and the Tonkawas, scouring the trail for signs and looking back to signal to the long column of riders lined out for miles along the wide bend of the river winding its course back to the frontier settlements and on to the distant sea beyond.

They rode through a dry mesquite plain and slogged across the quicksand streams within sight of the Double Mountains and took a northwest course crisscrossing the Salt Fork until late on the fourth day they came upon the mouth of Duck Creek as the sun slipped slowly into the desert. The slopes of the valley rose gently above them and the dugouts of the abandoned Comanchero trading stations scattered among the bluffs were bathed in the afternoon sunlight. That evening the scouts were sent out to search for the indians and on the distant prairies they could hear the bison bulls in rut bellowing out there in the failing light.

They followed the Freshwater Fork of the Brazos and as they neared the mouth of Blanco Canyon they began to come upon signs of the village. A few faint tracks of Comanche ponies scattered in the sands of the thin trails that led from the water. A sapling bent along the ground to point the way to a spring. In the middle of the afternoon of the sixth day they saw a small band of riders observing them from the bluffs but these spies were mounted on fresh ponies and easily made their escape. The scouts turned back and rode briskly for the supply camp and arrived an hour before dark to find the command sidelining the horse herds.

Dozier and RL surveyed the camp and when they took their supper by the fire that evening they invited Carter over to share their mess. Well Lieutenant, said Dozier, you might ought to let the colonel know to ring this camp with sentinels on account of them injuns. Carter looked out over the herd. He looked back at Dozier. It was a struggle to take him seriously. His mustache was tangled up in globs of snot and grime and tobacco and yet his bloodred eyes scrunched up confidently as if he'd just spoken the absolute truth of God. Dozier handed him up a plate. Hep ye self, he said. Carter nodded and took the plate and sat down and commenced to eat.

After supper RL sat watching the moonset and someone called to extinguish the fires and soon the command had turned themselves in for the night. It was very still, barely a whisper of breeze, and when it died he could hear the voices of men mumbling and the horses grazing at the end of their lariats. Before long all was quiet but there was movement in the hills and just after midnight as they slept soundly in their blankets they were ridden upon by a band of Quahadi raiders under the command of Quanah. An all-out stampede ensued in which Mackenzie's fine gray pacer was stolen and another sixty or more of the herd ran off in a panic.

The remainder of that night was spent getting the animals under control and assessing their losses. They untangled the maze of lariats and picket pins and kept watch to guard against another attack and in the first gray light they saddled up to hunt for the stray horses. RL followed the faint trace of a trail to the west and headed off alone. He crossed the Fresh Fork and followed it up through the sagebrush to a bluff with long views of the camp and the distant sunrise.

Silence hung on the prairie and the air smelled hot. Damn, he whispered. Already beads of sweat were pouring down his face and neck. He took off his hat and shaded his eyes and studied what lay before him. Then he heard a shot ring out. He looked out to the northeast for the noise and he heard a man shout and he kicked the horse into a hard gallop down the far side of the hill where after a short ride he came upon two detachments of soldiers gazing far off down the valley. The horses were blowing lightly from the trot. RL stood tall on his horse with his pistol drawn.

A dozen or more indians were riding with a large herd of loose horses on the north side of the river valley and they were moving west. They were hardly visible in the glare but they could make out the galloping forms and they could hear their hooves pounding into the prairie a half mile away. They nudged their horses forward and took off after them.

The freshest horses took the lead and those riders scattered in the chase and were able to gain ground on the indians rapidly. When the two lead riders opened fire the herdsmen abandoned the stolen herd and leapt off a ledge down into an arroyo and kicked up their ponies and sprinted out for the high bluffs beyond. Men were shouting and some of them reined up at the ledge but RL and Carter and a small contingency of riders cleared the ridge down into the scrabbled watercourse through the clouds of dust rising in the early light. They lengthened the reins and cursed the horses on. The sun was now up and rising behind them. They seemed to be gaining ground when they lost sight of the indians again over a ridge up ahead and they spurred the horses on. They ascended the hill and as they drew rein on the ridge their jaws dropped and they stared in awe at the scene before them. They began looking about frantically at one another as if someone might have a plan but no one seemed to be able to utter a single word. They could not believe their eyes.

A horde of a hundred or more mounted warriors were galloping toward them from the base of the bluff and they had begun to fan out and circle around their flanks. They were naked to the waist and decked out in trinkets of bells and feathers, shells and bones, and they had done themselves up in warpaints of every design and color, their ponies adorned with stripes of paint and flashy strips of flannel or calico and while they may have been poorly armed with rusted old pistols and muzzle loading rifles they came charging up the ridge like a swarm of angry bees, whooping and howling, flurries of arrows and pistolfire, all of them rushing to take the first scalp. Quanah was in the lead on a coal black racing pony and keeping pace about ten yards on his right flank rode Samuel *Pahvo* Terry.

Carter shouted. The company spread out and commenced firing with their carbines but the Quahadis tactically weathered this initial line of fire and as they advanced their line the soldiers began to let off rounds and duck low on their mounts. Their line was forced to fall back slowly. Several of the horses had been struck with arrows. One man took a bullet to the hand. When some of the panicked recruits turned their mounts and ran for their lives the Comanches began yapping and rushed them in a crazed flurry.

By now the lead Comanche riders were drawing near. Fire damnit, fire! yelled Carter, and the remaining handful of soldiers began to let off a desperate volley of gunfire. When the indians fell away in confusion he called for them to make a run back for the main column but there was a lieutenant named Gregg on an old gray horse and it wouldnt go. She's give out! he shouted. Then it took a few steps and swayed and crumpled to the dirt.

RL had checked his horse and was holding his Smith and Wesson in both hands and letting off shots to provide cover for Gregg. Quanah was closing in with his pistol held aloft, zigzagging his mount and using the fallen man as a shield. Gregg pulled frantically at the lever of his carbine but the cartridge had jammed and as he fumbled with his holster to receive the charge with his pistol Quanah shot him point blank through the head. Gregg slumped over and fell into the dirt with a thud. Quanah turned his mount aside, sitting tall atop the horse and he stared down the soldiers and let out a long, crazed howl. Bullets were whizzing by. When Quanah whirled back and broke into a zigzagging run they could see the long headdress of eagle feathers jinking and bobbing and flowing in the wind. Pahvo and the other warriors wheeled their mounts and followed him, howling out in a frenzy of short, sharp yips and the clouds of dust from the loping ponies rising slowly in the dry desert air with the bullets nipping at their heels.

Now the Tonkawas could be heard yelling out bloodoaths from out of the valley and beyond the dust from the advancing main column rose above the sunlit prairie like a golden veil when suddenly Boehm and the Tonkawas came flying atop their mounts from over the ridge. Take that side! he yelled, and they recharged their pieces and scattered out into a skirmish line fifty men strong. They whipped them on and urged their horses up the butte to where it leveled off and widened into a broad plain and they pressed on after the fleeing Comanches as they scampered for the scrabbled breaks of Blanco Canyon.

Mackenzie urged them on. For the next hour the Comanches stayed just out of rifle range, single warriors circling back in diversion, the squaws in the rear lines screaming insults and taunts and leading the fresh ponies. Now and again one of the Tonks would dash to the front lines to invite a duel and a Comanche would rush out to meet him, each of them firing imprecisely before whirling back to the battle line. Up in the rugged hills scurrying among the rocks were snipers with old target rifles, their bullets zinging the air and plunking the dust like random hailstones.

By the time the entire cavalry force arrived the horses were too weak to continue and the Comanches were gradually disappearing up over the rim onto the Llano Estacado. Mackenzie kept the Tonkawas on the trail but turned the command back. They marched back down the valley to bury Gregg where he lie sprawled out and stiffening in the dirt and they dug a hole in the earth and rolled him in his grave and covered it with large stones and said a prayer. They spread the horses out to graze with pickets on strong guard and settled down in the shade of the butte to gather themselves. Two hours later the scouts returned. The Quahadis had broken their camp and were moving the entire village across the Staked Plains.

Mackenzie gathered his staff. They walked to a vantage point where they could catch the breeze and they studied the rugged crags of the escarpment at the far mouth of the canyon.

How many of them are there? said Mackenzie.

Boehm shook his head. They have their women and children with them. Ole Henry thinks two, maybe three hundred. They wont be able to move fast.

How far can we push it from the supply camp?

Hell if I know. Sixty miles. Eighty. What do you think, Bob?

Carter did not know. Mackenzie looked at RL. What do you know about the terrain up top?

RL stepped out and shielded his eyes from the white sun that now sat pulsing high above the rim. He put his hand out and waved it like a conductor. There's good grass, he said. Playa lakes with water. And the meskins cross it pretty regular.

How far can we make it?

Well, our horses are shot. But I'd say at least another sixty miles in that country up there.

Mackenzie turned and looked out over the command. RL pinched a nostril and blew a hunk of snot into the dust. If we can get going and set camp this evenin at the base of the Llano, he said, we ought to be able to get up and make a run at em in the mornin.

Okay.

But we best get goin.

Have you thought about your boys being with them?

We'll just have to spread the word, let the chips fall where they may.

Peter, make sure the Tonks know about the Terry boys. Remind the men to be on the lookout for white indians.

Yes sir.

If they get close and encounter a man that looks like he might have white blood.

Yes sir.

Or a woman for that matter.

A gust of hot wind picked up out of the south. Large flocks of mallard came soaring off the Caprock whistling through the blue zenith of the sunbaked sky.

Let's go, said RL.

They rode out within the hour and by late afternoon they were scouting the fertile banks of the White River where it flowed clear and clean from the base of the Caprock. They bivouacked there on the grounds of the recent Quahadi campsite, a series of springfed pools swimming with fish and ducks and geese and all about the small grass shelters of the Comanche herdsmen nestled among the sheltered rocks. A detail of men was assigned to inspect the trails leading up to the canyon rim and they hiked carefully in the dusk, testing a trail here, a trail there, and stopping now and again to look back down and study the routes they had taken. They broke camp by first light and the sunrise found them pushing further up the valley again.

They followed the trail set by the scouts who were riding out an hour ahead and in the afternoon they came upon the trampled ground where the large indian herds had been grazing in the lush grasses of the valley floor. The trail turned up a tributary stream and by and by they came upon the remains of the main village that had seemingly vanished into thin air.

They dismounted and made their way slowly through acres and acres of trampled grass circles near the remains of small charcoal fires where the tipis provided shelter from the wind and rain and sun.

The Comanches had not been gone long. The camp was littered with refuse and the remains of bison and deer and antelope. There were piles of dried dung and chunks of mulberry and mesquite roots. Discarded stone hammers and forked sticks with strips of drying meat. Mortars of freshly crushed seedpods and rows of newly scraped hides and a boy's first bow that was broken.

The dragmarks from the lodgepoles converged at a central point at the western edge of the village and from there a broad trail leading up the canyon clearly marked the start of the village's frantic escape. Already the scouts were scouring the trails up out of the valley to the rim of the plains, their ponies sclattering through the scrabble of scrub and rock. All afternoon they scouted the diverging trail along the breaks of the escarpment. A pair of large black ravens soared high above as if to warn them with their deep and throaty croakings echoing off the canyon walls. They rode along a trail that would split, a faint track leading south and another north and then west, up gentle inclines and down steep ridges and crossing and recrossing and then converging again. They rode around giant sandstone columns and boulder-strewn wastelands and they rode through a run of low-lying hills that led them east down a fresh path that lured them along a backtrail that terminated when darkness overtook them and there they bivouacked at their place of origin.

They set out pickets and herded the packmules inside a squadron of guards and they slept that night without fires. Mackenzie stayed awake studying into the early hours of the morning. He looked at maps, he scribbled in his journal, he read a biography of Napoleon. He consulted a tattered book of poetry that he carried with him. In the morning when they rose the sky seemed to hold a strange light and when the sun appeared they could see the Tonks signaling urgently from the edge of the Caprock on the plains a thousand feet above. By the time they ascended the great mesa a strong north wind was blowing down from the arctic and the faint squall line of an immense sandstorm could be seen looming like God's own anvil above the horizon.

The Tonkawas had picked up the lost trail and reckoned the Quahadis on the move only three hours due west across the plains with several thousand horses and their entire village in tow. As far as the eye could see the booming void of the prairie stretched out before them. The company marched on into the face of the norther. The sky turned gray. By early afternoon the first great shock of cold, dry wind struck them and within minutes they were visited with icy drops of rain out of that darkening sky.

They nudged the horses on. Already the temperature had plunged forty degrees. They pulled their hats down tight and leaned in and hunkered low. They rode all day across that vast sea of grass and the freezing rain and sleet and snow would not let up. They began to come upon abandoned lodgepoles scattered across the trail and the hailstones on that endless prairie were soon piled inches deep and the summer clothes they wore were stiff and frozen and coated in ice and their feet were numb and still it was growing colder. Then two hours before dark in the shimmering flare of a long flash of lightning they saw something in the far distance. At first ones and twos and then dozens and then hundreds. Mounted men galloping slowly into the storm. Little figurines shambling along in a dark and dreary dream. The entire Comanche village was moving out there on the plain in silhouette only a few miles before them.

18

— ★ —

Cleo, Texas

1876

How many of there were you? That day on the plains above Blanco Canyon when we found you?

All of us. The entire village.

Rode through that norther all night?

Most of it.

What about the old folks?

We mounted them on horses behind the younger boys.

They were sitting in the shade of an old oak tree, hats off and taking the breeze, leaning against a sprawling branch that skirted a soft patch of grass. There was a bucket of spring water with bottles of beer between them and RL pulled one out of the cool dampness and placed it to his cheek.

I couldnt make sense of it, he said. None of us could. Mackenzie not keepin after you. But I spose it was meant for to be that way.

Sam drained the last of his beer. What?

RL had learned Sam was more prone to talking with a few beers in him and he handed him another. How things play out, he said. There were six hunnerd soldiers. It would have been a slaughter. And you wouldnt be here with me right now.

Sam popped the top with his teeth and sipped the beer. I dont know, he said. Quanah has a way about things. He would have figured something out.

RL pinched his lips together with a pained face and he was shaking his head slowly.

Tell me something. How in the hell was an orphaned half-breed able to command the respect of the Comanche people?

Sam sat there looking out, thinking for a long while. Something circling very high in the sky above them. A massive thunderhead forming in the afternoon heat. Well, just the look of him was intimidating, he said. He was a head taller. The muscles in his arms and shoulders. He could run, wrestle, handle a bow and a rifle. We could all ride but not like him. Well, maybe I could.

I seen him ride. God knows I saw that first-hand when he blew that ole boy's brains out.

He was a cold-blooded killer when it counted but you'd never find anyone with a bigger heart. Never hurt women and children. Never tortured a captive, which was unlike most every other Comanche. He'd just make it so that they understood there'd be no harm if they didnt attempt to escape.

Is that right?

Yes. We once had a white man roaming with us for months and Quanah took a liking to him. Eventually, he had one of his wives slip him a little tip that helped him escape.

RL did not say anything. A breeze picked up and he tilted his head back to feel the air. Sam was flicking the lip of the bottle lightly with his fingernail in a rhythm as he spoke.

There was hardly ever a situation that caused him concern. Riding that night into the norther, it was like a dream. It almost seemed like he was enjoying himself. I watched him. He rode around, this way and that, talking to people and directing things. No one questioned him. The other chiefs followed his lead. We did what he said and did it without fear because we trusted him.

Did you know that when you stampeded our camp there were four or five hundred sleeping soldiers armed with Spencers and Colts, all of them with hundreds of rounds of ammo? Was that his idea?

Yes, it was. And most of the other chiefs were against it. But he convinced them we could leave the bluecoats afoot, and the possibilities of what that meant were almost too good to be true.

What about that weather? Did he know that front was coming when he led the village up across the plains?

Well, it had been so warm. But most of us overlooked that. Quanah was the one who pointed out all the ducks flying down from the west over the Caprock earlier that day. Flock after flock. We were always taught to hone our instincts, but with him there is just something different. He has a knack for making decisions.

RL had been looking down but when Sam paused to take a breath he looked back up at him. Look son, he's just a man, he said. Like any other. Luck plays into things.

Luck?

RL watched him. Sam dipped his hand in the bucket and wiped his face with a splash of cool water. Sam was shaking his head.

He knew that storm would punish the taibos in their summer clothes, he said. And he weighed the risk. No matter how many of you there were. We had fresh horses. Even so, I dont think he felt like the Tonks would find the trail up across the plains. But he never seem worried. Not one bit. He'd sent a bunch of us out on the rear guard to scout. To create diversions. And he calmly pressed the village on as if it was the perfect time to move, on the perfect day. We were able to make out the halt of the command when the storm broke. But then it became impossible to see from the sleet and snow and darkness. I was with a group of scouts trying to locate your exact location. Where the packmules had been huddled up. We were blinded by the storm and couldnt hear anything for the wind and we accidentally stumbled right into your camp.

I remember. I can picture it plain as day.

I've never turned a horse and run out like that. Bullet grazed my arm right here.

He grabbed his shirt collar and raised it up over his head and looked at his left shoulder. See there, he said. Sliced it right where that scar is. We moved all night and just before morning as the storm cleared the most beautiful sun you've ever seen rose up behind us. Clear, blue skies. No wind. Ice crystals sparkling and the land so bright you had to shield your eyes from the glare. Quanah ordered fires built. He sat there smiling with the sun coming up, feeling its warmth. Like he'd just got up from a long night's sleep. He was smiling and loving on his horse like it was any other day.

Then after lying up for about three hours that morning he sent us on the backtrail to keep an eye on the bluecoats. What a beautiful day that was. Could not have been more silent on the prairie. Just the crunch of the ice as we followed the tracks through the snow. We watched you all resting down in the canyon. Men lounging around and sleeping. Aseway-nah said we should have a little fun. But I didnt agree. I told him there was no use in us dying.

The Fischer boy?

Yes. Rudolph Fischer.

How many others were there?

Well, it was me, him, a Mexican captive about my age we called Babo-so. Never had much sense. His older brother. A few others. The Mexicans dismounted and were quietly leading their horses down into the canyon. We were working around for a better vantage point. But by the time they'd gotten closer the Tonks had spotted them and came running. I dont know why they did it but the brothers panicked. They abandoned their horses and ran for a ravine, scrambling into a thicket of junipers.

RL seemed to be picturing it in his head. He was thinking about that day and could picture exactly what he was doing in that specific moment. The view up toward the Caprock. The cold, empty sky.

They were in big trouble, said Sam. Surrounded. No chance to escape. It was a standoff. Firing back and forth. We crept down a little on the back side of a saddle. Crawled up to the edge. Peeked over. There was a line of men on foot scurrying toward them to drive them out. We werent sure what to do. So I let an arrow fly from way out to try and create a di-version and somehow it caught one of them flush in the thigh. And that distracted them for a moment. But some of them sniffed out Babosa and his brother in the brush and after a great rush of gunfire they were dead.

RL was studying Sam, a thousand thoughts racing through his head. He could not understand how anyone of right mind, much less his own flesh and blood, was able to move on so easily from such a horrible tragedy and then become one with the perpetrators of the injustice. They murdered your mother, he said. The other women and children. Your very own family. How come you to just look the other way?

Sam turned his head, one eye asquint. He did not say anything.

RL watched his reaction and when Sam took a long swig of his beer there was something he noticed in his facial features, something about the way he finished his swallow and savored the feel and taste of it that reminded him of Sally when they were young.

Do you remember anything about your mother?

Sam looked out into the pasture watching an old bull taking the shade of a mesquite tree. It was a while before he spoke.

When she would read from the bible, he said. I remember her bible and I remember the bible studies.

RL smiled. Yes, she had come to love the Lord.

But just images really, from when I was real young. Caring for me when I was sick. But those days before it all happened, I remember her being tired a lot. And now that I think back on it she seemed angry a lot of the time.

RL shook his head.

Mainly she was always getting on me for hassling with Charlie.

RL sipped his beer. When was the last time you saw your brother?

When Quanah saved me from the Kiowas.

And that was the last time you saw him?

The last time.

How was he?

He was little, but he had hung in there. He was tough.

You never saw him again?

No.

Do you think he's alive?

Well, there were other white captives wherever we went and I never saw him. Not once. So I wondered. But I had a dream about him once, when I was on the mountain. That he was okay. And the eagle told me that he went to the west.

What was the dream?

I dont remember the details. Just that he was okay.

Sam had risen and walked out into the pasture to relieve himself, standing in the sun in silence with his member out for a long while thinking about things and then walking back to get his beer from the bucket and sitting back down again in the shade.

Did you think I was alive all these years? I mean, what has it been like? Was there a point that you gave up and stopped looking for us?

RL seemed to be framing his response before Sam was finished. He was raising his eyebrows and sipping the beer. Son, he said. When I set out earlier that week, I think it was three days before them savages tore our family apart, your momma and I got to fussin. She was begging me not to go. The indians had been all over the country. But I told her not to worry, that it'd all be just fine. Normally she'd let things lie but not that time. She had a feelin that things werent right. And I have to admit I had a little voice inside that was saying the same thing. But I didnt listen. Those were tough times but we had such big dreams and I was drawn to chasin em. For her. For you and Charlie.

I made a choice. The next day I headed out and left you all alone. And I came back home but that choice couldnt be taken back. That choice will define my life forever. I couldnt go back. Not then. Not now. And it tore me up no end. Still does. But I'm a different man now. It got to the point where I'd convinced myself that the both of you were dead, mainly I suppose because it was the only way I could move on. Somehow accepting that fact allowed me to move on. For years I couldnt function. But it got to the point where I had to let go. I had to get on with life.

RL paused and took another pull of the beer. He looked at Sam's eyes. Hazel like his mother's. He was young and handsome and a little larger boned, unlike himself, and he wondered where those genes came from. He changed the subject. Where did you all go after Cañón Blanco? What was that winter like?

After working north we eventually circled back south. Hunkered down in the Palo Duro, recovering. We spent the next few months preparing to wage war in Texas in the spring. Quanah got word into the Comancheros that we were ready to barter for weapons. And we did. He sent me and some others toward Fort Sill to let the reservation Comanches know about our plans. For them to meet us out on the plains when the grass turned green.

Tell me something, son. If Quanah was so smart how could he not know what was comin at him? Those boys that burnt down the south. Grant, Sherman, Sheridan. Mackenzie workin for em. Mackenzie damn sure was no dummy. And him wounded. By the way he was the one you shot in the thigh with that arrow. And he was one to carry a chip on his shoulder, from being outsmarted.

Quanah didnt care.

Didnt care?

We got with the Kiowas. Zepko-ette'. Their chiefs were still incar... Incar... cer. How do you say it?

In jail.

Jail.

Was that Big Bow?

Yes. Him and Guipago.

Remind me who that is.

The whites called him Lone Wolf.

Yes. Okay, keep going.

We went on the war trail with the Kiowas. Split up into eighteen, twenty different raiding parties. We hit the road from Santone. The one from Fort Concho. And especially the trail up the Pecos from the crossing. We stayed west out in that rugged country and made runs on the cattle trains. The ranches that were breeding them. And endless supply. Cattle. Horses. Mules. We even raided the poor Navajos at Bosque Redondo. If we saw something we wanted we took it, then disappeared back into the Llano Estacado and traded with the Comancheros. There were hardly any bluecoats out west. The elders said it was like the old days. But better because there were so many horses and cattle and a market to go along with it. I remember that summer so well. The celebrations when we returned to the village with our loot. Everyone was so happy. There was so much hope.

RL pointed to the west where a big cloud had mushroomed in the heat. He looked at the thunderhead high and white with its dark sheet of rain hanging down over the prairie. He turned to Sam.

And yet there are always dark clouds looming, he said. Hardly any bluecoats? How about six cavalry and four infantry companies all headed toward the breaks of the Llanos to hunt indians. You see, the government was finally wising up. Determined to punish any hostiles roaming outside the reservation. Determined to put an end once and for all to the Comanchero trade. They'd unleashed Mackenzie. Told him whatever he needed was his. They damn near emptied the forts at Richardson and Griffin. McKavett and Concho. Thirty plus wagons. Endless supplies from Santone. And you'd asked me if I ever stopped looking. Three years prior I'd run into a Comanchero named Ortiz. The wily bastard led me into ole Mow-way's camp. Me and him ended up gettin along alright. Mainly on account of me giving him and his cronies a damn good horse and every last dime I had at the time to help locate you and your brother.

And that's when you met Asewaynah?

Yes, the Fischer boy. Showed him a picture of you and Charlie.

Sam smiled.

Where were you?

I dont know. I dont remember exactly.

Did you know there were people looking for you?

It didnt matter. By then I wasnt interested in going anywhere.

Well, the point I was gettin to was by that summer in 1872 Mackenzie was puttin it all together. I told them where they could find Ortiz and we tracked him down. Got him to talkin. He told em about the roads across the Llano. The details. The location of the trading camps. Where those stolen cattle were moved into New Mexico. Mackenzie now had a map. So I set out with Ortiz and we scouted them across the prairie. Explored the Muchaque. Up and down the Caprock. Up north then back to the supply camp. Didnt find any indians since as you said, you all were raisin hell out west.

And there were troops in the field all over. We laid up and prepped to scout the North Fork. The Palo Duro. But then we found the main road leading west across the plains. Sometime toward the end of July. Now I'd heard a thing or two about these routes from Ortiz but had never seen it with my own eyes. It must have been a wet fall up on that flat country. Grass as tall as man on horseback. An ocean of emerald green and the playa lakes full. I tell you what. We damn sure didnt lack for forage or water. From the Double Mountain Fork all the way across the plains to the Salada.

I remember how wet it was. I couldnt believe it was like that.

We were up there, oh, I guess about a week and a half. Ten days. Had no intention of pushing so far west but the damn wagon road was so wide and plain, there must have been a helluva lot of cattle run that way. So Mackenzie figured, let's see where it goes. Ortiz was doing his job and he seemed to have the route back wired pretty good. We followed the trail all the way to the Pecos. Up above Fort Sumner.

RL paused and sucked up a big breath of air through his nose. He looked to the west where a cool breeze had blown in the fresh smell of rain from off the prairie. There was a bolt of lightning. He looked at Sam.

You remember Charlie Goodnight from when you was a boy?

Yes. A little.

Well, me and him went way back. We were laid up in Sumner for three days that summer and he was there, as fate would have it. You know he always talked favorably of you.

He did?

You and him were real close when you were little. You know, you were almost named after him. Your mother talked me out of that, said she'd had her heart set on the name Samuel, from the bible. So your brother got the honor instead.

Sam sat there staring out. He was searching through his memories, fighting his thoughts, trying to get his mind to somehow grasp it all.

Anyhow, said RL. There was a big push to stop the trade of stolen cattle. We had driven the trail all the way up to Alamo Gordo Creek looking for a few of the fellas Ortiz had called out. The merchants. But it turns out, and Charlie Goodnight told me this. That another Texan by the name of John Hittson had raised a force of a hunnerd or so gunmen and was already on the hunt roundin up all that stolen Texas cattle from the goddamn greasers.

Greasers, Sam repeated. God. Damn. Greasers. He said it slowly and awkwardly out loud to himself.

That's right. Goddamn greasers. Them boys Hughes and Church who'd been buyin up the stolen cattle. Hell, you probly seen em before. They'd skedaddled. Apparently Hittson and his boys rolled into Loma Pardans looking for the greasers and when the man in charge there wouldnt allow em to inspect their herds things came to a head. Shot and killed the police chief. Pistolwhipped several others. Hell, Charlie told me they shot the damned alcalde as he begged for mercy. Shot him in both legs and left him there whimpering and bleeding. All the while those terrified town folk huddled up in their homes praying to God for help.

So you see, things were comin to a head. We took the northern road back east through Fort Bascom, then followed the Tierra Blanca across the Staked Plains to the head of Tule Canyon. Meanwhile the New Mexican authorities kept troops on patrol all that summer. A lot of the same country we were exploring. The groundwork was being laid. That country was no longer a mystery. Those roads. The trading camps. The manner of doing business being disrupted.

RL turned and looked at Sam. Son, I'd imagine you all were on the move quite a bit that summer.

Sam stood up and looked at RL. Yes, we were.

They were looking at one another and then they looked away and they were there together in silence with the sun going down in the magical light of the late day. They had finished the beer. Sam started walking out into the pasture. I'll be right back, he said. He walked on through the tall dry bunchgrass and along the edge of the little peach orchard and he ducked under the shade of the big old oak and on out into the pasture.

White sunlight framing the outer edges of the thunderheads rising in the heat. A caracara perched on a gate post. Beyond the fence the rolling oak covered hills framing the stock tank in symmetry like a perfect painting. RL sat back against the tree and watched Sam walk with the clouds moving slowly in the distance beyond. Slow shadows sliding across a smooth grass prairie. Deer bedded down in the shade. Out there to the north a low thunder rumbled. There was a whistle and soon a horse appeared from out of a grassy swale trotting briskly out to Sam where he welcomed it with his open hand.

RL watched them as the horse eased its nose to Sam's chest and nuzzled him. Sam talked to it and its ears went back. A gust of wind blew up and the anviltopped clouds slid apart slowly with the breeze and the sun's sharp slanted rays beamed through and showered them in light.

RL rose and headed toward them but then he held up. The sun's spotlight now brightening over them in the field with the storm clouds looming darker all around. He thought about his life and all that had led to this moment. Big dollops of rain began to drop. Sam was patting and rubbing the horse's neck and it stood there with its head stretched up looking into the light. He stopped. The horse lowered its head and stood there looking at him. He stepped to its side and grabbed its mane with his left hand and crowhopped up, using the withers to pull himself up and over to settle atop the horse. A hard rain began to fall. He nudged the horse and leaned in as it broke into a trot and when RL called out to him he looked back to see the man with his hand held out but then he turned and held on at a full gallop, he and the horse growing smaller in the storm and then soon vanishing altogether into the driving sheets of rain.

19

— ★ —

Clarendon, TX

Spring 1927

After the wedding Corrine and the colonel settle into their lives in Clarendon. There are signs of spring and the joy this brings infuses new energy into the household and their work. She helps her husband maintain a voluminous correspondence and methodically records many of his recollections, amassing several hundred pages of typed manuscript material over the course of a month. Each day they receive a letter from Haley with questions related to his research and the next morning these are dutifully responded to in great detail and promptly mailed. He calls them from his office in the small college town of Canyon and visits whenever he can. With this information he produces several papers and articles based on these ongoing dialogues. He will give a lecture about the origins of Plains place names later in the month at the spring meeting of the Texas Folklore Society. In the summer, the Capitol Reservation Lands corporation will commission him to write a history of the XIT Ranch and as a result his interviews with the colonel will extend in new directions.

> *Mar 5: Married at Henry Taylor's home at 9:30 AM, a beautiful day. Taylors served a lovely dinner for us. South Ward school sent carnations. Lorena Stegal brought candy and flowers in the afternoon. Cakes from Mrs Crockett. Taylor and Mrs Beverley (Walter's mother-in-law).*

Mar 6: Numerous letters and telegrams and callers and a very pleasant surprise. Resign from my railroad position after 8.5 years of service. Telegram of congrats from brother, Beth, and Mrs Spry. Other dispatches too.

Mar 13: Very delightful trip over ranch, see buffalo herd (207 of them). Enjoy the lakes and dinner at Cleo's.

Mar 14: See lawyer on business. Wrote 40 more letters.

Mar 15: Company for dinner from Amarillo.

Mar 16: Mr Ellerd from Phoenix calls on us. Coles goes to Goodnight on behalf of G's interest in Merc loan.

Mar 17: More letters and visits.

Mar 18: Mr Coles comes to house. Interview with Mr JM Collins, reporter from KC Star newspaper.

Mar 19: G tells me some very wonderful and interesting things about his scientific discoveries and operations. Plans for accomplishments in the future. We write doctor at Baltimore, MD in regard to these things. Also merits of the buffalo tallow. 'Goodnighting' discovered on a cattle drive to Colorado, on Pecos River, July 1867 after losing several valuable bulls. This extremity proved to be his opportunity. Loving, his beloved partner, was wounded on this trip which caused his death. Sex, power and vibrant health. Inevitable and sure result of above operation on both animal and man.

When the old cook in the Taylor home passes away the colonel and his new bride accompany the family to the town of Jacksboro to fulfill their lifelong promise to her that she be buried with her family in the old cemetery. After the service, a small gathering drives back east to Black Springs to visit the place where Sheek Tavern once stood, source of so many fond memories of the colonel's formative years. They file out of the cars, slowly spreading out into the fringes of the property to survey the site. No one seemed to say anything, as if they were stepping into a hallowed place.

Goodnight shuffled from out of the car and settled himself upright with his cane. Corinne reached out to help him along but he waved her away. I'll be alright, he said. Thank you darlin.

She stepped aside, watching him, letting him have his space. Wind blowing his white hair. There'd been rain and he could smell the grass and the weeds. Something seemed to catch his eye and he started walking, his big frame gimping along one foot in front of the other. After a few steps he'd stop to catch his breath and turn this way and that taking in the scene. Pecan trees blooming out healthy and strong. The chinaberries had taken over and their new blooms were flowering and smelled sweet. Clusters of the little yellow berry-like fruits scattered about his feet. He shuffled off again, making his way to where the foundation of the house he built seventy-one years ago once stood, now just an overgrown jungle of weeds and a heap of stones that marked the chimney of the fireplace that kept them warm on those cold nights so long ago. Voices in the distance, voices from the past. Field larks singing in the sunshine. He turned himself around, leaning on the cane, shielding his eyes from the sun, peering out. The old man stood there a long time.

He saw the old, rusted windbell still hanging from the live oak, clanging gently in the breeze. The old water well covered in rotted boards. What was once a flourishing garden now a jungle of weeds. Out beyond the road the once fertile pastures he had cultivated as a young man. The fence he'd built still sturdy and straight, the cedar posts weathered in the sun but otherwise as good as new. He thought about his life. Tears streamed down his face. He whispered slowly to himself. It's just goddamned pitiful, he said.

It is midmorning after a strong line of storms has passed and a brilliant sun rises over the land that is wet and fresh and cool. Corinne comes inside from the garden with a basket full of onions and shallots, sets it down by the sink, and begins to wash them. She lays them out to dry and sits down at the breakfast table. The diary is there sitting in the sunlight that filters through the window and she opens it to April and peruses through the passing of the month.

Apr 7: 10 AM long distance from Mr Haley at Canyon.

Apr 8: Haley and Doris stay until 10:30 PM.

Apr 9: 8AM Haley and Doris interview until 11 AM.

Apr 26: Reading articles on chemistry and showing great passion for that subject.

Apr 27: In evening enjoy exchange of thoughts on various subjects. Religion, womanhood, manhood, sex power, passion. His scientific use of this led him to be well preserved at eighty.

Apr 29: G says he wants to let up on the smoking and take care of his health as he has so much to live for and so much to accomplish.

She turns the page to the April Memorandum. Clean, white, a blank canvas. She thinks awhile and starts to write but her thoughts are distracted and she gets up and leaves the room but comes back directly and sits down with a new pencil. Brand new, sharpened, waxy smooth. Eberhard Faber Blackwing 602. She taps the eraser on the table, staring blankly out the window. She rolls the pencil between her fingers, thinking, and then she begins to write.

G says no president ever equaled Lincoln. Were neighbors and knew him well. Has felt modest and timid in meeting big people because of feeling mortified by lack of education.

Saturday afternoon an hour after lunch. When he opens his eyes he is not sure where he is and he lies there looking at the ceiling until his mind comes to. The little alarm clock on the bedside table is ticking. It is cloudy outside and the pale light in the room is peaceful. He turns his head and sees her sitting there, reading, her eyes intent, she is fully absorbed in the story. Her soft, parted lips. When she has her hair up it shows off her beauty. Sweet, youthful face. She smiles at something that she has read and when she looks up in pause to appreciate the soulfulness of the words she sees that his eyes are open.

Well, hello there handsome.

The old man smiles sleepily. How long have I been asleep?

Oh, not long. Maybe twenty minutes or so.

It feels nice in here.

Yes. Yes it does. Very relaxing.

I had a dream?

What did you dream?

It was springtime. We were on a weeklong cow hunt. Me and Loving and all the other cattle owners. Working the cows on horses with the saddle pockets stuffed full of bread and ham and sugar. Just out in the sunshine working the country. And I remember we nooned by the creek and broiled some steaks and drank coffee.

Oh, how wonderful.

And then in the late of day, you see, I'd gotten sidetracked huntin some big ole mossbacks who'd seen us comin and hauled ass into the breaks, and my horse caught that flash of sunlight on their horns and he just puckered up and lit after em and boy howdy, here we go.

And what happened?

Well, the next part… it was after dark, you see, and we were all singin to a herd of yearlings.

What was the song?

Shall We Gather at the River.

Shall We Gather at the River.

That's what it was.

That must have been quite a scene.

Yes, those were some good times.

Goodnight has a sleepy, wistful smile and he lay there for a long while looking into her eyes as she waits for him to completely awake from his nap.

What are you reading?

She closes the book around her thumb and shows him the cover. Oh Charles, she says. It's such a special book!

He smiles back at her. What's the name of it?

To the Lighthouse. This came with Mrs Adair's package the other day. She says she loves Virginia Woolf.

I dont remember you reading that.

Well, you say you dont like women writers.

Try me.

Are you sure?

Yes, of course. I'd like to see why you like it so much.

She opens the book back up and flips through, searching for the passage she is thinking of. Let's see here. No, not that one. Oh where is it? Okay here it is, listen to this. It's from the section, *Time Passes*. It's just beautiful.

> *Listening (had there been anyone to listen) from the upper rooms of the empty house only gigantic chaos streaked with lightning could have been heard tumbling and tossing, as the winds and waves disported themselves like the amorphous bulks of leviathans whose brows are pierced by no light of reason... In spring the garden urn, casually filled with windblown plants, were gay as ever. Violets came and daffodils. But the stillness and the brightness of the day were as strange as the chaos and tumult of night, with the trees standing there, and the flowers standing there, looking before them, looking up, yet beholding nothing, eyeless, and thus terrible.*

She looked up at him to gauge his reaction. He was smiling, deeply in love with her voice. He may not have even cared about the words because the sound of her voice was so pleasing to him.

20

— ★ —

North Fork of the Red River

Fall 1872

On the twenty-first of September Mackenzie, informed with intel from Ortiz and the Tonkawa scouts, marched for the headwaters of the Red River in the heart of Comancheria with the mission of punishing the hostile Comanche and Kiowa who'd been depredating from out of the friendly confines of the reservation. There were seven companies of soldiers and they set out at dawn, riding up from their camp at the mouth of Blanco Canyon and watching the sunrise paint the canyon walls in shades of vermilion and yellow and gray.

The trail up out of the plains toward the head of the Salt and North forks of the Red River led them through the canyons and mesas of the Quitaque where the Comancheros kept their trade camps. The route followed the base of the Caprock and the springs that flowed down from the high plains rolled into quicksand streams and they crossed these continually and their progress was slow. Sculpted sandstone spires bled out from the red canyon walls into mazes of mesas and drywash arroyos dotted with the blooming desert plants of early fall. In eight days they saw no signs of indians. On the ninth the Tonkawas discovered two fresh trails along the banks of McClellan Creek, one from a packmule and the other from two horses. When they lost the tracks in a tall run of grass they halted and RL dismounted and walked his horse slowly along the banks of the creek where tangles of vines hung heavy with grapes and he followed the scatterings until fresh tracks appeared again on a trail heading north and he called out to the other scouts.

They rode briskly and within the hour the tracks led them to a narrow rise where they could look down upon the distant village of the Kotsotekas camped in the beautiful river valley far below. The simple things in life a few hours before sundown on a lazy fall afternoon. The villagers at peace ambling about and the smoke from their fires wafting in the fading light and the riverstream sparkling along in a slow swirl. Far away echoes of laughter. Children swimming, women bathing, old men sitting and smoking. The distant shadows of three hundred some-odd lodges slanting from the sun and the sheets of meat drying and the herdsmen in the fields prodding the little horses farther into the recesses of the valley grasses. Mackenzie when he rode upon this view dismounted and led his horse out upon a ledge and shielded his eyes from the sun for a long while studying the peaceful scene before him.

They eased back on the downside of the promontory, sending runners back to the main command and awaiting their arrival. A Mexican named Carrion was selected to proceed on foot to better scout the advance into the village. They sat in the shade tending to their weapons as the captains made their way among the groups of huddled troops detailing points of strategy. Ten minutes later Carrion returned and reported that the herd of indian mules he had spied upon were the ones taken from the wagontrain burned at Howard's Wells earlier that spring.

The Tonkawas had assembled separately, selecting their favorite war ponies from the remuda and dressing them for battle. They were passing small tin boxes and a piece of looking glass among themselves and like old master painters they carefully adorned their faces in dobs of paint as they conferred with one another for approval. Then the ponies were painted up in geometric designs of various shapes and colors or striped in white and strung with bright strips of flannels and feathers and when they had done they mounted up, prancing about proudly with their weapons at the ready and their headdresses flowing.

Mackenzie had been walking about the command observing the finer details of their anxious preparations and when he finished his inspection he called for his lieutenants and they huddled around a patch of soft dirt as he drew lines in the red sand and addressed them.

It'll be getting dark before we know it, he said. We must work fast. Ease the men down behind that break of cedars toward the bottom. Keep them quiet. When I give the command to charge, dont dally getting down there because it wont take them long to hear us.

Sir, which of us is assigned to the horse herds?

Now goddamnit Powell, how many times do we need to go over this?

I'm sorry, sir.

Lieutenant Lee will manage the horses.

Okay.

Now, remind your men to try and have some restraint. No need for this to be a free-for-all on the women and children.

Yes sir.

And remember, be on the lookout for anyone with white skin dressed up like an indian.

They nodded. It took the company another quarter-hour to get into position. They walked the horses down single file and lined out in the draw in columns of four to prepare for the charge. Mackenzie made his way to the head of each column and muttered final words of encouragement. The wind had shifted and blew lightly against them and doves were whistling overhead on their way to water. They mounted up. The horses were stomping and snuffling. The riders shifted in the saddle, pulling their hats down low and adjusting their weapons and taking last accounts of their ammunition. The captains at the head of their columns looked at one another and then they looked at Mackenzie and when he nodded they surged on.

When the women drying meat on the edge of the village first heard the rumble of the hooves they rose from their work and stood dumbly. They could see a light sheen of red dust rising over the mouth of the valley. One of them mumbled something. They could barely hear the boy herdsmen yelling from the fields and then they saw them running desperately toward them from out of a stand of woods. Behind them mounted soldiers began to appear, roweling their horses with their pistols held high and quickly bearing down on the barefoot boy runners. The women dropped their things and turned and ran.

The first handful of soldiers each fired once in close succession sending five young boys down to bleed out in the soft green grass. The Comanches were scrambling madly for their weapons and places to hide and groups of angry camp dogs came on the attack, barking wildly and charging at the advancers, one rider deftly veering his mount at the last instant and crushing one brave dog underhoof. Men were yelling and women screaming and the elderly waved flags or fell to their knees begging for mercy or laid out on the ground feigning death.

The early riders from Company F had made their way into the center of the village and at close range were met with volleys of bullets and arrows from a line of warriors hidden away in the grass. One private took arrows in his shoulder and arm and leg. The two on each side of him had meanwhile met with a line of gunfire and they were shot through the face and neck and fell strangling on their own blood and yet this would be the last of the Comanche's resistance. Warriors were caught running without weapons and women cradling infants ran shrieking and the loose ponies stampeded through the camp in a crazed rush of chaos and dust. Upward of three hundred mounted soldiers unleashed a battery of furious pistolfire into the defenseless village. Some of the men had dismounted and were herding up the elderly and children yet these mercies would not be exercised by the bulk of the command. Some were already scalping the dead or slicing off ears and fingers as trophies and others had begun to set the lodges afire.

By now a large crowd of Comanches had fled the burning village and they hunkered down to defend themselves under an embankment on the far side of the river pool. Mackenzie ordered a company of troops to the head of the ravine to cut off the escapers and he flanked his men on the ready with their carbines. The warriors were preparing their weapons for a desperate charge and as soon as the first line of runners emerged there was a brief and great battery of gunfire and they were shot down within seconds. That fleeting flash of silence was the only break in the bedlam from the moment the first shots of the battle were fired. Again! he shouted, as another line of advancers came out howling and were gunned down on the banks of the water.

Lieutenant Thompson called out to them from the bluff. A small band of indians were scurrying like a covey of quail into the thickets of the river bottom and there were women coming out of the brush howling with their hands in the air. Other Comanches were throwing bodies into the deeper recesses of the river to keep their dead from the Tonkawa scalping knives and glassy patches of red were emerging on the surface like subterranean thunderheads. Troopers galloped off in ones and pairs pursuing single runners. After a while the shooting and the shouting seemed to echo across the valley at a slower pace. Some of the Tonkawas were dragging bodies from the bloodstained waters and lining them out along the muddy bank to await further butchery. They knelt over them and carved them up like surgeons, taking first the scalps and then the ears before slicing squares of skin from each breast. Another company of riders passed back through the battlefield and surveyed the corpses strewn about and most anything moving or breathing was dispatched without pity. Mackenzie knew that his legacy would hinge upon any ill-formed impressions that would result from rumors of mass carnage and he rode among the men and demanded restraint.

Suddenly a handful of little indian boys came out of a burning lodge running crazily for the cover of the woods. Old Henry had been turned away from them but he had eyes in the back of his head and he whirled around and called out to his companions and they sprinted out in pursuit. The smallest of the boys stumbled and fell and scrambled up trying to run but he was limping slowly like a wounded fawn and by the time he could right himself they converged upon him in a caterwaul of yips and yowls with their knives flailing and clubs whirling and when they were done they set out on the run for the other boys but RL appeared galloping from out of the creek bed and warned them away with his pistol.

He pulled the reins and walked the horse slowly through the smoldering lodges studying the scene about. The sun was almost down and billows of black smoke were rising in the somber evening light. Women and children lay heaped and scattered all through the village and then something else caught his eye. It was a soldier kneeling over the bloody form of a squaw that had a hole in the side of her head and there was an infant in her limp arms suckling the breast of its dead mother. RL nudged his horse and approached him and the man looked up at him with tears in his eyes.

Get away, said the man.

RL kept on, turning back to keep watch, and as he did so the man pulled the child's head from its mother's breast and placed his hand over its mouth. He pinched the nose and pressed his other hand down and held the pressure firmly while the last of the life passed out of the child. RL shouted back at him. The man stood up with his shoulders slumped and his head down. He did not look up. RL watched him, the last of the sunlight shining through the haze of smoke, the man looking down somberly over the life that had just passed before him.

RL rode back to the command on the outskirts of the camp where they had gathered to assess their losses. It had not taken them an hour to seize the village. A strange calmness settled in, broken only by the random shouts of the captains or an occasional murmuring of a contentious crowd of frazzled soldiers. Strips of jerked meat hung from sticks throughout the camp and because the men had hardly eaten they were bickering over rations. A young Frenchmen from Louisiana had his bowels perforated from a gunshot wound and he writhed in agony as he was attended to and a team of men were lashing poles to a pair of packmules to prepare the litter that would carry him the seventy miles back to the supply camp.

Mackenzie urged them on, brandishing a flaming torch and holding it out to assess the details of their work. Burn it all! he kept shouting. The men were rounding up the assembly of hostages inside of a makeshift corral of supply wagons and the squaws were wailing hysterically and ripping out chunks of their hair. When he'd made his rounds he saw Boehm standing alone. Boehm had his hat in his hands and he was studying two holes from bullets that had passed clean through either side of the high-crowned brim. He put the hat back on and addressed Mackenzie.

Sir, if you're looking for the chief he's over that-a-ways.

Which chief?

Boehm nodded the way. Mow-way.

Mackenzie shook his head. No, Mow-way's in Washington.

Well it sure as hell looks like some sort a chief and whoever it is is shot all to hell.

Lieutenant, do the Tonks think this was the only village?

Boehm glanced north and then his eyes veered to the west where the sky bled a deep red. Oh, there's more of em out there. And you can damn sure bet they heard this jackpot.

Quahadis?

Quahadis, Nokonis, Kiowas, no tellin what all else.

Have we found any white boy captives?

Boehm knew the question was coming and was already shaking his head. Thompson swears he got a glimpse of some young man. It was early on.

He did?

But there's no sign of him now.

How old was he?

Sixteen. Seventeen.

Okay.

There's a few mexicans. Ortiz is talkin mexican to em right now.

Mexicans.

Yes sir. Boehm spat. He pointed to his hat. Can you believe my damn sombrero? he said.

Mackenzie ignored him. His head was on a swivel surveying the battlefield.

Sir. What do you intend for us to do with the hostages?

We'll drive them to Concho.

Boehm scratched his head and looked to the south. Well, okay, he said.

Mackenzie looked over the horse herd. I cant have another stampede, he said. Lieutenant, what's your thoughts on handling the horses?

Well, I'd recommend we place them under guard out in those sandhills. Down in the sink. Ole Henry's goin through em now and pickin out the ones he wants.

How many are there?

I dont know. Half a thousand or so.

No, I believe there's more than that. Mackenzie was doing the math in his head as he stood up to survey the herd. Helluva lot more than that, he said. He heeled the horse and hurried back out into the sacked camp. The troops were looting the lodges in the last of the light and he called out to them to leave nothing of sustenance behind. He reined the horse and looked over the men with their torchlights and he surveyed the work in a slow walk. He was snapping the stubs of his fingers, thinking, when he heard the commotion of excited voices out in the darkness. He sat the horse and took in the scene and awaited their approach. It was the camp surgeon riding in with the black field cooks, a crowd gathering around, each of them carrying gunny sacks with a severed Comanche head to be boiled out and donated for scientific study.

The following morning the command clustered the prisoners behind the wagons and surrounded them with mounted riders, herding them on foot like cattle on the long journey south through the land of inverted mountains. As they drove them on a pregnant Comanche woman jostling along in one of the springless army wagons began to have contractions. She was breathing heavily and biting down hard on a small mesquite branch and when her water broke she began to gush a pale yellow puddle of fluid all over the filthy splintered floor. The rugged walls of the Caprock were shimmering in the late morning heatrise and the weary hostages with their hands and feet bound slogged along silently and without expression.

Inside the stinking wagon the sweating squaw lie sprawled against the sideboard groaning and squealing like a stuck pig until at once there was a long and violent snarl as if some evil demon had been exorcised. The wagon stopped. The prisoners came to a halt. The riders on escort reined their mounts and grimaced at one another and their startled horses snuffled and shook their heads from the terrible sound that echoed across the prairie. Mackenzie had allowed an old medicine woman inside the wagon to serve as an accoucheuse and as she took hold of the baby the mother's painful cries slowly faded into a peaceful moment of silence and then all they could hear was the gentle humming of the midwife. No one spoke. Suddenly the newborn let out its first shrill and piercing cry and when it died off the command took up the march again, descending the course of the river valley and wading the stream bed and turning to the south to continue the march down into the rugged red breaks of the scabrock plains country.

The following day after the bluecoats had moved well to the south the Quahadis made their way among the carnage. The smokehaze of the still smoldering fires wafted slowly in a light breeze and the stench of death consumed them. Pahvo knelt beside the charred corpse of an old woman who had once cared for him and he waved back the flies and flipped her onto her back and began to drag her from the simmering coals. He hauled her slowly through the smoking ruins of the camp. There were dead and dying horses strewn in the ashes and dead dogs scattered about in the bloodstained grass. He pulled her by the seared frames of tipis where women and children lay inside bloated and scalped in every manner of stiffening contortion, reeking and buzzing with flies.

He dragged her along, weaving through the rubble of the camp, the dragmarks winding around broken crates and shreds of clothing and random tools and slain warriors splayed out face down in the dirt clutching their weapons. When he laid her out by a heap of corpses he stood up to catch his breath and looked west along the dry gulch where some of the village had fled. Bodies strewn up the arroyo all the way to the high ridge.

He picked up a white flag stained with smatterings of blood and peppered with gunshot. He walked along slowly. He saw a warrior with his intestines spilling out and a wounded dog came along whining in a frantic pant and stuck his nose in the guts as a massive swarm of maggots squirmed from the goopy entrails. He stood there a long while listening to the squaws moaning and wailing in their horror. He dropped the flag and went on, stepping around the bodies toward the river.

A wounded horse was struggling to its feet and neighing out, stumbling up and falling back down. He wandered among the remains of lodge after lodge. A swaddled infant lying by its mother's corpse. An old chieftain, hands clenched tight in death, one arm raised stiffly in the air. There was an entire family under the charred remains of an overturned cart, their faces burned up beyond recognition. A mule still in the shafts with its legs crushed, scraping at the dirt and squirming in agony. Corpses floating up from the bottom of the river pool. The headless bodies of two warriors.

Buzzards soaring above in the glistening sunlight, buzzards huddled among the trees. Shadows growing long in the killing field and the wolves lurking hungry in the hills. Dusk consumes the prairie and the yellowed haze of the horizon is sucked into the burning glare of the sun. Wisping clouds slowly passing, fading orange in last of the light. A light breeze carries the scent of death in the cool dusk and the early stars are shimmering. A voice calls out. He ignores it, gazing at the heavens and listening to the wind.

21

— ★ —

Clarendon, Texas

Summer 1927

Over the course of the summer Haley continues to endear himself to the storied plainsman. Consuming pot after pot of scalding black coffee they relive his histories while the wall clock ticks and ticks along. Goodnight leans forward rubbing his fingers through his beard and Haley slides a map across the breakfast table and spreads it flat.

When you decided to cut ties with Colorado, whereabouts did you settle in the Panhandle?

At first we set up two camps along the south bank of the Canadian. In Eastern New Mexico. Rano Creek. Another ten miles west. December 1875.

That soon? There were still renegade bands of indians roaming around then.

Of course. And outlaws and Comancheros. Also the New Mexican pastores and mustangers.

So how did you find the Palo Duro?

Paid one of them mustangers.

Really?

Goodnight places his gnarled finger on the map. There was a route drawn in pencil from the Arkansas down by Two Butte to the Black Mesa region where the Carizzo Creek meets the Cimarron. The name Coe had been scribbled, marking the location of a well-known cave, the outlaw hideout called Robber's Roost.

He follows the line all the way down the Canadian valley into Texas southward below the Caprock breaks. He moves his finger a quick jog back northwest near the mouth of the Tule. He taps the spot with his finger.

Right here. We found the brink of the Palo Duro. That wild gorge that cuts the Llano in two.

What had you been doing during the early 1870s? When the indian wars were playing out?

I had my eye on a range where the Arkansas cut through a rock canyon into the plains. I abandoned my camp on the Apishapa and situated a new swing station up there above Pueblo, recruiting cattle and building a new ranch home. I registered the PAT brand on the county records and brought Mollie over in the summer of 1870. Those early years up there were happy times. I ran water, had an apple orchard, farmed a little. At Mollie's urging we helped fund the school and influenced the building of the first church in that territory, Methodist Episcopal. We grew the herds and established camps on the Hardscrabble and St. Charles. Babcock's Hole. And then as I've been apt to do over the course of my life I got in over my head.

I had money in the bank, a meat packing house, various real estate interests. The ranges had been overstocked. I hung in there and waited for things to turn, all the while getting reports of what was playing out between the military and the indians. Particularly Mackenzie and his Fourth Cavalry.

Haley, I tell you what. That depression in '73 about wiped me off the face of the earth. Like the Comanches and Kiowas were a year later when they were run out of the Palo Duro.

Haley looked up from his notations. I've been meaning to ask you about that, he said. I've heard different accounts. Was it truly a battle?

Depends on who you talk to. But you goddamn sure caint dispute what followed. The indians skedaddled out of their stronghold and Mackenzie took their horses. Some say a few thousand of em. Herded em to the head of Tule Canyon and spent all the following day shooting those ponies. I told you about this. They had to shoot one horse at a time. Those bleached bones lay there for years until the bonepickers came along and sold em for fertilizer.

Eventually all of the indians made their way into the reservation at Fort Sill and that was that. I'd been hearing rumors for years of the range in that canyon. Comancheros told me they'd seen ten, twelve thousand Comanche horses grazing on the lush grasses in its recesses. All of it there wide open, free for the taking.

So you had decided to move there?

Yes. When the spring of '76 came we drifted the outfit down the river into Texas. Summered on the Alamocitos. We had to have a little come-to-Jesus with the sheepmen and let them know they best stay away from the Palo Duro. In the fall we moved toward Tascosa on down to Las Tecovas, where the Frying Pan Ranch is now, and worked our way across the Red River. That was the first time I laid my eyes on the canyon, the ancestral home of the Comanche. I knew instantly it was the range I had been seeking.

We drove the herd into the depths of the canyon and I left the boys to build the headquarters and I got my ass back to Colorado as quick as I could, to get things in order for a permanent move. It was a long winter. Everything unsettled. I sent Mollie to California to spend time with her family. And of course I was worried about the well-being of my ranch hands back in Texas so I made several runs back and forth delivering supplies, planning, checking on things. Also during this time I was introduced to the Adairs. I had a notion that with the economy turning the time was right to expand my cattle operations on a large scale.

In the evening Corrine poked her head into his room to check on him. The old man was lying in bed staring at the ceiling.

Darling, is everything okay? He lifted his head and smiled sleepily and waved her in.

Is there anything I can get you?

When she got to the bed he raised his arm and she sat down and took his wrinkled hand in her palms and kissed him.

Well, she said. How are you feeling?

I'm just fine.

She felt his forehead and then his cheek. His fever was very high.

How are things with our writer friend? he said.

He's doing well. You know, Charles, he truly does care a lot about you.

He's a fine young man. I have to admit I've taken a liking to him.

You wouldnt believe how much respect he has for you. This region and the history, your life and times. I can really tell how much appreciation he has for being able to spend time with you.

Well, it warms my heart to hear that. It truly does.

You know, he has been talking more and more about doing something with your story, to weave your life into the history of the region. Has he talked to you about that?

Not really. But I can tell that's where his head is at.

You should really think about it. You receive so many inquiries from those who want to publish an account of your life. It's obviously important to the people of the Panhandle. Especially for future generations. He seems to have the perfect vision to undertake such a project.

I agree.

I truly believe that if anyone was born to do it, it's Evetts. And of course I'll help out as much as I can.

She stroked his arm as she spoke. He gazed at her with far away eyes and perhaps it wasnt her beauty he saw but something deeper into all that was in the world. He looked away. I dont know, Corinne. My life, he said, has mostly been a failure.

They camped that night on the mesa that overlooked the great chasm of the Palo Duro, a thousand or more bison stampeding down in the depths of the canyon, their mating grunts echoing up the walls of the Caprock into the moonlight. The lightning flashing through the wagonsheet kept them awake and before long it began a cold, heavy rain. They made a bonfire of dry cedar and hunkered inside the wagons and watched the storm pass.

The following morning a full moon set in the west just before light and soon they went to work. It took them four days to route a winding trail to the base of the canyon. Late in the day when they arrived at the main camp the ranch hands had cleaned themselves up and laid out a feast of bear and buffalo meat with biscuits and honey and a big celebration commenced.

In the morning he set out alone following the trace of the river to scout the country. Tall grass, cedars in the draws, cottonwoods along the river, the slivers of water on the smooth, red sands of the canyon floor. Signs of the old indian encampments. His eyes scanned for sign and he watched the sky. He was working toward a spot at the mouth of a side canyon where it looked like a spring gave life to the landscape.

He was among the weathered artifacts scattered about from the final indian battle. Cartridges and bullets. Rusted metal utensils, bridle bits, buckles. A silver, crescent-shaped naja once worn on a necklace. The Pueblos had told him such pendants came from the bridles of the conquistadors' horses. This was sacred country. He'd planned to stay out a while and he spent that entire day soaking in the beauty, exploring every nook and cranny of the canyon. The rugged draws and the flat grassy plains. The trees, the springs, the lazy flowing streams. Down in its depths and all over its sides and up on top where the plains flowed on forever.

Corinne had been in to check on them, bringing a platter of donuts from the bakery in town and a fresh pot of coffee. Dont these look delicious, she said.

Thank you, little girl. You sure take good care of us. What would I do without you?

Why, you're welcome. I'll be back after a while. I dont want to disturb you two.

Haley smiled and rummaged through his files as the colonel bit into his donut. He weighed the consequences of the topic he wanted to bring up and he considered the timing.

Okay, let's see, he said. I made a note here to ask you about the Terry boys.

The colonel's lips tightened and he cocked his head.

Was there ever any news of them after the raid?

What do you mean?

Did they ever surface again?

The colonel shifted uneasily, thinking, chewing on the donut. He swallowed and picked at his teeth. He seemed to sadden.

Well, it's a mystery what happened to the little brother, Charlie. He never turned up. It was as if he was lost to the world. And the oldest boy Sam, he was discovered on the reservation at Fort Sill. Two years after the Comanche were defeated in the Palo Duro. He had held out with the last of the renegade bands. It took several months for the agents to understand who he was exactly. He'd been with the Quahadis. It was Quanah Parker who convinced him to be open to a new way of life.

Goodness. And so he'd been living with the Comanche for what, almost ten years?

Yes. His Comanche name was Pahvotaivo. White boy. Mackenzie sent him to Fredericksburg in an escort where he arrived back home in time for Christmas in the winter of 1875.

After nine months of attempting to reacclimate into white society, the boy, now a strapping man of twenty-two years, had been showing more and more signs of odd behavior, refusing to accept the rules that were being imposed upon him to make him something that he was not.

RL in his desperation had sent word to the Panhandle to ask his old friend to visit, to try and connect with his son, to somehow get through to him. At first it was as if the boy remembered nothing from his youth. He did not seem to recognize the man he had looked up to so much as a boy. Goodnight stayed in San Antonio for a week and before he left he spoke to RL and he did not mince words. You're going to have to let it go, he said. He could not bring himself to tell RL what he felt in his gut.

It took a few months for the newness of Sam's return to Texas to wear off. Everyone felt great hope for his recovery and there were positive signs early but slowly, he withdrew. He avoided the company of others. He could not stomach the food they tried to feed him. He refused to wear his new clothes and paraded about in his buckskins and moccasins and preferred to decorate his face with his war paint. He let his hair grow long again and refused to bathe. While he could communicate in english he would only speak comanche. There was a novelty to him that fascinated and tempted the public. In town strangers would crowd around him to gawk and ask questions.

He constantly thought about various strategies to escape, to get back to the people he loved. Over time he became more and more reticent. No one understood him. He was not like the whites. He felt like they saw him as a wild animal, as an enemy. There were other former captives who had been returned to their families in the Hill Country but he had no interest in them. He trusted no one. RL tried to keep him busy working outside, handling the horses and doing ranch chores, yet he would slough off the work and spend his time taking target practice at the farm animals. He would wander off in the woods around San Antonio and stay gone for days. RL kept a close watch and once stopped him as he was leaving but he just turned back glaring in contempt and kept on walking. All he wanted was to be outside. To be alone, free, like the hawk, soaring in the sun in the blue depths of the sky, listening to the music of the wind.

During those last days before he left for good they had sat down one evening with Goodnight to discuss the new plan for his future. Richard King had learned of the Terrys' story and he had compassion for their plight. In a few weeks he would hire out as a King Ranch hand on a cattle drive to Kansas.

Goodnight introduced him to the cattle baron over supper at the Menger, relaying details of how he knew the young man when he was just a boy, describing his nature, detailing the tragedies of his life and the troubles he was having and how it had all led up to this point. Sam ordered his steak raw and ate in silence. When he talked it was in english but he spoke few words. After supper in the hotel bar he stole a bottle of mezcal when no one was looking and after finishing it in the early hours after midnight he slipped into a neighbor's stable and ran off the horses. It had gotten to the point where the local law enforcement officers had threatened RL, he would need to do something about the situation. He looked at his son, defeat in his eyes. Heartbroken because he felt as though he was hated by his own son, that there was no good way for this to end.

Still, Goodnight held firm in his beliefs in their plan for Sam, kept his demeanor guarded in front of him to avoid fueling his behavior. The last time he saw him he and RL made a point to show their trust. Bragged on him, gave him money. Outfitted him for a short trip to the ranches south of town to bring back a herd of cattle for the drive north with the King Ranch vaqueros. When they wished him well the following morning they felt like they had done the best they could. Sam even smiled and waved goodbye. He was expected to return in a week but he never came back.

I told you it was a mistake to trust the kid, RL tells him when it becomes clear Sam is not going to return, his angry tone showing his frustration at Goodnight.

You did the right thing.

I should've gone with him.

He needs his space.

I actually had some hope. There were some positive signs.

He may very well come back. But he's been through a lot, and now having to come to grips with this way of life again. Give him time. He needs it. Helping that boy right now might work against you.

I was packing my bags to head back home. He wanted me to adjust my plans to try and help track him down. I told him it wouldnt be the right thing to do. There was something else I wanted to tell him but I didnt.

Early evening. The old man stands up slowly. He leans on the cane and limps to the counter where he pulls out a liter of whiskey and two tumblers. He nods at Haley. To get the juices flowing, he says. The writer comes over and opens the bottle and pours the glasses full. From a drawer he pulls out a double cigar cutter made of camel bone and steel and he eases back over to the table to sit down again with Haley. He sits there for a few seconds thinking.

All you've ever thought about is yourself, she hisses on that hot summer night seventy years ago, her voice, her eyes cutting through him. You never cared about *me*. You cared about yourself and you cared about the sex.

I wasnt begging you for it.

But I always felt like we had such a bond, such a connection. That there still can be.

Your connection was, and is, with RL.

I was just stupid about things. I was only with RL because of your indifference. To get to you.

RL is a good man. He loves you.

Come here and kiss me.

Not this time.

There's something more I need to say.

No, it's time to move on now, Sally.

I walked away that steamy August night in 1856. She was trying to tell me something that night but I wouldnt listen.

He clips the wet end of his cigar and lets it fall into the spit can at his feet. Haley sips his drink and watches him. Goodnight lifts his drink with both hands. They are shaking, and he puts the glass to his nose and smells it and lets it touch his lips and he takes a sip.

I moved on for good that summer of '66 when we made our first drive out on the trail around Comancheria up into New Mexico, leaving behind the chaos in Texas and the tragedy of the Terrys, the unopened letter she gave me a decade prior stuffed away deep inside a trunk somewhere. Ten years later that innocent little fling back in the summer of '56 would come back to haunt me.

You never knew what you might run into out on the plains back in those days. In the late seventies. I was scouting the country west of the Palo Duro, for my brother-in-law, Leigh Dyer. Spring Draw in what became Randall County near the junction of Palo Duro and Tierra Blanca creeks. All open country that needed to be claimed and my preference was for it to be folks I trusted. It eventually became the T Anchor Ranch, after the

Dyers claimed it and sold it to the surveying firm of Gunter, Munson, and Summerfield in 1878.

It was that time of year with summer winding down and you know fall is right around the corner. I was studying the draws for timber, looking for a place where they might set up a headquarters of their own. The sun was getting low, the day cooling off a little. I was generally enjoying myself and admiring that great ocean of grass and then I saw a man on horseback riding toward me from out of the east.

He was riding real casual, having trouble making me out for the glare of the sun. Shielding his eyes, I'm sure he just thought I was another cowboy on horseback in silhouette against the sun. I waved him on and he came up. It was RL Terry.

The old man pauses, staring blankly, looking back into the recesses of his memory into that moment of time.

He sees RL's face in the firelight telling him what he'd been told about his boy and what had transpired down on the King Ranch. All of his frustrations building. RL is very inebriated, just like the old days. Irrational. He takes another pull on the bottle of whiskey. But this time somehow the conversation had taken a turn and they were no longer on the same side. A lifetime of disappointments boiling up in a rage. A madness that had been craving some outlet and now he was sitting across the campfire from the man that would receive the brunt of it all. So many subtle things that were said, the collection of all of that building up. Then the lashing out. Finger pointing. Accusations. Goodnight realizes there is deep, deep resentment inside his old friend and now it's coming out. But why now is it so difficult to recall the specific details of what all was said? Somehow, in the moment he must have thought it would help to let the truth come out. His side of the Sally Johnson story. Her character. What happened on that Friday night in 1856 on the Fourth of July. What happened the rest of that summer. That somehow being open about it would force RL to begin to come to grips with some of his losses. Some nudge to help him move forward. Or was it the relief of simply getting it off his chest?

RL stands up from across the fire and approaches him angrily with his hand on his pistol. Goodnight stands up and welcomes the approach. Charles Goodnight is not one to back down from any man, anything. Then they are nose-to-nose, old friends now enemies, waiting to see who will make the first move.

In the first half of May Corrine neglects her diary because she is continually in discomfort as a result of her pregnancy. Persistent pain in her back and abdomen. Hardly an hour goes by that she does not experience cramping. She is young and healthy, does not smoke and rarely drinks, doing everything she can to take good care of herself. She rarely lets on, fighting through the episodes by telling herself that everything is normal, that everything will be okay.

Corinne, how's our little Goodnight doing in there?

Oh, pretty good, I think.

Are you feeling okay?

She just smiles, looking down and rubbing her belly. Inside, she fights the guilt.

Her discomfort comes in waves but whenever she feels like her old self she tries to sit down with her diary again. Perhaps what she writes is a way to heal her bad conscience.

May 18: About pre-natal culture: G has such splendid ideas about these things. Should have a mighty fine kiddie. Sure do want him bad enough. Unpacked my things from Livingston today, brings back memories.

May 19: Story of big snake at Quitaque from Dr. Galloway... G's chief lament and worry is that he cannot do things as he once did, so much ambition. Wrote four hours this morning on G's history.

She looks at the old man sitting outside under the sun, eyes closed and breathing deep so that he can soak up the fresh smell of the High Plains air. Almost smiling, completely immersed in nature.

Honey, are you doing okay out there?

His eyes are closed. She wonders if he's fallen asleep but then he opens them and smiles.

Can you believe how gorgeous this day is, little girl?

Yes, it is just wonderful!

I dont know that I've ever seen a more beautiful day.

Would you like some coffee?

Yes. Thank you. That'd be real nice.

May 20: Complains of back problems.

May 21: Just various household duties, etc. Read the interesting account to G in detail of aviator Lindberg's daring flight.

Whenever the weather permits it is a habit for them to spend the late afternoons outside, no matter how chilly it might be, tidying up the yard and the garden and enjoying the intricacies of the light in the west when the sky becomes yellowed and infused in the evening afterglows. They go inside and set the table for whatever has been prepared, generally something light for her and for him, some sort of variation of buffalo meat garnished with heapings of homemade pepper sauce poured from an emerald green bottle. Red Mexican peppers from the garden soaked in spices and vinegar. The colonel eats quickly, without talking, and for his dessert he takes a shot that consists of a mixture of buffalo meat extract and whiskey. Then he settles into his chair by the fire and thinks while he waits for her to clean up the kitchen.

She walks in and sits down with the copy of *The Sun Also Rises* they have been reading the past few days.

Not that book, Corinne.

She looks at him. She can tell that he is very tired after the long day. He's irritable and misses his tobacco. He'll be in bed soon but something overcomes her and she cannot subdue that little something inside that wants to push back, but before she can utter a few words in response he cuts her off in his gruff manner.

All that goddamn book is about is a bunch of damn rich kids tootling around Europe, getting drunk and wasting money and having sex with one another.

Oh Charles, now stop that! she says, a little flirtatiously.

Well by god you know it's true. The only part of it worth a damn is the bullfighting. I'd like to meet that Montoya fella.

She suppresses her disappointment. She has been looking forward to absorbing herself in the streets of Paris, the cafes of Spain, the pleasures of Lady Brett Ashley. She's always wanted to go to Europe and she tells herself that she's still young and there will be time for that one day.

And so they talk about the weather and science and psychology and the hidden powers of the subconscious mind and other things and finally another hour has passed and he tells her the story about the time the Kiowas came to the ranch a decade ago for the big buffalo hunt and Chief Long Horn gave him his shield as a show of appreciation and how surprised he was when the old warrior's wife planted a big kiss on his cheek. After a while he wears out and she helps him down the hall and into his room and into bed.

Back in the den she dims the lamps and lights a few candles and settles in by the fire with her diary in her lap.

May memorandum: Passion and sex the foundation of accomplishments if rightly used and controlled and applied. Creative purpose only.

But what after all is one summer? When the winter fades and spring brings new life, new hope, and yet the season is short and the long days and burning heat of the summer set in. And then somehow the summer is gone. Incidental ongoings or life changing events put on paper referenced as haphazard jottings, dictations, one-line parentheticals or nothing at all.

Aug 9: Lewises come over this morning. Then Dane Coolidge (writer)—also meet J Frank Dobie's wife—sister and brother in law.

In the middle of a hot summer night Corinne rushes down the hallway clutching her abdomen, straggling into the bathroom. Excruciating stomach cramps and vaginal bleeding and her cervix opens. Then the fetus flows away with the bleeding like a shadow lost when the sun is gone.

And then life moves on. Time. It is impossible for her to speed the time, to accelerate herself through the tragedy or any other trivial in-between part of her life. Nor for the old man that she cares for who is facing his end. Nor will time slow.

After they were informed by the doctor that her pregnancy had ended he left them alone to hold one another close and sob in sadness. Pure, private, palpable grief. Each of them in their own way, losing something, as the world carries on around them.

Aug 20: Read 'Six Years with the Texas Ranger's (Gillett) and 'Oregon Trail' (Meeker).

Aug 23: To Amarillo. Evening with Lewises. Met Hamner earlier.

Aug 24: To Canyon.

Aug 25: Met the old timers, impressive.

Only in the diary is there the chance to preserve the fleeting moments of time.

August Memorandum: Have been in bed all summer and not able to keep up the diary. I regret this exceedingly.

22

Fort Sill

October 1872

The man chartered to deal with the Kiowas and Comanches at Fort Sill was a Quaker named Tatum. He had long come to terms that the holy experiment of applying Christian principles to his dealings with the indians was a fool's errand and other than issuing weekly rations he now believed his primary mission was to recover the indians' white captives. There had been a buzz about the post over the last month since the capture of Mow-way's village on McLellan Creek and several bands had been moving near the post for lack of winter food and clothing. One hundred and sixteen Comanche women and children were being held prisoner at Fort Concho and this man they had nicknamed Bald Head expected that they would be willing to do whatever it took to get their families back from Texas. He was standing outside of John Evan's trading post on a pleasant fall afternoon when he saw them lined out on the western horizon. The ragtag assemblage of tradesmen and soldiers and indians that were milling about the store abruptly stopped conducting their business to watch them draw near.

It was a delegation of friendly Nokonis led by a man the whites called Horseback, a dozen, maybe fifteen. They were dressed in buckskin and a few had bows and arrows and there was something about the way they rode that seemed to engender feelings of empathy among the pilgrims that attended their arrival. There was a large man in the middle of the procession and he was much older than the others and his countenance was that of an enlightened being, a wise sage who had seen many things, experienced many triumphs, endured many tragedies. He was a proud man who had come on a mission and as they neared the post his escorts lined out alongside him halted and he continued forward, proud but somber, he and the two white captives that were on either side of him. Tatum called for someone to fetch the interpreter and he stepped forward to greet them as a crowd gathered around. The old chief dismounted to formally address the agent and approached him and extended his hand. Ma- ruawe Pot-ta-wat Pervo, he said. Buenas tardes.

Tatum regarded him and rubbed a hand over his shiny bald head, getting a good look at the boy captives and then the line of riders behind them. He held out his arms in welcome. The interpreter arrived and awkward pleasantries ensued. The whites' called him Horseback and he was repentant and spoke softly. When the shopkeeper stepped forward and handed them candies the old chief made the boys dismount and urged them forward. He was tubercular and fighting a persistent cough but the size of him made for an imposing presence. He looked at the agent and he looked at the boys and placed his hands on their shoulders. He patted them warmly and urged them forward like a loving father. He told them to go forward and be with their people.

The assembly held their breaths silently in anticipation of the next exchange like worshippers taking the gospel in a tent revival and yet they had no notion of the meaning of his words. The boys stepped forward nervously and Tatum leaned down toward the youngest and touched his cheek, peering into the depths of his eyes. The boy jerked back fearfully. After further questioning the chief made it clear that his intent was to exchange the two boys for the release of the Comanche prisoners that were incarcerated at Fort Concho.

Tatum shook his head, glaring back wistfully at the man. Where are the other captives? he said.

The crowd murmured. The boys looked at one another. They put their heads down and stared at the ground. Mas taibos? said Horseback, impishly. He pursed his lips and raised his brows.

The agent's eyes narrowed. We can talk about the release of your people when the other captives are delivered to me, said Tatum. The interpreter was translating before he'd finished.

Horseback skinnied his eyes and stared through Tatum for a long while. The gallery watched him. He took a big breath and tried to speak but he couldnt fight back his choking wheezecough. No mas taibos, he barely muttered.

Tatum glared back. Bring me the taibos, he demanded.

The chief's warring tribesmen were depending on him to plead for the release of their women and children. His eyes shifted back and forth between Tatum and the interpreter. He was in no position to make demands. Among those held prisoner were his wife and daughter, his mother-in-law, other relatives and their loved ones.

Tatum told the interpreter to take the boys to his office and he turned and walked off.

Horseback was angry and he called out to implore that he had no other captives.

Tatum stopped and looked back. He did not need a translation. Of course, and I have a full head of hair, he said. A few of the onlookers chuckled. The interpreter nudged the boys forward. Tatum headed off, calling back as he walked.

Bring me all of the taibos, he said. Every single one of them. Then we'll talk about releasing your women and children in Texas.

Horseback just stood there. Perhaps he'd been thinking the agent would release at least a few of the prisoners. He turned for his horse and looked at his men, muttering. None of them spoke. They sat their horses somberly. He waved them on and they mounted their horses and the post guards and the shopkeeper and the onlookers in attendance all watched them, Horseback and his chaperons riding slowly off into the tall buffalo grass prairie that waved gently under the sun with the light autumn breeze.

Tatum sat the boys down and shut the door and he and the interpreter pulled chairs from the wall and took seats directly in front of them. The boy warriors sat there like cornered animals and their eyes glanced around restlessly looking through the thin glass windows and studying the cold stone walls and the strange things hanging on them. The older boy was long and lean and brown-skinned with wild tangled hair bleached blond from the sun.

The interpreter spoke to them in comanche and Tatum put forth a basket of candy but they just sat there. Do you speak any english, son?

The boy seemed to nod.

The interpreter asked him in comanche and the boy responded. He says he can speak some english, he said.

Do you remember the name your momma and daddy give you?

He thought for a while. He shook his head.

Is your name Charlie Terry?

Still, he sat there thinking, hesitant to speak.

Son, think hard for me. What was your name?

He looked at the floor and then up at the ceiling and then he began to enunciate his given name.

Cli… Clin… ton, he said.

Tatum's eyes brightened. He was studying the boy closely. Clinton Smith?

The boy nodded.

Yes? Clinton Smith?

Ya… yea… yesh.

Tatum looked at the younger boy next to him. Is your name Jeff?

The boys sat there.

Son, is this your brother Jeff? He touched the boy's knee but the boy jerked it back. Horace, ask him where his brother is.

The interpreter translated the question and listened to the boy's response. He turned to Tatum. It's not his brother, he said. He says he last saw his brother with the Apache.

Tatum stood up. Horace, this boy looks to me like puberty's hit him full on. I'd give him twelve, maybe thirteen.

I'd agree with that.

And this little feller here is just a child. What do you think? Seven, eight?

Eight.

I'll be right back. I'm gonna see about fetching them something to eat and drink. Maybe that'll loosen em up. See if you can get the run down on the little man.

Yes sir.

The boys watched him go and they had a steely coldness to them despite their youth. When Tatum returned and handed them each a cup of water and strips of jerky they barely gnawed the meat before swallowing and then slurped down the water like thirsty mules. He looked them over and he looked at the interpreter. Well Horace, what'd you find out?

He's pronouncing his name as Toppish.

Toppish. Toppish who?

Just said Toppish. The boy dont know a lick of english.

Where's he from?

He aint sure. Somewhere south of the river. Mother and daddy dead. He's been with the savages three winters.

You ask them if there were other white children among their people?

Yes sir. They said that there were.

Horace, see if you can get these boys to understand that we're going to help them.

Okay.

And make the Smith boy to know that his daddy's been looking for him.

Tatum watched the boy. He was picking at a piece of meat stuck between his teeth and when the interpreter finished his translation he just sat there as if he'd not understood a word of it.

Poor kids. Tatum said it under his breath as he shook his head. Well Horace, only thing I can think is to get em cleaned up and in the mission school while we figure out what to do with them.

What about the weapons?

We better take them dont you think?

I'd say so.

Okay, you sit with em a few minutes. I'll get some of the fellas in here to help us. Let's get these rascals in the guardhouse. Get the barber in there and cut that hair off. I'll send for a tub to get em scrubbed up real good. And let's get em in some normal clothes.

Yessir.

I dont know about you, Horace, but I cant hardly stand the smell of em.

23

— ★ —

Fort Concho

1873

In the early spring of eighteen seventy-three RL was leaning on the wall of the stone corral at Fort Concho. He had been out west on the Butterfield road on escort with a surveying party and returned here the previous day to find the post busy with the preparations of the Fourth Cavalry. Five companies of troops had just arrived from Fort Richardson and there had been a celebratory buzz about the post and a group of these new arrivals had lined out alongside him to peek at the prisoners inside. The stockade held the Comanche women and children taken from their village on the North Fork six months prior and the officers' wives and children were paying them a visit. They were very excited and followed along behind the post chaplain who guided the goodwill proceedings.

The observers outside the walls were whispering observations and crude remarks to one another, befuddled by the philanthropic affairs being conducted inside. An old blind indian with long gray hair was the first in line, hands outheld, receiving an armful of shirts and blankets. Young boys and girls were jostling for a place in line behind him. The stack of goods was meant for the adults but the children had been prodded by their mothers to get all they could. Along the inside walls of the corral sat a line of elderly men lounging in the sun. Shirtless, heavyset. Dirty and dark brown. All of them smoking and observing the goods. In the far corner of the corral there was a pocket of shade where a pack of mongrel dogs lay sleeping. RL was watching the women. A man walked up and slid beside him and put his arms up on the rock wall.

I take it you've never been to a zoo? he said.

RL slid his eyes to get a look at the bystander without turning his head. He saw it was Carter. He'd pushed his hat back and smiled.

No sir, I hadnt come across one lately. RL turned and smiled and patted Carter on the back. How in the hell are ya?

Doing just fine. Just fine. How about you?

I'm gettin along alright, thank you.

We were talking about you just the other day.

Oh, really?

Well, we were wondering if you were ready to go to Mexico?

Mexico?

You haven't heard?

No, I've been out. Just got back.

Mackenzie has orders to take the Fourth down to the Rio Grande.

The Rio Bravo del Norte?

Yep. The Kickapoos have been raising all kinds of hell down there. We're pulling out as soon as we can refit the pack train.

RL shook his head. No sir. No more scout's wages for me.

There was a commotion inside the corral. One of the soldiers hollered something out and all fell quiet again.

So, what are your plans?

I dont know.

Now if it's a fortune you're after you might want to sit down with the fella that rode with us from Griffin.

And who would that be?

Goes by the name of Charleaux. He spent the winter up north with the buffalo outfits. Says eastern buyers are paying up to four dollars a hide. Three cents a pound for the meat. Hard to believe but he said he'd been with an outfit killing two thousand of the big shaggies a month.

RL took off his hat and scratched his head. Four dollars a hide!

Can you believe that? He says that range up there is about hunted out. So his backers sent him south to scout these ranges.

RL watched the women as he did the math in his head.

After the presents were distributed two of the officers' wives handed over their babies to the indian women. They were passing them around lovingly and stroking their soft blond hair as if the little papooses were their own. Bueno, heap bueno! they cooed. More of the squaws gathered around *oohing* and *ahhing* over the babies. The mothers were proud and they had big doting smiles. One of the baby girls was *googooing* softly but then the other started to cry. Her mother took her back and held her close, talking sweetly to the little girl as her cries subsided.

Just then Doc Notson entered the stockade on his rounds, walking briskly with his head down carrying his medicine bag. The dogs bristled up barking when he passed them for the smell he carried and he veered away, weaving through the indian children who were begging for candy. He walked toward the assembly. One of the babies had spit up and all the women were laughing but the doctor interrupted them with a scowl on his face.

Excuse me ladies, he said. How many times do I have to tell you that being around these Comanche squaws is going to infest you and your babies with the lice?

The smiles on their faces vanished.

Now go on, y'all get on the hell out of here!

He'd met Riverhorse Charleaux that night at the baile, a helper for the Mooar and Wright hunting outfit out of Dodge City. He was a French-Indian half- breed on the lam for having killed an army contractor in a quarrel over a whore and his bosses had sent him south to avoid the law and scout the southern ranges for the coming season. Now he stood with RL on the periphery of the evening festivities sipping whiskey, watching the dancers step and twirl to the "La Paloma", and that night he told him of his exploits along the Arkansas and Cimarron, long, frigid winters but extremely profitable. He'd been on the fringe of the Texas plains in the fall where a great herd that numbered in the millions stretched a hundred miles long and eight miles wide and he told them how all of the nearby cows and calves would stop when the leader was shot and how he lay on the ground with his rifle nestled in the crook of a shooting stick dropping three or four with only a handful of shots and adjusting his position and wiping the gun as others nearby would lay down in the middle of all that chaos as if to sleep while other groups would wander up and stand dumbly by the dead.

He said that one east coast tanner had given them an order for two thousand hides and with only a small crew of hunters and skinners and a few wagons freighting their hauls to the railroad at Dodge City they damn near met that order in the first three weeks alone, killed thirteen hundred buffalo and sold the hides for three dollars and fifty cents apiece and then moved north and killed another twenty-four hundred in a month and kept on killing just like every other outfit that had flooded that country looking to make their fortunes and there were so many hunters up north the men he worked for were planning on getting out of Dodge and heading to Texas where there were still some buffalo and a lot fewer hunters.

What about the treaty?

Treaty's ass! We're solving the injun problem our own selves, said Charleaux. Post commander told us to hunt the goddamn buffalo where the goddamn buffalo are. Not that I'm pretendin them injuns'll like it. We had one ole boy, Bashaw, couldnt shoot for shit but he went off and found him a herd. Got into em. We heard him shootin and when we run out to skin em we saw about thirty Comanch circlin and whoopin and firin at the poor bastard. Then they rushed in on the ole boy and that was the end of Bashaw. Thing of it is, he was one of them ole boys that had it comin to him. But that's another story. So we turned back and the injuns started after us. The wagons were too slow and they were gainin on us. Ole Boss White, he just said to hell with the wagons and we took to the brush with our guns. Held those sumbitches off till dark and they finally left us alone. We found Bashaw the next day stretched out dead stiff on the prairie. Thirty bloated buffalo carcasses around him within a two hunnerd yard radius. He was scalped. Cut up somethin awful. They'd cut a hole in his navel and taken out both eyes. Broke his restin stick in three places and stuck em down in his body. We commenced to cut up the dirt with butcher knives and pull out the earth with our hands. Three feet deep. Rolled him in and covered him up. Said a quick prayer for his sorry ass and started lookin for buffalo again.

They downed their cups and headed back toward the party for another whiskey. Charleaux stopped. He nodded at the middle finger of RL's left hand.

How come ye to have yer finger there nubbed off? he said. It get froze up?

Damned ole mule. The sumbitch wittliffed me.

They'll do that to ye. Charleaux sighed and shook his head and then something caught his eye. He pointed at the dancers. What'n the hell is that? he said.

What, the hat?

Yeah, the hat.

Oh, somebody said the general was given that sombrero by the citizens of Matamoros, down there on the border of Mexico.

Damn. Looks like he's got it all done up, his name embroidered in gold and silver bullion fringe.

RL filled their cups. Have another'n, he said. Listen, tell me more about the hide business. How'd you all get along in the thick of winter?

Charleaux took his cup and drained it and told RL about how hard the winter was and RL swug his whiskey and took it in, making mental notes of the nuances of the trade.

Them northers'll kill you as quick as the injuns will, said Charleaux. Come out of nowheres. Hell I got caught just before Christmas, following a wounded bull, up on the head of the South Pawnee. Late of day. It was dark and gloomy and when the snow hit I got all turnt around. Big herd of antelope come a runnin from the storm and damn near trampled me. Spent the night down in a draw inside of a green buffalo hide and it froze up on me. Damn thing werent thaw for me to crawl out until the sun got up middle of mornin.

RL glanced at the man's necklace. A beaded collar with various accoutrements and a dark pair of shriveled human ears. What do you have there?

What?

There, on your necklace.

Oh, thems from that ole boy I was tellin you about. That little tango in Dodge City. That's all. Anyhow, there was another storm come end of January. We was already worn out from the long winter. We was headin back to Dodge. A thirty-mile run. No, forty. Wagons loaded to the hilt and we're pushing hard. Was a clear day and we got to Mulberry Creek. Saw that line of gray clouds and then a big wind hit. Well, here she come. We hunkered down and before long it was such that we couldnt see for the ice and snow and the mules couldnt keep their feet and then we lost the trail. We were lookin for the Hunt Ranch which we knew had to be close by, but the mules kept comin to a halt. It was that ornery sumbitch we called Poncho. Damned if he didnt freeze to death in his tracks. Anyhow, we ventually made it to Hunt's and stabled the animals. Huddled up inside all cozy by the fire. Alls of us had frozen hands and feet but Baker was the only one that lost anything. Post surgeon at Dodge nubbed off a few of his toes. Damn doctor told him he'd lost count of the amputations he'd done that season. Said they'd counted over a hunnerd hunters frozen to death along the Arkansas last winter.

Charleaux was eyeing a rough looking soldier who was attending the colonel. He took a big swig of his whiskey and gulped and then he slapped RL's shoulder with the back of his hand.

Tell me somethin, he said. What are the odds that feller there would take a wager on a little knife thowin contest?

24

— ★ —

The Summer of 1928

The colonel and Corinne take a trip with Evetts Haley and his fiancé to Taos in the colonel's new car to visit some of his old Pueblo indian friends. The trunk is full of buffalo robes and meat and other old relics intended as gifts. Taking advantage of the old man's inspiration in seeing the wonders of the high desert and the Sangre de Cristo mountains, Haley inquires about his time on the trail in northern New Mexico in the sixties and seventies. Corinne is jotting notes in the backseat as the colonel tells them a story about the time when the old chieftain Standing Deer wandered into Texas.

What on earth was he doing in Clarendon? said Haley.

He was heading back from a trading trip with the Kiowas. You see, somehow he'd lost his way.

They pass long stretches of fenced ranch country and Goodnight is gazing at the distant mountains and studying the barbed wire that fences in the vast grassland pastures where large herds of antelope are grazing. My god, look what we did, he said. Those poor bastards fenced in.

They sit there quietly pondering the thought and watching the distant mountains as the car hums along the highway. After a while Haley breaks the silence.

Colonel, so how'd exactly the folks in town take to Standing Deer? That must have been a bit of a surprise in those times.

That's right, the entire damn town was all up in arms. Thought him and his boys were Comanches. When I first rode up I just hung back, taking it in. There was a big mob and it seemed that some of those folks had a mind to try and kill him. He was babbling about in spanish and they werent getting a lick of that lingo. Buenas noches, buenas noches! he kept saying. You see, he was looking for me.

Haley was chuckling, the girls in the back smiling.

You didnt help him.

Why, of course I did. Called out his name and everyone turned and that ole rascal broke into the biggest smile of relief you've ever seen. Everyone went on their way and we got to visit. After we'd caught up on general goings-on he asked me something. He said, how do I get back to Taos? I couldnt believe this old man who'd spent his whole life up in this country didnt know his way. But what it was, you see, was all of the damn fences. He couldnt find his way for all of the goddamned barbed wire.

They walk down the main street of Taos after leaving Doc Martin's home. Across the street a man stops cold in his tracks when he notices the striking presence of the old plainsman, weathered and tanned with his goatee and wild white hair glowing in the bright mountain sunshine.

Hello there, excuse me! he calls out.

The man scurries across the street with his hand out. Haley and the wives hold up but the colonel limps along shuffling, oblivious to the stranger.

Name's Buck Dunton, he said.

Haley shakes his hand and Corinne hurries along for the colonel, calling out to him to stop.

I'm very sorry to bother you all but I'm an artist here in town and I just took a bit of inspiration here. I was wondering if perhaps the gentlemen there might allow me to sketch his portrait.

Haley smiled at the idea and waved him on and they made small talk of the beautiful day as they made their way over to make formal introductions.

Pleased to meet you Mr Dunton, said the colonel, but I for damn sure dont have any interest in sitting for any portrait.

Dunton's shoulders slumped. He turned his head. He had a pained expression.

Oh Colonel, said Corinne. I think it's a wonderful idea!

Mrs Haley said so as well and Evetts was nodding his head approvingly. Goodnight bit off the end of his cigar and spit it out, muttering.

Corinne put her arms around him and gave him a big hug and then kissed him on the cheek. Dunton said something to Haley and then the writer chimed in.

Listen Colonel, this is a real treat. I've heard many fine things about Mr Dunton's work. And a piece like that would be a fine donation to the museum.

Why yes it would! said Corinne. He's right! Now Colonel, oh pretty please! With sugar on top. Just this one time for me.

She was bouncing on her toes, practically begging. Goodnight smirked a little and waved them off.

Well hell, I suppose I'll have to submit. But there's about as many damn pictures of me in Texas as there are buzzards, and just about as useful!

Dunton's studio was filled with western relics and natural light and the French accordionist Jean Vaissade was playing on the phonograph. The ladies were looking around. Haley was impressed with the soulfulness of the room and he could not help but break from his interviewing of the colonel to comment on their surroundings.

I must say Herb, this is a real fine place to work in. And the music, I really love the sound of that. What are we listening to?

Dunton was intently sketching at his easel, looking up from time to time to study the colonel, who was sitting there restlessly, fidgeting like a restless old hen.

Let's see, this tune is… I believe it's called Ma Régulière. I cant speak french as good as Blumenschein's. Or Sharp's for that matter.

Beg your pardon?

Oh, a few of my artist buddies here in town. They studied together in Paris and have turned me on to this stuff. It's street music, the stuff they play in dives over there. Fella on lead is Jean something or another but they say the kid playing backup banjo is the one to listen for. Django something-or-other.

Haley looked at his notes but glanced back up to wave at the girls through the window who had excused themselves to step outside.

I'm about done gentleman, said Dunton. Just a few more minutes.

Okay, let's see Colonel, said Haley. Yesterday, when we were discussing the indian wars, we didnt talk too much about the Kiowas.

What about em?

Well, did you ever deal with them much? Get to know any of them?

The old man bit his lip, thinking, searching through his memories.

Well sure I did, he said. Back when things were hot I'm sure we had our fair share of run-ins. Them and the Comanche hassling us for our stock. And there was a band of em came into the lower reaches of the JA in '78, looking to hunt bison off the reservation. That was when Quanah was there. They were with him.

So once you set up a run in the Palo Duro, they wandered from the reservation with Quanah and his boys?

That's right. And ever since then we were friends. As a matter of fact, what was it, twelve, fifteen years ago? Up on the old ranch we arranged for some of em to come over from the reservation. It was big doins. Had em kill and butcher a buffalo and then we put on a big barbecue supper for all the neighbors.

You made a film of that, didnt you?

Yes sir. We sure did.

Dunton stood up to stretch his legs and after he took a sip of water he had a question. Say, is it true the big Kiowa chief killed himself in prison? What was his name?

Satanta.

Yes, Satanta.

I did hear that, come to think of it, said Haley.

The colonel bowed his head, a little melancholy.

Well, the story I got was they wouldnt let him out of the penitentiary, even though once he turned sixty he was very, very sick and had been appealing to be released. To go back and die with his people. But of course by then they werent going to let him out, and he knew it. And then one day they found him with his wrists cut up, bleeding out.

Oh my. What a shame.

Just then the music stopped. The colonel took out his kerchief and wiped his mouth and brushed his nose and folded it up and tucked it back in his pocket.

Well, I dont know. Anyhow, they patched him up. Had him upstairs in the infirmary and when they wadnt lookin he finagled himself out on a landing and jumped to his death.

Jumped to his death? It couldnt have been that high.

Well, you know how those deals shake out. Apparently that was the official report from the prison.

They sat there. Goodnight tapped his boot on the floor. Dunton went back to work. Voices outside in the streets. The scribble of Dunton's pencil on the canvas. Haley broke their silence.

A few years before that, not long after they all surrendered, they hauled a lot of them off to Florida in chains. Fort Marion I think it was. Dr. Barker told me this. In Austin. The medicine man, Maman-ti, I think they called him the Owl Prophet or some such because he carried around an owlskin puppet. Well, the consumption got him. And Barker told me that Maman-ti's old nemesis, Kicking Bird, died just before that. They think of the lead poisoning. Some said at the hands of Maman-ti or one of his cohorts.

I did hear about that.

And apparently Lone Wolf got the malaria.

They all sat there nodding their heads thinking on things. Haley began jotting notes in his journal. After a while Dunton stood up, finished with his little masterpiece of the colonel. It was silent and Goodnight was staring at a fine piece of plaited rawhide hanging on the wall. When Dunton noticed this he reached up and grabbed it and leaned over, handing it over to the colonel as he turned back looking at the sketch on the easel.

Well, now that's a beautiful piece of work, said Goodnight.

Dunton stopped. He turned back to the colonel, pleasantly surprised, thankful. He thought the colonel had intended to compliment his portrait. But Goodnight grabbed his cane and pushed himself up in a rush, wobbling and flustered. He realized he'd been facing the drawing of himself and he shook the rope emphatically.

Now goddamnit I'm talking about this goddamn rope here! he said.

Then he pressed his cane forward and stormed off for the door, shuffling along and stomping on the hardwood floor and cussing to himself.

In the fall the colonel and his wife are in Austin at the home of J Frank Dobie on their way to the gathering of the Old Trail Drivers Association in San Antonio. Dobie, an aspiring folklorist and professor at the university, will be escorting the Goodnights on their trip to the annual meeting and he has to give a short speech honoring many of the old-time legendary cow people, the colonel and his accomplishments being of particular highlight. After small talk Corinne steps outside with Mrs Dobie for a tour of her extravagant flower garden and as the men continue their visit Dobie asks about a few of the colonel's contemporaries.

Well let's see. Ole Bose Ikard's hanging on. He's up in Weatherford. And I get to see Rumans ever now and then up in Amarillo. You know we're old as hell but we've got a helluva lot of life left in us yet.

Dobie chuckled. Well, I must say Colonel, you sure look great. But inside he was absolutely overcome by the physical appearance of the old man before him. He'd seen him two years ago and the changes were drastic. The frailty, the often distant, even desperate wander in his eyes as he faced the final journeys toward his ultimate fate, whatever it would be. Dobie's mind was racing, a thousand spontaneous thoughts and flashes of his own mortality. He could see the fleeting hints of fear that he'd seen in so many elderly and yet the old plainsman fought it back.

Dobie, I feel better than I've felt in years. Yes sir, I am one lucky old man. I've no doubt I'll live beyond a hundred. And I owe it all to that pretty little gal. If it werent for her I dont know how these past few years would have played out. She's been such a godsend to me.

Well, congratulations. I tell you what, we're sure happy for you. Corinne sure seems like one mighty fine gal. And smart as a whip!

Yes sir.

I can sure tell how much she cares about you. And I must say Colonel, she's very attractive!

Well she's back to her old self after a little rough patch last year.

Oh, is that right? How so?

The colonel gripped his cane, his knee jimmying and shaking as he thought about what he wanted to say. He sucked in a big breath and he caught himself up in a fit of coughs and then he cleared his throat and spit up a chunk of yellow-brown phlegm into the trash can at his feet.

Dobie, I'd appreciate it if you'd keep this between you and me. I haven't said much about this to anyone.

He leaned forward. Dobie did as well.

The little girl, he whispered. She had a miscarriage.

Dobie's face went blank like he'd seen a ghost and then he caught himself. He bit his lip, pained his face, shook his head in sympathy.

Oh Colonel, I'm so terribly sorry to hear that.

Well it's been a long haul getting over it. It was just meant to be that way, I suppose. But that's behind us now and there's hope yet, God willing, that we'll have some little Goodnights running around here one of these days.

Dobie forced a smile. He was nodding slowly. Goodnight looked out the window where the women were laughing in the sunshine and Dobie felt like he could actually see the old man picturing kids of his own running around and playing in the yard. He was trying to piece it all together. What, if any, basis in reality the story might hold. He was at a loss for words and he tried to change the subject.

Listen Colonel, tell me, how are Haley and Nita doing? I heard their wedding out in Alpine was a real nice time.

October in San Antonio, Texas. Goodnight is sitting on the long lounge in the lobby of the Gunter Hotel. He can hear the infectious spontaneity of a raucous fiddle tune emanating from the ballroom, courtesy of the Cockle Burr Band. There are onlookers lingering nearby, sneaking glances, fascinated by the presence of the old plainsman.

A stranger walks up with his hand out, smiling.

This is Colonel Goodnight, I take it?

No sir, this is Charlie Goodnight.

Yes sir. Well, it's an honor to meet you Mr Goodnight.

He shakes his hand and hurries on. The photographer Erwin Smith is on his right and he is listening to the old West Texas cowhand Blake Alexander, seated left, tell the colonel about what all transpired at last year's event.

By god Charlie, it was a shindig like you never seen! Whole town turned out, damn near. All the old Comanches come in from Oklahoma. For the wild west show. Right down the street. Right there. All the old timers put on their outfits. The Smith brothers, you know those boys that were raised as indians.

Yes. Yes. I remember. How were they gettin along?

Looked good. Real good. The Lehmann feller too. They were hawkin their books. Firewater was flowin. It was sure something. Seein all them old warriors, old and fat now, chattin it up with everone.

I'magine it was.

Boy howdy, talkin to em about them old days. Hard to believe how far it's all come.

I know it.

Where'd the time go, Charlie?

Hell I know Blake, its seems like it was just yesterday.

Just then another smiling man walked up with his hat in one hand and his other held out in greeting.

This is Colonel Goodnight, I take it?

Goodnight, gripping his cane like a vise, looking the man up and down, paused before he returned the exchange, trying to determine his place of origin by his accent.

No sir, this is Charlie Goodnight.

Well, well, it's such a pleasure to meet you sir. Names Gutzon. Gutzon Borglum.

He pressed his thumb against the top of Goodnight's first knuckle-joint and the old man was awkward in the doing but he returned the grip just the same. The photographer spoke up to ease the introduction, ever supportive of a fellow artist.

Colonel, Mr Borglum is the man who created the fine bronze monument to the old trail drivers.

I see. I see. Very well then.

And he's been commissioned to sculpt the nation's first presidents up on Mount Rushmore.

Ah, the Black Hills. Another slice of heaven we stole from the indians.

Well I suppose…

And now you're going to make it so that the great white fathers are going to look down on all that sacred country for all of eternity.

The sculptor demurred. He started to say something but a group of ladies from the Women's Auxiliary came up on a fast walk, worried, and interrupted the proceedings.

Mr Borglum, so sorry to bother you but Mr Chambers is ready for you in the office.

Yes, okay. Thank you ladies. Gentlemen, if you'll excuse me.

He nodded and put his hat on and the men on the couch nodded him on his way.

The photographer stood up and stretched his legs. I'm headed to the boy's room, he said. The two old men nodded. He walked on. The music in the ballroom had stopped and now the lobby was filled with the murmurs of the patrons. Alexander leaned over and whispered to Goodnight.

Charlie, that ole boy. The sculptor. Ye wouldnt of thunk it...

He looked around as if to see if anyone might hear them. Goodnight leaned toward him, hand to his ear the better to hear.

Klu. Klux. Klan, Alexander slowly whispered.

Goodnight's face strained. KKK! he yelled in surprise.

Alexander jumped back. Goddamn, Charlie, keep it down would ye. He leaned back in. That's what I've been told, that the ole boy was one of them knights that sits on the Imperial Koncilium.

Goodnight was shaking his head. I knew from the get-go there's somethin wadnt right with him.

Mm-hmm. Say, where's that good lookin young wife of yours?

Hell if I know. I'magine she's with Mrs Dobie and some of those other women over there at the Alamo. Actin like a bunch of damned tourists!

You know it's about all any of the ole boys are talkin about, Charlie. She is young and she sure is purty to look at.

Well, that's awful nice of you. Thank you, Blake.

Charming as hell and looks the spitting image of a flapper.

Goodnight smiled.

Right, straight-ass outta New York City!

Goodnight chuckled. He was studying the bell boy bringing suitcases in from outside. Another man walked up with his hand out, smiling.

This is Colonel Goodnight, I take it?

No. No sir, this is Charlie Goodnight.

Yes, yes sir. Well, it's an honor to meet you Mr Goodnight.

25

— ★ —

The Hide Men

1874

In the spring of eighteen seventy-four RL was with the hunting outfit of J Wright Mooar heading south from Dodge City. They had three teams of wagons and a herd of fresh saddle horses and they left at sunrise, trudging the caravan across the newly built bridge and looking back at the town and then prodding the mules slowly through the wet morning grass under a clear blue sky.

They rode for six days into the hostile indian country and crossed the neutral strip and drove the wagons into the Texas Panhandle and located a permanent camp on the west side of a small stream in the middle of a broad meadow covered in wildflowers and overlooking the valley of the South Canadian. Their wagons were heavily loaded with supplies and the large black dog they'd brought with them trotted alongside them panting. A herd of antelopes descended a distant ridge in single file to water and in the distance they could hear the endless muffled boom of the big buffalo guns echoing out across the endless plains.

Sunset found them scampering about organizing the camp, a haggard crew of dog-tired men wary of hostile indians, mumbling to themselves or cussing out loud and bickering with one another. They cleared a patch of grass and gathered wood and built a fire. The skinners unhitched the mules and began to unload the wagons. Tents put up, bedding spread out. Others were sent for water as the mess box was opened and the cooking utensils were laid out and set just right.

They settled in under the late orange sky and the first star twinkled and the top half of a big harvest moon appeared glowing in the east. RL wandered up on a little hill to the back of the camp with good views of the rolling country and he called them over. There had been rain and the little playa lakes to the east were glistening and full in the last light and down along the creek in the strands of cottonwood and hackberry there were turkeys flying up to roost. The hide men lined up alongside one another. Lookie there, someone said. To the north and west into the endless horizon the prairie was blanketed in a solid mass of slowly grazing buffalo.

That first morning the hunters crept to the top of a rise to spy out the herds. They saw from the broad plain to the northwest a thousand or more buffalo in a pell-mell run for the creek and they watched them lumber into the water and drink. Mooar was a stickler for not wasting lead and he carried a sixteen-pound Sharps rifle fitted with a german-made ten power scope sighted in at two hundred yards. With this he was well-equipped to ward off the indians and when the bison herds moved up from the water onto the plain he would crawl like a snake in the grass to get within range and settle the heavy octagon barrel into a custom fit steel bipod shooting stick and commence firing upon these animals as they bedded down in the sun or stood grazing three hundred yards below him. The rifle shot a five hundred grain bullet at sixteen hundred feet per second and he would eye the herd and pick out an old cow and shoot her in the lungs. The bunch of them would startle with the report and she would stand there wobbling in the trace with her eyes glazed slowly bleeding to death as the others nearby would smell the blood and mill up around her. Then he would jam another shell into the breech and closely study the herd for his next victim.

Mooar was business-like and methodical in his approach, buying bullets by the thousands and powder in twenty-five pound kegs. Every shot was a chance to prove his craftsmanship. He wrapped a piece of patch paper around each bullet before he put it in the shell to protect the interior of the barrel from becoming fouled with lead and to this end after every three shots he would run a wet rag through to keep it clean and cool. He also carried a set of alternate rifles in seventy and ninety grain weights and he would rotate the shooting of these pieces as he kept the herd in stand.

They were loaded for bear, carrying a month's supply of goods and running five wagons that could haul ten thousand pounds of hides over firm ground by teams of mules. There were mess kits of tin plates and pots and pans and sacks of flour and coffee and sugar and a dutch oven made by the Seldon-Griswold Manufacturing Company and barrels of salt and cases of bacon and beans and ten-gallon kegs for water and two barrels of pure Kentucky bourbon that wouldnt last. The caravan was armed to the teeth, each man carrying a unique assortment of guns and knives, each weapon with untold histories of travel and death. Bullets by the thousands. The wagons carried four hundred pounds of lead and the ammunition boxes stamped with the initials of its owner, filled to the brim with patch papers and lubricants and primer extractors, reloading kits with tamper and swage.

By the early afternoon they were done with the day's killing. The shooters had littered the field with dead bison and they signaled the skinners and watched them roll in with their grindstones and knife kits and commence slicing up the carcasses in the bloody grass where they lay, fastening a rope from the wagon to the thick skin on the back of the head, whipping the mules to rip the hide from the flesh. By late afternoon the bloating bison lay glistening under the warm sun and the fully loaded wagons were jostling back to the camp with fresh meat from the humps and hams and tongues and the stinking and fleshwet hides ready to be pegged out to dry and scraped and sprinkled with arsenic. By the steaming fires with a cup of whiskey and plate of tongue fried in marrow, twelve haggard men telling stories under the stars, a fiddle and a song and the buzz of the booze, setting them free for a brief moment in time.

They stayed in camp each day until midmorning to let the herds graze and they ate bacon and biscuits and sipped coffee as they loaded shells. The fourth day of hunting and already over three hundred hides stretched out on the prairie. Lines of hide camps along the banks of the river for miles and miles and the endless stench of rot and death lingering in the air. The savvy skinners worked the killing fields swiftly and with precision leaving piles of skinned bodies shining in the sun like a thousand giant mirrors. The smoke of the snipers wafted faintly over the perpetual plains breeze and they came to love the smell of gunpowder in the morning, these hide hunters slaughtering with no mercy with their big fifties and bruised shoulders, caring for nothing but hunting hides while the hides could be had. The lone man atop a ridge looking down on a hundred carcasses inside a semi-circle of a three-hundred-yard radius knows that time is fleeting and like the eagle he keeps watch on the skinners as he studies the hills for indians for he knows they are out there lurking.

It was late the following day when the hidepegger left the camp to claim a buffalo of his own. After sunset when he had not returned they searched for him in the dark to no avail. They found him the next morning in a bog of bloodied dirt just a short distance from the bull he'd shot but his face was mangled and his body was a mush of blood and flesh and bones and his clothes were shredded such that they could only make him out for the model of his gun. Someone went back to camp for picks and shovels and they dug his grave and wrapped him in blankets and placed him in the earth with his possessions and covered him with large flat stones and piled a cairn of heavier rocks all around him. They prayed. *Dear Lord, we trust you'll look after old Joe as he was a good man. He was hard workin and sure nuff knew how to peg out a hide and was genrally purty nice. He loved the ladies and never talked down to no whore. Amen.*

They shifted their camps with the herds as they drove east to west along the divide, shaggy beasts darkening the horizon like a plague and with a vantage point of ten miles in every direction the eternal sky blending into one boundless mass of buffaloes milling about and devouring grass and passing for days and days and days as if God had somehow created enough of them to last forever. In the fields of death where the cows lay skinned, stacked up thick like logs around a sawmill, piles of fifty, sixty, warming in the sun and the little bawling calves wandering about in confusion or suckling at the teat of the dead. Seventy shots and sixty clean kills in two hours, arms and shoulders bruised yellow and black and blue, pouring water on the barrel to keep it cool. One morning one of the Powell brothers exploded his rifle from repeated firing and he rode into camp with his head down and his hands mangled and bloodied, his days as a hide man done.

In the night packs of wolves appeared from the bottoms, flooding the fields and surrounding the camp to feast on the reeking flesh. Snarling about the fringes in the glare of the firelight, white teeth snapping in their tormented frenzy. Sullen and haggard men unable to sleep. One evening the skinners rummaged through the medical bags for vials of strychnine and they scattered poisoned meat all about the outskirts of the camp. All that night they could hear the blood curdling howls and in the morning the sun rose over a meadow of wolves in seizure, writhing in spasm and struggling to breath as they fought death.

Mooar kept track of the days of the week and the month of the year like a banker with his logbook and each day was much the same. When the killing and skinning was done the hides were hauled into camp and pegged out to be scraped and treated and all afternoon they'd stack those that had cured in piles eight feet high and run strips of green hide through the bottom peg holes and they'd draw them down and tie them up smooth and tight. They sat down with their ledgers, comparing their tallies by type and number for each man. In ten days they had five rows two hundred yards long of drying hides lined out from the east side of the camp. The profits had begun to add up.

Five days later when the herds thinned out RL set out southeast with a light team of his own. Two wagons and three men to work the canyons and valleys of the Canadian. He'd had his head down working the knives when he looked up and saw a group of mounted warriors observing their camp from the top of a distant ridge. He told the boys to keep on with their work and he walked out toward them, cautiously, and raised his arm in the air as a sign of peace. They watched him. He waved for them to come into their camp and he stood there waiting with his hand over his eyes to block the sun but after a while they turned their mounts and vanished behind the hill.

He turned back and made his way into the camp. The men were cussing him under their breath.

What the hell'd you do that for, RL? said a skinner named Harsh from South Texas.

I dont know, he said. He'd had a feeling. Something strange. He stared back at the ridge. The men were nervous.

What are we gonna do now, RL?

Well, let's get the horses between the wagons. And we better line them hides up for breastworks just in case.

In case of what?

Hand me the glass, said RL. He put it to his eye and squinted and looked out.

You see anything?

RL was silent. He lowered the glass and eyed the rise with his naked eye.

Harsh spat. What do you think?

I think you better get your bite ready.

Goddamnit, RL.

Harsh reached into his shirt pocket and pulled out a small glass tube filled with powdered acid.

Hell, I dont know how to use this.

RL took the tube.

Look here, he said. You're gonna slide this outside casing off. Then when it comes time just bite down on the vial.

Harsh looked at it, picturing what that moment might be like.

How quick does it work?

Depends on the man.

Damn you.

RL turned and called the others over. Now listen, he said. If the injuns decide to make a run at us, Ellis, you and Davis cover that south side. Harsh, you take that corner. I'll take this spot here.

How soon you figger they'll be back?

Well, given there's only a few hours of light left I imagine if it's goin to happen it'll be right quick.

You reckon we can hold em off?

What else are we gonna do?

Damnit.

We've got good cover and plenty of ammo. Let's just hunker down and wait for em to make their move.

They took their positions, loading their gun belts and pockets with bullets.

They spoke softly and placed wagers among themselves as to who would earn the first kill and they watched the rise for any movement.

There were no buffalo and the prairie was quiet with a warm wind flickering up the grass. A quail whistled. RL had risen to his feet and taken rest with his rifle on a wagon wheel and he began to settle in for action.

What is it, RL? You hear something?

It took him a few seconds to answer. He spat. His nose was up, nostrils flared, feeling the wind and breathing in the prairie air. Nope, but it sure smells like injuns, he said.

They watched the horizon a mile to the north and soon a cloud of dust rose and they heard the faint rumble of hooves and then the savages came riding over the ridge and began to move in.

They broke into a wheel formation, fifteen, twenty of them, their hellish war cries came down from an empty sky and echoed out over the valley. RL leaned in and set the rifle into his arm and looked through the scope and watched them circling. He made out the headdress and picked out the leader. He stood up and stretched his back and lowered the breech block and inserted a shell, looking back at the men, grinning and mumbling some sort of acerbic invocation under his breath. He settled back in and thumbed the trigger and pressed his cheek against the stock.

They were closing in now, a quarter mile out. The tip of his barrel was moving in a slow circular motion and he seemed to be gauging the timing of the leader's turn. He felt the breeze crosswise toward him and he pictured the lead to about twenty feet and then he held his breath and squeezed the trigger.

The recoil bucked him backward. Over that prairie the explosion was immense and a haze of black gunsmoke wafted away. The chief on his war horse galloped another few feet. Then the bullet blew him off spinning headlong into the grass with a splattering of blood. Harsh had been watching through the field glasses and he let out a low whistle.

Goddamn, what a shot, RL, he mumbled.

The other hunters had readied themselves to fire and RL reached for another shell but the scope had banged him in the eye and it was bleeding and beginning to swell. Another long shrill wail rang out from over the ridge. Above them on the plain they could see the indians rein up and scamper toward their leader who had been shot. RL wiped the blood from his eye and shouted encouragements to the men. Give em hell boys! he said. Dont let up on em now!

A cluster of indians were pulling the chief up to carry him off when a shot rang out. A pile of dust flew up at the feet of the fleeing ponies. RL set his barrel to rest and glanced to his left out of the corner of his eye. Harsh thumbed back the hammer and let off a shot and they heard the sound of the bullet flying but it seemed to vanish in the air, the indians in full flight ducking on their mounts as they descended the far side of the ridge. Another shot rang out and hissed away into silence.

RL stood up. You boys caint shoot for shit, he said. He made his way over to Harsh and grabbed the glasses and looked out watching the last of the savages galloping on the horizon in silhouette into the pale orange sky. They gathered alongside him.

We better pack up, someone said.

RL was nodding his head slowly. He put the glasses down and looked carefully about the camp, considering the state of the animals, the amount of hides and gear, the state of their hunt in general.

What do you boys think?

I think they're pissed and they're gonna regroup real damn quick.

They gonna gather a shitload more warriors and come right back here for us and then keep on the warpath.

Yep. We best get back to the Walls.

RL nodded. Okay, we pull out tonight.

It was agreed. The sun slipped off in the west and Mercury sat twinkling in the eastern sky before the moonrise and somewhere out there the Kiowas and Comanches were gathering by their fires to plan for war.

They rode all night, the dipper sliding along its path around the polestar above them, distant lightning flaring silently in the west. That morning they struck the breaks of the Tallahone where they watered and moved on, scattering turkey and herds of deer from the depths of the timbered coulee up onto the grassy plains. They could not move fast. The indian scouts had tracked their progress through the night and in the dunes to the east the hide hunters could make them out walking their horses in leisurely observance. They crossed the quicksand beds of the Canadian and turned to the west, riding with the big guns across the pommel of their saddles, keeping a wary eye on the indians a mile away on the south side of the river casually imitating their path. When they halted to take their bearings the indians would halt as well, sitting atop their horses like phantoms, watching them, and they rode in this manner most of the afternoon but in the evening the painted riders turned their horses and rode away. They cantered at a leisurely gallop, from time to time slowing down and looking back at the white hunters. Then they stopped again, turning back, and one of them raised a hand as if to signal some sign or warning or perhaps to simply pay his respects in farewell to their fellow pilgrims on the wind-whipped plains.

What'n the hell is that all about? said RL.

They rode on and turned in the saddle one last time, for one last look. RL spat and rubbed his fingers through his mustache, watching them nudge their horses into a trot until they were swallowed up by the country and could be seen no more.

An hour before dark they reached the breaks of the Canadian, riding down off a rugged butte through a timber of chinaberry and willow and into the squalid trading post of Adobe Walls, thickwalled buildings of sod, a stockade corral of logs, men at work moving freight and loading hides.

It had just stopped raining when they entered the settlement, escorted by chickens and pigs, hands waving and shouts from the greetings of the idlers. The sloshing of the mule's hooves splashing in the mud. A man called out to them and pointed the way to the well and they halted and looked down the path. A trio of longhaired skinners stumbled from the saloon arguing and against the walls of Rath and Wright's store sat a number of men either passed out drunk or asleep. They went on through the slop leading the outfit. Intermittent gunfire of target shooting echoed across the valleys outside the post. When they reached the corral they unhitched the teams and turned the animals over to a crew of men employed as hostlers by the local merchants. RL gave them some coins and limped toward the building. A number of dogs were sleeping beside the open door and they raised their heads lazily when he entered the Leonard and Myers store. He walked along the hardpacked dirt floor, perusing the goods, and he made his way to where the proprietor held court at his bench.

The only man before him in line had at the heel of his boot, unbeknownst to him, a shiny silver coin. RL bent down and picked it up and as he rose the man had turned to leave.

Excuse me mister, said RL. Did you drop this?

RL handed it over.

Thank you kindly, said the man. My name's Dixon. Billy Dixon.

RL Terry. It's a pleasure.

They shook hands. The proprietor scribbled numbers in his account book. RL nodded and patted Dixon on the shoulder and stepped forward to place his orders. Dixon smiled and headed on but then he stopped at the door and called back.

I'll tell you what, Mr Terry. When you're done in here why dont you come on over to Hanrahan's and let me buy you a drink.

RL raised his hand. You got a deal, he said.

When he entered the saloon he heard someone call his name over the roar of the patrons. He made his way across the room to the far side of the bar where Dixon had pulled him up a chair and called to the bartender for another round and he introduced RL to the table. Gentlemens, this is RL Terry, he said.

Acquaintances were made and whiskeys were served. Most all of the outfits were in town. A few of them he'd heard of or met before. Jim Cator, Jim White, their skinners and teamsters.

RL, where'd you pull in from?

Well, we done pretty good for a few weeks. Out on the middle Washita and on to Gagesby Creek. I was out with Mooar. But then I took a team further east and the hunt petered out.

It was the same for us working west. It's been a late spring. Signs of injuns all around.

They all nodded and gulped their cups.

Anybody seen Mooar?

A man named Sisk spoke up. He's out on the Salt Fork. I just hauled in a good load for him but there's a helluva lot more. Goin back day after tomorrow.

So he got into the herds on the Salt Fork?

Yessir. We was seein more and more of em. Wright thinks the big herds will be movin in any day.

He got room for all of us?

Gollydamn boys, no reason we caint all make a fortune! We gonna need all the men we can get. Hunters, skinners, haulers.

RL chimed in. And we need em on account of the injuns. They came at us a day's ride from the Tallahone.

Really?

Yessir, damn sure did. But I sent that chief a message with the big fifty. Let em know that cleanin us out wadnt goin to be worth it.

I heard they made a run at the Causey camp.

There was a freighter named Jones at the table who had just arrived from Dodge City with a team of wagons loaded to the hilt with supplies. That's the word up north, he said. The injuns are leavin the reservation to come fight the hunters.

No one spoke. They were all nodding, sipping their whiskeys.

A hunter named Dudley spoke up. I dont know fellas. It seems to me only a plumb fool would head back out there.

Jones pushed his chair back and stood up. He downed the last of his whiskey. Now goddamn Dave, if you was born to be kilt by injins you'd be kilt by injins.

You believe that?

Well by god, I know it. It dont matter if you was in New York City or Californy. It dont make a damn bit of difference.

They pulled out for the buffalo range two days later riding south with twelve teams of wagons and twenty-two men, many of whom were red-eyed and reeling from their early morning debaucheries. The sun was an hour up and the way down toward the Canadian led them through low sand hills covered with thickets of wild plum bushes where thousands of little yellow butterflies flittered and fluttered in the sunlight. They crossed the river and the trail followed a ridge from the mouth of a stream and the streambed was sandy and trickled along lightly against their course and they watched it shimmer under the continual arc of the sun all the day long.

They moved out onto the plains. There were deer and antelope grazing the valleys and many birds and they heard their ceaseless chirping amid the occasional screech of a hawk or the call of a bobwhite cock. The wind was warm and dry and it soughed through the tall green strands of bluestem and buffalo grass and the country fell all around the flat and treeless plains prairie.

In two days they saw no buffalo. On the third they were moving west when they began to see a few small herds now and again grazing in the valleys to the south below them. A handful of cows, a bull. They shot them dead and skinned them and left them bloating in the sun. Then they set the first camp and then another until they spread all four outfits running north along a creek where they could keep an eye on one another and the long views of all that good country.

Two days later RL awoke to a deep sound coming up from the plains like thunder rumbling in the distance but there were no clouds overhead nor lightning beyond and the air seemed still and peaceful. He walked out on a high point behind the camp looking south, watching with the new risen sun a golden sheen of dust billowing slowly into the empty sky and he called for the men to rise. They lined up alongside him, rubbing their eyes, the deep steady roar growing louder.

That aint indians is it?

I believe it's buffalo.

You sure?

Listen for the bellows.

I dont hear no bellows.

Just listen.

They stood there for a long time listening. RL walked down and stoked the fire and after a while he came back with a pot of coffee and four tin cups, his field glasses dangling from his neck. They poured their cups, taking turns watching the horizon through the glass and slurping their coffee. RL turned to the Mexican that he'd hired on as his assistant.

Well Jesús, what do you think? RL pronounced his name with a hard J.

He shook his head. I no see natheeng.

RL was grinning. Nothing?

No, no hay búfalo. No hay nada.

Well, you caint see em but they're for damn sure out there.

RL glassed the skyline again. Jesús, go rustle up the other camps. Boys, get us lined out and I'll be back right quick. I'm gonna have a look.

He saddled up and was galloping south on the plain and after a while he saw dark clusters of animals grazing toward him perhaps two miles away. He ascended a ridge riding more slowly and then he saw more and could make out that they were bulls. After a while he saw them stretched out in a great mass as far and wide as he could see and here he slowed his horse to a walk and then he halted. There were thousands of them. Hundreds of thousands. Millions. They were steadily moving north and with them came a constant roar like an endless thunder. By the time they began to pass him he heard the sounds of the bulls in rut, a bizarre chorus of booming bellows reverberating over the hills and plains. He felt the deep bass rumble of their hooves in the earth. The soft, tonal calls of the cows and calves. He sat there for a long while watching them pass and the beauty of it all struck something deep inside of him. Then he turned the horse smartly and rode back to the camp.

He found the hunters on their saddle horses riding out to meet him.

Did you find em, RL?

Did I find em? I may have just run into the largest herd of bison any man has ever seen.

Come on now.

Dixon rode down past him for a view of the valley. Tell me the wind is in our favor, he said.

It is.

How many in the herd do you figure?

You caint count that high.

Dixon took out his snuff and put a pinch in the crook of his gums. The greaser is bringin your gear, he said.

Are the skinners getting the wagons ready?

Yes they are.

RL took his hat off and looked up at the sun. Well fellas, this is what we've been waitin for.

They went on, following him down the trail of trampled grass from whence he came, the rifles bobbing gently in the scabbards as they walked the horses, softly swishing through the still wet grass. The trail came onto a long flat where up ahead lay the ridge that would overlook all of that vast, broken country that led down to the valley of the great herd. They dismounted and hobbled their horses, gathering their gear and edging up slowly to the high rimland of the plains. It was perhaps ten miles to the other side of the valley and every square inch was filled with bison. Nothing needed to be said. There was a light wind blowing up the canyon from the south. The sun was still rising behind them, lighting the rugged breaks and stretches of meadow that fed down below. They began to line out and scout for position, every man with a pair of guns and hats and shirts the color of the prairie grass, some with helpers hauling ammo and essentials and a third rifle for backup. The lead herds were now pushing up into the side canyons and cuts of the Llano toward them. Dixon was the first to slide off down the slopes. Plummer and Dudley were walking east and they were next. Then Galloway, Wilson, and Sisk each disappeared down somewhere out into the western breaks. They slowly spread out along the ridges surrounding the canyons, keeping eyes on their collective positions and working to cut off any potential escape route.

RL had picked out a spot straight down the slope due south and he slipped off with Jesús behind him, hunched over in a slow walk, sliding on his rear, crawling on his hands and knees. Five minutes later and they were in position hunkered down behind the cover of some scrubland junipers and a jumble of boulders. Thick grass. Good vantages of the thirty-acre meadow below and all of the surrounding slopes. A thousand yards across from him he could see Mooar in the grass on a knee with his rifle in the crook of his shooting stick. Around the ledge Sisk was sprawled out on his belly, propped on his elbows and looking through his sights. The others were somewhere out there and had set themselves up much the same. They waited. The herds were grazing slowly toward them in bunches of a hundred, two hundred, snorting and bellowing. The air was full of the strong, musky smell of the bulls in rut.

Mooar seemed to signal at him from across the way with his hand and RL slid carefully up the bank so he could have a better view of the herd that was now gathering in the valley before them. He took a long swig from his flask. The slope was such that he'd sat down and rested both elbows on his knees. He was holding the big .50-90 Sharps ready and in the grass beside him was a .45-90 model that had been rechambered with a one-twenty load. He also had at his disposal the .45-70 Springfield that Jesús was holding at the ready. All were chambered and the spare cartridges were neatly spread in the grass around them.

The first of the herd moved into range, perhaps only a hundred yards below him. At first glance he told himself there were a thousand, so thick in certain bunches they seemed unable to move, nibbling at tufts of grass as they nudged along. There were cows and bulls of all shapes, sizes, colors. Young and old.

He cocked the hammer and scanned for the leader. There was a rustling and a portion of the herd quickly spread and then he saw the big one. Massive head and forequarters. Two tons. Dark and shaggy with wide shoulders and a shredding winter coat with heavy mats of sandburs and bullnettles. Curved horns like two-foot daggers shining in the sun.

A younger bull had squared off to face him and they'd nudged heads, the elder now stepping back to draw his momentum. RL through the sights was holding on a mark where his neck joined his shoulder. Hulking muscles on his hips and thighs throbbing like welts. He shook his head, snot flinging from his nose, panting. Long strings of froth dripping from his mouth. He snorted and rolled his eyes and then like a bolt of lightning made a great lunge at the challenger, knocking him back to his knees wobbling. The old bull drew back heaving and snorting. RL touched the trigger lightly. My god, you are one helluva goddamned bull, he said, and then he held his breath and squeezed off, jerking back at the explosion that he did not feel and with the slap of the bullet a puff of dust exploded from the shaggy coat and the bull bucked and stumbled forward. He gave out a deep guttural sound and took two steps, wobbling in the trace. An edgy panic broke out in those nearest him. Now the big boom of guns began to resonate out all over the valley. He handed the rifle to Jesús and he picked up the .45-90 and set it against his shoulder. The bull swayed and dipped his head back and forth, up and down. Eyes bulging and rolling in anger. He pawed at the earth and tossed chunks of dirt and dust up with his horns. Then he stopped and crumpled down onto his front knees and fell over and died. With the smell of the blood in the grass the challenger plunged back in with his head down, circling and hooking his horns into his cold dead brother to tempt him to rise.

The animals on the fringes had turned up their tufted tails in a brief, agitated gallop and as they settled back into a mill RL slid to his right and set up toward the northern edge of the herd and began to fire on them where they stood or leaned with their heads down munching up the lush green grass. Jesús worked by his side and watched for walkers and wiped down the barrels and reloaded their rotating arsenal of guns and RL leveled the rifle against his shoulder and let the lead fly. With his second shot he caught a mother cow full on in the lungs and she just stood there bleeding. The next shot broke the foreleg of her mate and it jumped back awkwardly and galloped around in a three-legged frenzy. Jesús cursed some spanish slang about the accuracy of the gun and RL reached for the .50-90 again and then Jesús handed him his flask to steady his nerves and after he'd taken a nip and dropped it he swung the big gun up and squeezed off again. He'd swung the lead just right on the wounded runner and his shot dropped him dead. Jesús let out a long, highpitched wolf whistle with his tongue as if he was admiring a beautiful woman.

Eso es tan bonito, he said. Los búfalos son muy estúpidos.

Goddamn, Jesús. Back off a little, would ya. I dont need you lookin over my shoulder right now.

With each shot the surrounders would scatter briefly and then lie down or mill about again and gather around the dead, nudging at them with their horns as if to make them rise. RL moved about here and there, up and down, side to side, finagling himself for places of vantage and calmly taking dead aim, lost in space and time, shooting them down one by one and within the hour the meadow that lay before him was completely filled with dead or dying bison.

He'd only stopped because something caught his eye, or perhaps he had some rogue thought that what he was doing was somehow horribly wrong. The guns were smoking. He stood watching the herd. His clothes were soaked through with sweat and a breeze swirled up and cooled him. He wiped the sweat from his eyes. From every direction came the uninterrupted sound of riflefire and the sky was slowly filling with thin, black, wispy strands of smoke.

Down valley the sun broke through a bank of clouds, shining down upon the portion of the herd that he had spotted before. He saw something flicker like a brief flash of white. A goddamned white buffalo, he said aloud. He hurried over and grabbed the glasses and came back and scanned the country. He had seen it out there a long way off but now it wasnt there. He had a good long look at the valley and the mass of shaggy beasts still moving in from the rear was thick as sardines in the ocean, pushing up into the forward herds who were moving into the gullies and hillsides and the small flats where the hunters lie concealed above them in wait. He looked out over the distant fields, the ones that he could see, where the hunters had been at their work of death, figuring up the totals in his head. Hard to tell but about the same as him.

Last year Rath told him he'd shot over one hundred in a single stand and he figured he was more than halfway there. It was still long before noon. No reason to rush things. The number two hundred stood out in his mind. He did the math. They didnt have enough skinners. They'd have to leave them out there overnight and there would be wolves. He sat there listening, thinking. I caint believe that goddamned white buffalo, he said. He looked at Jesús.

You wouldnt think we'd be able to kill all of em in a hunnerd years, would ye Jesús?

No, no, he said, turning his head from side to side slowly. No creo que sea posible.

RL took his shirt off for the clean, cool feel of the fresh breeze and hung it out to dry in the sun and sat on a boulder and sipped his flask while he waited for the herds to settle. His naked torso looked like it had never seen the sun. His shoulder was black and blue against the sheer whiteness of his skin and his trousers were shredded and black with blood at the knees. Forgot my goddamn knee pads, he said. He felt certain that they could kill buffalo for as long as they wanted that day and he wanted to get his bearings and not wear down. He wanted to be the man that had downed the most. He also loved the sting of the mezcal on his tongue and throat, the feel of it in his head, how it made him feel better against any subtle feelings of remorse he might have for whatever role he had in the senseless slaughter of those animals. Then he thought of that day long ago when he rode upon his home in flames and how he came upon his pregnant wife limping along and he remembered what she looked like dead in that room and what it felt like throwing dirt on her grave, and as his thoughts turned to his boys a butterfly came flittering lightly from out of the sunlight, circling around him, resting softly upon his bloodied knee. He sat thinking, studying the deep yellow color, the red patch on the hind wing.

He did not say anything for a long time. He'd become numb to the shooting all around him. He finally spoke when the swallowtail fluttered away and he watched it and he spoke slowly as if he could not lose his thoughts. Let's clean up these guns, Jesús. Fetch me the water, por favor.

No hay agua. Está en el vagón.

RL stood up and began to put his shirt on. He looked at the sun. He pulled a pained face. No hay agua? he said.

Aye can go get eet.

No. Get me the Fifty. Bring the other guns and all the stuff.

RL stepped up onto the boulder and took the gun from Jesús, gripping it mid-barrel and lowering the butt to the ground where he commenced to unzip his britches and urinate down the muzzle. When it was full he pulled down the breechblock to let it run out. He swabbed the barrel out with a greased rag and set the gun down with it and opened it up to dry in the shade. Then he repeated this process with the other guns.

Jesús had been going through the ammo until he had the bullets organized and they sat in the shadow against some rocks waiting on the guns to cool and watching through the glasses as the guns boomed and dropped the buffalo dead in the meadows.

After a while Jesús got up and walked off, leaving RL alone with his thoughts. He scanned the killing grounds as there was a respite in the shooting and then a lone shot rang out and two seconds later he saw the animal that it struck. He put the glasses to his eyes. He saw the big black bull on the outer edge of the herd, left hind leg blown out above the knee, hopping around circling in a crazed half trot with its leg flopping about wildly. Bucking and tossing its head, ramming madly into the other animals and then it began to settle, turning slower and slower, leg spraying a bright red circle of blood in the fluffy spring grass.

When he saw it calmly lay down on the prairie with its head up looking about as if all was well in the world it struck him. How would it feel? The shock of the blow and the blood and the pain and then the coming to terms with it all. Mortal wound or not. Bleeding out, unable to move. The suffering. Facing that. Facing death. That beast had done nothing to deserve its fate. But a man might have it coming to him. Or not. Lying crippled waiting around to die. Something's going to get you, he said. The old bull didnt think that way. But he did.

Then as he sat there thinking he heard from somewhere over the coulee to his left a rattling scrabble of hooves among the cliffs like a rockslide or a herd of mountain sheep on the run. He turned back. Nothing. He stood up. He watched the cliffside a half mile off and then suddenly he saw them running headlong off the canyon wall, at first singles and pairs then handfuls of them, massive, shaggy beasts dropping soundlessly in the empty air. Silhouettes against the great blue, twisting and turning, floating in the sunshine as if it were some freakish dream and in the order of their falling they came thudding into the earth, blowing up in bursts of bones and blood and guts. When the last of them fell a strange silence consumed the valley. Piles and piles of them. A ton or two tons of muscle and hair. Broken backs, shattered legs. Some alive, some dead. The breeze died and a big heat had kicked in under the high sun and perhaps the hunters had paused to consider the events at hand and then a shot rang out and the slaughter resumed again.

26

— ★ —

Canyon, Texas

October 1929

Haley, it was the damndest thing I ever saw when we pushed that first herd into the Palo Duro in '76. I'll never forget it. That canyon was plumb full of big shaggies, probably ten thousand of em, and as we drove the cattle in we took to firing upon the canyon walls, pocking up the red dust and generally using our guns to stampede those hungry beasts from that range. All hell broke loose, the junipers snapping and the echoes of the gunfire with the roar of the hooves hauling straight ass down what was at many points pretty much a cliff. A goddamned red cloud of dust rising up over that canyon like you never seen, and ever other kind of animal scurrying around like the world was a comin to an end—jackrabbits, paisanos, foxes, javelina, bears. Coveys of quail, prairie chickens.

There was one helluva range back up the canyon near a little stream that trickled from out of the Caprock. We picked the spot for the house and corrals. Plenty protection from the cold winds off the plains. Plenty of trees. Hackberries, chinaberries, cottonwood, junipers and such. And so we took to settin up the Home Ranch and that meant clearing the buffalo to save the range for the cattle, which meant of course killing em and whatever else was going to get in the way of us raising cows. So yes, I had a role, albeit a different one, when the slaughter was at its height. And it liked to have killed Mollie. She just couldnt stand it and over time I started to come around to her way of thinking. She was one wise woman in her day. But it wasnt long before we had a buffalo herd of our own. To try and preserve em because otherwise they were doomed to extinction.

We built out a buffalo range. The first bull was Old Sikes. That big bastard didnt give a goddamn about barbed wire and boy howdy would that sonofabitch roam, I tell you what. I cut him and de-horned him. Out in the pasture he fattened up and in time the herd began to grow. Now, there's absolutely no question their meat is better than beef. Dont let anyone tell you that. And their hides are the warmest. I learned so much watching them grow over the years. My god what a tragedy it was, that slaughter.

He is sitting in Haley's study being interviewed for the planned book about the Texas Panhandle region centered around his life. Mrs Haley and Corinne come in with armfuls of recently typed reminisces, stacks of them from the previous months, Corinne's notations of the colonel's oral histories. They set them down and as the women walk out the door Mrs Haley says, It looks like Mr Baird just drove up with some other gentlemen.

Okay, thank you. The writer does not look up as he is writing furiously and there is more the colonel has to say on this topic.

You see, a buffalo has a helluva lot more sense than most folks give it credit for. Tougher than a cow. Wont get sick. Could give a damn about a heel fly. Smell water better and go without it longer.

About how many are in your herd right now?

Oh I'd give it over two hundred for damn sure. Maybe two fifty. Yessir, it's no wonder the indians believed them to be sacred. As we should've all along. Like ever other animal.

When the visitors came in they urged the colonel to stay seated and they greeted him with handshakes and gifts of books and jars of pickled peppers and old ranch relics and pats on the back. The room was loud with laughter as the ladies brought in extra chairs and the men took their seats. The colonel knew Ed Baird from back in the eighties and Haley had invited the local printer, Horace Russell, as well as another Amarillo man who plied his trade as a geologist searching the High Plains for oil. His name was C Don Hughes and while the colonel was anxious to meet him on account of his dreams of striking oil on whatever remaining property he had in his name he was leery of the camera equipment Hughes had lugged into the room.

What'n the hell do you have there, Hughes?

Oh this. Well, we thought it might be a good idea to get some of the session on film.

Goodnight raised his cane and pointed it at the man.

Now wait just a goddamned minute! he said. Rage in his eyes, he was fuming like an old bull and started to say something else but stopped himself and looked at Haley, incredulous.

Aw hell, Charlie, said his old friend Baird. Lighten up a little.

Haley shifted in his seat. Listen Colonel, it was my idea. Don is a damned good photographer and that equipment is pretty rare. And expensive. And I just thought having a little of this on film would help me in writing the book.

Goodnight leaned back, sighed a little, settled back in. Haley appealed to him.

I know how you feel about unnecessary publicity and I can assure you there's no plans to get this out to the public.

Well…

It's only for me and my work, that's all.

Alright then. My apologies Mr Hughes.

Oh no. No, not at all.

Haley knew that certain topics lent themselves to the colonel's favor and he quickly changed the subject. Say, Colonel, while we're getting settled here why dont you tell them that story about the old bull?

The colonel grinned. They all leaned in, interested. They'd likely heard the old joke in some form before but to hear the colonel tell it would be a real highlight. The colonel leaned back and smiled wide. He looked at the door as if to make sure the ladies wouldnt hear.

Now, you see, there was this old bull and a young bull sittin up on top of a bluff, looking out over the long views of the country.

He paused and wiped his nose with his kerchief as he chuckled to himself. The men were smiling.

And this pasture was just gorgeous! I mean goddamned gorgeous! Tall spring grass from recent rains. Clouds floatin by and they were warm in the sun, and you see, they were looking down at this big bunch of fat heifer cows who were grazin there, lookin all pretty out in the pasture before them.

The colonel was beaming, looking at them excitedly, waving his arms and painting the scene for his audience like a true storyteller.

That young bull, see, was all excited, chomping at the bit. Hornier than a two-peckered billy goat. And he says to the old bull, Hey, why dont we run down there and put it to one of those heifers?

The men chuckled and slapped their legs. The colonel scooted to the end of his chair and leaned forward to deliver the punch line.

And that old bull, you know what he says? He's looking down there, enjoying that view, with his discriminating and unsentimental eye. Like a goddamned impressionist painter. Or a poet. And he says to that young fella, No. He says, no, now look here young feller. Here's what we're a goin to do. We're goin to mosey on down there, take our time, and fuck em all!

They roared with laughter and with all of the noise it wasnt long before Corinne and Mrs Haley poked their heads inside to see about the ruckus and the laughter died down to an awkward chuckle. Goodnight looked at the geologist. Hughes, he barked, Is your movie camera there picking up what we're saying?

The women left the room with orders for iced tea and coffee and small talk ensued. Russell asked Haley about his recovery from a September car wreck near Mineral Wells that had left him in a bad way. Well, if you ask me you look pretty damn good, he said.

Well I was cut up something awful. Lost a few teeth, broke a few ribs. And of course, this leg is shot.

He pointed at it and told them a little more about the wreck.

Well, it just goes to show you, he said, got to soak in each and every moment because you just dont know when it'll all be over.

They all nodded in agreement. The statement wasnt lost on the colonel. Which is why we've been working like niggers to get this damned ole book done! he said.

Yes we'd been at it pretty good until this little set back, but thankfully Mrs Goodnight has been putting all these papers together and now the colonel has been kind enough to stop in on his way to Arizona for the winter.

Hughes nodded at Haley to let him know that he'd started filming and the writer looked at his notes to pick the next topic. Baird spoke up.

Charlie, you gettin out there by way of Albuquerque?

Yes, Ed. Straight shot there and likely down to Las Cruces before heading west.

Mmm-hmm.

But the little girl might talk me into a more scenic route.

Yes, it sure is purty country out there.

Haley here knows a little about it of late, dont you son? He was out there before his little dust up.

Oh yes. I certainly appreciate the desert but most folks dont understand there's mountains out there. Alpine country like New Mexico, Colorado. And down south there are places that remind me of the high desert in West Texas. You know, that area down around Marathon. Alpine and Marfa.

Where bouts did you hunt them peccaries?

East of Nogales. In the Huachucas.

Do any good?

Shot a few, but you how it is, Ed. The best part about those trips is not the hunting. It's sitting by a big ole campfire and dinking a little mezcal, watching the stars and telling stories.

Baird let out a long, high whistle with his tongue pinched against the roof of his mouth. You got that right, he said. And that's some drivin now, aint it?

Yes it is. Ask the colonel about their trip out west this time last year.

Same route, Colonel?

No. No, we were down state, in the south country. Through Austin. Santone for that ole cow punchers deal. Then Corpus, Brownsville. Followed the Rio Grande all the way to El Paso and then shot west.

Oh boy!

Three thousand miles and only one flat.

Now that's really some drivin! I'll tell you what.

Haley perked up, lifted his pencil. Colonel, what was the longest drive you ever made on horseback? In a short amount of time?

Goodnight took a big slurp of coffee and set it down and wiped his mouth again with his kerchief and stuffed it back in his pocket. He sighed.

Well let's see. That'd have to be after Loving's jackpot. I guess I set out two to three hours before sundown and reached Sumner the next morning a few hours after daylight. What's that, Ed, seventy-five miles?

Gollydamn, Charlie.

Well, I had me one helluva saddle mule.

Baird was shaking his head trying to compare some of the rides he'd made.

Charlie, when's the last time you was horseback?

Oh hell, Ed. I dont know. I'd say it was nine, ten years ago.

Russell chimed in, looking at Hughes. Now that's the picture you need to get Don, he said. Get one of the colonel up on horseback.

Everyone was nodding at the idea and looking to the old man to gauge his response.

Now it's funny you say that because I told Cleo that before we leave for Arizona I wanted to get out there and see that canyon on horseback again. See the land and feel the climate. Feel that cool, dry wind bending the trees. See the dancing shadow patterns of their branches on the ground. Like the old days. All that dazzling sunshine burning down on a broad clean pasture of High Plains grass dancing in the breeze.

Baird could picture it. Damn, Charlie, where'd you learn to talk like that? That sounds like poetry, he said. What a mighty fine idea!

Goodnight was looking out the window, nostalgically, picturing it. There was a moment of silence as Haley looked to his list of topics. Baird spoke up to keep things going.

Charlie, I was thinking you told me a time or two that you ran into Richard King from time to time in Santone?

Well, yes. Of course, the Menger Hotel was his home away from home. He was a tough old cuss. Like Shanghai Pierce. Those South Texas sumbitches were absolutely void of principle. You know King, they called him… what was it, damnit? My españole has never been worth a shit.

Haley looked up. Didnt they call him El Cojo?

Yes, yes! El Cojo, said the colonel.

You see he'd been crippled in a steamboat accident. I forget what it was that bothered him. But the thing I got a kick out of was he'd apparently bought a parrot down in Mexico. Bought it for his wife and he was playing with the little sonofabitch in the stagecoach. On the way back to the ranch. And that damned parrot took a chunk out of the side of his nose!

This tickled the colonel. He had a giggle that would wrangle in from time to time and when it took hold of him it was a joy like no other. The joy of his laughter became contagious and they all joined in, guffawing and wisecracking. El Cojo, they'd say, repeating it, laughing. The colonel kept on.

So Captain King had one nostril biggern the other and that's why he grew the beard. Now, first off, if I ever I took occasion to handle any damn bird the little sumbitch is a goin to know surenuff who's boss and we'll be the best of friends from the start. Birds just know. And then if a man has a sorry enough nature to worry like a damned ole woman about some insignificant abnormality, whether loss of hair or a birthmark or whatever the case may be. I mean hell, just act like a grown-ass man and let your light shine. No need to be covering it up like King did by growing that beard.

Suddenly Corinne appeared at the door and called out to the colonel.

Now Charles, we're guests here at the Haleys'. You are cursing something awful.

He heard her just fine but he cupped his hand over his ear and leaned forward as if to hear her better.

Hey? Now what's that little girl?

His audience was smiling sheepishly. She repeated the request. Please, she said, but he fired back impatiently.

Oh hell, Corinne. I'm not cussin.

Why yes you are, Charlie!

The men were chuckling, waiting for whatever might come next. The colonel had a twinkle in his eye.

I haven't cursed not one goddamned time.

Now, Charlie. She was smirking back at him, a flirtatious little plea.

Well you'll just have to excuse me darlin, I haven't seen ole Baird here in a long time and I have to use the kind of language he can understand.

She waved him off and slipped down the hallway.

Now where was I?

You were talking about the ranch men from South Texas.

Oh, yes. Those bush cowboys. You see they grew up at a time when our state was maybe the most lawless that it ever was in the time of its history. Up to 1870 there was no law or order down there in the cattle bidness. You see, so those South Texas boys grew up with no morals, no education. Encouraged to drink, gamble. Now I'll give it to them for knowing their trade. They know the cattle and the horses and are loyal as hell to their cause. Just no discipline. King's just one of many, a damned outlaw. Now take dear old Loving by way of contrast. Oliver was the most modest, unassuming, polished gentleman you ever saw. The highest of morals. Unbelievably fair. For as brave as he was, hardened to the frontier, he was the cleanest man I've ever known. Never drank, never smoked, never chewed. Strong as an ox. Hell in his middle fifties he looked twenty years younger. I've been lucky in my life to have some damned good role models. And it's partially on account of men like him that us cowboys of the plains handle ourselves so much better. That, and the fact that things got settled out here later and our young men were fairly well educated. The flatlander boys understood the economy and industry and were generally raised by good folks. The fact is they're just more intelligent, more cultured. Better mannered. They understood a little about discipline.

Haley was scribbling on the page with his pen and the others were nodding their heads, letting the old man talk.

Now see, what sense is there in a general habit of gambling or drinking when you're working on the range? I mean I'll enjoy a toddy now and then when the setting calls for it but when there's work to do habits matter. Hell I didnt hesitate one damn bit givin leave to Mollie's brother when word got back he'd been raisin hell. Same for Mrs Adair's boy.

You fired Mrs Adair's boy?

I damn sure did. Well, I demoted him. I got word he was gambling with his men. But I did fire Walter Dyer on the spot.

Gollydamn, Charlie. That couldnt of been easy lettin go of your brother-in-law.

Well, in fact it was. Whiskey, cards, cowboys. They dont mix.

What did Mollie think of that?

Why, she knew to stay out of it.

Hughes kept the tape rolling. Another hour passed, the morning wore on. They broke for lunch and when it was served the colonel ate quickly without speaking and promptly stepped outside to enjoy the sunshine. He'd not bathed in the morning and so as the men settled in for the afternoon sessions he excused himself to clean up, coming back in freshly washed, in a clean set of clothes and his hair nicely combed. He looked good. Life in his eyes. Haley was like a maestro, flipping through his notes or the correspondences detailed by Corinne, bringing out little relics or clippings to spur some topic, orchestrating their dialogue with mastery. The talk turned to the Red River War.

Colonel, did you ever meet Ranald Mackenzie?

No. Unfortunately I never had the occasion.

Goodnight sat there looking down, hands clasped between his legs and rolling his thumbs around, working his tongue around the inside of his mouth, thinking hard.

I wish I would have, he said. He did more for the settlement of this country than anyone will ever know. It's a shame how it all shook out for him, the poor bastard. What he did to deserve his fate, I'll never know.

What happened exactly?

Well, I'll never forget when I was in Santone, in the early 80s I guess it was. Whole town was talking about poor Mackenzie this and poor Mackenzie that. All sorts of rumors. He'd been talking crazy. Some said drinking heavy, which he wasnt generally known to do. His injuries must have caught up with him. But somehow he got hisself in a tussle with some civilians. Apparently he was harassin them. Lord knows why. He was givin them all kinds of hell and so when they'd had enough they ganged up and beat the hell out of him. Of course, they didnt know who he was and they'd bound him up to a wagon wheel and called the authorities.

Good God almighty.

Yes. Brigadier General. Commander of the Department of Texas. The greatest indian fighter the military ever produced. Ended up in and out of the crazy house in his last years. He was only forty-nine when he died.

They were all shaking their heads, save Haley who weighed in with a comment as he made his notes. I heard there were rumors that he died at his own hand.

Well, I hate to think of that.

It may not be true as there wasnt a whole lot on that.

Colonel, didnt you tell me that he and Quanah Parker got along well?

That's what Quanah told me. Mackenzie helped him get on his feet, on the reservation. Taught him the ways of the white man.

Imagine what it was like when they first met.

Well, Quanah was smart as a damn whip. One look at him and you could tell it. He was practical. He damn sure knew where his bread was goin to be buttered.

And you interacted with him quite a bit over the years, didnt you?

Oh, sure. Sure. We'd write each other from time to time.

Tell the fellas here about the first time you met him.

Well, it wasnt long after we'd set ourselves up in the Palo Duro, in '78. He was out off the reservation with a big group hunting meat, killing our cattle, as there werent hardly any buffalo left. Anyhow, we had us a little meetin and they were asking this and that, trying to see if I was Tejano. But see I knew the ranges out west and convinced em I was just in from Colorado, which I was. And I told em it wasnt my land, but the state of Texas', as I was payin taxes and all. The deal was, I said they could camp and do what they pleased but to keep order and in return, I'd give em two beeves every other day until they could find the buffalo. And that was that. We were friends ever since.

The men were smiling. Haley was studying his subject's mannerisms. The gray-blue eyes shining brightly under that heavy brow, thrusting out like a rock.

And I sent Haley here the clipping of Quanah's granddaughter getting married in Phoenix this past summer. Now imagine that. You know the thing I got a kick out of the most with Quanah was his women. Six wives I think it was. Last one was a real good looker that he'd stole from some ole warrior. She was quite a woman. Mighty lively personality. The last supper I had with him she put on like a white woman. Sat next to me and we had us a big time. Afterward Quanah and I got to talkin about his wives and I asked him, I said now Quanah, how in the world did you learn a Comanche squaw to keep house so well? And he just grinned. But you see, I found out later he'd hired him a servant white squaw to teach her.

Goodnight was chuckling and he leaned to the side and pulled out his kerchief, dabbing his nose and then wiping around his mouth and then stuffing it back in his pocket again. He gave out a long, loud sigh as if to give himself pause and he looked at Haley scribbling in his notebook and waited for the next question. The old man's energy seemed boundless and his storytelling became more graphic as they talked the hours away. Wildlife, flora, fauna. He told them about the proper management of a trail herd and all of the fine men who'd worked for him over the years. He told his favorite stories of his beloved longhorn steer, Old Blue, and he told them stories about his favorite buffalo bull, Old Sikes. And he talked breeding—how he'd bred the horns off cattle and what all he'd learned by crossing cows with buffalo and how down in Mexico once he'd seen a cross between a hog and a sheep. The observations flowed on. How he'd built the ranch in Colorado, the JA, the big house for Mollie up on the Caprock near the railroad. The churches, the college to educate the nesters. All of the fortunes made and lost. But as the afternoon wore on his spirit seemed to wane and as Haley interviewed him about the last days of the JA his voice grew softer, more nostalgic.

Now think about what all had transpired in such a short amount of time, he said. I just caint hardly fathom it now.

The colonel seemed to be forming questions to himself. He was staring straight ahead, out into the sweeping prairies of his mind. He spoke slowly, softer. I fenced it in, he said. Well over a million acres and a hundred thousand cattle. It made it easier to control the herds and ensure my prize bulls could do their job. It was the best beef herd that ever existed. Built it all up and then the drought took hold. Then things went south in the mid-eighties. Useless politicians were against us. Banks wouldnt lend money. The railroad was comin and I knew what that meant. Land squatters. More and more problems. I was too old and worn out to start all over. I was torn up physically. And I didnt realize I was only halfway done with my life at that point. Hell, believe it or not I had an eye on winding things down there for a while. I was beat. And how could I have known how much change was on the way? Those sorry ass goddamned nesters. Didnt have any tools, didnt know how to farm up here. They had no fences. Had no sense for that matter. And if we bought what little cattle they had more would fall in and take their place. And they made it against the law to fence in the so-called *school lands*. They wanted to tear down all my damn fences. Those were dark days, I must say. They went so far as to say I'd been stealin money from the school children. Dark days. I felt like I had to get out from under it all before it all went to hell in a handbasket and it wadnt easy. I was desperate. And so what did I do? I let Mrs Adair take the Palo Duro range and I kept the Quitaque and sold half of that off to LR Moore. Then all of it. It was my biggest mistake. One helluva of a big mistake.

He stared blankly at the floor rubbing his white goatee with the back of his hand. Knee jimmying. Silence in the room. The men watched him.

Well, maybe not the biggest. Goodness, it still riles me to no end though. Makes my heart hurt.

He bit his lip, slowly shaking his head. Thinking about his life and what all had passed, what little left there was to come.

Anyhow, we moved over on the railroad. Started our new lives. Good memories of the early days in the big ranch house, but that was overshadowed somewhat by me having pissed away a lot of my life savings in the mining bidness down in old Mexico. And those days were about settlement. Towns growing. Water wells drilled. We pastured the cattle out on the plains and used the windmills to get water to the ground tanks. Agriculture became big. Hell, we had to help the nesters make a livin to keep em from dyin on our hands. And then you wake up one day and there's automobiles. And telephones. Radios. Airplanes. What are they gonna think of next? Flyin a man to the goddamned moon? And to think of a 'World War,' where how many people died? Ten million? Fifteen? Twenty?

He shook his head. His arms were stretched out wide, his big hands open. His audience shook their heads.

And to think we were only thirty to forty years from the indians being run out of the Palo Duro. If there was a first world war you can damn sure bet there'll be another. The way I grew up it was ingrained in you that if a man works hard and holds up his end of the bidness he's got some control of how his life plays out. But that aint always the case, on so many levels.

The colonel looked his audience over. Today he did not look ninety-three years old to them. Baird was an old timer and he got it but the other two, they might as well have been babies.

Damn boys, he said. Dont let me to get to preachin like that.

Outside in the yard the shadows had been growing long and the haze that had moved in over the setting sun had the western horizon glowing pink. The old man pushed himself up on the cane and shuffled to the window and the other men stood up, rubbing their hands and pressing their pockets and thinking about how to turn the subject.

Well, it's been a full day, said Haley. I'm plumb tired.

They all agreed. Hughes thanked the colonel for allowing him to film and he told him what an honor it was to spend the day with him. Baird had to get home for supper.

Well it's just been one helluva visit Charlie, he said. It's been real nice catchin up. I can sure tell you're feelin good. By god, you're just lookin great!

Well, thank you Ed. I love my life. I've never felt better, in fact. This summer I had a spell but the little girl worked like hell to get me through it. And my damned ole feet swell up from time to time.

He sat back down and set his cane against the wall and reached into his shirt pocket, hands shaking, and pulled out a small pill box and opened it and put a few in his mouth and put it away. Haley was filing his papers away.

And I caint see for shit anymore. Got the bursitis in this shoulder. And when the gout gets to actin up I get stove up. Caint hardly move. Which is why I take that liver extract.

What sorta pills are you takin there, Charlie?

Hell if I know. I forget. The little lady keeps me stocked with em. Vitamins or some such. She's studied it. Holds the damned doctor accountable. He's liked to of kilt me with all of these damn pills though, enough of em to kill a goddamned mule.

Well now, aint that the truth.

And you know, I do everthing I can to keep going strong. Get outside and walk around in this heat. Get the ole blood pumpin and sweat a little.

Hughes hadnt said much in a while and he felt the need to chime in.

Down in the oil fields of Mexico, he said, they talk about taking shark liver extract.

Well now, I'd sure give that a try, said the colonel.

Ed nodded in agreement and he thought of something. Say, you're not on the cigars anymore are you, Charlie?

No sir.

When was it that you…

I quit on October 10, 1926, at nine o'clock at night.

They broke out laughing.

I'll tell you what boys, the little girl's even got me to join the church. This weekend I'll be going under the water, whole hog.

Baird was incredulous. Now Charlie, you're full of it! You are damn sure not going to get baptized.

The hell I am.

Well, then tell us what church it is?

Hell if I know, but it's a goddamned good church!

The service was on a warm and blustery Sunday, late in the morning. A handful of Model T's lumbered slowly down the dirt road toward the stock tank, an old buffalo wallow damned up so it could hold more water. A windmill hummed in the wind. The passengers knew from the weather that a strong norther was bearing down from somewhere out on the plains and they kept looking to the horizon for signs, talking about how warm it was for that time of year. The road made a sharp turn and headed up a slight ridge where down below they could see the water for the first time, reddish brown and shining under the noon sun, the steady wind whipping up little whitecaps.

The cars turned off the road and lined out alongside one another looking down on the tank. It had been six weeks without rain and the earth was slowly sucking up the moisture and the soupy mud that lined the banks was pockmarked with cattle hooves, some dried, some still wet. The colonel opened his door. He took in a big breath and sighed and fumbled for his cane. He tried to turn and get his leg outside but his old bones stove up and he let go of the cane and fell back in a huff.

Goddamnit! he growled. Old age hath its honors, but it's for damn sure inconvenient.

They helped him out of the car. He had on his favorite work shirt and his old chore pants were held up by suspenders. His britches were unbuttoned, as it was just more comfortable to ride in the car that way, and his white socks were tucked inside a pair of old house slippers because he was planning on getting wet. His white hair was blowing wildly in the wind.

The preacher hurried down and set up a table and got out his things. He studied the mud, listening to the wind and the voices of the small congregation as they made their way toward the tank. They'd come in their Sunday best, the preacher and his helpers and a small group of close friends. Everyone held their hats to their heads. Goodnight's foster son, holding his arm, led him down the slope as the witnesses took their place.

Cleo, what'n the hell have I got myself into? he whispered.

They both smiled. Some of the women broke into song to pass the time until all was settled. It was an old majestic Christian hymn of poetry and song and it set the mood as the witnesses made their way to the stock pond. The preacher plodded through the muck and entered the water, sloshing along down to about mid-thigh where he turned and surveyed his audience. He watched the colonel, he looked at the mud.

Larry, he called out to his young assistant. Run'n git me that board yonder. Over there by the windmill.

It was a two-by-six blown down in a storm and they laid it out across the mud as a bridge for the colonel to enter the water. He waited for the colonel to make his way down to the water and he looked at the people lined out on the ridge at the top of the tank. They stood side-by-side, waiting expectantly with heartfelt and thoughtful faces, every eye studying the great presence of the old man and his great white shock of hair gleaming in the sun. The song ended just as the colonel reached the edge of the water. The preacher welcomed them and opened the proceedings with a bow of his head and a few short words of thanks, a solemn moment of silence. He looked up and smiled and he held out his arms.

Friends, we are so very blessed to be here on this special day as we pay tribute to God's word as the authority for all that we do and say. Then he delivered a short sermon about the forgiveness of sins and the fulfillment of God's will. When he was done he paused and looked down at the water and he listened to the murmurs of amen before he addressed them again.

The gospel! The good news of Jesus Christ promises…

Suddenly a big windgust blew through and drowned out his words but the preacher did not stop. Hats were flying and clothes were flapping but he kept on. The colonel lost his balance but the handlers were there to steady him and as the wind died down the tail end of his pronouncement could be heard again—and the fulfillment of God's will. Listen to me, people!

He wanted them to feel his passion or perhaps he was just angry at the wind.

The gospel of Jesus Christ, he cried, the good news of Jesus Christ promises that if we in obedient faith call on His name in baptism, He will forgive all sins.

As he preached the colonel's eyes gazed out far beyond the minister up into a heaven of endless blue. In the northwest waves of geese were flapping their way south in wrinkled waves of V-shaped flocks. He knew there were larger flocks above and beyond them, naked to the eye. To the east a peregrine soared above the plains, diving and flashing through the sunlight, rising in the warm breeze. He smelled the wind, the muddy water. He had tears in his eyes.

The preacher called to him, waving him into the water with both arms.

Now it is time for you to be the recipient of God's one and only plan of salvation.

As the old man stepped onto the board the handlers walked beside him reaching for his arms but he waved them off, grumbling. I can handle this my ownself, he barked. The board squished in the mud from his weight. He stepped into the water, slipped, righted himself. A few gasps from the witnesses and the preacher stepped forward to help but he was alright, taking short little shuffle steps, hunched over and off balance, he'd stop every few steps to get used to the coolness of the water.

The preacher put his arm around him gently and turned him so that he was sideways, the preacher facing the witnesses. The colonel knew to clasp his hands and the preacher took hold of his wrists with one hand and braced the back of his neck with the other. They were waist deep. He said something about death, burial, and resurrection but the patrons could not hear this. Just the mumbles. Then the wind died down and all was quiet save for the gentler breeze, the squeaking and creaking of the old windmill, a thin strip of metal clanging.

Charles Foxwing Goodnight, do you believe in Jesus?

The old man had been told that he was supposed to say that he believed that Jesus Christ was the son of God but he was lost in the moment. The preacher waited. He felt the full weight of the great old man and he took a big breath and braced himself and called out loudly for all to hear—Through baptism we put on Christ—and without warning, he seized up the colonel and dunked him backwards under the water.

The old man held his breath and then opened his eyes, watching the stream of bubbles swirling up through the sunlit chocolate brown water. The distant sounds of hallelujah from above so sharp and clear. He sensed a great presence, a peace, as if all time and action had been compressed. He was thinking about his life, all that had passed and whatever was left to come. The preacher called out, I baptize you in the name of Jesus Christ for the remission of sins, and then he pulled him up from the water again and looked proudly upon the sopping old man.

The colonel was gasping, his hair like a shaggy white mop, and he let out a loud, long whoop and wiped the water from his eyes and opened them wide.

Praise Jesus! said the preacher. There were shouts and the witnesses broke into applause and the two women assigned to sing the hymns broke into song and held their arms out looking up at the heavens to receive the light.

In the weeks to follow the Goodnights wrapped up loose ends and packed up their bags for the annual winter trip to Arizona. Afternoons found them on the porch enjoying the late summer sunlight dropping down over the plains, talking and dreaming of the future ahead and waving hello to passersby. Corinne kissed the old man on his check and rose up to step inside the house to begin preparations for supper and the colonel's foster son took her place to sit with him and visit.

Colonel, I believe things are about ready for us to head out in the mornin.

Thank you, Cleo. I sure appreciate it.

Yes sir. I sure hate this time of year when you head out for Arizona. We miss havin you around.

It'll go by quick though, like everything. Before we know it it'll be spring again.

You still feelin up for a ride?

I caint think of anything else I'd rather do right now.

They walked out to the barn and went into the tackroom and while the old man waited in the bay Cleo got the old saddle the colonel had given him when he took over as foreman of the ranch. Cleaned and conditioned, looking new despite its legendary history, the smell of leather and saddle butter all about the room. He carried it out and set it on the rack and pulled up a chair for the old man. Then he walked down to the third stall and after a while he came out walking the gentle old horse they called Buttons. The colonel smiled.

Buttons, you old fool. What do you say we go check on the pasture?

Cleo bridled and saddled the horse and then led him over to where he had provisioned a makeshift staircase out of some old crates. Well, we best get goin, he said. We're burnin daylight.

The colonel rose up with his cane and eased up the stairs, groaning and grunting with each step. He traded the cane for the reins and grabbed the saddle horn, leaning on the horse with his foot wobbling in the stirrup. Cleo hopped up to push the old man up into the saddle.

As they were walking out from the barn Corinne hollered out at them from the house.

Oh Cleo, would you please get your camera and take some pictures of Charles?

Yes, of course I will. Colonel, I'll be right back. You sit right there.

Aw hell, he grumbled.

The old man nudged the horse into a slow walk, leaning down and patting it, talking to it as they went. You sure are a good ole boy, Buttons. Dont it feel good to get out. You needed some fresh air, didnt you? Where do you feel like going?

It was a short ride across the last of the level land out to the Caprock rim. They took it slow with Cleo walking alongside and the colonel telling him again about the time that first spring fifty-three years ago he and Mollie had camped there overlooking the canyon. They pulled up along the edge and the colonel sat the horse and looked out as Cleo got in position to take the photo.

Colonel, turn this way for me please.

He pulled the rein and faced the camera, pulling in a big breath and sitting up tall and proud. Take a good'n now, you may not get too many more chances.

Cleo snapped the photo and then sat back, looking at the old man, his eyes watering up at the view of the old plainsman as he soaked in that fleeting little moment of time.

Cleo, son. Now give me just a second here to myself, would you. No need for you to have to watch the great Goodnight shed a tear.

Why of course, you go on now. Take your time.

Cleo watched him go. The old man walked the horse out along the ridge to the west sitting with his hands on the pommel, looking south down the rugged slopes, the horse stepping slowly through the tall plains grass. There'd been some high clouds and a steady breeze but now the sun was burning through. It was clear, bright, still. He gazed upon the pillars and the mesas and the gulleys glowing red with the glorious afternoon sunlight coming on the Palo Duro.

That's God speakin to us, he told the horse. Then he sat there for a long while gazing out across the canyon. He took in a big, long breath through his nose, smelling the High Plains air, and he exhaled long and slow and whispered to himself.

I wonder if this'll be the last time I'll ever have the chance to do this, he said.

26

— ★ —

Adobe Walls

1874

The saloonkeeper at Adobe Walls was an Irishman named Hanrahan. He was also in the business of running hunting outfits both in Kansas and Texas. He had recently been giving the bulk of his personal attention to his tavern and as such was busy making good money off the large crew of hunters that had just arrived at the post to sell their hides and celebrate their success. Of late there'd been several hunters killed and maimed by the indians and yet the herds were now so plentiful on the range that most men were willing to risk their scalps for the profits to be made dealing hides and Hanrahan was desperate for hunters who could keep his skinners busy.

Leaning on the far corner of the bar with RL and Dixon they drank pints of beer poured from a keg shipped from the Brandon and Kirmeyer brewery out of Leavenworth, Kansas and as they discussed their final preparations for the upcoming trip the saloonkeeper asked them if they had any interest in joining him as formal partners. He also relayed to the hunters some intelligence he'd received about an attack upon the trading post that he believed was imminent and he urged them mightily to get out on the range as soon as possible.

Dixon nodded. He asked the date and time of the attack and he asked what sort of shares he had in mind for the partnership. Hanrahan said it could happen at any time and he offered him thirty percent of the outfit plus room and board and drinks on the house. Dixon rubbed his chin and looked at RL. Something did not sit well with RL and he asked Hanrahan why he hadnt warned the others. Hanrahan said it was on account of him needing folks around to help fight off the indians. RL did not mince words. He accentuated the potential profits to be made with their skilled marksmanship and he also affirmed that not only did they know exactly where the big herds would be located but they were already fully packed and ready to pull out early the following morning. Hanrahan poured them more beer, made a toast, discussed logistics. Word was spread to the skinners. When they finished drinking and headed outside to settle in for the evening they had Hanrahan's word that all profits from the partnership would be split fifty-fifty.

They tended the horses and mules with extra helpings of oats and corn and arranged their possibles and then bedded down under a full moon, drifting off to sleep listening to the hoot of the owls and the muffled sounds of the stock rummaging in the corral.

The next morning at dawn the indians swarmed down upon them from the surrounding hills. The men inside the saloon had been up early repairing the sod roof's main support beam and others were out readying the horses and wagons to pull out with the first good light. The warparty came charging in the darkness from out of the early morning sunrise yipping like coyotes, fanning out across the trampled grounds toward the buildings. Sprinting all out for the saloon before them were RL and Dixon and a man named Ogg and they barely made it safely inside amidst a flurry of gunfire. The defenders inside were barricading the doors with sacks of grain and chinking portholes in the sod as the windowpanes exploded broken shards of glass upon the hardpacked dirt floor. The hunters were clamoring about for their gunbelts and pistols when the indians began firing through the windows and they dove for cover or backed up against the walls with legs and arms splayed flat like spiders.

In the early heat of the fight they held them off with their sidearms. Dixon shot twice up into the roof where he'd heard a clamoring of footsteps and others were firing out the windows with any flash of movement and when the front door nudged open from the weight of the backside of a large warhorse every man inside began to empty their revolvers. There was a fleeting moment of silence as smoke drifted through the building and they reloaded with their backs to the wall. Ogg slivered on his belly and reinforced the door. They could hear the highpitched tongue trilling of the savages receding from the periphery of the saloon and out there now continual gunfire emanating from the other buildings. The hunters hunkered down or slid along the walls and posted themselves about the windows with their pistols drawn and peeked outside at the wild chaos of dawn. It was getting light now and the indians were swarming around the other stores, stealing horses from the corral, pilfering the Sheidler brothers' wagon and killing and scalping them and slaughtering their dog. There were more mounted warriors in silhouette covering the skirmishers from the hills, howling riders circling the sod houses amidst the call of a bugle, others scurrying about on foot dispatching the horses and shooting from close range into the supply stores. Hanrahan crawled through the haze of smoke and around the overturned tables and chairs and shouted across the room at the bartender where he lay curled up behind some shattered crates of whiskey near the storage room.

The big guns, Oscar! he yelled. Get in there and break out that case of Sharps!

Suddenly a rider appeared from the ravine and charged them, zigzagging his horse and ducking the hunter's gunfire, dismounting and making for the side of the saloon where he jammed his revolver through an open porthole in the sod wall and let loose a flurry of bullets. But Dixon was at the near window and he craned his torso out, twisting long and lean and shot him square in the side of the back. He ducked in just as a bullet launched from the hills exploded into the wall nearest him and when he peered back out the warrior he'd shot was coiled up and humping along in a waddlecrawl and when RL put two more bullets into him he crumpled up and died. Now there were two men shooting out each window and two at the door and others had taken positions firing through portholes that had been chinkered through the walls. A great and lethal barrage of pistolfire beset the ill-fated attackers all through the middle of the morning and the noon of day and the hunters in their dishabille began to gain the advantage. Words of encouragement were exchanged. They watched the attackers fall back. The exterior walls had meanwhile been getting pounded from distant riflefire and great chunks of sod were exploding with each blast and it seemed as if the building would be blown apart. Hanrahan scurried about the room distributing the big fifties. Clods of dirt were dropping from the ceiling and the sweating hunters now commenced loading these guns. At the west-facing windows Dixon and RL were taking rests with their rifles as if they were lining up to kill bison. RL looked up from his sights and yelled out through the noise across the smoking room at Dixon where he squinted an eye down his barrel with his finger on the trigger.

That bunch up on the ridge, Billy. Way out there. You take left and I got right.

Quanah and his warriors were so far out they may not have even heard the boom of the big guns that were unleashed upon them. He and Isatai'i sat horseback looking down from a half mile out and three other riders rode up alongside them. They were discussing strategy and studying the dead and wounded sprawled out between the stores and in the fields. Dixon shifted his knees ever so slightly and rested the big rifle on the sill and let off a shot, the recoil bucking him back enough that he struggled to gather himself in the two seconds before the bullet struck its mark. By the time he had refocused his gaze he could see the far-left rider's head pitch back and then he fell from his horse. The indians nudged their ponies over to see about him and RL reckoned the wind and squeezed off a shot and when the bullet struck Quanah's powder horn the blast grazed into his shoulder and blew him off his horse. RL let out a slow whoop and stepped aside to make room for the nearest man. This was an englishman named Charley Armitage and his shot exploded the head of the medicine man's horse. The white warpony that Pahvo sat was now splattered with blood and the Quahadis began stepping the horses back out of range with their chief and the medicine man crawling through the tall grass behind them.

Hanrahan rummaged through the supplies searching for ammo. He cursed at a crow that had flown in and had been cawing from perch to perch inside the sweltering saloon. Boys, he said, I hate to say this but we aint fixed much for ammo.

What?

You heard me damnit. Somebody's got to make a run for bullets.

There was a lull in the fighting although any careful line of sight a mile out or more seemed to reveal clusters of mounted warriors milling about in confusion or gathering in council.

RL spoke up. Well, I'll make a run for it by god if somebody'll shoot the damn bugler.

I'll go, said a man in a tattered Knudsen hat named Masterson.

Someone shouted. Dixon stuck his arm out and fired his pistol at a runner but it blew up the dust at his feet. He pulled back. Jim, let's you and me run to Rath's. He turned to RL. RL, you and Bat get over to Myer's.

They stepped back from the windows and gathered themselves and the others took their place with guns at the ready. RL reloaded his forty-five. I'm goin with you, he said. There aint a hunter one at Rath's.

Alright.

When they broke from the saloon a great chorus of shrill cries rang out from the hills. The warriors on the rise began firing upon them and gunfire rang out from all three buildings to provide them cover. They ran all-out with their gun belts flopping, a pistol drawn in one hand and a big fifty in the other, bullets whizzing by and bullets pocking up the dust at their feet.

There were six men inside of Myer's and three of them were fighting in their underwear, huddled behind piles of corn and flour sacks and whatever else they could muster for cover. Myer's partner Fred Leonard greeted them.

What'n the hell did you do that for?

We aint got no ammo, said Dixon.

Well sumbitch. He pointed across the room. Help yourself.

The new men looked about the room. Everybody all right in here? said RL.

Well, they kilt the Sheidler boys in their wagon. And they shot Tyler. He's alive but it dont look good. And it's hotter'n hell and we aint got no water.

And Old Man Keeler's pet crow has put the hex on us.

Where's Tyler?

He was lying slumped against the wall calling out for water in a gargle of blood. I'm dyin, Bat, he said.

Along the west facing wall were stacks of crates and supplies from the storage room and RL climbed up to have a look outside through the transom. There was a lull in the firing and in the quiet he could hear from behind the ricks of hides near the store the painful and plaintive wail of a wounded warrior calling out to his comrades. Somewhere a shot rang out and there was another sequence of bugle calls. Then he saw a rider appear from the low hills in the west, a lone warrior on a white horse five hundred yards out and moving fast. RL turned around and reached back for a rifle. Masterson had loaded it and handed it up. By the time he had settled back in to take aim Pahvo was already riding amidst the hide yard and was leaning down and lifting up Asewaynah. He turned and flailed at the horse and they tore off back across the field. The shot roared and with the whack of the bullet the right hind leg exploded and the horse staggered and veered, Asewayhah hanging on perilously as Pahvo whipped it forward toward the safety of the hills.

O'Keefe, I've got line a sight up here. I'll cover if you want to take a sack of bullets back to the saloon.

Awlright dammit, he said. He checked his gun and stuffed up the sack with lead. Then he crawled through the window and they handed him the sack and he set off at a run.

The indians may have backed out of the fight sooner if it wasnt for their desire to recover their wounded and dead. Five of them were trapped behind the Sheidler's wagon and RL noticed some movement. They could see them through the gunports on the north wall. Leonard along with Charley Armitage and Dutch Henry lined their rifles up through the loopholes and on the count of three let the lead fly, the bullets blasting through the wagon and dropping the indians dead in a smattering of blood and shattered boards. A sixth figure scampered up from out of the rubble. There was a bugle slung across his shoulder and Armitage took a spare rifle from Leonard and slipped outside through the storefront and leveled the gun. He judged the pace of the runner and made note of the hot wind against the side of his face and when he let off the shot he'd had the barrel ahead of the runner a good five feet. The shot was fired from such a close range that the impact blew the indian sideways completely off his feet. He rolled over once in a convulsion and then lie still. Armitage scurried back through the doorway into the cantina where the hunters leaned into the portholes looking out into the hills for more assailants. Leonard went for his looking glass. He poked it through the porthole and put it to his eye and squinted. He put it down and rubbed his eye. He wiped the lens on either end with his kerchief and looked again. He chuckled.

What'n the world are you laughin at, Fred?

You wont believe this Charley, he said. You shot the damned bugler.

I shot the bugler!

And he was a goddamned yellow nigger painted up like a Comanch!

There was a hurrah at this and despite their fear they knew they had the upper hand and their spirits were high. They settled in to continue to hold off any charges and as the day wore on the fighting subsided.

It was four o'clock in the afternoon when they began to cautiously emerge from their shelters. They pilfered the clothing and accoutrements of the dead, curiously walking from body to body and scrutinizing where they lay stiffening with glazed eyes in the bloodslaked dust. There were handfuls of warriors spread out around the grounds of each building and a dozen more in the hills including the five at the wagon and the bugler Armitage had shot. Comanches and Kiowas. Some Cheyennes and Arapahoes. Billy Tyler had passed and they dragged him to where the Sheidlers lie and wrapped them in blankets. They took shovels and dug a common grave and covered them with dirt and Jesús said a simple prayer in spanish and traced the sign of the cross on his head and lips and chest. They turned to the corrals. All of their horses were dead. There was work to do before dark and the hostiles were still out there watching them somewhere beyond the hills.

27

Palo Duro Canyon

1874

It did not take long before the indians had regrouped and set out to seek their vengeance. The Kiowas under Lone Wolf, the Comanches and Cheyennes under Quanah. White horse thieves and hunters who had remained in the field that summer were systematically tracked down and butchered. Their warriors formed into smaller bands and unleashed an unprecedented brand of guerrilla warfare upon the settlements. The hunt for hides ceased indefinitely and the hunters and settlers fled into the safety of the posts. Stagecoaches were robbed and their passengers slaughtered and the wagons were left burning on the prairie. Mail stations and ranches were burned, women raped, children taken captive. The Texas governor appealed to the legislature to appropriate three hundred thousand dollars to resurrect the frontier battalion of Texas Rangers under Major John B. Jones. In Washington the pro-indian factions and peace advocates fell under intense scrutiny and the wheels churned in motion to make changes to military policy. As the body count began to pile up throughout the frontier four hundred and fifty fighting men under six companies of Rangers took to the field to exterminate the indians.

In early July the superintendent of the Cheyenne-Arapaho reservation knew the indian conflict was coming to a head. The Cheyenne hostiles had been on the warpath and he felt an attack on his agency was imminent. He was desperate for help. He sent runners south to Fort Sill requesting reinforcements and then left with a small command scouting north. They had been seeking a wagontrain run by a man named Hennessey but the Cheyenne Dog Soldiers had attacked the outfit and Hennessey's charred remains were chained to the rear wheel smoldering in the sunlight, his skin shrunk up and cracked black and the fat leaking out in strips of shredded clothing hot like a wick fueling a candle flame.

By the middle of the month news of these latest uprisings had spread east and the War Department began planning a full-scale campaign. The failed pacifist policy of the Quakers was terminated, the agencies and reservations were placed under military control. All the tribes would be required to register and enroll at the agencies by the first of August and report for daily roll call. General Sherman lifted all restrictions on the army and left his commanders at liberty to pursue and kill the horse indians wherever they were to be found.

With Mackenzie's now seasoned knowledge of the Comanche's secret wintering grounds in the rugged breaks east of the Llanos, Sherman authorized forty-six companies and three thousand men with official orders to relentlessly pursue the indians in converging columns through the heat of the summer and the cold of winter, burning their villages, capturing their horses, giving them no quarter.

On the nineteenth of September Mackenzie had the Southern Column of over six hundred men staged at their old supply camp on the Freshwater Fork of the Brazos awaiting the order to march north and hunt for indians. They set out following the Tonkawa scouts and they left at sunrise, pushing up the canyon of the Blanco and looking up at the rim of the Caprock and watching great masses of billowing clouds blowing up from the plains.

It had not rained in this country for sixty-three days and the tracks leading up from the foothills took them through the Caprock canyonlands where a rough wind was blowing and the sky was stained bloodred. The trails skirted the base of the red rock walls through a maze of arroyos and the trails were fresh and they scouted for sign off and on the edge of the Caprock sunup to sundown those first few days.

On the third night they awoke to a howling wind and the boom of thunder overhead, sheetlightning flashing the night skies white and sheets of rain and sheets of hail pounding the fragile canvas tents. When they set out in the morning the land was silent and still and the air was warm and smelled of wet sage and thunder rumbled away in the distance. They plodded through the muck, nothing but soupy red mud with the wagon tires sinking to the axles. The little desert frogs were chirping in the dawn and droplets of rainwater dripped from the chollas and in the east lightning flared the distant thunderheads above the new risen sun.

In the afternoon they were visited by another line of storms and then a cold wind began to blow down out of the north. They took refuge under the wall of the Caprock and waited for the supply wagons. The wind blew down cold sheets of rain and in their wet clothes they froze to the bone, struggling to keep the fires burning. In the deluge great hunks of earth began to crumble from the sodden escarpment walls and they were wary of falling victim to these random landslides. Another hour and the rain had slacked and by the time they had dried out by the fires the rains would come again. A pale sun in a cool gray sky lingering in the easy moving clouds. They only made three miles that day. On the day following it was much the same.

Mackenzie fell under a spell of darkness. He railed at his lieutenants and cussed the weather, reeling from the lingering pains from old injuries. He spoke poorly of the other commanders in the field. He walked his horse out along a ridge with long views of the country and their camp. Dull, gray sky. Heavy clouds hovering and the west a mustard yellow from a sliver of dusky light. He watched the last of the light and the darkness falling over the land and the light of the campfires and the plaintive singing of his bone-weary men. He turned the horse back for the camp, walking along slowly and coming to terms with the suffering and carnage that would be required to put an end to the endless guerilla warfare of the mounted tribes.

Early the next morning as the front cleared they left the supply train behind floundering in the mud and pushed the cavalry battalions out ahead on a nonstop twenty mile march to the north. Crisp, clear skies and the sun upon the rainsoaked canyon country. Hawks circling in the cool north breeze, taking the thermals, and mule deer on the mesas silhouetted against the sun looking down upon their procession. In that day's ride they reached the mouth of Tule Canyon where the creek was up and muddy and the cottonwoods were glowing gold in the autumn light.

Late that day the scouts rode in and reported finding numerous signs of the Comanche, one a trail of perhaps a thousand ponies or more heading prominently to the east. Mackenzie consulted his maps. It began to cool in the early part of the evening and he walked out to where he could see the moon rising and he studied the sky for the weather and thought about all that he'd learned two summers ago. Winter coming on. The people he hunted would need shelter. All of their horses. All of their women and children and elderly. He looked to the north and awaited the arrival of the other scouts, who returned just as the sun went down. They had a Hispano captive with them. He was disheveled and his shirt was bloodied and he seemed to ponder the size of the military camp before him with great wonder. He was riding a swaybacked mule and his hands were bound at the wrists. It was Jose Tafoya. They took council and RL lined out for Mackenzie the details of his past run-in with the Comanchero trading camp. He said that Tafoya was someone he had dealt with before and that they should take advantage of his intimate knowledge of the Comanches.

Mackenzie ordered Tafoya to dismount and his hands were unbound as a show of goodwill and the colonel told him that he best get ready to talk. He led him off a little ways so they could stand face-to-face and discuss the matters in private.

Tafoya was at least half a head taller, an aging man with wise eyes and when he played coy Mackenzie sucked in a slow, deep breath and grimaced. He looked down and exhaled loudly. He stood there shaking his head and when Tafoya spoke up again, feigning ignorance, Mackenzie reared back the clinched fist of his three-fingered hand and backhanded the broadside of Tafoya's jaw with a violent blow. Blood shot out of his mouth and he slammed into the ground with such force that his head bounced back up listlessly like a broken rag doll. It appeared briefly as though he was dead. Mackenzie kicked him all out in the kidney with his boot. Then as he reared back again but held up. Something had caught his eye right before impact. It was the burned orange color of the late evening sky and a dead tree bent over like a skeletal sentinel against the setting sun. An idyllic portrait of a blackened tree burned to a crisp in the passing storms. Tafoya was coming to and rattling in spanish about mercy and family and God. The side of his face was swelling and he'd put his forearms to the sides of his head and curled up into a ball babbling on. Mackenzie held his bootheel firmly on the man and he called out.

Thompson, bring the man's mule over here and bring me a rope.

He gave Tafoya his foot again. Now get up, goddamnit! he said.

The rope was hung from a sprawling branch and Mackenzie took the other end and fashioned a noose and directed Tafoya to mount up and he led the mule over to the hollowed corpse of the tree's trunk and handed him up the rope.

RL, tell him in spanish. Tell him to fasten it right about there.

We better get Jesús.

Get him then.

RL came back with the Mexican, wide-eyed and perhaps ashamed about his duty.

Go on now, tell the man.

Sí, por supuesto, said Jesús, and then he nervously went about his impromptu role as interpreter for the colonel.

Hacer el nudo allí.

Tafoya held the rope and nodded dully and stood looking at them.

Tell him nice and tight.

Agradable y apretado. Mira la holgura.

Tafoya did as he was told.

Mackenzie took the reins and set the horse just right. He stepped back. Now tell him to slip it over his head. Make sure he sets it ahead of his ear.

He pointed. Right there, he said. That spot beneath that lower left jaw, right there.

Jesús translated. Tafoya warily slipped the noose over his head and he was pleading now in a rapid and frantic spanish, who knows if Jesús even understood, and when he'd done they stood in silence, their eyes on Jesús who was trying to make sense of it all in his head.

Mackenzie pulled the reins of the horse, stretching Tafoya off balance and craning his neck and holding onto the horse with his feet, reaching to take hold of the rope above his head to support himself.

Madre de Cristo! he pleaded. Un momentito!

Mackenzie was gritting his teeth. He spoke in spanish slowly and his pronunciation was poor. Dónde está Quanah? said Mackenzie.

No sé! gasped Tafoya.

Mackenze kept a slow pull on the mule. Tafoya's feet slipped off, flailing and kicking, and he held on as the full weight of his body now dangled and swung. He was trying to say something.

Mackenzie led the mule back to where the Comanchero could just barely support himself with his outstretched foot. He spoke slowly. Dónde. Está. Los Quahadis.

Ellos no estan aquí. Ellos estan al sur. Muy lejos.

Where are they?

No sé! No hay Quahadis!

Mackenzie pulled the mule out from under him but Tafoya in his struggles had somehow been able to loosen the slip of the knot and he dropped to the ground in a thud. RL had his sidearm pointed and cocked. They bound his hands and mounted him back up. They sent Jesús for a horse and he was made to pull up beside the man and set the noose good and tight.

No, said Tafoya. You no understand. Quanah no here. Pero todos los Comanches están, y Kiowas.

Where?

He did not in fact look like a man who felt compelled in this moment to fabricate the truth. He gestured frantically with his eyes to the northwest. Un viaje de un día. El otro cañón. En el Palo Duro.

Mackenzie studied him. His shirt was bloodstained and the right side of his face was swollen a mottled blue and black. True and desperate fear in his eyes. He left him there and walked out with RL and Carter and after a short council they returned.

Now listen here Jose, said the colonel. You work for me now. You understand? You will lead me to that canyon and when you do, God willing, I will allow you to continue the privilege of breathing and you will have your pick from the Comanche horse herds. Tell him Jesús.

Jesús told him.

You understand, Jose?

Sí, sí señor.

Good.

He looked at the other men.

Carter, get him settled and fed. Then get him outfitted.

Yes sir.

And send the Tonks out to confirm the location of the camp.

Yes sir.

Mackenzie turned and surveyed the command. He weighed his options. In that lost and broken country the late sun flared redly and then died and as the night's darkness consumed them they studied the soft evening light around them where a newborn harvest moon rose upon the canyon lairs of the hidden Comanche spies.

Mackenzie looked at RL. You believe this man?

RL nodded. Yes sir I do. They're all settlin in for the winter. And their scouts are watching us right now and worried we're headin their way.

Can we make it there if we push through the night?

I dont advise it.

Why not?

Well, where's Lawton?

Mackenzie turned to Carter. How far out is the supply train?

Carter looked to the south. He rubbed his chin. If it keeps drying out they'll be here tomorrow, middle of the afternoon.

I believe we should push on.

I dont know, sir. The men are beat. We need rest. We need Lawton's supplies.

Mackenzie turned and looked to where the canyon fed up from the southwest. RL stepped alongside him and spat. Sir, if we can get them thinking we're marching up the Tule, he said, I believe them Comanche scouts'll pull off and head on back home. But you can bet they'll make a run for our horses real soon.

Well then, let's push on for a few more hours.

But tomorrow we should wait for Lawton.

Yes. What's the best route to the Palo Duro?

The moon was higher now, turning from deep orange to yellow as it drifted over the plains. We'll push up this canyon and come out the headwaters of the Tule, said RL. Then it's a straight, flat shot across, maybe a day's ride across the plains.

Good. And we'll do it overnight.

They made another five miles up the mouth of the Tule as planned and that night the horses were picketed under guards and they slept with their clothes on and their weapons at hand. All the day following they stayed in camp and Lawton's supply wagon arrived and that night with sleeping parties posted around the horse herd the Comanches rode upon them howling from out of the darkness but the attack failed. When the command rode out the next morning they could see horsemen watching them from atop the northern rim of the canyon against a high blue and windless sky. Mackenzie ordered the Tonkawas to attack. The Comanches spies were scattered about the country and after a brief skirmish in which one warrior was killed and several horses wounded they vanished like ghosts into the recesses of the plains.

The column set out to the southwest deeper into the canyon of the Tule. A pair of eagles circled above in the warm south wind, cruising high in the sun and watching over them like spies transmitted by the spirits of the medicine man. They ascended the sandy, gypsum-encrusted stream all day, the horses picking their way through boulders and brush, forests of cottonwoods golden and glistening in the sun. They rode through a series of winding defiles of sheer redstone walls and they passed waterfalls and seepsprings and little pools of cool clear water and at four o'clock in the afternoon they set the horses out to graze in a small side canyon that was showered in a brilliant haze of yellow sunlight. Here they restored themselves from the day's long journey and scouted the way up out of the canyon onto the plains.

Two hours later the scouts that had been sent out the evening prior came straggling in with the report Mackenzie had been waiting for. The Comanches and Kiowas were camped in the depths of the Palo Duro a day's ride to the north. Two hundred lodges, thousands of horses, all of their women and children and the food that would sustain them through the winter. With this news Mackenzie walked up alone along a solitary slickrock precipice and stood watching downcanyon for a long while the shifting hues of twilight.

They turned the command north and marched up onto the barren high plains in the cool blue dusk and rode all night keeping watch on the stars, the wary eyes of the creatures of the night glowing in the moonlight, silently watching them pass. Two hours before first light they reached a shimmering playa lake a half mile from the rim of the Palo Duro. The moon was very bright and they dismounted and set the horses out to graze and water. They spoke quietly and as they tended to their weapons Tafoya escorted Mackenzie and his lieutenants to the rim of the canyon.

They lined out along the sheer edge, peering down into that dark chasm. Dead silence. A soft wind came up low from the canyon and they could hear the gentle rustle of the junipers down below. They stood watching for a long time. Too dark to judge anything save for the waning embers of the scattered campfires gently glowing far out in that utter blackness. They spread out, carefully snaking along the sheer canyon rim, vainly scouting the terrain just below them for trails that would lead them down into the darkness.

Mackenzie kept watch on the stars and for signs of light in the east. He pondered his options. After a while he turned without speaking and they followed him through the grass back to where the troops were waiting and he addressed his captains in council.

We dont have much time. Maybe a half hour before light. They're sound asleep and we've got to be on them before they're up.

How many are down there?

It doesnt matter.

Mackenzie paused and looked them over. Now listen, he said. Thompson's scouts will lead us down. Beaumont, I want you and your men focused on their horses.

Yes sir.

Let's go. We need to be back on that rim so we can see it at first light.

They made their way in the last of the darkness out upon the escarpment and stood looking out as the blue dawn seeped from the edges of the world and favored light upon the sleeping village. The small thin tipis like toothpicks following the gleaming curve of river for miles up the canyon, the water slow and silent and faintly shimmering in the new light. A pale flash flared across the sky and faded into darkness. The men were whispering to one another, trying to make out the distant horses, tiny and speckled, now being strangely revealed by their eyes as in a stereogram. Mackenzie pointed at something. They followed his gaze. The early song of the morning canyon wrens below flittering and fading with the gentle wisps of wind. They could see the first village of perhaps four dozen tipis directly below them. Mackenzie turned to the lieutenant on his right. Thompson, take your men down and open the fight.

Thompson stepped his horse along the promontory until he came to a crease on the ledge that fed into the boulder-strewn descent down into the canyon. The Tonkawas followed. He stood looking down at the precarious cliff hanging trail as it switchbacked and dropped out of sight into the depths of the dark canyon. He took a deep breath and leaned over and whispered into his horse's ear and then he started down.

As the advancers clambered and scuttled headlong down the rabble-stone trail the deer that had been bedded down in the brush darted up bounding away like jackrabbits. Gravel and rocks began to tumble and fall, clattering out over the canyon. A lone Comanche sentry sat up dully from the lookout where he'd been sleeping and as he fumbled for his rifle Thompson shot him down and now the soldiers on the rim came scrabbling down single file like an army of ants scampering for the canyon floor with their horses following and the men and horses stumbling and falling and falling again, crashing and thundering downslope among the boulders and junipers and cactus like some barbaric medieval horse race.

The indians were scrambling from their lodges shouting and running with whatever goods they could carry. By the time the troops reached the bottom and they had mounted and set off at a gallop through the first camp with their revolvers raised the panicked villagers were scampering like goats for the upper reaches of the canyon with the new sun now up and spotlighting their ascent. Mounted warriors covered their rear guard and took shelter high up behind the boulders and prepared to fight.

Within minutes every lodge in the entire encampment had been abandoned. Their camp goods were strewn about in every manner and the crazed packmules were stampeding wildly about the camp. Mackenzie shouted orders and the troops formed skirmish lines in pursuit and set out at full gallop, firing their big Walker revolvers and pressing the snipers concealed in the bluffs above them.

By now Beaumont and his troops had already rounded up the bulk of the remuda and were driving them back through the abandoned encampment amidst the pandemonium and sniper fire. Mackenzie urged his men on and sent detachments of sharpshooters to provide cover for the front lines but the indians were well sheltered and kept a steady fire down upon the soldiers. Bullets came hissing down from the cliffs, thunking into horseflesh and peppering the dust and pinging off the rocks. The wounded horses screamed and reared, milled and circled, threw their mounts, and the bugler was shot through the stomach and fell from his horse in a pool of blood crawling like a slug for cover. The marksmen of Troop I had meanwhile reached a favorable position across a deep branch of the canyon and with a great volley of gunfire had the indians falling back and scampering for better cover. One of the warriors took a bullet in the shoulder, falling from his perch atop the high ridge, flailing and threshing in a long slow drop and crumpling into the rocks like a mangled child doll.

A Tonkawa squaw gave out a yelp and quirted her horse forward. Four other scouts followed. The fallen man had tried to get up but he now lay prone with his ears bleeding. She dismounted and knelt beside him. A bone was sticking out of his arm and he turned his dead eyes toward her, mumbling something weakly.

Get the hell away from him, shouted Mackenzie.

But the squaw was leaning down and whispering something evil into the man's ear and then she rose up yammering out in a rage and she gripped her warclub with a firm fist and reared back above the man and swung down with all of her force and crushed the side of his head with a shuddering blow. Blood splattered and pooled where he lay. She howled out and wiped the blood from her eyes and face and crowhopped back onto her horse. Then the scouts put their heels to their ponies and rode off again in pursuit yipping like a cackle of hyenas.

By now the sun was high up and butter yellow over the canyon. Mackenzie sat his horse and studied the retreat of the indians. Gunfire falling off. No signs of their families. A group of riders disappeared behind a sharp bend of the canyon and single warriors were bounding from rock to rock and scurrying out of sight as the bullets pinged the slickrock walls all around them and on the upper bluffs a dozen riders were making their way to the rim in an effort to block the paths by which the command had entered. He called to Troop H.

Captain, take your men and hold the ridge.

He turned to McLaughlin.

Keep enough men deployed in the bottoms to handle the snipers.

What about all these lodges?

Burn them.

Burn them?

Dont leave anything behind. Burn it all.

Yes sir.

Mackenzie stood tall in his saddle. Deserted tipis on either side of the river as far as he could see and their entire horse herds and all of their winter goods at his disposal. Soldiers were tearing down the lodges and hacking up the poles and pulling them into large piles for the bonfires. The wives of the Tonkawa scouts were dashing from lodge to lodge ahead of them looting for anything of value. The shelters were filled with buffalo robes and blankets newly issued from the reservation and they gathered up shields and lances and quivers of arrows and metal cartridges of assorted calibers and baskets of roots and a Confederate cavalry officer's saber and a knife and fork silverware set that had never been used. The captured horses from the remuda were being beaten and herded into bunches of twenty at the base of the canyon wall and driven up the scrabbled trails in single lines to the top of the canyon. Groups of men were lugging great handfuls of miscellaneous paraphernalia and heaping them onto the burn piles and others were walking about with torches and lighting them afire. One of the scouts rode past with a herd of mules like some wayward Mexican trader, the animals loaded down with bales of calico, bags of flour, gunnysacks of dried fruits and berries. Mackenzie knew that his legacy was unfolding before his eyes in the chaos of that canyon and to capture their horses and strand them afoot with no supplies for the winter would be a fate worse than death. He rode up and back, cursing them on. Through the noon of the day and as the shadows grew long over the canyon until the final horse was driven onto the plains in the last light of day. Fifteen hundred horses. They formed a living corral around them and set out just before sunset, riding south into the plains and looking back down at the black smoke rolling north out over the Palo Duro and the distant bonfires flickering in the dusk.

In the west the sky was seeping red and the cool dry air of evening settled over them and then it grew dark. The moon had not risen and the stars sparkled and fell. They followed the trail coming up from the plains from which they had ridden in the early morning before dawn. Thirty hours in the saddle and counting, riding along slumped and jostling and the images of that day reeling vividly in their mind and still a long, long way to go. RL was riding beside Carter, the Tonkawa scouts lined out behind them. Carter had just returned from a council with Mackenzie and he had taken off his hat and was rubbing his temples thinking of what lay ahead. He looked at RL.

He wants to finish the job.

Finish the job?

Carter nodded and RL peered into the darkness taking stock of the herd. A mass of black shadows in the night plodding through the grass.

Kill off all these horses?

Yep.

How in the hell are we goin to do that?

Carter shook his head. He looked at the stars. Well, apparently Custer did it at Washita.

Custer did it?

He damn sure did. And besides, there's no sense in trailing them all the way to Concho. Because sure as hell they're going to try and take them back.

They aint takin nothin back.

The hell they wont. You were there at the Cañón Blanco.

Yeah but it's different now.

Maybe.

Think of what all that horse flesh is worth. It's such a waste.

I know it.

What about the Tonks?

They're going to get their pick.

RL leaned and pilfered about in his saddlebag. He handed up a handful to Carter. You want some jerky? he said. It'll be a while before we're back at the Tule.

Thank you.

They rode for a long while. No words. Just their thoughts. Then Carter looked over at RL dozing in the saddle.

RL. You alright?

He rode slumped and tottering but the question seemed to rouse him and he mumbled. I just need some place... He opened his eyes and turned to look at Carter. I just need some place... where I can lay my head.

In the morning it is still and cold and with the first glimmers of red out on the rim of the plain the little prairie birds sing and flitter about in the wet grass. The camp sleeps lightly. The air smells of earth and horses and smoke and they can hear the soft snuffle of the herds grazing gently in the accruing light. After a while the sun slips above the plains. Reveille calls. The men rise and a new day has begun. One fine morning.

The infantry had formed a makeshift corral inside the supply wagons and herded it chock-full with the captured horses of the indians and Mackenzie granted the scouts their pick of the lot and selected another dozen strong saddle horses and mules to remain with the command. There'd been much discussion about how to proceed with the day's events and after breakfast Lawton formed two long lines of mounted men leading from an opening in the corral. Four men were stationed as guards to manage passage through the tunnel. The horses were munching quietly and milling about, tails swishing at the flies, the foals nursing, the yearlings playfully stomping their feet and nudging one another. Another two dozen men stood waiting their turn at the far end of the run a hundred yards out. They held .45 Springfield carbines and had .44 caliber Smith and Wesson sidearms on their belts.

The sun was well up now, flashing brilliantly on all the pretty horses and their colorful coats. Blues and duns, reds and yellows. War ponies with faded remnants of battle paint. The finest race horses. Dapples.

Whites. Yellows. Paints. Young and healthy and handsome.

Men were climbing on the wagons and looking for places of vantage. Somber. Curious. Other riders had been positioned on the outskirts to help herd up any escapees and stragglers. Within the hour all was ready and the firing squad milled about uneasily where the chute fed out and they drew lots to determine order. The first man up was Claude Bernard and he offered anyone a half month's wages to take his place but there were no takers.

Shitfire fellas, he said.

It'll be okay Bennie. We gotta start somewhere.

I never signed up to be no horse killer.

The gatekeepers let the first few horses through. A handful of mares and a weanling. They went along innocently and walked right on down the line calmly, perhaps even curious as to what might await them.

Bernard was a young, red-headed man, as fine a soldier an army could enlist. Make sure y'all stay out that-a-way boys and I'll try not to shoot ye, he said. John, slide that halter over nice and long and let the lead out gently, full slack. He watched the horses coming toward him and judged their gate. Good god, what a fine herd of horses, he said.

The near man serving as gatekeeper let the first horse slip through. It was the weanling and it took the rope uncertainly and walked the slack out tight. Bernard spoke to it and stroked its neck and when he put the muzzle of the forty-four to the animal's temple and fired and the little thing slumped dead he swung back away from it and bent down gagging in disgust. The next horse in line reared and screamed. A panic spread through the entire herd. There were a hundred men in the immediate vicinity and perhaps another four hundred in the extended camp and to a man they stood in silence. The Tonkawa scouts were nowhere to be found. Mackenzie sat his horse near the firing squad. Let's get on with it, he said. A man ran and undid the rope. The next horse came out jerking its head and stomping, a gorgeous milk-white mare. The lead rope ran out again and Bernard blew a hole through its head. When it fell its legs doubled under and its arched neck turned down aside, its muzzle resting gently in the trampled and blood-splattered grass. Four more horses came down the line and Bernard emptied his rounds and stepped aside for the next man, shuffling to the back of the line to reload and watch the carnage. By now it was chaos inside the stockade, the white-eyed horses foaming at the mouth, pacing and prancing with their ears pinned back and nostrils flared. Squealing and grunting. Bunching and milling. Tails switching hard and fast. At first the shots were slow and steady. Each man took their turn, six shots each. They were deliberate and shot well and the dead piled up a horse per minute but the math did not add up. Mackenzie ordered another killing line to the east and another running west. The pace of shooting picked up and by mid- morning they'd established a rhythm to the work. The big breeder stallions required two or three successive brainshots, collapsing like freight trains, flailing their legs trying to get up, they groaned like humans. Counters tallied the horses as they entered the lines and teams of draggers kept the piles in check. Wagers were made on the final reckoning. Slowly the herd thinned out, becoming more and more desperate. A colt made a rush to hurdle the blockade and clipped its legs mid-jump, crashing down in a flurry of flailing whips and then it was shot. By noon the sun was full up and it was hot. No time to break for lunch. Their food was brought to them in the field and they ate as they worked. Flies swarming and the constant pistolfire and the smell of urine and blood and runny manure. The prairie grass trampled to dust now and a thin brown haze floated in the sun. In the early afternoon there was concern the ammunition wouldnt last and they began to separate the colts and one by one knock them in the head with hatchets. They kept the horses moving. Shouts and yells, cane poles and whips. Grunts and squeals and the mares crying out for their foals. At three fourteen the last horse was led from the slaughter line, a gentle old sorrel mare. She was rolling her eyes and snorting softly but otherwise seemed to accept her fate. The hostler led her out, she stood still, head down. When the man fired she crumpled down heavily and fell to her side. From any angle she looked asleep. Lying there peacefully, a thin trickle of blood oozing from her mouth. The man stood there looking over her. He put his nose in the crook of his arm. Others slowly began to gather around. Nothing was said and the new silence from the lack of shooting hung over the killing field like an evil pall. After a while the dust cleared and the sky was blue all over the prairie. Gradually they wandered away from the killing fields, talking quietly among themselves like men returning from a funeral. Mackenzie sat his horse watching them. Thinking, planning. He looked to the north where on a rise he thought he saw a lone Comanche scout observing them but he paid no mind.

28

— ★ —

The Reacclimation of Sam Terry

1876

In the middle of July eighteen seventy-six Pahvotaivo was camped along the shores of the Laguna Quemado high on the Llano Estacado. He was with a small group of runaway Comanches making their way up from the Casas Amarillas and they had joined up that night with some bedraggled Apache families who had been wandering for days through the sandhills in search of water. A low rise overlooking the shores of the brackish lake with the sun going down behind them and a steady summer breeze from the south to cool them from the searing heat. As they sat in the dusk roasting jackrabbits over the fire they saw on a rise a party of riders casually cantering toward them from out of the darkness. Pahvo rose from his seat and walked out from the fire and the others followed and they studied their approach. Six silent riders and three packmules loaded with supplies. At a hundred yards out they slowed the horses to a walk and then they stopped, a white flag rising above them flapping in the breeze.

Pahvo heard the mournful call of a hoot owl in the night from a long familiar voice. The sizing up and silent moments of speculation. He returned the call. Then he heard a whistle.

Piajuhtzu? called Pahvo. He heard that distinctive whistle calling out from the dusk.

The riders dismounted and led their horses into the camp and their hosts walked out to greet them. It was Quanah and a peaceful commission of Comanche friends from the reservation at Fort Sill and they were carrying official papers from Ranald Mackenzie that sanctioned their travels. There were smiles and hugs, slaps on the back, tears in the eye. They sat down to eat and to discuss their journeys and afterward with the fires glowing low and the stars passing overhead Quanah told them of how the year had passed on the reservation and there was much speculation of how it had all come to this.

He'd been sent on a mission to locate the renegade Comanches who had refused to surrender after the defeat at the Palo Duro now almost two years prior and he told them that the roaming way of life was over. Forever. He preached of the black iron horse that carried an endless stream of taibos from the land of the rising sun and he urged them to follow him to a new way of life on the reservation.

And out there above them the stars were falling. The plains breeze blew cool and the moon rose and the embers of the fire burned low. They took council until the early hours of the morning and the next day when Pahvo arose with the sun it was decided. The following morning they would set out on the long journey to Fort Sill.

They took their time and it was a nostalgic journey, riding carefully with lookouts by day and traveling at night to evade the soldiers and hide hunters on the plains. It took them three weeks to reach the Indian Territory and when they were nine miles from Fort Sill they saw the dust cloud from the soldiers riding to greet them. Quanah told them that the soldiers would not hurt them but Pahvo turned his mount and galloped off alone to the north. They watched him go, vanishing into the prairie and riding on through the rolling foothills and up into the boulder-covered buttes of the Wichita Mountains.

Hundreds of miles of open grasslands stretching to the horizon. Herds of grazing bison. Calm blue lakes smooth and shimmering under the high sun like shining mirrors. He stood atop a jumbled mass of boulders and watched a lone bull elk standing in a stream taking water. Overhead clouds like cotton drifting with the breeze. The varied songs of the vireos. A collared lizard scurried along and stopped, standing up and looking out on its hind legs. After a while he could see a lone horseman out on the plain riding toward him, escorted by an eagle sinking up into blue depths, flapping its wings and soaring in the sunshine.

He sat there thinking as the distant figure floated silently across the prairie in the sunlight. Shadow of horse and rider growing long beside it. He laid on his back looking at the sun and closed his eyes, dozing off to the strange patterns of the phosphenes and when he woke another hour had passed and the sun was much lower. He rubbed his eyes and looked out. Down below him at the base of the mountain he could see a familiar horse, the magnificent gray pacer of the bad-handed chief of the bluecoats they had stolen five years prior at the Cañón Blanco. He did not wave him on. He knew that Quanah sensed where he was at, understood what he was thinking, perhaps had already spotted him.

After Quanah arrived they sat together for a long time while the sun sank into the plains and the sky grew pale. Pahvo said very little. Quanah spoke to him sagely and in a fatherly manner but his young apprentice was sullen and cold and he spoke back to his mentor in a way that made Quanah so frustrated his only recourse was to advise the white warrior to take refuge in his camp.

In the ensuing months he kept quarters with Quanah and his family in the mountains near the post, laying low and avoiding the soldiers at all costs. He tended the horses and hunted. He wandered off alone for long periods of time and he watched the land and the weather and the animals and the sun in its course across the sky and he thought about his life. He heard news of the poor treatment of his tribesmen. Plowing fields, grading roads. Warriors placed under guard inside the icehouse, soldiers tossing raw chunks from the meat wagon each day to the prisoners inside. He kept a low profile and did what he could to conceal his Anglo features but it did not take long for rumors to spread. There was a white warrior somewhere near the post. Mackenzie had issued orders to locate him.

One afternoon as he was bent over attending a wound on a handsome bay gelding he looked up to find himself surrounded by a detachment of soldiers who had noticed traces of his wavy, blond hair. Some untamed instinct compelled him to run but he did not get far before they took him down, shackling his hands and dragging him against his will into the agency headquarters. They gawked at him like some caged animal. Someone brought in a warm dishrag and three men subdued him as a fourth wiped his face down clean. They looked in his eyes and studied his skin. They looked at one another, nodding assertively. He glared back, spouting threats in comanche but they did not understand. They hardly said anything to him.

Before long Mackenzie walked in with Agent Haworth followed by the interpreter Horace Jones and when Jones began to relay the colonel's respectful demeanor it seemed a bit of calm settled over him. The colonel ordered for him to be unbound and he dismissed the guards. A few minutes later Quanah arrived. He looked around the room and was greeted warmly and then he spoke cheerfully to Pahvo in comanche, smiling wryly with his comments as if to lighten the mood of the room. The kid grinned. Jones chuckled.

Mackenzie gave the interpreter a quizzical look. What'd he say, Jones?

Well sir, that gray pacer you were partial to. The one they stole at the Cañón Blanco in the stampede back in '71. Said you didnt want it back.

Mackenzie shook his head slowly, smiling. Pahvo watched them. He could tell there was a mutual respect between the men and Quanah seemed to have his charming old air of confidence he'd come to know so well. The interpreter pulled up a chair and he sat in front of him with the others looking on from behind and he told the boy that there would be no harm done to him and they wanted to learn more about him as it was believed his true father was still alive and searching for him. He talked for a long time. Quanah nodded his reassurances. The general and Agent Haworth had been leaning forward listening intently to try and pick up whatever details of the language they might understand and they looked at him as one might look upon one who has been struck by great misfortune. When he was done he asked the young man if he could remember his birth name but Pahvo just stared back at them blankly. Quanah muttered something. They waited in silence.

Mackenzie spoke up. Son, is your name Samuel Terry?

Pahvo sat there silently.

Mackenzie asked him again and Jones repeated the question in comanche.

Quanah said something and then finally Pahvo stood up and patted his chest, looking the general in the eye. Me, Samuel Terry, he said. Then he repeated it. He sat back down and Mackenzie exhaled, dropped his head, closed his eyes.

Jones pressed on. Son, he said. Do you know what happened to your brother Charlie? He repeated it in comanche.

Sam stared out, thinking, then he shook his head.

They asked him what he remembered about how he had come to be there and Sam began to piece together for them his recollections of what that day was like three thousand eight hundred and twenty-seven days ago. He remembered being clubbed down and thrown onto a horse and he remembered watching his house burning as they rode away. His grandfather lying dead with arrows sticking out of him. He never knew what happened inside the house but the men that took him made him carry the scalp of a woman and he was made to understand that it was his mother's. Then he stopped talking. He was calm, perhaps annoyed at it all, even angry with Quanah. Quanah, the others, they were looking down at the floor solemnly.

Well, said Mackenzie. He sighed. He considered his approach. I suppose I should get word to Mr Terry. Give him the news. Make arrangements for this young man's return. And Agent Haworth, let's get him cleaned up and ready.

Sam was watching their body language and if he picked up a word or two he kept quiet and trusted in Quanah.

Mackenzie turned to the young chieftain. I need you to help this young man understand that I have no choice but to send him back to his father.

Quanah thinned his eyes and turned his head thoughtfully, nodding slowly, lips pursed.

Now if you'll excuse me gentlemen, he said. I have work to do.

He placed his hand on Sam Terry's shoulder and told him that he was in good hands and would be taken good care of and then he exited the room with the others in tow. Quanah remained behind. Two soldiers stood on guard just outside the door.

In that room Sam began to talk crossly to Quanah in a manner in which neither of them would ever begin to believe was imaginable and Quanah knew that his psyche had been dismantled by the profound reality of being randomly thrown once again into another world. Sam questioned his manhood to his face. Quanah listened patiently. Sam pressed on. He told his mentor that he would never go but Quanah with his innate gift of diplomacy softened his message. He told him that he had been several times to Texas to see his people and that he had enjoyed himself. Then he told him it did not matter because they were going to take him anyway.

Late that day he was allowed to go back home with Quanah and they talked long into the night and all the day following and as he was going through his possessions some of the officers' wives came with a bag of clothes and baskets of gifts and candies and then led him to a room in the hospital where the post surgeon told him that he would be given a bath and examined. The doctor turned as if to leave but stopped himself and looked back, giving a good long look at his patient in consideration of his care. He nodded at an old sheetmetal washtub, he looked at his watch. Sit tight young man, he said. Aretha'll be here shortly. She'll draw you a bath and get you cleaned up.

Sam didnt understand a word of it but he looked at the tub. The doctor stepped out and after a few minutes another man came in, all business. He said hello and pointed at the kid's feet. Sam just sat there. It was the cobbler and he knelt down with a tailor's tape and took measurements of his feet and stood up and jotted notes and numbers in his memo pad and turned and exited the room without a word.

Sam sat on the doctor's table listening to the soldiers talking somewhere down the hall. He lay back and closed his eyes. A few minutes passed. When he opened them a line of men came in with steaming buckets of water and began to fill the tub. The doctor poked his head in and moved on. Other lingerers kept sliding by with furtive glances. Finally the old negro mammy they called Aretha came in and shut the door. She was twice his size and she meant business and she told him to take his clothes off and get in the tub.

Mr Terry, we's gwyne git you's cleaned up real geeuuud, she said.

He stood there, studying the specimen that she was.

Gwyne now!

When he just stood there she stormed over and gathered her arms around him and a brief tussle ensued until he wrestled himself away from the woman and hastily undressed himself and hopped into the tub. She took her rag and scrubbed him down with soap and hot water and she spoke to him as if he were her son and hummed an old soulful hymn off and on as she did so.

Now, take dis towel chil' and dry yo sef off, she said. She stood there watching him naked and dripping, his manhood. Her lips pursed, eyebrow raised and the whites of her eyes big and wide like she'd seen something unbelievable.

Lawdy, son! I bet dem injun gals sho take a liken to ya. Mmm-hmm.

She handed him the pair of britches and told him to dress. White cotton shirt and a pair of brown cord trousers. Underwear. Wool socks. He looked at the underwear and threw them to the ground. Just then the cobbler came back in with a pair of used boots, newly polished, and he handed them to Sam and pointed at his feet. Those ought to do it, he said. He looked at Aretha. They goin to cut his hair?

Mmm-hmm, she murmured flatly. Dis boy a-gwyne to look like a new man agin. Alls white en shiny. Mmm-hmm.

She leaned into the hall and hollered out for something, someone. The cobbler stepped out and thereafter the barber walked in with his kit of tools and began to lay them out. He directed Sam into a chair and placed a sheet around him neck down. Aretha oversaw the proceedings. The barber had set out a razor and cream and the mammy spoke out. Now Jim, he dont need nun dat, she said. Dey's hardly a hair en dat handsome face.

You sure?

Mmm-hmm.

Okay.

He cut his hair. It took him a half hour to finish the job for the length and the gunch and the tangles. Sam was fidgeting, his eyes shifting this way and that as he sat there trying to watch the man but some odd curiosity seemed to settle him. When the barber was done he brushed him down and swept off the sheet and looked his work over with much scrutiny, like a painter or a sculptor. Aretha, run get us a mirror, he said.

She came back holding a wooden pocket mirror, the doctor and his wife in tow. The barber had just finished combing Sam's hair and touching it up with a smidgen of oil and he made him stand up and he showed him himself in the mirror. They gathered around and watched him as he studied the reflection of himself.

Well son, what do you think?

I bet he aint never lookt hisself en de mirror afore.

Good Lord, imagine what this poor young man has been through.

Sam stared at the image of himself blankly. He put the mirror down, turned it in his hands, examining it like some holy instrument of the Gods. He raised it again, turned his head, shifting it around and looking himself over. Then he smiled. They all smiled. Aretha belted out a big laugh.

Deeply tanned and scrubbed clean. Smooth skin. Bright eyes of youth. He had a freshly washed head of combed blond hair and in his new clothes he looked healthy and handsome and you wouldnt find an ounce of fat on a frame so muscular and lean. The doctor's wife was a pretty woman of culture from the east who'd been bored in this place and as she looked him over perhaps such a specimen of youthful manhood and exotic history aroused something inside for when they made eye contact she bit her lip and blushed and looked down shyly.

He spent the next few days gathering his things and in his curiosity he was reluctant and circumspect, saying his farewells to those he cared for and assuring them that he would be back. On the night before he left he sat with Quanah in his lodge on either side of the fire while Quanah told him of the sacred spirit inside that was waiting to be found, the way of life when he would see the great chasm. He said that he was a brother and would care for his horses and that there would always be a place for him in his lodge. They talked long into the night. Pahvo had been prodding the coals of the fire between them and he was coming to terms with his journey. When they were finished they stepped outside under the moonlight and embraced. Quanah placed his hands on either side of Pahvo's face, looking deep into his soul, saying goodbye with his eyes. Then they walked away from one another for what would prove to be forever.

There wasnt much of a ceremony when they pulled out of the fort for the long trip to San Antonio. A few officers' wives and cavalrymen, some traders at the post. It was just another day. They rode south for Texas. At first the settlers on the prairie paid them no mind. For all they knew it was like any other army wagontrain plodding along the military road between the frontier forts. Yet in those times those that carried the mail did indeed spread news with stunning efficiency and by the time they rolled into Fort Richardson the populace anxiously awaited their arrival.

It was a late Sunday morning after the church service when they entered the post. He'd been laying in the wagon mulling things over when he heard the murmurs of the crowds. Sam rolled over and stuck his head out for a look. Soldiers and citizens lining the mud street. A crowd closed in around them. A woman in a bonnet started singing a hymn. They slowly tried to make their way through, his escorts shouting to clear the way among the gawkers, and after a while they came to the headquarters where they were greeted by the post commander, his men, their wives. He stepped down from the wagon and looked around, bewildered. The crowd broke into applause. He was led toward the home where a big noon meal had been prepared and the crowd of gawkers followed.

They were four days to Griffin and another four to Concho, rolling along the fringes of the fragile frontier settlements that he had come to know so well as a young warrior. Blessed by the sunshine of the mild days of fall out on the Texas plains. There had been rain and the grass was lush and little yellow butterflies hovered about in the sunlight as they rode. As the sun fell down each day the wind laid and in the cool nights by the fires his escorts discussed their lives and the times and they watched the stars.

He was with a good group of men about his age who carried themselves well but he kept quiet, eating alone and sleeping out away from their camp. He said to himself that he could slip them if he needed to. Or kill them. Halfway through his journey he began to pick up certain words that were spoken to him but he did not let on, watching their hand gestures and following their eyes, staring back innocently, blankly. They speculated among themselves endlessly of his state of mind and history. They debated his future and his fate.

By now the newspapers had been circulating accounts of his return and the citizenry had become fascinated with his story. When he arrived with the military escort at the town of Menard the populace had been awaiting their arrival. The entire town turned out to observe their passing, lining the streets as if they'd planned a parade and children running alongside the stagecoach for the chance to get a fleeting glimpse of the hometown boy, the returning white indian. When they passed through Mason two days later it was much the same.

They traveled southeast toward the German town of Fredericksburg and they crossed the Llano River as it was on the rise from a line of storms upstream. Ranchlands he'd been raiding since he'd become a warrior. He walked out alone looking back across the river at the rolling hills and the sprawling strands of oaks and the jumbles of granite boulders that led toward the plains where he'd been hauled away on that fateful journey so many years ago. He turned, studying the soldiers as they lunched and he looked back to the south and considered the path forward along the trail that would lead them to the city of San Antonio where he'd been made to understand that he would be reunited with his father sometime soon. The sun was warm on his face. He closed his eyes. The faded memories of being with him in the fields. The hazy images of what he looked like. He stood there for a long while thinking of what it might be like when they would meet again.

When they rode down the main street of Fredericksburg it was one o'clock in the afternoon. The soldiers tried to spread the word that they were carrying important military cargo and just passing through but their arrival had been foretold and all of the local children had been let out of school to attend the arrival of the white indian. As they pulled in front of the Nimitz Hotel there was a great commotion, the school children yammering out and rushing the stagecoach and the hotel guests and patrons of the bathhouse and casino hall filing frantically outside and now with the emerging pandemonium the booths of the farmers and traveling salesmen emptied as did the general store and saloon and there were herds of folks in a fast walk or jog clamoring down the street and filing from out of all of the stores and the Vereins Kirche and all of the newly built stone houses within a half mile radius of the hotel. The soldiers were shouting at the gathering to keep out of their way but were ultimately forced to hold up. No one seemed to know what to do. The onlookers murmured nervously and if there was the slightest indication of the stagecoach door pushing open the entire crowd would fall silent.

The owner of the hotel had been watching the proceedings from his perch atop the fourth-floor balcony and with the lull of the crowd and the caravan at a dead stop he removed his hat and called out to the people, waving both arms above his head to call their attention.

Now kood beople, he shouted.

Every head turned. He spoke in a heavy german accent. If vu vould bleaze kindly clear zee vay ve need to make room for zee schtage to bark itzelf here at zee hotel.

You heard the man, someone called from the gallery down on the street. A buzz swept through the crowd and the folks alongside the carriage began to shuffle aside. Someone shouted. A woman screamed. A shoving match broke out and just as the patrons were on the verge of an all-out brawl the owner pulled a pistol and let off a shot into the air. The horses stepped nervously, whinnying, and the soldiers pulled their weapons and waved them about the crowd as all fell silent and the owner appealed to them again.

Ladies und gentlemen I regret to inform vu zat in your ferffor vu haffe hunknovingly disvubted…

Suddenly the front doors of the hotel burst open. The crowd fixed their gaze on the man that appeared walking briskly toward the coach. Two men of military bearing were following behind yelling Mr Terry! Mr Terry! and scrambling to hold him back but when the carriage door opened they stopped.

A handsome young man in standard street clothes had stepped out of the carriage and looked about the crowds. His skin was tanned brown and he was strong looking and lean of build and his hair was bronzed from long hours in the sun. He was a hair under six foot and he turned his head slowly this way and that, surveying the scene with a wild look in his piercing green eyes that seemed a bizarre blend of fear and confusion, curiosity and rage.

The audience was silent, standing tiptoe watching with their jaws down. There was no sound in the street. All waited to see what might happen next. His eyes followed the path that had been cleared before him where RL Terry was approaching him with his arms held out. They made eye contact. The man that he once knew as his father was smiling serenely and there were tears in his eyes.

RL stepped toward Sam and put his arms around him and began to squeeze down hard and pat the back of his shoulders firmly, lovingly. Sam slunk back indifferently and stood limp. RL had him in a long, firm embrace and then he stepped back, resting his hands on the kid's shoulders. Sam was leaning back as if to avoid some evil spirit and when RL began to speak he jumped back, bewildered, and he muttered something in comanche.

The crowd gasped. A woman broke into song.

Speak to your father, called a man with a bible standing nearby.

RL fought to control his emotions and was carefully studying him, noticing the childhood scar above his lip and the distinctive brown mole on the side of his neck. He put his hand to his chest. It's me son, he said. Your father.

Sam ignored him. He was uncomfortable. His eyes scanned the crowd like a cornered animal. He may have been irritated or perhaps he did not understand.

RL appealed to him with his eyes. Samuel. Haden. Terry. He spoke slowly, enunciating each name clearly and gesturing at him with his hands.

Sam stared back, the audience leaning forward. A long silence before he spoke. He nodded as he said it.

Yesh.

The crowd was silent, stunned. RL's voice quivered.

Charles. Warren. Terry. Do you remember your brother?

Yesh.

Sam was looking at the lines on RL's face, the specs of gray in the fringes of his hair. Fleeting glimpses from his past flashed before him but in those images this man was thinner. He had energy. He was more youthful. But now the eyes were tired, the voice was aged. He looked just like any other white man he'd wanted to kill.

Son, is anything coming back to you? said RL. He tilted his head. Do you remember now?

Sam nodded slowly.

RL reached out and hugged him again, caressing the back of his head as Sam awkwardly bent his elbows to place his hands on RL's back to softly return the embrace.

RL was crying. Welcome home, son, he said. Welcome home. It is so very good to have you back.

Sam stepped back, confused. He turned and looked at the crowd. Women were crying. The hotel owner had made his way down and was conferring with the soldiers and Sam was looking about and wondering what might happen next. He turned back to RL standing before him.

I love you son, said RL. He was smiling and more tears streamed down his face.

The owner eased up and placed his hand on RL's shoulder and spoke softly. Excuze me Mr Terry, zee men haffe his trunks ready und if vu'll follow Mr Bedicek inzide vith your zon ve can enzure vu tvo haffe zome briffacy.

Thank you Mr Nimitz. I sure appreciate it.

Of course. It's mein bleazure.

RL motioned for Sam. He nodded toward the hotel entrance. Come on, son, let's get your things and get inside away from these folks.

Sam eyed the hotel nervously. The soldiers gathered around and the porter picked up the trunk. I'll get this in the lobby, Mr Nimitz, he said. The owner nodded. RL put his arm around Sam and nudged him on their way. A smattering of applause commenced from certain segments of the crowd and then the owner called out to them.

Now folks, let's ko on apout our puziness. Ve need to giffe zee Terry family zome privacy.

The crowd was restless and began to shuffle about, grumbling. A reporter from the San Antonio newspaper rushed forward. Mr Terry, Mr Terry, excuse me but if I could just ask you and your son a few questions. The good people of this state will…

The soldiers restrained him. Some of the crowd began to disperse but all kept a watchful eye on the Terrys as they entered the hotel, side by side, the father with his arm around his long-lost son.

It was quiet inside the hotel and Sam noticed how the stirring of the mob outside fell to a quiet murmur when the doors closed shut behind them. There was no one at the front desk and at this hour of the day, the hotel empty of guests. Mr Nimitz said something to RL and then walked briskly down the hallway and the porter headed up the stairs with the trunks that held all of his possessions in the world. RL stepped to the side and watched his son look about the lobby. The shiny wood floors and the ornately papered walls. A side table, ornamentally carved, of walnut and marble. Sam walked across the room slowly, awestruck, studying the painting on the wall above the table. A sailing ship on a glassy sea, an impressionist seascape captured in oil. He placed his finger gently on the canvas and stepped back, gazing at the clearness of colors with the wonder of a child. He noticed some very small seabirds hovering above the dancing waters, a little patch of billowy clouds floating in the afternoon sunlight. He muttered in a low voice, something in comanche. Who created this? Where was it? What could it mean? He turned back to look at RL. The father watching the son who had just returned from a world without time. The room was silent save for the ticking of a clock that had drawn Sam's ear. He slowly swung his eyes around the room searching for the sound, listening to the passing of time. It was a longcase clock made of mahogany, eight-feet tall with brass eagle and finials, long iron weights and pendulum. *Tick tock. Tick tock. Tick tock.* As he approached it he could see the reflection of himself in the glass and he stood facing it, the long hand just reaching its meridian and the chime sequence now mysteriously and beautifully striking the start of the hour. He stepped back, turning his head innocently this way and that, hypnotized. When the chimes stopped he heard the *clip clop* of steps coming quickly toward them from the hall and then Mr Nimitz appeared, hat in hand, waving for them to follow.

Now Mr Terry ve'fe zet zee taple up und zee food is ready, he said. I'll schow vu zee dining room.

RL held his arm out to gesture the way for his son but Sam just stood there. Come on, let's get you something to eat, he said. He motioned with his hand to his mouth and mimed his cheeks as if he was chewing.

They were seated at the end of a long table covered in cloth and set with china and silverware and simple dishes of food. The butler poured them glasses of water from a silver vase and stepped out and returned shortly with a fresh carafe of coffee. The small talk from the butler was returned with looks of impatience. When he left them they sat there, silent and awkward. RL did not know what to say and he raised his brows and motioned over the table with his hands. Dig in, he said. Sam pushed his chair back and stood leaning over the table with his face scrunched up. He reached over and grabbed the plate of pork shoulder, grimacing, and tossed it to the floor, porcelain shattering and the juices of the meat oozing across the floor. He looked at RL to judge his reaction but RL just sat there sipping his coffee as if he'd been expecting it. Sam took the lid off the butter dish, pinching off a great chunk of it with his fingers and slurping it into his mouth.

That's for that plate of bread right there, said RL.

Sam took two slices from the platter and stuffed them full up in his mouth, cheeks blown out like a squirrel gathering nuts as he chewed.

Help ye self, son. We'll worry about the manners part later.

He poured Sam a cup of coffee and pushed forward the bowl of sugar. Sam ignored the spoon, picking up the little bowl and pouring a heap full into his steaming cup. He stirred it with his finger. As he reared back and chugged it down he watched RL serving himself, stuffing his plate full of beef clod, mutton, a link of smoked sausage prepared as it was in the old country. He passed the plates to Sam.

He watched him pick the meat and eat crudely with his hands and by way of example RL began to cut his food with his fork and knife, gentlemanly, eating one bite at a time and chewing slowly.

Well, he said with his mouth full. How is it?

Sam didnt answer.

They wanted to know if I needed an interpreter to help us talk a little, said RL. I told em that werent necessary. That we'd figger it out. That you'd start to pick up on things eventually.

RL took the basket of corncobs and lifted the dishtowel and offered it to Sam. How about we get a few of the basics down, he said.

Sam had grabbed a handful of corncobs.

So if I was to ask you if you liked this here corn, you'd say, 'yes'. RL nodded his head slowly. Yes, he said again. He took his fist and put his thumb in the air, nodding, and repeated the word a third time. Sam, do you like the corn?

Sam nodded and spoke with his mouth full. Yesh, he said.

Okay good. Now I take it you dont like the pork.

Sam looked back quizzically. RL pointed at the mess on the floor. He shook his head from side to side. No, he said. He pointed at the corn. Yes, he emphasized. Then he pointed at the floor. No, he repeated. He nodded his head accordingly each time.

Sam pointed at the floor. No. No muviporo, he said, and he broke into a smile, that clever little smirk that RL had come to love such a long time ago and now that he was seeing it again flooded him with such vivid memories of his wife. There was something else there in that look that struck him and he sat there trying to place it but it was lost on him.

RL pulled something from the shirt pocket at his chest and handed it to Sam. Do you remember this? It was the studio portrait of Sam and his little brother. That was ten years ago, he said. Almost eleven. Can you believe that?

Sam held it in his hands. He touched it.

RL watched him. Dont it feel like it was just yesterday? he said. He reached over and pointed at the picture. Hard to believe, son, but that's you.

He waited for their eyes to meet but Sam just stared at the images, trying to unravel and piece together the past. RL pointed at the smaller boy in the photo. Do you remember your brother Charlie?

Yesh, he said, without looking up.

Do you know what happened to Charlie?

Sam looked up, thinking. He started to shake his head slowly. No, he said. He handed it back to RL.

RL studied the photo again. Sam watched him.

Now that I've found you, your brother is the only one from that day that hasnt turned up.

Sam seemed to be searching through his memories. He was peering into RL's eyes and biting his nails and then suddenly he stopped. Wa… Wil… Wil… ma.

Your Aunt Wilma?

Wilma, he said slowly.

Son, they found your Aunt Wilma just off the Butterfield Road near Fort Chadbourne. Starved. Beaten up and bruised. Unconscious. It was maybe ten, twelve days after they hauled you all off.

RL paused and took a sip of water and wiped down his mustache with his hand. Apparently they were able to revive her, he said. But by the time the doctor arrived three days later she couldnt breathe. Got the pleura all up in her chest and died shortly thereafter.

Sam glanced off across the room, eyes watering.

Son, do you remember how she fell out on her own?

Yesh, said Sam, but RL didnt push the conversation any further.

They ate on, mostly in silence. The clink of a dish, a gulp of water, the sounds of two men chewing in a silent room. RL would point at things and pronounce the word and Sam did his best to repeat the sound that he heard. Hand gestures. Awkward silences. Questions answered with a yes or a no. It took them a long time to finish the meal. When they were full RL wiped his hand across his mouth and belched long and loud and then he smiled. Sam chuckled. Then he began to laugh and soon they were laughing together and when the laughter died down a poignancy settled over RL. He became serious and spoke in a low voice.

Son, I know you may not fully understand what all I've been saying, what I'm about to say, but I just want to talk to you. Just be with you. Hopefully the spirit of all this will prove out. You'll hear the tone in my voice. See it in my eyes. Ever since that day I received the letter from Fort Sill saying that they had found you I've been thinking about what it all meant. What it all means. What to do. How to handle all this. I started conjurin all these scenarios tied to where I've been. What I've done. Where you've been. I caint get my head around it.

He paused and took a sip of water and gulped and they sat staring at one another in silence.

And I dont know, he said. I dont have the answers. How was I supposed to know? I admit there were times that I'd given up. I thought you were dead. It got to the point where it was easier to think you and your brother were dead.

RL shifted his position in the chair.

Think of all that we've been through. There's things been running through my mind I would have never thought I'd have ever thought. Deep, sincere feelings. Son, I aint gonna live forever. I want to make the most of things. To spend time together. And I want more than anything in the world to make things right.

He reached across the corner of the table and touched his hand. He smiled earnestly.

It aint like me to feel like this. Hell I know I caint fix what alls happened. But I know I can be a better father, a better man, moving forward. I want to know who you are. Where all you've been. What you've become. You're my flesh and blood, Sam, and I took that for granted when you and your brother were little. Not anymore. I want to know everything about you and what you've been through. Help you figure out what you want to do moving forward. I know all this is going to take some time but I want you to know I'm here for you now. I want you to know that I love you.

Sam was looking at him. He did not understand but he could read the face, the rheumy eyes. The deep shade of melancholy.

RL said it again. I love you, son.

29

★

Tucson, Arizona

Winter 1929

That last winter the Goodnight's rented a home in Tucson, Arizona for their annual extended winter vacation out west to keep the colonel from suffering with his asthma. Their lives were much the same, burning the days in the warm desert sun with Corinne serving him dutifully. She guarded his time, protecting him from unwanted visitors, and she waited on him patiently hand and foot, cooking, managing all his correspondences and especially ensuring that Haley's inquiries were responded to promptly and in great detail in order to do everything they could to assist the writer in completing the biography of the colonel. All in all it was a very pleasant winter and the old man held up well physically in the dry, mild climate and he used up all of his energies in dictations to Corinne.

Dear Evetts,

I'd be happy to contribute to the society's museum and applaud you very much for all of your efforts. A few items off the top of my head: A very nice buffalo head and robe, the buffalo hair blankets woven by the Pueblos, also miscellaneous items I've moved on from (my old pipe and tobacco can and the copper coffee pot). There are other things I am sure and when I return in the spring we'll sort all of that out.

As always, Goodnight

On a Sunday morning she left the colonel alone, as he had not been feeling well, and she walked the two blocks down the street in the new morning sun to attend the tent preachings of the Friends and Workers Fellowship. She returned two hours later to find a surprise visitor in the living room talking with the colonel. The man was sitting in the big mesquite chair, a well-dressed intellectual, legs crossed and very distinguished looking, and when she entered the den he jumped to attention to formally make her acquaintance. The perfect gentleman. He was perhaps a few years shy of seventy with a full head of sandy-blond hair with streaks of gray. Corinne was drawn to his dazzling eyes set in a handsome face, weathered nicely, and it occurred to her that he was one of those men who appears twenty years younger than his actual age. His suit was white, wide lapels, a shawl collar waistcoat and a spear-point collar dress shirt. The Panama Optimo hat he wore about town was on the floor.

The colonel stayed in his chair when she arrived. He was trying to smile but he looked like he had seen a ghost from an earlier world, as if he was having one of those episodes where he seemed to not know where or who he was, or perhaps he was so taken aback by some of the things he may have heard. She knew he had been feeling bad but something seemed different. She also was put out that the visitor appeared unannounced, irritated that he had entered their lives while she was away, and yet she was curious, taken aback by his good looks and charming smile.

Mrs Goodnight, I'm Charlie Mathiessen. It's very nice to meet you.

Charlie Mathiessen, she repeated back. It's a pleasure to meet you as well.

Please accept my apologies for showing up unannounced.

Yes sir. Well, it looks like the two of you are getting along alright.

Yes, yes we are. We've been having a nice visit.

The colonel waved his cane from the chair. Dont worry Corinne, I gave the young man a good cussin when he showed up but decided to talk with him on account of his fine first name.

They chuckled. Corinne looked the man up and down, glancing from time to time trying to get a read on her husband.

Charlie Mathiessen, she said again. Why I know I've heard that name somewhere before. May I ask what you're here to see the colonel about today?

Why yes, of course, I was just getting the colonel up to speed. You see, I have business in Hollywood, and I wanted to visit with you a bit about some ideas I have of making a movie about the colonel and his life.

Over the course of the afternoon he told them about his fascinating path through the world that had led him to this place. A lifetime ago he'd faced a great tragedy, some had speculated in Texas, and he had vague memories that he was told matched the description.

I remember bits and pieces, little flashes here and there, he said. But I was thankfully too young to really remember anything in detail.

The indians had attacked their home and hauled him and his brother away. He did not know what happened to his mother or father. What few images he could recall were of his brother.

It was a warm summer morning, said Mathiessen. No wind, a light fog, everything bathed in a yellow haze. He was on the back of a horse riding away and I called out to him.

He remembered being with another band of indians who took him west into the mountains. The face of a woman who seemed like a mother. They told him that somehow he ended up at Camp Grant in the territory of Arizona. He could recall images of the desert but otherwise all he knew was what he'd been told by the man who raised him. Doctor Henry Mathiessen, the assistant post surgeon. Apparently a wagontrain of emigrants heading toward California had picked him up on the trail. Malnourished, in terrible condition. They took him into the post where he remained under the care of Doctor Mathiessen who nursed him back to health over the course of months. They did not know who he was, where he was from. He'd been traumatized and they could not get him to talk.

Corinne was shaking her head slowly, wistfully, like she was looking at a little baby or a wounded animal.

Why Mr Mathiessen, my Lord. Did they ever find out about your folks? Your brother?

No. Nothing ever turned up. It was always just assumed that they were dead.

He turned to the old man who was staring at him blankly, seemingly deep in thought and yet he could have been having one of his episodes of confusion or fatigue that had plagued him of late. Charlie Mathiessen felt compelled to expand on his story.

You see, my first consistent memories as a boy are of San Francisco, after my father adopted me and took me there where he established his own practice. Such beautiful memories. It was a boomtown. Gold, silver, railroads. Walking up Powell Street to Nob Hill and the views of the city. The weather. I would sit in his office all day reading books. Encyclopedias. Newspapers. I'll never forget reading *The Adventures of Tom Sawyer*. I must have been ten, maybe eleven. I really couldnt have asked for a better childhood. Whatever power placed me in his hands, I suppose you could say it was a miracle. I cant imagine a boy having a better father. Such a caring, loving, intelligent man. Very spiritual and in tune with the way of things. He was quite successful, making good money and well established in the community. And yet he was a very humble man. He married an amazing woman and she became my mother. She was very social and they were constantly entertaining. All of San Francisco's elite families. They were never able to have any children, so I received all of their energy and attention. Private school. Weekend trips to the coast. By the time I enrolled in the university I was ready for the adventures of the world.

Corinne was captivated, following every word intently, picturing his life in those days in the city of San Francisco, the Paris of the West.

Mr Mathiessen, what university did you attend?

The University of California, in Berkeley.

Oh, my brother Thomas, he's told me magnificent things about that place. What did you study?

Architecture, and philosophy.

Oh, what wonderful areas of study.

Charlie Mathiessen kept trying to turn the conversation back to the colonel but Corinne's curiosity wouldnt allow it. The colonel was quiet, contemplative. Corinne kept looking back at him as if to bring him along in her enjoyment of this surprise visitor but he just sat there, smiling serenely, nodding politely at little details here and there as the man answered her questions. Perhaps there was an image of a tow-haired little boy from somewhere in his past but he did not trust his mind on those sorts of things anymore. He was clenching his teeth from some sharp shooting pains in his chest and he wanted to go lay down but then they'd subside and he sat there patiently, more as a courtesy to his wife who seemed more excited than she'd been in a long time.

Yes, I've been very, very fortunate, Charlie Mathiessen kept saying. The colonel would look out the window, his mind in and out of the conversation. There was a lizard tiptoeing through a maze of thorns on a young saguaro cactus and just above it a finch had landed on a newly blooming flower and it was feeding from the nectar.

Were you in San Francisco for the great earthquake? Corinne asked.

Oh no, no. I was long gone by then. After school I spent time in Europe.

He was hesitant to talk too much about himself but Corinne continued to pepper him with questions.

Really? Whereabouts in Europe?

The south of France. Italy. Spain and Portugal. Yes, it was another impactful time in my life. Once I was back in the states I spent a year in New York. And then I took my time wandering all over the country on my way back to the West Coast. My folks were worried about me. I passed through Texas on my way to Mexico, which is by the way, when I first heard of Mr Goodnight. Eventually I found my way to Los Angeles and settled in. I'd seen a bit of the world and it was time to get to work.

In architecture?

Well yes, as an architect initially, which eventually led to other business interests. I was fortunate to become acquainted with a man named Fred Rindge.

Oh, oh, is he the gentlemen who purchased—oh, what do they call it? Malibu Rancho?

Yes, yes that's him.

When I was living in Montana there were families that would visit in the summer and apparently they knew him. They would talk so fondly of him and that area. Someday I'm going to go to Los Angeles. The City of Angels.

Yes, yes. It is special. At least for the time being.

And how did you meet him?

Well, let's see. We were members of a few of the same social organizations locally. History. Archaeology. He was President of the Harvard Club and he brought me into all of that, which led to so many other things. Real estate was natural for me. The San Fernando Valley. Stockton. It led to oil, life insurance, whatever. I have great memories of those years but I was just too busy. I should've taken more time to relax. And so this last decade I've slowed down and I've really grown to appreciate all of the time on my hands.

Mr Mathiessen, were you ever married?

Yes. Yes I was. But unfortunately my fair young lady became very sick just after our honeymoon, with the cancer. She was gone within months. I was devastated, which is one reason I devoted myself so much to my work.

Oh, I'm so very sorry to hear that.

Well, thank you. I suppose it was just one of those things. It was just in the cards. A cruel hand. It seems there's always something lurking right around the corner that can change things in a heartbeat. You get through it and go on though. Life goes on.

Suddenly the colonel leaned forward as if to say something, clutching his cane, studying the man. They turned to him. He was pulling at his goatee and thinking hard. Something in the man's eyes but he could not place it.

How'd you get yourself into the movie bidness, Mr Madison?

Yes, yes. About the movies. Well, I've always been interested in photography, film. Following the technology over the years. And oh, I guess it was a decade ago. Maybe more. All of the film producers moved to Southern California on account of Edison's monopoly. All of his film patents. And of course, the weather and the fact that Western films were becoming so popular. I was fortunate to have the resources and so I funded new forms of production, backing a man named Thomas Ince, who broke the process into all of its forms—writing, costumes and makeup, directing, publicity. It's amazing what a big business it's become, and now with sound it's only going to get bigger. Does Tucson have a theatre? Have you seen *The Jazz Singer*?

Corinne was pouring a pitcher of tea into three freshly iced glasses.

No, we haven't but I would love to! Oh Colonel, this summer we should go to Amarillo and see a picture.

The colonel was grimacing, feeling bad. He acknowledged her idea with a nod. Excuse me Mr Madson, he said. I should go lie down for a bit. I'm just not feeling well. But feel free to make yourself at home.

Why yes, of course.

It looks like you and the little lady have a lot to talk about.

Here honey, let me help you.

Corinne put her glass down and offered her arm but the old man wobbled himself up on the cane and waved her off. He shuffled to the doorway and then stopped and turned back.

Mr Madson, I appreciate you stopping by and it's sure been good meeting you. I'm sure you're a fine gentleman, and I wish you well. But there's something I have to tell you.

The old man paused. He raised his cane and pointed it at Charlie Mathiessen to emphasize his point.

It'll be a cold day in hell when I consent to a movie about my life.

The old man is weak because he is fighting a low-grade fever. What started as a cold progressed into acute lung congestion and he fears he has pneumonia. He is ninety-three after all, and they've had such a hectic schedule since the long drive from Texas, hosting an endless stream of visitors and getting settled in their new winter home.

Corinne is almost finished taking dictation on the last of fourteen letters for the day and the songbirds flittering in the sun outside the window catch her ear.

Oh Charles, listen to those birds would you.

What?

The birds singing outside.

She gestured at the window. He did not hear her or the birds. He put his hand to his ear.

What's that you say, little girl?

She spoke loudly. The BIRDS, honey. Outside the window. Can you hear them?

Oh, oh. Yes, the birds.

Have you ever noticed that the littlest birds sing the prettiest songs?

Corinne, darlin. I'm sorry. I caint hear you. What'd you say?

She leaned up from her seat and got a little closer to him.

I just wanted to know if you want me to write anything else in this letter to Evetts before we're done for the day.

Well, yes. Tell him that I am not feeling well. That I've not been feeling up to myself lately but will try and write next time about the day I met ole Sam Houston.

Okay. Anything else?

Yes. Remind him that while I'm not getting any younger, and I'm anxious as hell to have the book done, he's best served tending to his business there in Austin at the university before he turns any more attention to the book. Tell him to take his time with this thing, work it out to his satisfaction.

Okay, I like that.

And one more thing: Tell him to by god do it right and it'll serve him well for the rest of his life. You never know, it might just turn out to be his masterpiece.

The colonel had insisted they bring plenty of buffalo meat with them to Tucson for the winter and this served them well when they had the big Thanksgiving supper. He insisted on preparing the main dish, cutting up beautiful medallions of meat and dousing them with oil and salt and pepper. And he was a master with the parry knife, perfectly slicing little incisions in the meat so that he could embed little chunks of garlic and when this was done he completed this magnum opus with a layer of bacon freshly processed from a wild boar that had been shot in the Rincon Mountains. Pastor Ralph Blackburn and Frank Dennison had been down at Tubac and they'd brought back a basketful of sweet potatoes and carrots and green beans and Corinne skilleted all of that up along with a dish of potato gratin. She made buttermilk biscuits and two pies. Pumpkin and chocolate, the colonel's favorite. Her brother Tom, just back from California, brought over a few bottles of wine from the San Jose Winery in Santa Barbara County. Mae Dennison made a caramelized onion galette and her close friend Elma Wiebe brought over a batch of her famous homemade cornbread dressing and a dish of citrus-cranberry sauce.

This little dish has been in the Frigidaire for two weeks, she said. It's from my grandmama's recipe I stumbled upon last month. Can you believe that?

Hmm-mmm. I caint wait to try it!

It was a big feast. The colonel was on his best behavior at the head of the table and they ate like kings, telling stories of the old days while Louis Armstrong played in the background on the phonograph. But after dessert something was off with the colonel. He was tired and full and he was fighting waves of intense chest pains and he seemed to be having trouble breathing. He sat there staring blankly, trying to get his bearings. Corinne was concerned.

Honey, are you feeling okay?

I think my damned pyrosis is actin up.

Oh no, I am so sorry. Can I get you anything? A little bourbon?

He shook his head. Mr Blackburn weighed in.

Colonel, I've got a bottle of sotol from down south. It'll settle your stomach.

That's a damn good idea, Frank. Yes, I believe a little pull of that'll do me some good.

They poured him a nip of sotol and they put him to bed and they sat around the table after the dishes were done talking about what they'd done earlier on that day of Thanksgiving.

Ralph, what all d'yall do down at Sasabe?

Well, the colonel wanted to see the La Osa Ranch. Lots of history there, as you know. All the way back to the Spaniards. It was part of the Gadsden Purchase. So Mr Finley arranged for us to have a tour even though he's sold it of late. Bunch of damn greenhorns bought it. And you should've heard the colonel cussing the condition of those cattle.

Oh, I'm sure.

You see, the mugs of those darn cattle were all ulcered up from hunting for grass under the cactus. Stickers all up in their noses. And the colonel was out there stomping around in the desert with his cane, cussing to himself, loving on those cows and pulling the stickers out of them.

Aww.

Boy howdy, I liked to have never got him outta there.

Four days later the colonel suffered a heart attack. He had been in the courtyard on an unusually warm day and he had been pushing himself. It felt like the old days. He figured it was good for him. He could not remember the last time he'd sweat like that. She left him alone to get him a big cold bottle of beer and he leaned his cane against the low cinderblock wall and bent down to pick up a heavy-potted fishhook cactus. He wobbled along, unsteady, grunting, and after he set it down by the fountain he stood up, lightheaded, and as he tried to catch his breath he felt a squeezing on the left side of his chest. He was sweating but it wasnt from the heat. A cold sweat. He sat down on the bench by the fountain and closed his eyes. The tightness in his chest seemed to be spreading over his body. His jaw, his neck. He put his elbows on his knees, head hanging low, sweat dripping onto the warm pavers.

When Corinne came outside and saw him struggling she rushed over and knelt in front of him.

Honey, what's wrong? Are you alright?

He didnt answer.

Did you hurt yourself?

He barely got anything out. I'm okay, darlin, he said. I just overdid myself a little I think.

She called Dr. Wyatt at the Desert Sanatorium and he was there in twenty minutes with his assistant.

Colonel, are you experiencing any tingling sensations in your arms?

I dont know. Maybe a little.

Have you been having any pain the past few days?

No, he said. He shook his head. He was lying.

How is your chest feeling now? It seems like you're breathing a little better.

It comes and goes, but when it comes it feels like there's a goddamned buffalo bull sitting on my chest.

I want you to have a sip of water and take these.

He gave him the glass and some aspirin and a morphine pill. He replaced the cold wet rag on his forehead with another.

It's important for you to relax and breathe deeply. Dont push yourself too hard. Dont talk too much. Try and get some rest.

What'n the hell is in that water?

Just a little sodium bicarbonate.

What's that?

Baking soda. I want to try and prevent any build-up of lactic acid.

Okay, doc. You're the boss. Whatever you say.

He looked at Corinne and feigned a smile. After a while he was asleep. The doctor was serious and spoke softly.

I really think he's going to be alright. He's strong as a bull but apparently, well, he just overdid himself.

It's my fault.

No, no. You cant think that way. Just let him rest and we'll keep him on the medicines.

Dr. Wyatt, thank you so much.

Listen, I dont want to disturb him any further but when he wakes up I'd like you to give him some of this. He handed her a little green bottle.

What's this?

Campho-Phenique. I'd like you to massage a good coat of it all over his chest every four hours or so.

But I thought this was for bites? Or burns?

Well, it is. But just trust me. Hopefully he'll be much better in the morning.

She sets up a bed with cushions and blankets so she can be with him in the night but she cannot sleep. So she watches him sleeping, his mind probably somewhere long ago and far away, trailing a herd of longhorn cows up the Pecos, watching for the Comanches. She imagines what he must have looked like at thirty.

She walks to the kitchen and grabs the candle and the copy of the new book her brother had just sent them. *The Sound and the Fury*. She returns to the room and nestles into the rocking chair and opens it to the marked page where she last stopped. Silence in the room save for the little alarm clock that is ticking on the bedside stand. She reads the last paragraph she had read before she had stopped. Then she picks up from there, reading slowly, paying attention to the bumps and flows of the words, the inner music of each sentence. Becoming lost in the book helps her make it through the night.

It was propped against the collar box and I lay listening to it. Hearing it, that is. I dont suppose anybody ever deliberately listens to a watch or a clock. You dont have to. You can be oblivious to the sound for a long while, then in a second of ticking it can create in the mind unbroken the long diminishing parade of time you didn't hear. Like Father said down the long and lonely light-rays you might see Jesus walking, like. And the good Saint Francis that said Little Sister Death, that never had a sister.

Eventually she closes the book and blows out the candle, listening to the patterns of him breathing against the ever-steady ticking of the clock. Goodnight Charles, she whispers, and she slips out the door into the room across the hall and crawls into her bed.

He opened his eyes to the sunrise, the bright new light gleaming into the room, a brand-new day. She was beside him, smiling, holding a fresh steaming cup of black coffee. She helped him sit up and he sat there getting his bearings. He didnt say anything. He took the cup with both hands and put it to his nose and breathed in deeply, smelling the nuances and beauty of the aromas. Sunrise on those first cattle drives with coffee and campfire biscuits and bacon. He took a long slurp from the mug and swallowed and let out a big sigh.

Charles, darling. How are you feeling?

He swallowed the coffee slowly, feeling the heat on the back of his throat. He gulped it down. Another big sigh.

I feel like a new man, he said.

Every six hours she takes his temperature and gives him his medicine. She puts the back of her hand to his cheeks and forehead, ignoring him as he grumbles about being confined to his bed rest. His eyes still show the trauma. Sunken and tired and hollow.

She has nursed him back from the dead other times and she knows his body well, but something inside told her this was different. What will I do if he dies? she thinks. He has become her life. He sits up in the bed, restless, looking out the window at the birds and the sun, watching the splashing fountain bathed in sunshine and yearning to be outside.

She rubs the campho into her hands and massages it slowly into his massive old chest, paying special attention to the left side, his heart. He loves the feel of her soft young hands on his body and the pleasant smell of the eucalyptus oil. Otherwise the treatment would be forbidden, ridiculed as some sort of nonsense.

She knows he is becoming his old self again when he flirts with her, holding onto his virility. Subtle allusions to whatever imaginary sex life he dreams could exist.

Oh Colonel, she says, smiling.

He lets his old gray eyes wander from her lips down her neck to the cleavage of her breasts. The soft skin of youth. She puts her lips to his forehead. Then she sits back in her chair with her books and reads to him.

He lays back, watching her, watching the light in the room slowly change with the passing of each day, in those last days before he died.

Corinne, little girl. Now listen, I think I'm well enough that I can get out of this damned old bed and walk around outside.

I think that's a fine idea.

Let's set the chairs up by the fountain, in the sun. Maybe the hummingbirds'll be buzzing around.

Okay, let me help you. I'll come back and get these books.

The sun was warm on their faces. He sat back and closed his eyes. She had to get used to the glare of the bright sun on the page. The stories

Corinne read to the old man, riding along with the old plainsmen in *Chief of Scouts* or, *Thirty-One Years on the Plains and in the Mountains*, had infused him with renewed energy and inspiration—taking him back to the old days in hearing the adventures of his contemporaries. Kit Carson, Jim Bridger, General Crook. Indian fighters like him. Spending time with these books forced them to envision what it would be like for the latest generations of Americans to sit in the sun or by a fireplace, holding in their hands a book about the settlement of the Texas Panhandle Plains, turning the pages and reading about the colonel's life and times. They'd dream of the book, picturing it in their hands, and they talked about the possibilities, comparing the memoirs they had read and envisioning what Haley might do differently with his approach.

I wonder what that young man is thinking of naming the book? he said.

I know! And the cover. I sure like the idea of Mr Bugbee drawing something up for the cover.

The book she held included the descriptive sub-headings used by the author, sometimes simple, often elusive, offering clues into the contents of a given chapter's secrets. They'd peruse them leisurely, spurring random reminisces from the colonel, forcing her to pause and resort to pen and paper to capture them for Haley, then she would begin to read to him again.

Chapter 33: The Massacre at Choke Cherry Canyon - Mike Maloney Gets into a Muss - Rescue of White Girls - Mike Gets Even with the Apaches

Or from the latest novels sent to them by her brother or Haley. Some of them new, others well-used with their dog-eared pages, marked up, annotated with another reader's observations.

Corinne, read to me from the war book again, he would say.

I was always embarrassed by the words sacred, glorious and sacrifice and the expression in vain. We had heard them, sometimes standing in the rain almost out of earshot, so that only the shouted words came through, and had read them on proclamations that were slapped up by billposters over other proclamations, now for a long time, and I had seen nothing sacred, and the things that were glorious had no glory and the sacrifices were like the stockyards at Chicago if nothing was done with the meat except to bury it.

Read that again for me, little girl, there's something about what he's saying there. Did you tell me that the book was written by the same man who wrote about the young men and women wasting their youths in Europe?

Yes, Hemingway.

Well, he's really done something with this one. He writes as if he was there. It's a wonder to me what mankind is capable of in war. I just caint hardly fathom it.

His episode had happened on a Monday and by Friday he seemed completely back to his old self. The doctor prescribed him with a clean bill of health and warned him to keep taking things slow and easy. They were anxious to send as much information to Haley as possible, hoping it would speed whatever process he was following to complete the book.

Colonel, he has a few questions in here about the ranch house.

Okay, shoot.

Shoot? What do you mean?

The questions, fire away.

Oh. Well, let's see here. The paintings in the war room.

Those were done, I think, in the late '80s by a man named Cowles. He was a student of a man named Beer-stat or some such.

Albert Bierstadt?

Yes, I believe that's correct. Anyhow, he was one of the first western painters. Cowles took ill. Somebody said it was the consumption but I dont think that's right, and so Bierstadt finished them himself in his studio in New York City.

That's quite interesting.

What else does Haley need?

The mining in Mexico.

Yes, it was down in Coahuila. Came over on burros from the west coast and crossed the mountains. Lived there like a peon for six months or so. Never made a dime.

Okay, anything else on that?

No. I dont like to talk about it. What else?

The horses. He wants to know about the horses on the ranch.

Oh, I'd say we had several hunnerd. Half of em saddle horses, half of em mares. There were three heavy teams of horses and a large team of mules. Another light team for the buggy. Mollie had the gray mares, Nancy and Dixie. Black and gray teams of carriage horses.

Okay, let me see. He writes here, *Colonel, you've talked about Hawk as your favorite horse, but what other sires did you have at the ranch?*

Ahh, okay. Well, we had an imported French Percheon horse. Named France, of all things. He sired the younger grays. Curly, the fighting stallion, he sired the older bays. Sam Dyer killed him in 1892, or '93 I think it was.

You want me to put 1893?

Yes, that'll do.

Alright, one last question here from Evetts.

I'm ready.

He says, *You told me one day about a conversation you had with Jose Tafoya when he was an older man. About the wildlife. But we were interrupted for some reason or another. Would you please revisit that for me?*

Well, yes. Let me see. We were reminiscing about the buffalo being gone and he told me about the time he was heading back home after dealing some goods to the Comanches at Muchaque. He said between the Double Lakes and Tahoka Lake, he'd seen thousands and thousands of turkeys moving across the Llano. A half mile wide, horizon to horizon, with packs of coyotes flanking each side waiting on stragglers. Likely heading to the Simanola valley to feed on the shinnery acorns. But he told me that west of there he'd seen a big range of country completely bare of any vegetation, except that it was covered by thousands of dead grasshoppers.

It's hard to believe.

Picture it, darlin. Back then you'd hear stories of those massive grasshopper swarms. Hundreds of thousands of them glittering like snowflakes in the sun. And turkeys migrating like buffalo.

I'd give anything to be able to go back and see those turkeys. To see those buffalo herds.

Well, we messed things up pretty good didnt we?

Yes, it's shame. And I dont imagine we've learned much from it either.

No we damn sure have not. Hell, the Forest Service has essentially become a wolf extermination unit.

The colonel leaned over and grabbed his cane and pushed himself up, sighing, looking out the window, shaking his head.

It's hard for me to talk about it. Lord knows I've done my fair share of harm over the years. I'd bring those wolfers into my ranges and they'd shoot em, trap em, hunt em with dogs and drag em from out of their dens. Or lay out carcasses poisoned with strychnine as bait. And from time to time you'd be riding out looking over all of this beautiful country and you'd see a fox or a bear or an eagle that had perished from feeding on that poisoned carrion.

Now Charles, honey. No need to beat yourself up about this right now. Listen, let me go get us a glass of iced tea.

Goodnight turned to watch her go. He sat back down, stroking his goatee in thought. Well, he whispered to himself. I suppose mankind's about as damn useless as it gets.

On Saturday morning the colonel rode with Ralph Blackburn to the farmers market to pick up some groceries. Also, in the afternoon he had to make a run out to a ranch on Oro Valley road to check on some cows. On the way they ate a late lunch at a roadside stand that was known for its green hatch chile chicken enchiladas and cold beer. The colonel talked non-stop, sharing his endless observations about native game, cattle, buffalo, and his attempts to crossbreed the two. The cattalo, he called them.

When I was a little boy on the Brazos we'd trap the turtles. Make soup out of em. Sell em. Whatever. Damned if those things aint left-handed. I can only think of one we ever caught that was trapped with its right foot.

It was a pleasant afternoon, sunny and warm. The colonel was enjoying his day out and about. But out on the range as he was waiting on Blackburn to finish feeding he watched a dark line of clouds building to the west.

Blackburn, he barked, we best get back to town.

The pastor looked at the sky and shrugged his shoulders and hurried over to help the colonel to the car.

Back on the road Blackburn kept the old Packard cruising at sixty and was content with the pace. The colonel talked on, keeping an eye on the storm.

Now damnit, Blackburn. Is that as fast as you can go?

Well, I suppose not. We can go faster.

The old man had his cane in a death grip pounding it into the floorboard. Well by god, then let's get on it! That storm is ridin our ass and you're drivin like a damned ole woman!

Sunday morning.

Corinne, darlin. Listen here now, he said. I woke up thinking about something. About my will. I must have been dreaming about what Mr Cole said about Underwood.

But Charles, honey, remember the attorney said everything looked alright.

I just dont want there to be any problems for you. It nags me. Underwood's generally got a good feel for things.

It's probably just one of those dark dreams you have in the night. Those always make things seem heavier than they really are. If Cole says the Dyers have no grounds, you should sleep well. Dont worry.

You're probably right. But ole Leigh, he would roll over in his grave if he felt like his daughter had any notion of causing trouble with the will. He just wadnt that way.

After lunch the reporter from the *Arizona Daily Star* showed up late to interview the colonel about another old timer named Uncle Jim Owens and his mountain lion hunting exploits. He arrived when the Goodnights were walking out the door and the colonel read him riot.

Sir, you're late and about two blocks from here is some good preachin goin on and I'm goin to hear it.

He was holding out his large gold pocket watch as if to emphasize to the man that he was late. In his irritation he felt a sharp twinge of pain, a squeezing in his chest.

The man apologized. He tried to get a few questions answered ad hoc but the colonel wouldnt have it.

Mr Goodnight, do you believe he's truly killed thousands of cougars?

I told you, son, I'm goin to a preachin. Now you're welcome to wait until I get back or we can book us a little appointment for tomorrow.

The man was dejected, perhaps on a deadline. The colonel may have felt bad for his gruff demeanor.

Or hell, you're welcome to come along with us and listen, he said. Might do you some good.

On Monday well before it was first light he woke up with the old pains again. It was slight at first and he wanted to think it was because of the dream he'd been having. Something about a gunshot into the back of his shoulder, blood running down his upper arm, an intense stinging pain in his side. The blast had knocked him down and he was all alone in the desert somewhere near the Castle Gap. Just lying there, suffering in pain unable to move, no one to help and waiting to die.

Once he got up and had his coffee he felt a little better but after breakfast the pains came back again and it was much worse. He was extremely tired. Felt like he could go back to bed. He put it off to something bad in his food, tried to conceal it from Corinne. She was used to the ebbs and flows of how he felt, his moods. She brushed it off and all morning as it became worse he continued to fight through it. They read through the mail and typed up responses. Letter after letter after letter. But he did not have his normal energy. He was hopeful he was just having one of those days.

They lunched on leftover buffalo roast stacked between two slices of white bread with pepper sauce. Cold. He never ate bread but a sandwich sounded good. When they sat back down to work he could hardly function. He said he wanted to be outside in the sun for a while. It always made him feel better.

She left him alone on the bench by the fountain, bathed by the brilliant desert sun in the purest of winter skies, listening to the water. He closed his eyes, breathing deeply, smelling the desert. Dry. Sweet and dusty. Earthy. He opened his eyes to the pitter patter of a troupe of Gambel's quail scurrying through the desert scrub at the edge of the yard. He grabbed his cane and pushed himself up to have a look, dizzy and trying to catch his breath. Then all he could hear was a wash of rushing air as his chest seized up in a great rage of pain. He lay where he fell, crumpled up, gasping. Wind chimes tinkling in the breeze and the water in the fountain splashing in the sunshine, the mourning dove cooing softly from the paloverde trees.

When she came outside and saw him sprawled out on the hot concrete pavers she thought he was dead. She screamed in shock, the cold bottle of beer she carried dropped and shattered into a hundred tiny shards. She rushed over and knelt down and put her arms around him, sobbing. He could not say anything but there was life in his eyes and he was breathing.

30

★

Further On Up the Road

He opens his mouth, lips dry and quivering, waiting, for some respite or for the aspirins and those wondrous little pills of morphine. The taste hits his tongue and Corinne puts the glass of water to his lips. He slurps, swallows. It does not take long for the drug to alter his state of mind.

When they put him to bed that night after his second heart attack they truly believed that his death was imminent and yet he was somehow hanging on. He would revive. They sat with him all night, her and Doctor Wyatt and his assistant. Ralph Blackburn would relieve them every few hours. It was much the same the following day. It was difficult to tell sometimes if he was breathing. He did not speak. He somehow looked like he'd aged another decade overnight. Shriveled, translucent skin, his large frame wasting away.

She talked to them about what would be next. The reality of it all was sinking in. She feared coming back into the room to his lifeless body. How would she let those close to him know? What to say? Making arrangements to ship his body back to Texas on the train. What would it be like riding with him? The funeral? But early the next morning he revived.

Corinne, I vaguely remember dying. The pain numbed me and I gradually faded away, thinking at the time that it was the end. And then somehow this morning as the sunlight filled the room, I opened my eyes. Back from the dead. I dont understand it. Is it a miracle? A blessing? A curse? I lay there, listening to that voice. Promising myself, promising God, that I would face it all. Accepting that it was finally time to fully come to terms with all that my life has been. To ask forgiveness. Corinne sat with him and she held his hand and let him talk.

I must tell you about the young man I've talked so much about. Sam Terry. He had been struggling terribly to reacclimate back into white society. Just when it seemed as though he was completely lost, that he would be relegated to a sad life of depression and sorrow, he miraculously came back to life. You see, he'd fallen in love. It gave him strength, to be deeply loved. Is it not after all, the greatest happiness of life, to love. To be loved. I never understood this when I was young even though it fell in my lap with Mollie. And when you came into my life, I was a dying man. But love saved me. You saved me. And so Sam Terry, who prospered as a wild Comanche indian, likely because of all of the love the tribe bestowed upon him, lost the beauty of love in his life when he was forced back into white society. But there was a common path that changed that. Call it fate. Or God. The mysterious ways of the universe.

We'd arranged for him to have work in South Texas on the King Ranch. He obviously had that famous Comanche passion for horseflesh, a great knack for them. But it would get him back out in nature again. He was reluctant but he knew that anything was better than what he'd found himself in the middle of. The ways of the white man. White society. A circus of gawkers. And we had him in what appeared to be the perfect place, but then his life turned upside down again. He knew he could not go back to the old ways and I think by then there was trust between him and RL. And of course, he seemed to listen to my guidance.

By the latter half of the 1870s the King Ranch was sending tens of thousands of cattle up the trails. King had been fostering the Mexican vaqueros, feeding and housing entire communities of them on the ranch and paying the cowboys monthly wages. He set up a ranch school to educate the kids. Those boys knew horses and cattle, maybe as good as the Comanches, and they were generally an independent bunch of folks. Had their horses, saddles, ropes. Did their own business. But King brought them in and they were loyal as hell to him. They were knowns as, *Los Kineños*. One big family. One common cause. It made sense that Sam Terry must have felt some kinship with them.

They said they'd never seen anyone handle a horse like he could. And that's saying something from those folks down there. So he must have been appreciated from the start and I'm sure he grew close to them. Evidently one of the original vaqueros that King brought with him from Mexico in the Fifties, one of the most valuable caporals on the ranch, took a liking to him, as did his daughter. She'd grown up on the ranch, was coming into her own as a young woman. They say she was very beautiful. Silky black hair, green eyes, the light skin of a Spaniard. So here along comes a strapping young man about her age. Good genes. An Anglo who happened to be raised as a Comanche, and he could out vaquero anyone on that ranch. They took a strong liking to one another. They fell in love.

You tame a million acres of rough country and you're sure as hell going to have enemies. And Richard King especially, given his often-questionable character and all, had his fair share. Long before the Bandit Wars in the 1910s. Mexican outlaws wandered across the border. Military deserters wrangling horses. Just bad folks roaming the country. There was no law back then and King did his damndest, like we all did, to enforce order. But one night a band of outlaws came riding from out of the darkness with an eye on looting and plundering, burning buildings and stealing horses. There was a big fight. Men died on both sides. Helluva lot wounded. Sam Terry wasnt there that night. They said he was working one of the northern ranges. But his bride-to-be was. When the dust had settled they found her sprawled out dead with her drawers down, her throat slit.

It seems to me there were two paths there that he was faced with. Revenge. Or solitude. Who knows what pain he must have felt, what all was going through his mind. Think about what all he'd faced in his life up to that point. It's no surprise he disappeared. I imagine that's what I would have done at that stage of the game.

RL must have set out immediately to track him down once he'd gotten word of what had transpired. I've thought about that often over the years. What I would have done. I always think about him.

RL was quite a bit smaller than me, yet he was a man that you wouldnt want to underestimate when he had his edge going. He could be dangerous. I'd seen him get himself into situations back when we were young, jackpots I wasnt so sure he'd be able to work himself out of. But he always did. I'd tell him, Pardner, one of these days that's going to catch up with you. And he'd just smile.

He had a sweet face, that's what Mollie used to say. Lean with a scruffy beard and brownish hair. I'd seen his intense, determined eyes, and he could work like a dog. In fact he was loyal like an old dog. There's not many men I trusted back then to have my back in the heat of battle but he was sure one of them. I could learn more about a man spending a few days and nights on the prairie with them, hardly speaking, than I could talking to them on a daily basis. I saw that in him when we first started working cows together.

How I got caught up in the middle of him and Sally Johnson I'll never understand. There was nothing intentional. It just happened randomly. I told myself at the time, in those early years of their courtship and marriage, that it wasnt that big of a deal. But I suppose as it went on that summer…

The old man paused and looked down, biting his lip, his face squinched up as if he felt a great pain. Hell, he said, we werent even together all that much. I suppose the fact that I wasnt forthcoming with such a close friend, it was destined to catch up to me. Those things always do.

He used to ask me certain things about her, usually if they were having issues. But not always. He'd ask things sometimes, almost like he was testing me. I'd sit there looking at his facial expressions, thinking to myself, how much does he know? And I'd tell myself I was just reading into things too much. I dont know, maybe he had figured it out. How would I have felt if I were in his shoes?

When somehow our paths came together that afternoon, randomly, in the middle of nowhere, in the middle of I-dont-know-how-many-hundreds of thousands of square miles. And right when I'd first arrived in the Palo Duro to build a new life. I most definitely took stock of what the gods of fate were presenting me with in that moment. I had a feeling as he rode up. The power of the subconscious mind, I'll tell you what, you best listen.

We set up a camp like the old days, just the two of us out under the stars on a clear, cool night, the flames of the fire crackling, catching up about everything. And you know I'm sure he'd been thinking to himself, this sorry bastard has done gone off on his own up on the Apishapa and made a fortune. Which of course I had but then I lost it all in the financial panic. But envy, it'll eat you up like the cancer and it must have been building in him. Among other things.

RL told me that Sam had been missing for a few months. That he'd gotten word from the King Ranch boys that he'd up and left one day, that they thought it was on account of the little Kineño gal he'd gotten sweet on had died tragically as a result of a bunch of outlaws making a raid on the ranch. RL was hurting inside something awful. He was nostalgic about how they spoke so highly of Sam, about how good he'd been doing, how happy he seemed. How he was such a damn good cowboy. And that had to of broke RL's heart to know that Sam walked away from that.

I remember sitting there that night listening to him tell me all of this, and I'm looking this way and that over my shoulder, for a ghost out in the dark of the night. I sensed something. I knew the kid had to be out there somewhere on the range, probably not all that far from where we were. Hell, maybe looking at us sitting right there that night by the fire.

I dont know what I was thinking running my mouth that night. My mantra, especially when I was younger, was to not look back to where I'd been, but where I was going. I should've been talking through what we were going to do the next day to go find that boy. But I'd told RL for years and years it was time to move on. And now the boy was grown and he was done and gone. For good. I told him, RL, it's time for you to deal with that. He didnt appreciate my tone.

There's no way to recall exactly what all was said that night to enflame our conversation in such a way. Somehow I let myself get sucked into rehashing everything from the past. But I do remember that at one point I told him. I dont know what got into me, but I said, RL, I need to let you know something. Since we're getting things off our chest, I need to let you know that back in the summer of '56 Sally Johnson was playing both sides of things. And he said, what do you mean by that? And I told him that at the same time he was courting her, that she and I had a little thing. I said I was sorry about that, and that I didnt mean anything toward him by it. That it was just one of those things that happens in our youth. But he went wild, cursing me, threatening me, rage in his eyes. Tears. Perhaps it was just the alcohol, but as I said there must have been deeper things.

What exactly is he talking about? Corinne says to herself. She was having difficulty putting it all together. He looked bad. He was pale and gray. His voice sounded much older. Perhaps it was the morphine making him fuzzy. The agony of his recent trauma in his eyes. Sullen, empty. The glazed stare of a man who was facing some fear inside that he'd never known.

I truly dont even remember what he said. Just that he had the stare of a man who wanted me to think he was crazed. Or maybe he was crazed. A man capable of anything. But by then I was completely caught up in the moment. I know I said some derogatory things about him as a father, as a man. It's unreal how quickly that escalated. It's fuzzy, like I was in a dream. I remember seeing some teeth flying out with the blood and slobber, his head lolled, and then his body collapsed like a tree felled in the forest. He fell on his back. His eyes were wide open but he was unconscious. Then a strange thing happened. Something with his muscle memory. Just lying there, he started throwing his fists upward into the night sky. Both hands, like he was in a fight. I dont know that I'd ever in my life thrown a punch before that.

How did it all come to that? Was that how it was meant to be? Perhaps I was so lost in myself. Those years when I'd put so much into making my fortune. Only to lose it all. I keep thinking of those early years on the trail when he was trying to move on with his life, move on from the loss of what he felt was his true love. Searching for his boys. My god, he was going through a lot.

RL generally took things day-to-day. Didnt look too far ahead. I dont think he was all that educated. Or interested in expanding his horizons. Never saw him show much interest in a book. When we came upon something in nature that to me, would seem as though it were a miracle, it didnt really touch him. No deeper meaning. I suppose I looked down on that.

But I always loved how matter-of-fact he was about things. How simple. I would tend to overthink ever little angle, and he'd be able to boil whatever it was down to its most basic properties. He fought through any adversity we ever faced with dogged determination. He was fearless. True, maybe he wasnt that well rounded. Maybe he lacked certain things as a husband, a father. Still, he dug in and wouldnt give up on finding those boys. Meanwhile, I was selfish. All I cared about was myself. I'm haunted by that.

He holds up the back side of his right hand, the knurled knuckles, from the fracture, from his only punch. She watches him. His eyes are heavy. They slowly close and reopen again. Then they close again and he is asleep. She has been letting him talk but the energy in his voice is gone.

She no longer takes notation to pass along the beauty of his life to the man who will put it all onto paper and turn him into a legend.

When Mr Blackburn comes in to spell her she steps out into the courtyard and sits down by the fountain and puts her face into her hands, tears streaming down. She sits there sobbing, the water from the fountain lightly sprinkling about her ankles. The sun is starting to set, burning and yellow. She sits there for a long while, getting herself together as the sky is bathed in the afterglow.

When Corinne comes back into the room the old man is awake. Mr Blackburn has given him a steaming cup of black coffee and he seems a little more alert.

Ralph, there's something I've been meaning to ask you.

Of course. What is it?

Do you think the Lord will forgive me?

Well, Colonel, yes of course he will forgive you. Solomon asked the Lord to forgive his people if they repented of their sins with all their heart.

I think about the churches I helped build. Up in Colorado. In the Panhandle. It was sincere. It was from the heart, for Mollie and I to do what we could to help establish those communities.

Well, of course it was sincere. You were doing what you thought was right.

I just wonder. It means something to hear that from you, Ralph.

Dont worry, Colonel. You're going to be just fine.

When the pastor left Corinne sat down beside him, holding his hand, letting him talk. His mind had taken him back to the founding of the JA in the Palo Duro. He spoke slowly, as if he was remembering a dream.

Those were the days when the monied gentry in Europe were anxious to invest in America. The country had been coming out of the depression of 1873 and they were hearing good things about all the land. All the cattle. By 1877 Jack Adair's people in Denver put us in touch and we agreed to visit the Panhandle and discuss our partnership. Mollie had given me the ultimatum. She wrote me from California—settle somewhere in civilization or she was coming to the Panhandle. We outfitted at Trinidad with six months supplies and a light ambulance. Just two hands and us and the Adairs. It was a time of much hope. I just knew, felt it in my gut, that prosperity was around the corner.

Mollie even drove one of the wagons herself. Three hundred miles across those plains. Unbroken grama grass and buffalo turf from the base of the Rockies to the plains of western Texas. Yet unclaimed by any man. The Comanches and Kiowas routed out of their ancestral homelands. Across the Raton range, Cimarron Plaza, and across all that wilderness where we crossed the Canadian at what was then the new town of Tascosa.

I was anxious to see the view from the northern side of the great canyon. It was noon of a bluebird day when we worked our way across the tablelands to the rim of the gorge. A thousand feet down the Prairie Dog Town Fork were the headwaters of the Red River. Somewhere out there on the other side was the new ranch house. I gazed at the range way off on the other side, across the canyon named Palo Duro.

The rank smell of death riding a stiff prairie breeze. This was three days after he had seen the white buffalo. When he heard the rifle shot and fired back spontaneously in self-defense. Perhaps one of Dutch Henry's boys or some other rustler. Or a rogue Comanche scout wandering from the reservation. He wasnt sure if he'd hit his target. He was alone. He thought he saw some other riders and he made the choice to ride away with his scalp intact. Now he was back near the spot where he had taken the shot and something caught his eye. Looked like a horde of vultures. Not the direction he'd been aiming. He nudged his horse and trotted toward the stench. Soon they began to scatter. Flapping their dark wings and hopping about. Singles flying up and circling. Groups of them bounding to nearby vantage points.

It was RL Terry, dead in a bed of bloodied grass. A bloated, reeking body facing the sky. He had been shot through his left shoulder. He was wearing the same outfit from a few nights before and his rifle and sidearms were sprawled out alongside him. The trampled grass around him was dark with blood, bloodied footprints of vultures and wolves extending from the fringes. He looked all around. A lone wolf observing from the horizon turned and trotted away.

Clothes shredded. The vultures had been picking at the flesh of his wound. They had also been at work at the eyes and the abdomen. Shredded, gaping. His pants were mangled and ripped but his boots were still on. Goodnight stood there in the breeze with his face buried in the crook of his arm, studying his old partner.

He opens his eyes, sleepily, and discovers the doctor attending to him. The cold stethoscope is on his bare chest. Corinne stands behind him, her eyes bloodshot and watery from crying. She wipes the tears from her eyes, sniffles, feigns a smile of encouragement. She is relieved to see his eyes open, that he is still breathing.

When he awakens again Mollie is there, her gentle smile, the loving assurance in her eyes that he is going to pull through, that she will be with him no matter what until the end. How did he get so lucky? he thinks. He thinks of all the years she put up with his smoking and cursing. All his bad habits.

Corinne watches over him faithfully as he sleeps. The labored, shallow breaths. A wrinkled, shrunken body. It is time for him to pass. But he has faced death before. In earlier times of despair he always showed that great desire to live on. There is so much more life he has dreamed he can live. Was that desire still there?

Dont die on me, Charles, she whispers. You're going to be alright.

She sits with him, hour by hour, listening to the melancholy in his ramblings. She can hardly hear his voice, at times barely a whisper wasted away by illness. A feeble old man, desperate to cleanse his soul to prepare for whatever is next. This was not like him. Reeling with pain, confused, hallucinating from the rush of the morphine. Or perhaps not.

With each piece of the story she follows along, piecing the little slivers together like some infinite puzzle. Putting the fragments of his past together. Pulling them apart. Everything he'd seen, all of the triumphs. And now whatever ghosts remained of his earlier worlds.

When RL came back to consciousness the fire had died and the moon was out. He was alone. Maybe four in the morning but he wasnt sure. He heard his horse grazing but when he turned toward it everything was a blur. His face was swollen and throbbing and his head felt like it was going to explode and he could taste the blood in his mouth. He stood up, wobbling. Slow steps to test his balance. He looked around. He spat. His lip was so swollen and numb that the bloody spittle just slurred out onto his shirt. He could see a little better by tilting his head and squinching his left eye. All of his possibles were still there. Under the moonlight he could make out the trail of a lone horseman heading east. As he gathered his things and packed the horse he wasnt really even thinking about looking for his son anymore. He was going to track down and kill Charlie Goodnight. He took a pull from the bottle of whiskey and packed it away and mounted the horse and set out into the darkness.

An hour later he had lost the trail along the lip of the Palo Duro just as the sun was rising. He sat the horse, searching for sign, thinking. He watched the great sun pierce the rim of the plains. Huge and red. Pulsing. Rising. Floating. He looked back to study the tracks. All the new light shining clean upon the prairie, pure and flat, stretching to the south and to the west. Long yellow grass dancing in the cool morning breeze. He scanned the country to see if anything was moving, studied every wallow and draw with a hawk-like vigilance. Nothing else out there. He turned the horse, stepping along for something he might have missed. Suddenly a lone prairie grouse flushed up, flapping and cackling, soaring on. And then only the whisper of a breeze that died, the faint rustle of a field mouse in the dry grass.

He worked his way back east, then south, picking his way along the edge of the canyon for another hour, looking down for any sign of Charlie Goodnight. Nothing, not even any animals. His head pounding. You're out there somewhere, he said. You sumbitch. And eventually I'm goin to find you. He looked back to the west. No, he's down in the canyon.

Then from the corner of his good eye the rising sun seemed to flash on something far out on the prairie. He turned the horse, scanning. He spotted a small herd of buffalo on the horizon. A few dark blotches, one white, like a ghost. Grazing. He rubbed his eyes. Well now, he said, fancy seein you again. He took the bottle from the saddlebag and unstoppered it, looking out and admiring the scene, admiring the white buffalo. When he raised the bottle to his lips and drank he felt a great punch into his shoulder that spun him reeling off the horse. It was just a thunk. Whitehot. Spontaneous. He lay squirming in the grass clutching at his shoulder, the horse stamping and snorting anxiously, the echo of the shot shearing out over the canyon and then silence. He clambered about, cowering low in the grass, looking around wildly. Blood everywhere. He sat up and looked out, gasping. He had no line of site but somewhere out there Samuel Pahvo Terry stood atop a rise watching him through the foresight of his smoking rifle.

Why are you telling me this? Do you mean to tell me that Sam Terry shot his father?

The old man didnt answer.

Charles?

Yes, he whispered.

I dont understand. What makes you say that?

I was there.

You were there?

He stared out the window, saying nothing. Last light in the west flaring briefly.

Charles, honey, you were there?

I was back out there trying to find RL. To make amends. It was such a beautiful morning. I was watching a herd of bison but must have had a different vantage point. Incredibly, there was a white buffalo. The terrain was such that my view funneled straight down to that herd. It must have been that way. I prided myself on having the eyes of an owl, able to pick up anything in my periphery, regardless of where I was looking. There was nothing. Just the magnificence of that rare creature white in the sun. That's when I heard the shot. Very near. I thought that someone was shooting at me. My heart hammering. The first thing I thought about was RL Terry. I jerked the horse back, to get moving, to get to a line of sight. I didnt know whether to try and defend myself or ride out of there. The country was dead flat. Some long, gentle rises. Hardly noticeable. I finally got myself to a point of vantage and saw something. A lone man out on the prairie. Two hundred yards out. My instincts kicked in. I didnt hesitate. Not one bit. Just instinct. I unsheathed my rifle and took dead aim and fired. Just like that.

Corinne wants to close her eyes and make his pain go away, for it to be over, the agony of the last days before the end. She feels helpless. She knows that she needs to be back in a young world again, where there is no fear or pain and anything is possible. She wants to put her arms around the old man, tell him that she loves him, and make it so—the way he always talks about dying. To place him back out on the range where the grass is green under absolute sunshine and the blue sky is pure, his cattle are grazing and fat. He'll dismount the big black horse, Hawk, his favorite, and set it out to graze. He'll stretch out on the grass and slide his hat down over his face and fold his arms across his chest. Then he'll close his eyes, at peace with life, and die. But we dont get to choose, she tells herself.

Corinne leans over and touches his leg.

Sweetheart, I dont understand.

What?

After you heard the shot, and you swung around, you shot RL Terry?

No.

No?

It was… Sam.

She says nothing, trying to piece his words, his thoughts, together.

You see, the Quahadis were known to stray from the reservation under the supervision of Quanah. With General Mackenzie's permission. When the boy left South Texas, with his broken heart, he must have been seeking a return to his old life. To return to his true family again, thinking that he could find them in their ancestral homelands. In the Palo Duro. Quanah used to tell me that he would speak to Sam about this. Before he left the reservation. That he would always be there for him if it was time for him to return.

And that's where RL found him?

What RL was searching for found him. Although I suppose after what had transpired between us it was very likely that he was hunting me. In any event, as impossible as it is to imagine, somehow our paths led us to that common destination.

It is dark outside, dark in the room, silent. A petal from the wilting lily falls, twisting, floating gently to the floor. The lamp is dim and the candles are flickering lightly, a soft, sepia light and the tears that pour from Corinne's soulful eyes glisten and stream and drop. Her flowing brown hair is up, highlighting the beauty of her face in the candlelight.

She had sat down on the edge of the bed so she could be closer to him, to touch him. To just be there for him. She would wipe her eyes with a tissue, trying to be strong, suppressing her urges to cry, choking up when those poignant thoughts struck. She leaned down and put her nose to his cheek, a peck of a kiss. It was her compassion that he needed as she leaned toward him holding his old, trembling hand in hers, stroking it lovingly with her nails.

You sure have been good to me, he told her. You make me feel loved, and that, no matter what anyone says, is worth everything. It's all that matters. I pray that I've done the same for you.

Yes, my love. Of course you have.

He smiled weakly.

I hope that someday, when I'm gone, you'll look back with fond memories of our love. And I know that you will find another love, even stronger than ours.

The old man lays there in the silence, squeezing her hands, looking deeply into her eyes so that she could see all the way through him into his heart, as if this was his one last chance to cleanse himself, to relinquish all things into her hands. His hands.

All of this, it can no longer stay inside of me, Corinne. My heart is old and sick. I'm broken. Is it useless to try and tell someone of my child's death? At my own hand? I could never bring myself to tell anyone. To acknowledge it myself. Such a dark secret. I admit, I lived the rest of my life trying to forget them and what had happened. Haunted.

A single tear streams down her face. He is confused, she thinks. I cant let him lie here and suffer with these thoughts.

Honey, Sam Terry was not your son.

His eyes turn to the bureau. Over there, he said. In the desk. Bring me the bible. Please.

There was a rifle and two pistols lying in the trampled dirt around the body but the first thing that caught his eye was the bible. The instant his eyes focused on the book, its ornate leather cover and the distinctive metal clasp, his subconscious instantly ran through a lifetime of memories. Loving used to take this very same book and hold it reverently, fascinated by the randomness of its path, tactfully using it to emphasize its spiritual lessons when their conversations became reflective. But the old plainsman was always cautious with his faith, exploring its mysteries at his own pace, in his own style. Then at one point it occurred to him that it was better served in the hands of someone else. He'd grown to appreciate the malleable nature of the boy in his youth, looked inside himself and explored his own faith a little more because of him.

Sam's spirit was infectious. On a cold, snowy day on the streets of Fort Worth, under the stars by the campfire, after a cussing from his father on the front porch when talking meanly to his little brother, talking back to his mother. The colonel's own mother had spoken often of the Good Book's lessons when he was a kid, as did Sally Johnson back in those days when they first were getting to know one another. And then of course, Mollie. Giving the book to Sam just felt like the right thing to do. You would never believe that anything so tragic could possibly be tied to such a gift, but he had failed to understand the turns that life could take no matter what choices one might make. How could he have possibly imagined that it would turn out like this. And now the book was in the dirt by Sam's dead body, near his hand, as if he had been clutching it in the throes of death.

I knelt down beside the body as a father, studying him closely, thinking through it all. Feelings in my gut that could never possibly be described in words. All of the things I should've done differently. Choices made in the heat of the moment. Just innate reactions, seemingly so simple at the time. You can be sloppy drunk in a cantina staring down an outlaw with a gun, or with a pretty girl on a hot summer night. I've done both and did what I did in the heat of the moment. There are things in this life that are beyond our control. Moira. Even the gods cannot alter what is ordained. It's taken me a lifetime to come to make sense of the choices I've made.

The last time I had seen him he was so conflicted. Once again his life turned upside down. Caught between two cultures. I came back to Texas. To try and help. They had him dressed like a white man but he was still all Comanche.

The vivid images of him as a boy were cemented in my mind. Still are. They were with me when I went back to Texas and they were with me that morning I stood there looking at him dead in the dirt. You see someone dead, it's a pretty poignant thing considering them being alive, their life and all it was and then one day it's just over. It does not matter how much you know them, although it's a much heavier burden when you have ties to them.

I knelt down and picked up that family bible, opened it up just to make sure I wasnt dreaming. I saw the handwritten notations in pencil. The family tree, birthdays of relatives, highlighted scriptures. The book had made it all this way. Now back in my hands again. Somehow it made it through all those years and he had brought it back to Texas with him. I recognized the handwriting in the front pages from so long ago and I flipped through them, saw the more recent ones, notations from the early months of his reacclimation when they were helping him in his rehabilitation.

She sits back down beside him, cradling the bible. He takes it into his trembling hands, feeling its texture, paying tribute to its path. He opens it to where the pages are split by something that has been inserted. He pulls out the small, sealed envelope, yellowed with age, and hands it to her.

What is this?

Read it to me, please.

Why have you not opened it?

Because… I suppose because I know what's inside.

She carefully breaks the seal with her nail, sensitive to its fragility. She slowly unfolds the piece of paper and scans the lines, the beautiful cursive in the hand of a woman. She begins to read and with the beauty of her voice it sounds like a poem.

My Dearest Charles,

I will keep this short as I know you will not tolerate any ramblings. It is clear that your destiny has swept you away from me. I accept that. However if it is truly over, there is one thing I must force myself to reveal, for I cannot move forward with my life without sharing this with you—that our union has blessed us with a gift beyond all imagination, the beautiful little boy I have named Sam.

Corinne pauses to wipe her eyes, to catch her breath as she sobs, fighting back the pain and sadness that she feels in her heart. Then she begins to read again, slowly through her tears.

I know that I will be haunted by the poor choices I've made until the day I die. Yet it is a beautiful life that we are so blessed to live, and with this letter, with faith in the Lord, I pray that I will be free to move on and to make the most of the Lord's gifts, and I pray that we will bestow the spirit of Him into our child.

Always, with undying love, I will be with you forever.

Sally

The faint flickers of the candlelight dance softly about the darkness of the room. Another tear streams down her cheek. She wipes it with her hand, staring at the letter in silence. She whispers slowly.

This is the letter that Sally Johnson gave you.

He is staring deeply into her eyes, her tears streaming. He nods.

When you broke it off with her?

Yes. In 1856. And twenty-one years later I dug a shallow grave in the sandy red soil of the Palo Duro Canyon and laid our son to rest. And then I buried my old friend and partner who died at his hands, the supposed son he had been searching for all those years.

They sat there in silence. She turned the letter in her hands as if it wasnt real.

And you've been holding this in? All this time?

No response.

No. Charles, honey, it's not adding up. I just cant put it all together.

The old man just lay there. He turned his gaze away from her, staring out wistfully into the darkness of the room.

Corinne put her hand on his leg.

Tell me again what happened after you had the argument with RL. After you went back out there and you heard the shot.

When I left RL that night I was in a rage. He was out cold. Helpless. I was afraid I was going to kill him so I got myself out of there as fast as I could. My emotions reeling, I rode for a long time that night in the darkness looking out at the stars and truly pondering my existence. What it all meant. I slowly made my way back to the ranch house.

But by the time the sun rose I had convinced myself it wasnt that big of a deal. Two old friends in a fight. He would sober up. I would be sorry. It would blow over. We'd figure out a plan of action and track down Sam.

I checked in with Mollie, the Adairs, the ranch hands. And then I set back out again to make amends. That next morning. There was something about the beauty of everything that morning. The smell of the plains with the sun rising. A cool breeze. That something special about a new day.

Up on top of the Caprock there are places you can see for miles. I knew I would find him eventually. And then when the white buffalo caught my eye, like some spirit, I couldnt take my eyes off of it. Perhaps I didnt really see it. Afterall, I hadnt slept. And when I heard that gunshot my instincts, my emotions, they just took over.

I swung around and got a line of sight. Saw him. Shot him. Saw him buckle and stumble and fall to the ground. The echo of the blast hovering over the prairie. Then I thought I heard a rumble of hooves and I saw dust rising and right then I realized I was all alone, with no cover, and my gut said to get out of there, for it could be indians or horse thieves on the lam. More than I would be able to deal with. Back at the ranch I was out of sorts. Didnt tell anyone. It took me three days to get the nerve to head back out there.

What happened before I rode upon that view of the white buffalo? Did Sam know who he was shooting at? All I could ever think of was the white buffalo. It must have caught RL's eye. Just like it did mine. Sam saw it too, shining in the sun, and I believe that when he saw a man out on the plains to him it was nothing more than a lone buffalo hunter. That's why he shot RL. He was just a buffalo hunter.

Of all the things I've seen and done in this life, and now at the end of the long road, this curse that will never go away, lingering with me in death.

I cannot accept it. The curse, whatever I did to be forced to stand hand-in-hand with the devil. This despite all of the gifts life has bestowed upon me. All the beauty of the days gone by. Those will also be with me. Driving that first herd into the outskirts of the Bosque Redondo. All of those nights of storytelling by the campfire. Watching the great storms roll in from the plains. Sam's handsome smile when he was a young and curious boy. The way he would follow me around, look at me, take to whatever I was trying to teach him. The fifty-six years Mollie and I were together. Even these past several years, wonderful years, since you and Evetts came into my life.

Corinne's eyes teared up as she smiled.

And now, here I am, facing whatever road is ahead.

I knelt down beside him. He'd been dragged by the wolves. Chewed on. Picked apart by the vultures. I pushed him over to see his face. But it was already gone. Just a decomposing body, mind and thoughts forever gone. No more struggles. No more pleasures and joys.

A thousand faded memories. All those times you were following us around when you were a little boy. I brought you along, showing you the ways of nature, of range life. Everything I did, you went with me. I sat beside you when you placed the barrel of your first rifle at rest, taking aim at your first deer. You were nervous but brave and you were dying to shoot that big buck, and yet there was something inside of you that was respectful of the animal. I stop giving you instruction and sit back to watch, impressed by your patience and concentration. It is cold outside and your nose is running, cheeks red. You hold your breath and squeeze the trigger. The buck deer drops, kicking in spasm, and you are fascinated as it slowly becomes still, taking its time to die. You look at me and break into a huge smile. It was the most joyous smile I had ever seen. Have ever seen.

RL makes it back to the camp when we are processing the deer. He is beaming with pride. He heard the shot and was hoping it was from your gun. *Son, I just caint tell you how proud I am of you.* We celebrate that night by grilling the backstraps and re-telling the story of the hunt by the fire.

And I feel my own strange sense of fatherly pride, grateful for my role in the hunt. I prod you along, asking you questions, leading you to tell us in your own words what the hunt was like. It was a fleeting moment, the only time you would ever feel *exactly* like that, a boy who'd shot his first deer. Of course there will be many other first times, many other impactful moments. Your whole life is ahead of you.

The next day is a Sunday. I'm at your house. You're helping me. We'd just fixed a windmill and now we're pushing a cow and her calf across the pasture. Your mother calls out, urging us in toward the yard where all of the neighbors are congregating in the shade of that old oak tree where she's set up a service for the circuit rider to do his preaching.

Goodnight, you say, are you coming to the service?

Not today, Sam.

You take me by surprise with two questions out of the blue.

Are you religious? Do you believe in God?

Well, now Sam, I've read my fair share of the Bible. But I dont suppose I go to church much. There's just too much work to do.

You're looking at me with those sincere eyes, that childlike wonder, questioning it all. I'm thinking about how to handle it. Then an inspiration strikes me.

Before you go, Sam. Let me give you something to take with you.

We walk over to my horse and I reach in the saddlebag. I grab Mrs Sherman's bible and hand it to you. Thank you, you say, feeling the weight of it in your hands. I tell you the story of how I'd found it five years prior and the mystical fate of all that. I try and tell you my feelings about the way of things.

Sam, look around us right now. Take a breath. Really listen. You see, I believe in nature. Look up there on that windmill we just fixed, at that dove calling. Just watch it. Dont think about anything else. You asked what I believe in. I believe that life on this ole planet is driven by hidden forces. And you see, Sam, if we dont get in touch with em, if we dont somehow connect with em, now then we're missing out. We cant be truly, authentically alive. So, just pay attention to it all, whatever is in front of you, in that moment, without thinking about anything else. I believe that nature will remain.

You just looked at me, thinking. I didnt know how to handle that moment and at the time you had no way of grasping all of it, but I think you knew that I was speaking from the heart. That was a long time ago.

He was covered in a blanket of flies when I walked up and they rose up in a swarm like a black fog. Both of his eyes were gone. Hair matted up from the bloodied footprints. The maggots were already in there. The vultures and the eagles and the crows had been pecking away at him. Clothes shredded. Skin all torn up with pockmarks. They'd opened him up and the innards had been dragged out. I covered my mouth and nose and waved my hat about for the flies, looking at him.

I didnt have anything to dig a grave with. The Comanches had a notion to bury the body the same day. They'd wash it, dress it up with personal things. Pull the knees to the chest, bind it inside a blanket with rope. I was thinking about that as I studied the country. They'd find some elevation with a cave or some crevice at the head of a canyon. Place it in a sitting posture facing the rising sun and cover it with rocks.

I dragged his body down into the canyon, into a small niche under an overhang at the base of the canyon wall. The vultures would have devoured the corpse in hours. I covered the opening with cedar stumps and brush and rocks to keep the animals away overnight. I took off my kerchief and hung it up on the end of a mesquite branch to mark the spot.

The next morning, after another sleepless night, I went back out there. I brought along a shovel and a few things to leave with him. I pulled him out and took him back further up the side canyon where there was a pretty little spot near a spring that infused life to that rough country. Very peaceful. Water trickling at the base of the canyon wall. The sun came up over the draw and bathed the spot with an enchanting glow of miraculous light. Daisies and zinnias speckled about waving with the grasses in the breeze and wrens singing. It was his place. I found a soft depression in the soil where water had gathered and I started digging his grave.

I think back to Mollie's funeral. Listening to the songs. *Victory in Jesus. When the Roll Is Called Up Yonder.* During the sermon it was difficult for me to absorb all of the loving words that were spoken of her. I sat there with my head down but my eyes were wide open looking out through the window into our yesterdays. The coffin was open and she was just there, made up to look pretty with the best clothes she wore, but it wasnt her. The look of the dead, like a statue. Everyone lined up to file by and pay their respects to her one last time. But I'd had enough. I never did believe in showing off the dead. I got up and got out of there. You dont believe it's ever going to end and then one day there's that moment of reckoning, just like that. She had run out of time and it was over.

The old man looked out the window as if his eyes were watching for God.

Death finishes all of our stories, and after all of her suffering and the state that she was in, it was her time.

Oh, Charles…

But Sam's story wasnt meant to be finished.

The old man turned his gaze back from the darkness to meet her eyes, glistening in the candlelight. Somber, glazed eyes sodden with defeat. She caressed his hand and felt his wrist, barely a pulse. A bluish tinge to his fingernails. She kissed him. I love you, she said.

He squeezed her hand.

Charles, honey. It's getting late. Are you tired?

Yes.

Can I get you anything before you go to sleep? Some water?

No.

Anything?

No.

She put the back of her hand on his cheek. Cold to the touch. Pale, shriveled skin mottled with purple patches.

You know darlin...

What is it?

I think I'll have a bourbon. I dont guess it can hurt to have one for the road.

She feigned a smile and bent down and kissed his forehead. He grabbed her hand again. He squeezed it and held it for a long time. Then she left the room and he closed his eyes and lay there in peace. When she returned a few minutes later with his drink he was asleep.

THE END